PRAISE FOR ROB POBI AND *EYE OF THE STORM*

"A most impressive work, one that will linger, if not haunt outright."

—*Quill & Quire*

"Heartbreaking and chilling."

—Andrew Pyper, author of *The Demonologist*

"A *Sixth Sense*–like take on Thomas Harris in his prime."

—*National Post*

"This sparkling first novel has an ending few readers will see coming."

—*The Gazette* (Montreal)

"Dialogue keeps the pulse racing. Description pushes the energy and the conclusion stops you in your tracks."

—*The Hamilton Spectator*

"Intense, dark, and frightening."

—*Toronto Sun*

"An author to watch."

—*The Globe and Mail*

"Jake Cole has to be one of the most compelling and tormented protagonists in recent crime fiction. . . . The pacing is relentless, and Pobi's updates on the growth of the hurricane are almost welcome interludes amid the pervasive creepiness and horror of the growing body count and Jake's appalling past. . . . A remarkable debut."

—*Booklist*

"Pobi boldly announces his arrival as a cunning novelist."

—*Publishers Weekly*

"A very suspenseful novel."

—*O, The Oprah Magazine*

"A fantastic new voice in the thriller genre."

—*New York Journal of Books*

"It will surely make a lasting impression."

—*The House of Crime and Mystery* (blog)

"A gut-punch of a book . . . showing the grace and grit of ten first-time novelists. Try closing your eyes after digging into this one."

—Gregg Hurwitz, bestselling author

"Every element of this story feels like a ticking bomb that could explode at any moment, creating one heck of a riveting story that keeps pace right through to the end."

—*The Debut Review*

"A compelling, layered, gripping novel that can hold its own with the likes of Thomas Harris. . . . One of the strongest debuts I've seen in a very long time."

—*Spinetingler Magazine*

HARVEST

III ROB POBI

SIMON & SCHUSTER CANADA

New York London Toronto Sydney New Delhi

Simon & Schuster Canada
A Division of Simon & Schuster, Inc.
166 King Street East, Suite 300
Toronto, Ontario M5A 1J3

This book is a work of fiction. Any references to historical
events, real people, or real places are used fictitiously.
Other names, characters, places, and events are products of the
author's imagination, and any resemblance to actual events or
places or persons, living or dead, is entirely coincidental.

This Simon & Schuster Canada edition January 2015

SIMON & SCHUSTER CANADA and colophon are registered
trademarks of Simon & Schuster, Inc.

For information about special discounts for bulk purchases,
please contact Simon & Schuster Special Sales at 1-800-268-3216
or CustomerService@simonandschuster.ca.

Interior design: Lewelin Polanco
Cover design: PGB
Cover image: Shutterstock

Manufactured in the United States of America

3 5 7 9 10 8 6 4 2

ISBN 978-1-4767-2878-0
ISBN 978-1-4767-2872-8 (ebook)

It is an illusion that youth is happy, an illusion of those who have lost it. . . . [The young] must discover for themselves that all they have read and all they have been told are lies, lies, lies; and each discovery is another nail driven into the body on the cross of life.

—W. Somerset Maugham, *Of Human Bondage*, 1915

It is impossible to suffer without making someone pay for it.

—Friedrich Nietzsche, unpublished fragment from
Thus Spake Zarathustra, 1883–1885

HARVEST

‖‖‖ O N E

TYLER ROCHESTER enjoyed walking home from school alone; it was a hard-won privilege that had taken negotiation and persistence. Of course, his parents had insisted on a few conditions—which he was old enough to know was just a fancy word for *rules*—but in the end he had won his independence. And any ten-year-old will tell you that independence is almost as good as cake—the kind with sprinkles.

Tyler was on his way home from the Damien Whitney Academy for Boys on the Upper East Side. Summer break was only a few days away and the city already felt like it was on fire so he allowed himself the luxury of opening the buttons of his school jacket. He also wanted to open his collar but he had spent a lot of time getting his tie just right, with a perfect knot, like Tom Cruise had done in that old movie *Mission: Impossible*.

The taxi dropped him off a block from his home. Tyler stopped for a Coke at the deli, taking a can from the fridge by the fruit stand. He paid the man at the register with his debit card and walked out into the heat.

Tyler Rochester never made it home.

Tyler Rochester had just become a statistic.

||| TWO

THE SUN was dropping over the Jersey shore, staining the atmosphere with the orange of late afternoon. The day had been cloudless and only the vapor trails over Newark marred the perfect blue of the sky. The wind was dead and the Hudson was in one of those rare states where it looked like a gently rolling field of dark, heavy oil. Manhattan, stretching ahead and to the left, glowed in the last breath of the afternoon.

Alexandra Hemingway made good time, the swing and grip of the paddle pushing her south, the tide donating a little extra speed. Every time her right arm came up, her shoulder blade clicked, a keepsake from David Shea.

The water headed out to sea, pulled by the unstoppable schedule of the moon. Today the garbage wasn't too bad— mostly the mundane detritus of coffee cups and plastic bags— but every now and then she had come across some pretty grim things in the water. Anyone who spent time on the river had. When she worked days, she'd often have an early-morning coffee with the rowers from Columbia; their superstition was that the season didn't officially start until they came across a body in the water. Business as usual in the Big Apple.

She had crossed under the George Washington Bridge a few minutes back and the further downstream she went, the greater her speed became. The GPS hooked onto her vest clocked her at nearly three knots faster than she had been just ten blocks back. As the outflow of the Hudson sluiced between New York and New Jersey, it picked up a lot of speed, the faster troughs sometimes moving at twenty-five knots down near Battery Park. To offset the heavy pull of the water she stayed close to shore. Inexperienced kayakers sometimes found themselves washed out past Red Hook and under the Verrazano—not the way she wanted to spend a Monday night.

She had grown up on the waves, her first solo foray out on Long Island Sound in the Laser her father bought her for her tenth birthday. Her passion for the sea had deepened with each new year until now, at thirty-seven, it felt like an integral part of her own biology. She was out here every night before her shift, rain or shine, pounding the water. It wasn't just a way to keep her body from atrophy, it was one of the few places where she could be alone—a near miracle in a city of thirteen million people.

And other than the morning Mank had been killed, she couldn't remember a time when she had needed to be alone in her own headspace as much as now.

Today wasn't about grief, at least not technically. But that morning the little stick had turned blue; then the clear solution in the comparative bottles had turned blue; and finally the meter had registered a plus sign. By the time she had chewed open the box of the fourth off-the-shelf home test, she was going through the motions out of nothing more than morbid curiosity.

She had squeezed in an emergency appointment with Dr. Sparks for confirmation. She was *with child*, in the parlance of Hester Prynne's time. *Knocked up,* as Phelps would say. *And out of work,* as her boss would soon be telling her.

She made the nearly hundred blocks from the GWB to the 79th Street boat basin in a little less than sixteen minutes, not a record in her scull but good time in the clumsy kayak. She was tall, a little over six feet, and she found most kayaks uncomfortable. Even though this was only her second run with the new fifteen footer, it already felt like an old friend—a good sign.

When she paddled into the marina, the carbon monoxide migration on the West Side Highway was clogged to walking speed in both directions; rush hour had started and people were heading home to suppers of booze, antacid, and reruns of *The Simpsons.*

Hemingway pulled up to the launch, took off her Ray-Bans, and hopped out into the mid-thigh water. It felt like it looked—warm and heavy. She removed the wheels from the mount holes on the back of the Prowler, lifted the stern, and placed the support posts into the scupper holes. Then she pushed the kayak up the slope to her truck.

———

Hemingway pulled the Suburban off the southbound West Side Highway, wove through the Tetris-like traffic blocking the intersection, and barreled east on 27th. She hit the brakes at a red light on the corner of 11th and the truck slid on the condensation that beaded the asphalt, coming to rest at a slight cant. The moon roof and windows were open and humidity misted the leather steering wheel. She thought about running the light to get the air flowing again but didn't want to get pulled over by a cop—things like that were bad for business. So she waited.

Two kids ambled across the lane. Gangly teens in the standard-issue streetwear of the uninventive: low-slung jeans, old-school Run DMCs without laces, caps locked on sideways. One wore a Knicks jacket, the other was in a Yankees jersey. It was too hot for the heavy clothing and Hemingway found herself pitying their need to conform. They had that loose-legged walk that speaks volumes to street kids. They crossed in front of her bumper, close enough that a pant leg brushed the fiberglass. The one in the Knicks jacket gave the kayak on the roof rack a once-over. He said something to his friend who turned back, his eyes sliding over the hood, past the windshield, to the top of the truck, as if he were staring at a spaceship.

Hemingway reached for the MP3 player, cranked the volume, and Andrew W.K. told her that it was time to party hard.

There was a shadow at the edge of her vision that set off a flash in her circuitry; before instinct converted to action the warm end of a muzzle pressed against her cheek.

"Out of the car, bitch," the voice behind the pistol said.

The flicker of the second guy pulsed in the rearview mirror, heading for the passenger's door.

She took her hands off the wheel in an *I'll-do-whatever-you-say* gesture that she punctuated by pounding down on the gas.

The big SUV lurched forward, tires screaming. There was a brief snap of time where the muzzle slid back and away from her cheek and she reached up for the wrist holding the pistol. She pounded down on the brake pedal with both feet, throwing her shoulders back into the seat.

The truck bucked and she slammed the wrist down into the doorframe. There was a snap of bone and the roar of the engine was overridden by a scream as the kid flew forward.

His pistol bounced off the dash and ricocheted into the back-seat. There was a single panic-stricken flash of teeth, then he spilled forward with another howl. She hit the gas and something solid thumped under her wheel and the truck jolted. Before the back wheel finished what the front hadn't, she stopped the SUV and tumbled out of the cab with her pistol clasped tightly in both hands.

The kid was sprawled out by the back tire, his leg twisted under the truck. His foot looked like someone had unscrewed it. Bones poked through the cuff of his jeans like pale splintered roots. His shoe lay ten feet away.

She spun her head, looking for the second kid. Traffic had stopped fifty feet back, silhouettes behind windshields dropping below dashboards.

Through the windows of the SUV she saw the second target coming up on the back right fender. A little chrome .32 glinted in his fist.

She crab scrambled sideways and stood up with her pistol leveled at the bumper he'd have to come around. She stepped back from the sweet spot in four long strides, bringing her sight up to adjust for the increased distance. When she reached the apex of the curve, and the barrel began to drop, she stopped. Held her stance. He rounded the back bumper, aiming too low; she was fifteen feet beyond where he expected her to be.

"Freeze, idiot," she said.

But he went for it.

She squeezed the trigger once and he doubled over and somersaulted in a single disjointed cartwheel, capped off with a high-pitched screech. His pistol clattered to the pavement under the cyclopic gaze of the traffic signal a few feet away. He hit the asphalt and his hands went to his groin. Someone to her right honked.

Hemingway stepped forward to the kid under the truck. He had crawled from beneath the frame and was gasping for breath, like a boated fish. She raised the pistol to his face. "You want it in the head or the heart?" She lowered her sights to the middle of his chest with the second part of the question. It did not sound rhetorical.

The kid looked up, barking out a plea between his jack-hammer breaths. "No . . . please . . . Miss . . . I didn't . . . mean . . . no . . ."

Behind her, the low grunt of a wounded animal and the sound of a body dragging itself over asphalt. Metal scraping on street.

She turned.

Crotch-shot had crawled to his automatic, a black smear shimmering in his wake. He had wrapped his bloody fingers around the grip and was trying to lift it off the pavement. His arm moved as if he were suspended in acrylic; the gun looked welded to the road.

"Hey, fuckface," she said, and circled around the car, coming up on the kid's flank in her long-legged stride, gearing it up to a run.

She came at him from his left and he didn't see her coming; his attention was nailed to the pistol. She kicked the cap gun out of his hand and threw her foot into the wreckage that used to be his testicles.

He howled and puked a supper of what could only be beer and nachos all over his jacket. He collapsed back onto the pavement with a thud. It sounded like he cracked his skull.

Hemingway stood in the middle of the street, over the vomit-covered kid. She looked back at the one with the broken wrist and Captain Ahab foot. Then she checked her watch: her shift started in a few minutes. Someone honked again.

"You assholes made me late for work," she said to no one in particular. Then she pulled out her phone and dialed 911. "I should shoot you just for that."

A couple of tourists on the corner had their cell phones jabbed skyward in the universal YouTube salute. Hemingway raised her arm as if to wave. Then she smiled and gave them the finger.

HEMINGWAY CLIMBED the steps in morose silence, wondering what she had done to deserve an attempted carjacking. The Suburban was ten years old and not particularly valuable, which was why she used it in the city, so what had that been about? It had to be the kayak. But those kids wouldn't know where to sell a kayak anymore than they would know where to sell weapons-grade plutonium. Maybe it was the heat. It was like the surface of the sun outside and the humidity was floating somewhere around a hundred percent—with conditions like that it wouldn't take much to set off the crazies in the city of the dead.

She thought that she had changed her karma or juju or whatever they were calling it these days. But it looked to be just more of the same: old-fashioned bad luck. It had started when Mankiewicz had been killed and for some reason hadn't let go. Not in three years.

Part of her thought that maybe it was some sort of Faustian bargain that she wasn't aware of—the bad-luck payoff for an unremembered wish. Only she had never asked for a thing. Except for Claire to come back when she was twelve. And then, twenty-two years later, the strength to walk into Shea's and finish what Mankiewicz had started. Not much in the way of a wish list. Not really.

The fates had given her Shea. And his men. When she had been done, four of them were dead and Shea was squirming around on the terra-cotta in his own blood and shit. She had stood over him while her chest made a weird sucking sound. She had raised the pistol, looked into the two rivets of fear that were his eyes, and scooped his brains out with her .357.

Of course it had all been captured by the surveillance cameras and there had never been any charges because video didn't lie.

Nicky, Shea's right-hand man, had put one into her shoulder as soon as she had gone in. She didn't remember much after that, except that she had shot at everything that had moved and more than a few things that hadn't. When it was all done, there were five dead men on the floor and walls and Hemingway had turned and walked out onto the sidewalk with only that weird whistling coming from somewhere in her body to let her know she was not yet dead.

The sucking chest wound was louder than the whine of the approaching sirens and when she stepped into the sun she realized that the side of her face was lit up with 50,000 volts of pain. She tried to open her mouth and all she heard was a scream that she was sure had come from somewhere deep inside.

She sat down on the curb, leaned up against a garbage can and stared down at the pair of pistols in her hands. Then she passed out with her shield hanging from her neck on a length of bloody chain.

When she woke up in the hospital, the shield was still

there but half her left lung and a portion of one shoulder blade was gone. Along with a whole lot of blood.

The first thing the doctor said was that her golf swing would never be the same. She tried to tell him that the only time she had held a club was when she had smashed Skippy Cooper's hand with a Callaway driver when he had tried to feel her up in the pro shop on the night of her sixteenth birthday. But when she had tried to open her mouth, she heard that scream again.

Someone—ballistics had never been able to figure out who, exactly—had put a round into her jaw. It had shattered most of the left ramus—a scratch that sixteen hours of reconstructive surgery and some titanium hardware had managed to correct; she hid a lot of the scar tissue with a pageboy haircut that added a little extra architecture to her already angular features. She had only lost one tooth, now replaced with a nice porcelain implant. But it had taken eleven weeks for the damage to heal to the point where she could chew bananas. Three more months until she was able to speak properly.

When she had finally walked out of Flushing Presbyterian she had a lunch box full of narcotics to help her deal with her repaired body; apparently sedated animals were easier to handle. She had walked away with remarkably few scars—a shiny fifteen-inch strip down her sternum where they had cracked her ribs; four melted patches of skin where lead had burrowed into her flesh; an extra angle to her jaw. She dumped the pills down the toilet when she got home—she had never been a big believer in crutches and she wasn't about to start. She hadn't taken so much as aspirin since. Fuck the doctors. And the five men who had tried to put her in the ground with Mank.

She made the top of the steps, walked into the detective's office, and the room erupted in cheers.

"Nice shooting, Hemi," Papandreou hollered from the far end.

"Did you have to get the guy in the nutsack?" Lincoln asked. "You're already on the Interweb—you flipped the bird at two German tourists."

"At least I smiled at them." And she went to her office.

Phelps was at his desk, his big feet up on the beaten oak, fingers knitted together on top of his head. "Hey, Hem, you okay?" He was trying to sound casual but she recognized concern in his tone. The father of two boys, she always felt she filled the space of de facto daughter in his life.

"You really worried?"

Phelps smiled, shook his head. "Not about you. But the kid you shot in the pills is another thing."

She shrugged and sat down. "It seemed like a good idea at the time."

"Yeah, well, don't it always?" Phelps dropped his feet to the floor, reached forward and picked up a mug with a happy face on the side. Took a sip. "You hungry?" he asked.

"Do you have to ask?"

Phelps stood up and fed one thick arm through a jacket sleeve. "Let's go get us some food."

———

They sat in their usual booth at the back of Bernie's. The diner was the best place in the neighborhood for sandwiches and coffee and its proximity to the precinct had made it a recession-proof success since 1921. At any given moment—night or day—there were a dozen cops sprinkled around the place, reading papers, writing notes, or simply avoiding going home to bad marriages.

Hemingway was downing the last bits of a chopped steak with mashed potatoes, peas, and gravy while Phelps looked on, astounded. "You know, Hemi, I been eating with you for almost seven years now and I still can't wrap my brain around how much food you can shovel away."

"*Shovel away*?" She smiled over a forkful of peas. "You're smooth with the compliments, Jon."

"I'm not kidding." Phelps shook his head. "In the Marines I never seen a guy eat like you. And there were some big motherfuckers in the war. That was back before they let chicks into the forces. At least in combat positions."

Hemingway washed the peas down with a slug of coffee and pushed her empty plate to the edge of the table. "Yeah, well, now they give us guns and shoes and the right to vote. It's a brave new world out there. The times they are a-changin'."

"Don't steal my generation's music, too."

It was then that her phone rang. She wiped her mouth with a napkin and answered with her usual, "Hemingway."

Michael Desmond, the dispatcher for the detective squads, identified himself. Then he told her what had happened.

She felt the chopped steak twitch in her guts. "Jesus. Sure. We'll be there in ten minutes."

When she hung up, Phelps was already on his feet. "Where we goin'?"

"East River Park."

"Who we got?"

She pulled a wallet out of her jacket. "Dead kid."

"Sure it's a murder?"

"Unless he chopped off his own feet, yeah."

III FOUR

THE BONES of the bridge filled the sky overhead and re-
flected off the windshield as Hemingway rolled past the
police barrier. A uniformed officer in a yellow traffic vest
waved her through the utility gate and she parked the Suburban on the grass at the edge of a small park under the
shadow of the Queensboro. They sat in silence for a few
seconds, each going through a personal checklist of preflight
preparations. After a few ticks of the clock the internal mon-
ologues were done and they stepped out onto the manicured
green.

The circus was in full swing on both sides of the yellow
tape. Joggers took photos with their cell phones, excited that
something was happening to break the monotony of the health
train. A handful of news crews had set up camp at the tape-
lines on either end of the path, chattering into the cameras
like pageant contestants, rictus grins and polished hair competing with non sequiturs for attention. The reporters were
almost shouting to be heard over the traffic of the FDR a few
yards away. Two of the borough's big forensic RVs were
parked nose to nose, blocking off any chance of an errant

camera—cell phone or news variety—from converting death into entertainment.

They headed for the Jacob's Ladder pulse of the photographer's flash behind the RVs, ignoring the white-haloed forms of the newspeople bottlenecked at either end of the footpath. The esplanade felt weird without joggers whipping by or Rollerbladers barking *Coming through!* They stepped off the thin strip of asphalt that cut through the imposed green space and Hemingway spotted a stone on the ground. She reached down, picked it up. It was smooth, the size of a robin's egg. She slipped it into her pocket.

Phelps watched her, used to the ritual, then headed toward the screens. "When you gonna get tired of doing your Virginia Woolf imitation?"

They walked the rest of the way in silence.

The boy lay on a tarp, eyes pointed at the sky, chin on chest, the pose reminiscent of Caravaggio's Crucifixion of St. Peter—only there was no tension in the muscles, no flex in the little neck. His clothes were filthy and ripped and stuck to his flesh, one jacketed arm under the railing, reaching for the East River. Queens beyond. He wore a school jacket and tie. His feet were gone.

Dr. Marcus was down on one space-suited knee, practicing his arcane arts on the child. Unblinking. Unmoving. A photographer moved around the tarp, snapping frames. Marcus looked up, nodded an unhappy greeting, and turned back to the body.

Someone came out of the darkness between the privacy screen and the RV and the eerie strobe of the photographer's flash gave the shape a jittery, unhealthy cadence. Three steps later it morphed into Walter Afonia—an old-timer doing the tail end of forty years at the Seventh, most of it in the detective squad.

"Hemingway, Phelps," he said in way of a greeting, then nodded at the boy on the plastic. "Kid's name was Tyler Rochester. Some jogger found him about a half an hour ago."

"The jogger?" Phelps asked.

"Dentist. Name's Zachary Gizbert. He was out here doing ankle training—whatever the fuck that means—and found the kid. Called it in on his phone and a car was here in a little over four minutes. A pair of patrolmen from the Ninth pulled the kid from the drink. He was against one of the pilings to the utility bridge." He nodded at the world beyond the screens. "Gizbert's back at the station giving a statement. Guy shit himself." Afonia paused, waiting for someone to crack a smile or tell a joke or cry. No one did. He continued with the same flat tone that had gotten them to this point. "Kid was dumped upriver. Tide's been going out for three hours."

Hemingway turned to Dr. Marcus. "What's TOD?"

Marcus looked up, nodded. "Two, two and a half hours."

Afonia moved in beside Marcus and looked down at the kid. "Tyler here made a call from his cell phone at six twenty-one to tell the housekeeper he was on his way home. He took a taxi up Fifth. Got off at the corner, stopped at a deli for a Coke. Paid for the cab and the soda with his debit card. Stepped back out onto the street and off the grid."

Hemingway stared down at the child, her interpretive software trying to convert the image of the dead boy into some sort of approachable geometry. "What about his cell phone?"

Afonia nodded like he was just getting to that. "Wasn't in his pockets. Good guess would be the bottom of the East River. If it's not, it's turned off."

"Anything unusual about the body?" she asked.

Afonia shrugged. "Someone took his feet off."

Hemingway looked off into the water washing by, thinking of kayaking on the other side of Manhattan a few hours back. The boy had been alive then. Now he wasn't. All in a few short hours.

Afonia looked down at the kid for a second. Then he swallowed and turned away from the body. "All I know is he disappeared sometime after buying a Coke at six forty-three p.m. and less than three hours later he washes up here. Kid's family lives up near you. You want this case, you can have it." Afonia fished around in his pocket, his hand coming out with a pack of Parliament Menthols. He offered one to each of them, then excused himself for a smoke in the darkness beyond the privacy screens.

Hemingway crouched down on her haunches beside the medical examiner. He didn't bother looking over; for him, a crime scene was not a place of greeting, it was a place of solemnity.

Clear polyethylene bags were secured over the boy's hands with cable ties. Inside the foggy plastic his fingers looked scrubbed and clean, in direct contrast to the filthy clothing and matted, tangled hair that knotted on his forehead. Tyler Rochester had been a good-looking kid who would probably have grown up into a handsome man. Only now he would stay ten forever.

After a few silent moments of magic with a black light, the ME said, "His feet were removed by a saw of some sort. Small, serrated blade. Not a bow saw. Something smaller. Hacksaw most probably." Then he leaned in and pointed at the boy's left eyeball. "There's a small puncture through the sclera, right here. I'm guessing premortem but it might have happened in the river. I'll have a better idea once I have the body back in the lab. Right now, that's all I can give you."

Hemingway looked out across the river, to the lights of

Queens on the other side, dappled with the unblinking eyes of apartment windows. Over there it looked alive. She turned back to the dead boy. Then to the medical examiner. "Defensive wounds?"

"His nails look pretty clean but I'll know a lot more when I get the swabs under a scope. Other than his feet there aren't any signs of a struggle."

The feet were enough.

Marcus stood up and pulled off his latex gloves. "The first cuts are tentative, unaligned. After an inch he hit his stride and did a clean job. But the killer didn't have any practical knowledge of anatomy. The cuts are too high—he went through the bottom flange of the tibia. Half an inch lower and he would have missed both the tibia and talus—it's mostly cartilage and it's a lot easier to saw through.

"I'll have blood work and a tox screen in a few hours. Come see me in three hours." He dropped his eyes to the stumps of the boy's legs, one sticking out of a cuff that the river had not been able to rinse of blood.

Afonia came back in.

"You can go home. We're taking the case."

Afonia blinked once then nodded. "I thought you would."

She turned to Phelps, "Call Papandreou and have him put a list together." She nodded at the dead boy without taking her eyes from Phelps. "Anyone who's walked. Countrywide."

The big cop reached for his phone. "Released in the last six months?"

"Make it twelve," she said, "I don't want to miss this guy because he controlled himself for six months and a day."

THE ROCHESTERS lived in a remodeled brownstone that had everything new money could buy. The home vibrated with the comings and goings of busy people.

A wiry man sporting a well-tailored suit and the fluid movements of a street fighter ushered Hemingway and Phelps into the library. He stood at the door as if an invisible fence prevented him from entering the space and introduced himself as Benoit. Then he told them that the Rochesters would be with them in a few minutes and asked if they wanted anything to drink. Phelps waved it away. Hemingway asked for a Perrier. Benoit disappeared.

Phelps finished casing the room and asked, "How much a place like this cost?" Like any good detective, curiosity was built into his genetic code.

"In this neighborhood? Maybe six mil." She glanced around the room, then amplified the result to include the rest of the brownstone. "The renovating about two. The furniture and paintings another three. Some of it's good." She leaned over and examined a bronze jaguar sitting on a painted Pembroke table. "Most of it's just all right."

"No shit?" Phelps jerked a thumb at the library walls. "I checked and the books are in Swedish and German. This isn't a library, it's a movie set."

She shrugged again. "They're supposed to look good, not be read."

"The rich *are* different."

She shook her head. "They're like everyone else: insecure."

The low hum of ambient noise beyond the doors of the library went silent and a few seconds later the Rochesters came in, followed by Benoit who had Hemingway's Perrier on a small silver tray.

Mr. Rochester clocked in at a fit sixty and had the sharp black eyes and firm handshake of a Wall Street poster boy. Mrs. Rochester was younger by two decades and had the unfocused eyes and loose body movements of a Xanax and vodka cocktail.

When everyone was clear on names, the Rochesters sat down and Hemingway nodded at Benoit as he brought her drink over. "Mr. and Mrs. Rochester, I have some very personal questions to ask and you may not want Benoit—"

Mr. Rochester held up his hand and shook his head. "He stays."

She took a breath and began. "We are sorry for what happened to your son. We want to find who did this and we want to do it quickly. In order to do that, we are going to have to reconstruct his routine. We have one objective: to find the person who did this."

Hemingway focused on Mrs. Rochester—the mother usually knew the routines, tradespeople, help, and schedules—but she was staring into the past, her mouth open, her eyes red and black from crying through her makeup.

Hemingway looked down at her notebook. "The first thing we need is a list of everyone that you can think of who might have had contact with Tyler. The school has given us a list of their teachers and personnel but we'll need to know his extracurricular life as well. Doctor, dentist, piano teacher, fathers of friends who have driven him home, any of your people; tutors; maintenance; cleaning crews; household staff; tradesmen—as comprehensive a list as possible."

Mrs. Rochester's head bobbed up, as if gravity had let go for a second. She tried to focus on Hemingway. "God, you don't think that it was someone he knows—*we know*—do you?"

Hemingway didn't look away. "We don't know."

The woman's mouth turned down and her eyes began ratcheting back and forth, as if the gearing had suddenly skipped. The tears very quickly started. "Why did this happen to us? All I wanted was a baby."

Her husband leaned over and put his arm around her. It seemed an awkward, unnatural gesture.

"Just a baby," she said, hugging herself and rocking slightly.

Hemingway thought of the cells dividing in her own body and she felt a flush of weird shame. "Have you, or any of your people, noticed anything unusual lately?"

Mr. Rochester turned to Benoit, the replicant, who simply shook his head and said in an even tone, "Nothing unusual."

"At what time did Tyler usually get home each day?" Hemingway kept her eyes locked on Mr. Rochester. A man like him would want to be certain that the detective investigating his son's murder had backbone; when they had shaken hands he had squeezed a little too tightly, one of those sexist tests men threw at her every now and then—probably his version of the acid test for competency.

It was Benoit who answered again. "He was usually in the elevator by four thirty-seven. Tonight he stayed late to use the library. Tyler is one of those rare children who likes books." He paused, then corrected himself. "*Liked* books." The man had a precise foreign accent that she couldn't quite place. It had a lilt of French to it but his Rs were a little hard.

"Did he walk to school unescorted every day?"

Benoit again. "Since January."

"And before that?" Hemingway kept her eyes locked on Mr. Rochester, ignoring Benoit.

Benoit opened his mouth and Phelps interrupted. "Mr. Rochester, you were his parents, *you* are the best source of information."

At that, Mrs. Rochester snorted. It was a loud farm girl guffaw. She stopped when her husband hit her with a hard stare.

"Unfortunately we have been occupied with other things as of late. Of everyone in his life, Benoit knew him best."

Hemingway's eyes flicked to Benoit; his face was still molded into that flat battlefield stare his type always had. His head rotated toward her, and she could almost hear the metallic click of gears and grease in the movement. "Until last week I followed him to and from school each day. I think he knew. I discussed it with his father, and Mr. Rochester agreed that he should spend the last month of the year learning what independence was. This was the first time he walked home without my presence."

And Hemingway recognized something else going on behind the flat eyes. She knew the type; Mank had been like that. If she really wanted to think about it, she was like that, too.

"Put a list together of everyone who saw him on a

regular basis. Highlight new people in his circles—the last six months or so."

Mrs. Rochester was nodding off into Mother's Little Helper Land again and Mr. Rochester looked like it was starting to sink in.

"All I wanted was a baby—" She sniffled, a loud inelegant pop, and wiped her sleeve across her nose. "How could someone do this to him?"

Mr. Rochester's face tightened.

Hemingway tried to get the interview back. The next question was a tough one, but standard operating procedure. "Is there anyone who would want to hurt you? Past business dealings, maybe?"

Mr. Rochester stared at her for a blank moment, and then his software was back up. He didn't hold up his hands and give her an emphatic *no fucking way* and he didn't think about it as if it had never crossed his mind, he simply stared at her and said, "Detective Hemingway, I can in no way think of anyone who would feel that something like this could be even remotely justified. This is beyond retribution, Detective. In any capacity." And for an instant his eyes found Benoit. They shook their heads in unison.

"Has anyone noticed anything out of the ordinary recently? Anything at all? A new delivery man, or florist, or car detailer? Any new spouses or boyfriends in your social circle? Anything at all might help, no matter how insignificant." Phelps kept his tone even, direct.

"What can you tell us about Tyler?" Hemingway automatically looked at Benoit but it was Mrs. Rochester who answered from behind some unseen curtain of communication.

"He was a good boy. Funny. Thick brown hair, big brown eyes . . ."

Hemingway remembered the boy's stare pointed up at the sky and the knot of hair on his forehead.

Mr. Rochester added, "He was gifted. Brilliant."

His wife waved it away as if that didn't matter. "He was the fastest runner in the hundred yard dash at the Randall's Island track-and-field day."

An image of the chop lines through his bones flickered in Hemingway's head.

Mrs. Rochester continued talking as the medication and misery gave her a momentary reprieve. "Loved baseball and eggs Benedict. He was my gift. And now he's gone."

Hemingway folded up her three by five, pocketed it, and nodded for Phelps to do the same. These people weren't going to be any help. Not yet. They were in the early stages of shock. Maybe tomorrow morning. Maybe tomorrow night. Maybe never. "We'll need to speak to you sometime tomorrow. If you think of anything in the interim, please let us know."

Mrs. Rochester repeated, "And now he's gone," then faded out again.

———

Benoit walked them to the door and Hemingway watched the way the rest of the people in the house shied away from him, the alpha among the omegas.

Benoit stopped in the foyer with them and asked, "What are the chances you'll find the man who did this?" There was no hope in his voice, no false buoyancy.

Hemingway did her best to sound confident but Benoit looked like the kind of guy who had well-honed bullshit detecting skills. Besides, they hadn't started to connect the dots yet. "We'll pick up a lot of evidence as we move upstream with this. We'll find this guy. I promise."

Hemingway held out her hand.

Benoit stared at it for a second before nodding perfunctorily and saying, "I hope you catch this guy before he sets his sights on another child. Have a good night, detectives."

Then he opened the door.

HEMINGWAY AND Phelps were in their booth at the back of Bernie's again. It was late. Bernie had put on his monthly Fiesta Night, ramping up the décor with greasy Mexican souvenirs hung around the joint like props in a film. The place had been packed with Corona-drinking cops with red eyes for most of the night. Now only stragglers remained.

Hemingway had talked Bernie into warming a Tourista Trio up for her—a culinary sculpture consisting of three burritos and three tacos on a bed of nachos and cheese topped off with fist-sized scoops of guacamole and sour cream. It was past its prime, and the cheese tasted like electrical cord, but she was grateful for the meal. Phelps was finishing a diet soda and a single soft-shell chicken taco adorned with lettuce and a little salt. Alongside the food their improvised office was littered with notes, case jackets, and photographs.

Hemingway knew who would be sitting where without having to look. Most cops were superstitious about things that civilians took for granted, including where to sit in a restaurant. Some chose defensive positions against walls and in corners; some stayed close to the coffee machine so they could order as fresh pots came off the burner; some sat near the windows to watch the world outside. According to the unwritten schedule, this was Hemingway and Phelps's booth every day from 6 a.m. until 3 p.m., from three to midnight it belonged to Donny Lincoln and Nick Papandreou, switching squatters' rights to officers Diego and McManus from midnight to 6 a.m. In a life filled with uncertainty, it was nice to have a table you could depend on.

Hemingway spotted Lincoln and Papandreou ambling over.

Phelps pointed at Hemingway's plate. "We're almost done."

Papandreou threw an orange file on the table, pulled up a chair, and nodded at Hemingway as she put a mouthful of nachos away. "You know, Hemi, for a woman you sure eat a lot of fuckin' food."

She wiped her mouth with a napkin and smiled. "I get that a lot."

"How's it going with your boat?"

The time Hemi spent out on the water was a rolling joke with some of the other cops. She smiled. "Still floating."

"You got a fridge on board? You know, for snacks and shit?"

Hemingway stabbed at the guacamole with her fork. "Sure. I keep Pop Tarts on board, just in case."

Papandreou tapped the orange folder. "Here's the list you asked for."

Phelps slurped the last of his soda out of the waxed paper cup, moving the straw around with his lips to vacuum the dregs, then reached for the file. "How many names you come up with?"

"You don't want to know."

Hemingway's fork stopped halfway to her mouth. She eyed the two cops, then put her fork down with a clang and wiped her mouth again. "Yes. I do."

"In the past twelve months, there have been eleven hundred and thirty-one men paroled countrywide who have violent and predatory histories with children. One hundred and eleven women. We ran the MO through the system and came up empty. Lots of child predators out there but none that seem predisposed to this kind of pathology." Papandreou jabbed a finger at the pile of files on the table. "A lot of bad people on the list but none of them seem right for the job."

Desmond, the dispatcher, came running into the diner. He looked angry which, along with the wet crescents staining the underarms of his suit, was the usual state of affairs with the man: bad news personified. He spotted Hemingway and headed over, eyebrows knitted together in an indignant V.

"Here's Desmond," she said, and pushed her plate away— Desmond was also a spitter.

"Whyintya guys fuckin' tell me you found them?" he snapped at Papandreou.

"We just got here."

Desmond fastened his eyes on Hemingway.

"What's up, Dezzy?"

Desmond's eyes stayed on her face for a moment, then focused on her plate, then looked back up to her eyes. "Where's your fuckin' phone?"

"In my jacket. Right here." She tapped the pile of linen beside her on the bench. She never carried a purse.

"You ain't fuckin' answerin'," Desmond snapped.

She pulled the iPhone out and scanned the screen. "It was on vibrate. Thirty-one messages."

Desmond turned to Phelps. "You, too, fat man?"

"This ain't fat, it's muscle," Phelps said. He eased his

mass back in the seat and his jacket fell open, exposing his substantial gut and an automatic in a shoulder holster. "My phone's in the car."

Hemingway's eyes shifted from Desmond to Papandreou to Lincoln to Phelps then back to Desmond. "Will someone please tell us what's going on," she said.

Desmond held out a dispatch sheet. "The medical examiner's office called. He wants to see you as soon as possible."

Phelps started to slide out of the booth. "What gives?"

Desmond threw his arms up in the air. "You'd know if you had your fuckin' phone with you."

Hemingway pushed the table away and stood up. "You can stop with the histrionics and get to the point."

"Marcus finished with the kid. The tox screens had a lot to say."

Hemingway was up now. "Such as?"

"Tyler Rochester was alive when someone chopped off his feet."

THE MEDICAL examiner's office was unusually busy for 1:30 a.m. Hemingway nodded a few hellos to personnel as she and Phelps worked their way through the hallways on their way to the lab, a bright space where the white-coated acolytes pried secrets from the dead.

Dr. Marcus was in his usual lab—a meticulously appointed subway-tiled space that contained a dozen glass booths, each with a single stainless steel table over an eighteen-inch square grate in the floor. Several of the cubicles were occupied, the inhabitants covered by opaque plastic sheets. When they walked in, Marcus looked up from a cup of coffee he was examining as if it held great cosmic meaning.

"Hemi, Phelps," he said.

No matter how many times Hemingway visited the morgue, it always seemed as if its walls off-gassed disinfectant and death.

After a thorough cleanup that involved changing his lab coat and gloves, Marcus walked them to the far end of the lab where the Rochester boy was laid out.

The boy was pale and bloodless. There was a cut on his

eyebrow that Hemingway hadn't seen down by the water because it had been hidden by his hair—a white gash filled with pale pink flesh, like a third eye not yet formed. His mouth was slightly open, the almost white tip of his tongue protruding between perfect teeth.

Tyler Rochester did not look like he was sleeping. Or in a coma. Or in God's arms. He looked like what he was: a dead child with no feet.

The sheet was folded down, covering him from mid-chest to where his legs stopped at the nub ends of bone. Hemingway took up position at the boy's side. Phelps, looking like he'd rather be anywhere else, stood on the other side of the body. It was clear that no one wanted to be here. The job of examining the dead always held a certain intrinsic sadness but seeing a child lying on the slab was tough for everyone, even Dr. Marcus, a man who had spent his career examining tragedy.

Marcus indicated Tyler Rochester's left eye. It looked like a dried-out cocktail onion pushed into his socket with a little too much force. "The boy had an anesthetic injected into his left eye. Downward trajectory—right-handed. Barbiturate-grade anesthetic. It will take another week for the lab to match the compound but I'd say something like thiopental. And at this point there is no indication of an analgesic, so he would have felt what happened to him." Marcus dictated from memory, ignoring the notes on the trolley.

"How long would it take for something like that to take effect?" Phelps's face was in work mode, an expressionless blend of angles.

Marcus's head bobbed back and forth as he calculated. "On a body mass like his? Twenty-five, maybe thirty seconds."

"Was he restrained?"

"No bruising under his throat, so he wasn't held from behind. No ligature marks on his wrists or ankles, so he wasn't cuffed or strapped down."

"And the kid would have felt this?" Phelps waved a hand over the space where the boy's feet should have been.

Dr. Marcus nodded. "Yes."

Hemingway ran a hand through her hair. "Have you figured out what he used to do this?"

"It was a hacksaw."

Hemingway took in a lungful of disinfectant-tainted air and tried to focus on the notes she was taking in her three-by-five. "You still think the killer lacks practical anatomical knowledge?"

Marcus nodded. "Like I said at the river, both feet were taken off too far above the ankle. Anyone with practice would know that half an inch down—between the tibia and talar head—is a lot easier to saw through because it's mostly cartilage and tendon. And if you look here, at the right ankle, you can see that he doesn't get the hang of the saw until an inch or so in."

Hemingway looked up from her three-by-five. She wanted to say that this didn't feel like the work of a first timer but kept it to herself. "He jabbed the kid in the eye, waited for him to drop, then went to work on his right foot?"

Marcus nodded. "The boy would have screamed, doubled over holding his eye. As long as the killer left him alone for thirty seconds, he probably wouldn't have run. He'd have wasted the last half minute of his life."

"The work was done on a smooth surface. The body was dumped in the water as soon as his feet were removed. There are some abrasions on the epidermal layer on the back of the ankles, near the cut line—the boy was dragged after his feet were taken off, dumped in the water while he was still alive."

"How long until he bled to death?"

Marcus shook his head. "The anesthetic slowed his heart rate, ergo his pulse. He didn't die of exsanguination. He drowned."

Hemingway looked down at the boy; he looked absolutely horrifying now. "How hard would it be to get a hundred-pound kid to a secluded spot by the river? An industrial lot, abandominium, grass yard? Go at sundown. Inject him. After he's out, place him on a wooden door or old tabletop. Maybe a sheet of plywood. Saw his feet off. Four minutes goes fast. Unless you're the one being sawed up." She stared down at the body for a few beats of her heart as the flowchart slowly came together. "If he had a lair, a place where he had taken the boy, there'd be tether marks on his hands. He would have a table for this—a surgeon's gurney or workbench. Something tailored to his needs."

"Maybe it's not part of his fantasy," Phelps suggested. "Maybe he's a sporting man. Maybe he gets his jollies from their helplessness—so helpless that they don't need re-straints."

Hemingway nodded at that. "Maybe."

Dr. Marcus eyed her over the frames of his glasses. "There are no signs of a struggle. No defensive wounds. No ripped fingernails. There are a few cuts and contusions, most notably the one on his eyebrow, but that is postmortem, probably thumped his head on a rock in the river." He took his glasses off once again and went through the same ritual of cleaning his lenses with a static-free wipe, no doubt a nervous habit.

Hemingway wanted to tell the boy that she would find

his killer but she settled on reaching out and touching his hair, as if contact with him would somehow let him know what she was thinking. "What kind of a human being does this to a little boy?"

Marcus shrugged. "If I knew that, you'd be out of a job."

III EIGHT

HEMINGWAY PARKED in the garage and turned off the engine. The tired rattle of the big V-8 mimicked her own exhaustion and she sat there for a few seconds, trying to build up the steam she'd need to make it inside. After a few moments of nothing but the ticking of her motor offset by her own breathing, she grabbed the plastic bag off the passenger seat, checked both mirrors, and stepped out into the dark. She closed the door, leaving the truck with the kayak still strapped to the roof in the cool confines of the little garage behind her building.

She had owned this place for fifteen years. There was a bakery downstairs—one of those Italian bread places that had been there since the heyday of Ellis Island and was now in the hands of the fourth generation. Like everything else that the American Dream had changed, the children of the Arigo brothers didn't see their future in flour and eggs. When Joe and Sal eventually retired or died, a McDonald's or some other soulless corporate sound bite would move in and another piece of what had built America would be lost in the name of progress.

She walked out of the alley, around the building, her jeans sticking to her thighs with the humidity that had gotten worse in the past few hours. Tomorrow—today, technically—was going to be a stinker. One of those days where you wouldn't be able to tell if you were sweating or if you had pissed yourself. She couldn't remember it ever being so damp and wondered if this was one of those fabled hormone-fueled sixth-sense abilities that came along with her special condition.

No, *special condition* was a misnomer.

Life changer was more fitting.

Holy fuck. How had this happened?

At six weeks, her body had not yet changed, not outwardly. But the clockworks hadn't felt right for a week or two. There were no monster cravings—at least not yet—and she wasn't depressed or impatient or any of the other emotions she had seen chew her sister's pregnancies into nine-month bouts of hysterics. But the humidity was bothering her, and it never had before—Mother Nature was finally fucking with her.

She passed the antique store on the corner, then the bakery, and came to her door. She paused for a moment, her forehead on the painted surface. The day had been one of the toughest she had experienced in a while. The discovery she was pregnant, a carjacking, and a boy with no feet seemed like a triple play dreamed up by an epic sadist.

She reached into her pocket for her keys and touched the stone she had picked up on the esplanade near the dead child. She pulled out her keys, unlocked the door, and pushed it open. Her hair blew back in a gush of air-conditioning. She stepped inside and headed up the wide wooden staircase in the dark, her shoes clacking on the hardwood.

Hemingway dropped the plastic bag containing her breakfast onto the island, pulled a carton of whole milk out of the fridge, and poured a glass. She walked over to the wall of arched windows that framed a wedge-shaped view of the West Side Highway to her left, a broad swatch of the Hudson beyond to the right, and Jersey in the distance. The sight of the river brought her back to standing over the Rochester boy. The awkward way his arm had reached out for the river, as if he were pointing at the secrets they would find out there. His bloodless complexion, punctured eyeball and legs that terminated in lopped-off bone only hinted at the madness he had endured.

Her damp clothes were getting cold and the milk almost cracked her teeth but she stood there, looking out at the world. She had been a cop long enough to know they might never know who had killed the little boy. The stars just wouldn't align and they'd end up with a shelf full of boxes moldering away in the Pearson Place Warehouse Facility in Queens. Another cold case. Another child who would stay frozen in time forever. Another statistic.

The sound of footsteps echoed somewhere behind her in the vast space of the loft and she turned. Daniel came at her out of the dark, tired but smiling. "Hey, babe. Helluva day, huh?" He came over and kissed her. He tasted of toothpaste and smelled good.

"You have no idea."

He put his arms around her and she buried herself in his shoulder. "I saw you on the news. The carjackers this afternoon. And I assume the kid they found on the East Side was yours, too."

"Okay, so you have some idea."

He squeezed her for a minute; she knew she could fall asleep leaning against him. "I picked up some shumai and a six of Sapporo. It's in the fridge. Want me to heat up the dumplings and pour you a cold one?"

She thought about the baby inside her, about Tyler Rochester lying under the Queensboro Bridge, arm pointed out at the current, and decided that it was time to talk to Daniel. "Heat the dumplings but the beer can wait." She held up the milk.

He held her at arm's length and stared into her eyes. "Why don't you take a shower? The dumplings will be ready by the time you're done, then you can get some sleep."

"I have to talk to you."

He backed up and crossed his arms—they had had plenty of "talks" over the past two years and she had learned that his standard MO was to listen. Not that he was the strong silent type, but there was a certain fortitude necessary to deal with the kinds of problems she came with: the job; the way she dealt with the world; her family; the gun she kept under the pillow; the times she'd be gone for days on end, chasing down some depraved monster. Daniel's way of dealing with her was to listen. The last one—Mike—had opted for throwing shit and screaming. That had lasted for precisely one argument before she had tossed his ass out. Before that it had been Mankiewicz and that had always been—what was the word?—*broken* seemed to be the only thing that fit. Their relationship had never been built on a healthy foundation.

Daniel looked at her, his head cocked to one side the way Phelps often did, and she wondered if it was a trait common to the men she ended up with in one capacity or another—the ones she worked with and the ones she loved. She looked into his eyes, saw the trust in them, and dug down into herself for the courage to tell him. He was incapable of lying and that innate ability she had to read people had never detected so much as petty jealousy in him. If anyone could take this—and let her deal with it in a way that made sense to her—it was Daniel.

"I'm pregnant."

His mouth broke into a shy smile then quickly flattened out as he realized that her tone had not been as happy as it could have been.

She continued. "Six weeks."

"And?" He reached out and took her hand. There was nothing possessive about it. It was simply his way of saying he was there.

"And tonight I had to talk to the parents of a boy who had his feet sawn off while he was still alive."

Daniel kept his fingers pressed into her palm while he examined her. He didn't look judgmental or angry or confused. But it was obvious he was waiting for her to say something.

"And I don't know if this world needs another child. The good is bleeding out of our species and when I look at all the messed-up things that happen day in and day out, I wonder if it's fair to foist this upon another human being. The notion of any kind of a god is laughable when I see what happens to good people all the time. Fuck free will. Any kind of a god who cared about us wouldn't let the shit that goes on happen."

She paused, waiting for Daniel to say something. All he did was look at her and in that instant, she realized that she had found *him*—the one for her. She thought Mankiewicz was the one but, like so many other things, that had ended when Shea put him in the ground. Daniel had asked her to marry him three times and she had turned him down. It had not driven him away, or made him bitter. He seemed content just to be with her. He gave her space, and he appreciated his. "I love you," she said.

That made him smile. "I know." And that was it. Nothing about the baby. Or about the shitty condition of the world. Or about her doubts. "You want those dumplings?"

She nodded. "Why not?"

Daniel went to the kitchen, turned on the lights, and opened the fridge.

"It's not that I don't want your input. I do. Just not now. I need to know how I feel about things before I ask you how you feel about them."

With that he stopped and turned to her, the foil plate held in both hands. He looked like a long-haired Oliver Twist in a pair of boxers and a wifebeater. "Baby, you don't have to explain this to me. But let me know where you stand before you do anything"—he paused, then added the word—"*decisive*." He stared at her. "Is that fair?"

"You amaze me."

He smiled, put the dumplings into the oven. "That's me—amazing."

"How long until the dumplings are warm?"

"Twenty—twenty-five minutes."

"That's just enough time."

He pulled a plate from the cupboard. "Enough time for what?"

She headed for the bedroom. "You'll see."

He followed her. "At least we don't have to worry about you getting pregnant."

But at the back of her mind she couldn't forget that somewhere out there a child killer was alone in his head. Thinking bad thoughts.

And planning bad deeds.

TREVOR DEACON couldn't take his eyes off him. He wasn't handsome, at least not classically, but he had that unnamable quality Trevor had always been drawn to, the vibe of a young Montgomery Clift. Trevor stared at the photo, at the way he leaned against the fence, hands in the pockets of his gray flannel trousers, tie loose, top button undone. His jacket was over his shoulder—it was supposed to look casual, unpracticed, but Trevor knew better.

The boy was maybe ten years old.

Eleven tops.

Trevor stared into the dark eyes, rife with mischief. The boy would be his. Like the others, a gift.

Trevor used to hunt children through one of the big Internet auctions but that had become boring—like injecting vegetables with hypodermics down at the market, it was too easy. No sport. No challenge. No adventure. *No fun.*

With the auction, it had been easy to find them. He remembered the first; standing on the lawn, holding up a pair of deer antlers that had a starting bid of ninety-nine cents. VeryHappyWendy1977 had 629 feedbacks. Trevor had cycled through some of her completed auctions, and had been able to put a decent file together. The house was white stucco with a small mulberry beside the porch. In the background, behind one of the trees, he could see the spire of a church—this one pale green with a crystal ball at the transept of the cross. There was a number on a porcelain plaque beside the door: 15891. There was a car in the driveway, an old Volkswagen Jetta in white (she had been smart enough to blur the license plate with a basic spray paint command). She also mentioned her son, Franklin, as her reason to live. This, of course, had made Trevor very happy. He was sure that Wendy would be thrilled to know that someone was going to love her little boy for the rest of his life. VeryHappyWendy1977 would have to add a second *very* to her moniker.

The very first time Trevor Deacon had plugged into the collective database of the Internet, his world had forever changed. Since then, there had been no break from the voices in his head. No reprieve from the throbbing between his legs. And he had to keep the spider happy. Always the spider. Or else.

And so he had started hunting.

That first one had taken a little creative thinking, but not much. He had stared a little harder, connecting the dots that Wendy had been happy enough to supply. The child was wearing a Carlyle Academy shirt.

He had tapped into Google and found that Carlyle Academy was located in Staten Island. He found a directory of churches in the area, then Google-Earthed them one at a time until he found one that had a distinguished color to it—green. From there it hadn't been difficult to find 15891 Kottler Road. All because of this wonderful thing called the Internet.

The Internet had helped Trevor go from being a lonely, frightened, frustrated man to being a world-class lover. With the advent of cyberspace—thank you very much, Mr. William

Gibson, for that wonderful phrase—Trevor no longer had to make do with used-up teenagers. Now he got the good ones.

When it came to his boys, Trevor was a benevolent god, teaching them true love with a patience they could never have found out in the world. And like all pure sociopaths, Trevor took this responsibility very seriously. In the old days he had felt special, as if maybe he was one of the last members of a tribe that no one knew about. But now, with the digital world of bits and bytes swirling information around the globe at the speed of light, he had found others out there; like-minded souls he probably passed every day on the train and in the aisles of the liquor store where he bought his mother her Yukon Jack. But along with its blessings, the Internet had also brought about a lot more competition. It was social evolution, and only the smartest would survive.

The rest would be carted off to prison.

A story on the *Times* website had recently reported there were eight million Facebook users under ten years of age.

Then YouTube came along.

YouTubers loved uploading videos of cute kids with the looks he wanted. And it was easy to find them. All he needed as a starting point was a car license plate or a fridge magnet or a grocery bag in the background. Hell, it was amazing how many people had the local news on the TV in the back of their videos and photos. And nothing helped nail down a region like the local news. Why did people insist on leaving it out there for him?

Because they secretly wanted to help.

Trevor clicked back to the picture of little Bobby brown-eyes and staring into that smiling little face made him want it. But Trevor didn't want to use him up in his mind before he got to use him up in the garage; he'd have to make do with one of the others.

On the way to the garage he passed the birthday present his sole friend had given him—a photograph of a duck decoy floating in the current. As he walked by he reached out, brushing the back of his knuckles across the glossy paper. It was the only present he had ever received. As he walked by it he decided on Simon Becker.

He paused in front of the garage door, his hands out on the cold steel skin. The only thing he feared in the world lived in there. The door was riveted quarter-inch steel plate but it was an empty gesture—nothing could keep the spider in. Not if it wanted out. Some nights he'd be alone in his bed—maybe with one of them to keep him company—and he would hear it, the watermelon abdomen popping as it squished under the door. Trevor would freeze. He had read an article that said spiders hunted by carbon dioxide output, so he held his breath.

It would rattle the bedroom doorknob until its claws found purchase. Trevor never looked at it—never made contact with its million and a half eyes. He would lie still, shaking as it came snuffing over, its hairy legs rasping on the carpet. Then it would crawl up into bed with him.

One spiny appendage would wrap around him from behind. Then another. Pretty soon it would be spooning with him. Trevor would shut his eyes and pray. But it didn't do any good. The spider was too powerful to wish away.

When he woke the next morning, it would be gone, back under the garage door to live in the damp shadows of the garage. Waiting for him to feed it.

In the fifty-six years Trevor had lived here, he had never seen it in daylight. When he was a boy he had asked his mother about it. She had lied. There was no spider, she said. And the beatings had gotten worse. So he had stopped asking her about it.

The only thing that kept it away was screaming. *Their* screaming.

Trevor opened the two deadbolts, the padlocks, and the metal crossbar. He swung the door in, waiting for the bloated insect to launch at him from the shadows. But it didn't; somehow it knew he was working on getting another one and it would leave him alone for now.

The wire-caged bulb overhead did little to illuminate the gloom of the space. He walked over to the big coffin freezer, lifted the lid, and took one out. A perfect little foot, frozen solid, five neat little toes bunched up in what looked like a Babinski reflex because the boy had still been alive when he had sawed it off. He had a recording of the screams that he would play back sometimes; Simon Becker had had an amazing pair of lungs. He had one of Simon's feet put away at the back of the box, kept in waiting like a fat blue Mr. Freeze for the perfect summer afternoon. An afternoon like today.

It was small cold beautiful magic in his hand, with five little toes. It would help him forget the one he was working on. Until he was here. Chained down to the workbench. Screaming for him. For the spider.

Trevor sucked the frozen little toes, brittle and hard as china against his teeth, and wept with happiness.

Soon there would be more feet for the freezer.

Oh, thank Jesus for the Internet.

Thank Jesus and Mary and Joseph and God and William Gibson and Montgomery Clift and his mommy and the spider. Thank them all. For the Internet and all the little boys. The boys most of all. Above everything. Thank you thank you thankyou thankyouthankyou. THANK YOU.

Behind him the coffin freezer full of little feet sat silent, a larder waiting to be enjoyed.

As long as people kept posting photos of their children on the Internet, Trevor Deacon would be able to keep the spider away. And in the process, feed his freezer.

And feed it.

And feed it.

And feed it.

‖‖‖ T E N

TYLER ROCHESTER'S fourth-grade picture had been destined to become part of the collective American consciousness from the moment someone with a hacksaw had fastened his sights on the boy. The information pipeline hammered every television, newspaper, magazine, tablet and smartphone with the boy's school portrait. The *Times* had carried a front-page piece on him, below a crisp image of the smiling face. Dark brown hair. Brown eyes. Blue jacket. White shirt. Striped school tie.

Hemingway threaded the Suburban through the staggered gauntlet of news vans. The main event was in front of the police station, a scattered collection of vehicles with one distinct purpose—to entertain. With the daunting task of feeding the twenty-four-hour news cycle, fact had already succumbed to fancy footwork and finger pointing. The reporters would camp at the precinct's doorway until the next tragedy scarred the American landscape and then they would move on.

Their first order of business would be to fault the police. Then, when they were done asking questions and pointing fingers, they would move on to the beefed-up police presence at schools in the city, signing off with the old barn door analogy, asking if the extra security was too little, too late.

Hemingway had slept for two hours, then gone back to the morgue to visit the Rochester boy before they released him to the family. She had been in homicide for ten years, promoted to violent homicide investigation almost seven years back. Not a lot of time under her keel in one respect. A lifetime in another. Many lifetimes, if she considered the dead.

Child killings were the worst. It was one of those things that always felt personal, no matter what you tried to tell yourself.

As a detective, she was, if not used to, then at least familiar with the twisted pathologies of killers; this was going to get worse before it got better. There would be no reprieve, no reassignment. The only break would come when they solved the case. Or it went cold. And if that happened, she'd lose everything she had worked for. She'd lose the street time and the exams and all the hard work—years of having to be just a little more careful than the other cops, always having to do something better than the men she worked with in order to get equal credit. If she messed up the investigation, the derogatory language would start. They'd call her scared or a pussy; the hardened lowlifes in the department would call her a bitch and a cunt. No way—she was not backing down. She'd stick this out because that's what she did, what she had always done. When the status quo were howling in pain, she kept banging away at it. Another trait inherited from her father.

The case would be media heavy to the end. When it came to murders, the value the media puts on lives was directly proportional to the entertainment value of the victim; it was about ratings. Drifters and homeless people got the leanest media coverage and, often, little in the way of investigative resources. The next layer up—another lost cause—were drug addicts. Then came the prostitutes, a layer of individuals no one cared about until the third or fourth victim. After that were drug dealers, followed by felons. The further up the social hierarchy you climbed, the closer you got to the American Gold Standard in murder victims: the rich white child.

She pulled into a reserved parking place and realized that her left hand was on her stomach. She stared at it for a while. Was she trying to feel a baby she wasn't sure she wanted? Or trying to shield it from the bad juju of the job? She rubbed her stomach, a new habit that felt oddly familiar. Then she grabbed her backpack and the Rochester file from the back and got out into the early morning.

She cut around back to avoid the news teams. She clocked through the gate and walked through the garage, nodding a good morning to Albert Chance, the car dispatcher. When she was inside she felt the familiar vibrations of the precinct, a building that never slept. But riding just below the familiar current of the place was a foreign species of white noise, that of interlopers.

The cops she passed on the staircase looked irritated, the natural defensive position of policemen under scrutiny. The morning was always busy as the collective mind of the hive geared up for the day but today it was in overdrive as the eye of the media dialed in on it. The usual hallway chatter was noticeably absent.

Hemingway climbed the back staircase to the top floor, doing the full five flights in a quick jog. With this case looming in front of her, she knew she would be doing little running and no kayaking. Spare time had just evaporated— what little would be left after the investigation was done chewing through her days would end up being spent on not enough sleep. And trying not to lose her mind. Stairs would be her only exercise for a while.

Phelps was at his desk, wearing another of his ubiquitous gray suits and a solid tie, this one a deep navy. He had a coffee in his hand and the same indignant look that the cops on the staircase had—siege mentality setting in as he prepared for battle.

"Detective Phelps," she said officially, handing him a paper bag.

"Hey, kiddo." He looked into the bag, finding four bagels stuffed with lox and cream cheese, all wrapped in wax paper. "Let me guess, one of these is for me, right?"

"Half of one." She winked.

He unwrapped a bagel and began fueling for the day. "You're the best."

She went to the window and looked out onto the street. From up here it looked worse than it had at street level—cameramen running around pulling establishing shots; reporters preening in handheld mirrors; yellow power cables reaching over the ground like tropical vines, feeding electricity to the lights. She put her hands into her pockets and felt the stone from last night. She wrapped her fingers around it. "You ready for this?" she asked.

Phelps took a slurp of coffee from his mug and shrugged. "I ain't never ready to deal with those pricks outside asking questions like 'did we find anything in the boy's ass?' I spoke to Dennet. He's making you PIO."

Being dubbed public information officer was a thankless job that every detective dreaded—it took time that wasn't available for people who didn't appreciate it. In the broadest sense, her job would be to feed the press tidbits of information meant to solicit their help whenever possible. But as the official talking head for the investigation she'd also be the official whipping post if things went screaming off the rails. Besides adding a lot of weight to her workload, it would also put her under a microscope, something she had learned to live with in the wake of the Shea investigation.

Her phone went off at her hip and she checked the message. "Dennet's here."

The noise five floors below rose in pitch as the captain's car pulled up in front of the precinct. From her bird's-eye perch she watched him step out into the glare of lights and he lit up like the Silver Surfer. She watched him shake his head, ignore shouted questions, disappear up the steps and into the building.

"Let's get this party started."

Phelps stood up, grabbed the second half of the bagel and lox he was working on, and pushed the paper bag across the desk. "Load up, you ain't gonna have time to eat after this."

"I hate the press." Hemingway kept her eyes on the group of reporters below. "Any suggestions?"

"With your education and family? Yeah. Go downstairs, resign, and become a Park Avenue plastic surgeon."

"I meant about the press."

"Just don't shoot anyone."

"Thanks."

They took the back stairs down to Dennet's office passing plainclothesmen and uniformed officers scuttling between floors, silent and on edge. Hemingway walked ahead of Phelps, a habit past the point of being unlearned; with Phelps in the back they both had a clear forward view—imperative in their line of work.

Ken Dennet was cornered in front of his office, trying to ease away from a duty cop hammering him with questions. When Hemingway and Phelps came out of the stairwell, he pointed at them, his thumb and forefinger miming a gun. "My appointment is here, we'll talk later." He ushered them into his office, waving Mike Babanel, the precinct's lawyer, over from a corner. When they were all safely inside, Dennet closed the door.

The captain dropped into his seat and stared at Hemingway. From down here the chatter of the media outside had the windows vibrating. "Where are you with the Rochester kid?"

No one wanted to hear that more killings were probably on the way. "We've gone through everyone who was even remotely connected with Tyler Rochester, from the school's personnel records to the Rochester family's list of help, through friends and business acquaintances. No red flags. We've hit all the registered sex offender lists—federal and state—and the recent parolee alerts. No one in any of the databases fits the MO."

Dennet looked up at the ceiling and the word *sonofabitch* came out of his mouth in a protracted hiss. "The good news is that the extra security we're putting on the street will help bolster public confidence. We've got a little over a week until the schools are out for the summer and anyone walks within two blocks of a schoolyard between now and then, I want them to see blue." Dennet leaned forward and pushed a security schedule across the desk. Hemingway picked it up and scanned it while he went on. "We've assigned a police officer to every school in Manhattan—our men are doing double shifts. After school's out, there's extra security around parks, day camps and anywhere else kids hang out."

"For how long?" Hemingway looked up from the three-page schedule, a stopgap measure to make the media think things were under control. Which they were. For now.

"Until you get a break or we arrest someone. I don't need to tell you that those news assholes outside aren't going to get tired, do I?"

The inference wasn't lost on Hemingway; for the three months the Shea investigation lasted, she had been under constant attack from reporters. "Nossir."

"Phelps tell you that you're public information officer on this?"

"Who do I clear my releases through?"

The captain reached for the coffee on the edge of his desk, took a slurp off the top, and nodded at Babanel on the sofa. "Mike will make sure you're golden." Then he made a point of looking at his watch and clapped his hands. "Okay, school duty starts. Go talk to Desmond downstairs—he's got the assignments. You'll handle the daily brief and we'll send a summary out to the other precincts. Then it's off to protect and serve the school children of this city—I want people to think that this is a police state. And above all, I don't want anyone else disappearing. One fucking kid goes off the reservation and those cocksuckers outside will do more harm than good. If you need help, or don't understand something, you ask. Clear?"

"Crystal, sir."

"Good. After school duty, you and Phelps hit the lists again. Do the rounds and ask questions. Find this guy."

||| ELEVEN

HEMINGWAY AND Phelps had pulled duty at the Lyle School for Boys—one of Manhattan's oldest private educational institutions and a fixture of the Upper East Side. It served the same demographic as the Damien Whitney Academy for Boys where Tyler Rochester had gone. Maybe the man they were hunting had a taste for the neighborhood.

Phelps leaned against the hood of the cruiser, going at his fourth coffee of the day. He looked like he was oblivious to his surroundings but two tours on a sniper team in Vietnam had honed his observational skills to near clairvoyance; if anything within sight was anomalous, he'd spot it. Hemingway paced the sidewalk and watched the street, her hands on her hips, her jacket open. The final bell had rung ten minutes ago but there was a fifteen-minute override in place to help with latecomers. This made no sense to Hemingway— the Lyle School was not the kind of place where the students were late. Especially not after one of their kind had been splashed all over the news.

The cops weren't out for surveillance. They weren't out as a deterrent. They were there so it would look like the NYPD was on top of things. It was a PR move that Hemingway and Phelps resented because it pulled them away from the case. Now that the coroner's reports were finished, there were things to do, places to go, people to visit. Their window was floating by and they were making sweetfuckall in the way of headway because they were stuck here, making an appearance to appease the news cockroaches.

The heat was in a dancing mood again and the day was a sultry motherfucker. Hemingway wanted to take off her jacket but a white shirt rendered invisible by perspiration was no way to keep the boobage dialed down—something she never forgot on the job.

Her phone went off, startling her with its shrill chirp. She slid it from her pocket and answered the call. "Hemingway."

"Yeah, Detective Hemingway, this is Marvin Stapleton, I'm with the Nineteenth. We got a problem."

"What?"

"I'm at the Huntington Academy. Detectives Lincoln and Papandreou just left."

Hemingway knew the school; she had briefly dated a boy who had gone there. It was three blocks north, two east.

"And a kid got snatched."

She felt her stomach lurch and she regretted the second breakfast she had pounded down after the briefing.

"The perp killed a driver and took a boy."

"Rope it off. We'll be there in four minutes." She whistled for Phelps as she ran for the SUV.

STAPLETON HAD cordoned off the street and put up screens
to conceal the mess from prying eyes. A single news team was
already there, drawn by the scent of blood in the water. His
cruiser was parked in the middle of the asphalt, beside the
crime-scene screens, lights thumping like a heart. The Suburban slid around the corner in a four-wheel drift, tires smoking.
Hemingway punched up the final hundred yards, screeched
to a stop at the perimeter, got out, and ran under the tape
with Phelps closing up her wake.

Officer Marvin Stapleton stood by the cruiser looking
shell-shocked. Another man—the school's headmaster, Hemingway guessed—stood off to the side of the vehicle. He wore
a good-quality suit and brogues.

"What happened?" was the first thing out of her mouth.

Stapleton jerked his head toward the wall of accident screens
he had set up. "Driver for one of the kids is dead. Kid's gone."

"We know the name of the kid taken?"

Stapleton shook his head. "I called you as soon as I found
out and been pulling out screens since."

Hemingway turned to Phelps. "Run the plate. Get us an

ID on this kid now." Her need-to-know programming was up and running and she ducked behind the screen.

It was a big Lincoln sedan, black, with tinted windows. The driver's door was open about a quarter of an inch. A puddle of blood had accumulated on the pavement under the sill, already scabbing over in the heat. She pulled a pair of latex gloves from a kit in her pocket and eased the door open. The stink of blood and shit rose out of the vehicle, made all the worse by the sour heat baking the street. Off in the distance the thrum of emergency sirens was nearly buried by the morning noise of the city.

A man in a black suit was sprawled across the front bench. He was a big man who had not yet been reduced by death. He was slumped sideways onto the passenger's seat, twisted and lying faceup. His left hand was on his throat, middle finger dipped into the long gash. Blood had pissed everywhere, splattering the steering wheel, dash, windows and carpets. His mouth and right eye were open. A jet of blood had squirted up onto his face and his left socket was a flat glistening puddle of red.

Hemingway scanned the interior. "What happened?" she asked Stapleton from the door of the vehicle.

The whir of emergency vehicles was gaining on the clatter of street noise, the distant Wagnerian thrum of police cars, fire trucks, and EMT vehicles: cavalry on the way.

Stapleton leaned in so he wouldn't give the news team at the fence ammunition and Hemingway gave him a point for that one. "Lincoln and Papandreou were here with me all morning. They had the back; I had the front. It's a big school, nearly six hundred students. The final bell rang and I saw Headmaster Sinclair outside," he nodded at the man in the suit standing at the edge of her vision. "He gave us the wave off and then I saw the car.

"It was just sitting here, idling in the drop-off zone. I came over. Rapped on the window. The sides are tinted but when I looked in the front . . ." He let the sentence die and swallowed loudly. "I saw."

Phelps was off his phone on the other side of the car, his body over the windshield at an odd angle as if it were electrified and he were afraid to touch it. He looked over the roof of the car at Hemingway. He, too, spoke softly. "Car is owned by a Jesse Grant."

Hemingway turned to the headmaster. "Do you know if you have a student by the name of Grant?"

He was rattled out of suspended animation. "Yes. Of course. Bobby Grant. Grade five. One of our brightest musicians—a pianist." His head ratcheted down to the car and his mouth went into a perfect O, making him look like an emoticon. "Is this the Grant boy's driver? Oh, Jesus."

Hemingway wondered how many black Lincolns turned up here every morning to drop off children. Since the recession, conspicuous consumption was out and low profile was in; a lot of the wealthier urbanites had traded their Bentleys and S-Class Benzes in for the less showy, and less costly, Lincolns.

"What's he look like?"

Sinclair's eyes scrolled up and to the right. "Ten years old. Brown hair, brown eyes. Thin. School uniform."

The description set off a tremor somewhere behind her eyes. She glanced up at the school and the windows were filled with the curious faces of hundreds of boys. Did any of them know how lucky they were?

Two patrol cars came around the corner, sirens blaring, pushing the early-morning pedestrians up onto the sidewalk. She was grateful that there wasn't much to attract tourists to this area at this time of day.

She grabbed the headmaster by the elbow and steered

him toward the school, gesturing Phelps over as chaperone for the man. "I need a picture of the boy and I need it right now."

Phelps took over steering duties and ran the headmaster across to the school.

The approaching police vehicles were a live presence that shook the earth, a cacophony of pulsing sounds and lights at the corner of the street. When they cleared the traffic lock, they barreled up the street in a cloud of scorched pavement and rubber that scared the news crew out of the way. The legion of flashing vehicles screeched to a halt. Doors opened. Officers spilled out onto the pavement and raced over.

"You see anything unusual?" Hemingway asked Stapleton.

He glanced at the car and shook his head. "Kids running up and down the street like they're on Broadway. The bell rang and they headed in. When the street was clear I saw the guy in the Town Car was just sitting there. That's it. No honked horns. No flurry of motion. No distraction—I watch for shit like that." He rolled up his sleeve, exposing an Airborne tattoo on his forearm. "Two tours in Iraq. You don't sneak up on me."

Hemingway glanced at the screens that hid the Town Car and thought, *Obviously*.

"Nothing unusual until I spotted the car idling here."

"How long was it running before you came over?"

He shrugged. "I don't know. Six, maybe eight minutes. It took me a few minutes to realize that it should have gone. It kind of fit in with all the kids in the formal wear. It belonged."

"They're not tuxedoes, they're uniforms." She turned away from Stapleton and wondered if the gap between detective and street cop had broadened since she had made it up through the ranks. She looked up and down the street, thinking that with a twelve- to fifteen-minute lead time the kid could be on the dark side of the moon by now. Or floating in the East River.

The uniformed cops closed in on her, a field of blue glittering with nickel and brass. She turned back to Stapleton. "They have a no-idling policy in front of the school?" She had done a lot of work with the board of education and in the big push to go green, a lot of schools had implemented a no-idling policy.

"The headmaster said they don't tell the parents how to behave because it would be 'counterproductive.'"

"You've got to be fucking kidding." Her eyes drifted over Stapleton's shoulder to the mouth of the street. Another cruiser rounded the corner, nearly taking out a cameraman. There were now six police cruisers, an ambulance, and a van from the fire department just over the tape. She was surrounded by uniformed police officers.

She took a breath and let it power her voice. "It looks like a little boy has been abducted. Brown hair and brown eyes. School uniform." Over the line, the reporters began chattering at the flurry of motion.

Her phone chirped and when she held it up she saw Bobby Grant's face smiling out at her—a citywide memo from Phelps. Within seconds all of the cops in front of her were staring at the same image on their own phones.

Bobby Grant looked so much like Tyler Rochester that they could have been brothers.

||| THIRTEEN

THE REPORTERS had a hard time finding fault with the NYPD's reaction time. Under Hemingway's direction, the police had fanned out from the Town Car epicenter like an antivirus program, scouring every shadow and dark corner in the neighborhood. The smart money was on a vehicular abduction but they went on a thin wedge of hope that the boy had been taken by someone on foot. It wasn't the smartest line of reasoning, but sometimes the easy money pays off.

The police didn't find Bobby Grant. He had been pulled into a wormhole.

No witnesses. No surveillance photos or video. No sign of him at all.

Hemingway and Phelps ended up in the headmaster's office, fielding calls while appropriating files. The room smelled of mahogany and ancient pipe smoke and history. The sofas were tufted leather and the Persian carpet was worth more than many homes.

The first order of business was to make certain that the Grant boy had been in the car with the dead man. A call to

the home verified that he had left for school with Desmond—
the man with the slit throat cooking in the heat-baked Lincoln
outside. It seemed like a silly thing to have to verify but it
was entirely possible that the driver was there to either pick
up or drop off homework—something the headmaster said
happened from time to time.

It took another ten minutes of no news before Hemingway
succumbed to the grim truth that they had lost Bobby Grant.
And there had been three cops at the school—two if you
discounted Stapleton. She wasn't prone to claustrophobia and
she had never experienced a panic attack, but she suddenly
felt like she wasn't getting enough air. She nodded at Phelps,
who was standing over the headmaster's shoulder as they
went through attendance logs. "I'll be outside," she said, and
turned to the door. "Get a faxed release from the Grants and
a copy of the boy's file. And I want a list of everyone who
has stepped foot in this school. Then we go talk to the parents."

Phelps, who looked like he belonged behind a tractor
instead of a badge, nodded and by the way his eyes narrowed
he confirmed that he understood something was up with her.
Like many partnerships—business or personal—they had developed a silent communication that transmitted more than
language often did. "Sure."

She cut through the outer office and was met by the
worried stare of two secretaries. Once out in the hall she was
hit with more uncomfortable looks from faculty and students.

Hemingway had firsthand experience with the immutable
pain of having someone taken: her eight-year-old sister Claire
had been abducted from their beach house when they were
kids. The police were called. Private detectives hired. Armed
bodyguards for the rest of the children. Her first taste of *too
little, too late.*

Claire was found in a field in East Hampton three days

later; she had been beaten to death with a framing hammer. The killer was a nobody—just a bad man with worse ideas and poor self-control. The loss of Claire had manifested itself as a weird presence on the periphery of Hemingway's mind, always ready to remind her that things went off the rails more often than anyone wanted to admit.

Her parents had brought in counselors. Dr. Bryce, the family psychiatrist, had talked to her for a couple of years. She still talked to him every now and then. But all the therapy and role-playing and talking it out hadn't killed the feeling that the world was a place that couldn't be trusted, not in any real sense of the word. All because someone couldn't stop his id from grabbing the steering wheel and punching down on the gas.

She stepped through the double oak doors into the tiny courtyard. The heat hit her from the asphalt up. Before she was at the fence—twenty paces away—her head was shimmering. She took off her jacket and the movement made her shoulder blade click and she realized that this was going to get a lot worse before it got a little better—something about the way it was unfolding was more oppressive and threatening than the heat and the helplessness.

The forensics guys in their space suits had set up a clean tent around the car and even with the pumped-in air-conditioning she knew it had to be a million degrees under the plastic enclosure. Cops had come back from their search for the Grant boy. They milled about like extras in a film who hadn't been given any direction other than to look defeated. She cut through them and headed across the street.

As she moved, she consciously avoided turning her head toward the news cameras set up at either end of the street.

Papandreou stood beside one of the big panels that blocked the crime-scene tent from the cameras, sucking on a smoke and generally looking like he was trying out for an I-don't-give-a-fuck-athon. "Hemi," he said flatly.

"Where are we?"

Papandreou took a drag, blew the jet straight up into the lifeless air, and nodded at the screens. "They just pulled the guy out of the car. ME's still in the tent." Hemingway stepped around one of the protective panels. Behind the barriers, where the tiniest breeze couldn't reach, it felt like a foundry.

She recognized Mat Linderer outside the blue tent in his static-free suit, his attention nailed to a Panasonic Toughbook.

"Find anything?" she asked, simultaneously checking her watch.

Linderer looked up, then went back to his screen; everyone knew the clock was ticking. "Bunch of prints, looks like two sets. The majority belong to Desmond Grossman, our driver. A bunch of smaller prints that probably belong to the child are all over the back door and seat belt buckle on the right side. Both passenger doors were wiped clean."

Hemingway filed that one away. Whoever had killed the driver and—presumably—taken the child, had not only touched the car but had the presence of mind—or training—to wipe their prints off. Which meant they hadn't been wearing gloves. "The body tell you anything?"

"Single swipe with a very sharp blade across his throat. Nicked the top of the larynx. Severed both jugular and carotid. Didn't know it was coming is my guess."

"How's that possible?"

Linderer stopped in mid-keystroke and turned to her. "I collect the data, you answer the questions."

"I thought Friday was let's-be-a-prick day; today's only Tuesday."

Linderer stopped typing. "I didn't mean—"

"Yes, you did. We exchange ideas, that's what we do. You

want to be an asshole, do it on someone else's time. I know it's a hundred-and-fifty fucking degrees out here but we've got a missing child and we just pulled a human Pez dispenser out of the Lincoln. I would like to find this kid before someone does bad things to him, understand?"

"Yeah. Of course. I'm hot."

"We're all hot, Matty. This weather sucks. But you don't see me being a cunt, do you?"

He opened his mouth to protest but something stopped him. "I'm sorry."

"What else have you got?"

Linderer tapped the screen of the laptop. "When I model the blood spatter, Mr. Grossman in there had his pipe cut on a downward angle."

"You mean a downward stroke?"

He nodded and the collar on his space suit rasped in the lifeless air. "Yes, but the cut was in a straight line—there's no sweep to it. It was pulled across his throat from a low angle. The killer was probably kneeling on the pavement beside the car and when Grossman leaned over—probably to get something from the glove compartment—the door opened and he was hit with the blade."

"What was in the glove box?"

"Two Charleston Chews, a cell phone, a handgun, and three shots of Cialis."

"What kind of a pistol?"

"Small automatic. Beretta. He had a carry permit."

Hemingway was once again amazed at how quickly the forensics guys were able to turn someone's life into the past tense—it always struck her as abrupt.

Mr. Grossman hadn't known much about guns—a Beretta was as deadly as far as you could throw it. But it was expensive. For some, cost equated to value; the pistol had probably been purchased by someone who wanted the best but didn't know what to look for.

Linderer continued. "I'll have a full report once we get the car back to the lab but don't expect any surprises. Whoever did this knew what he was doing."

Phelps was suddenly there, straightening his tie. "I caught Dr. Grant at the office. A car is on the way to take him home." He held up his smartphone, the photo of Bobby Grant smiling out of the screen. "It's already on the news."

She took out her own phone and cycled to a photo of Tyler Rochester. She held it up beside the phone in Phelps's hand and stared at the pictures of the two children. It was impossible to miss the similarities.

"We've got one break," she said.

"Which is?" He pulled off his jacket and his shirt was stained with a deep shadow of sweat down the front and under both arms.

"We know his type."

ACCORDING TO Dr. Grant's files at both the DMV and city hall, he was two weeks shy of his sixty-first birthday. He looked like a mummified fifty, a benefit of being one of the city's most prestigious plastic surgeons. Mrs. Grant was twenty-five years his junior and had the classic look of a certain kind of second wife, replete with breast implants and a flat expression that differed from Tyler Rochester's mother in that it came from Botox, not booze and pills. The resemblance to a ventriloquist dummy was hard to miss.

Unlike the ministry of help at the Rochesters' townhouse, there was only one other person in the apartment—Mrs. Grant's mother, who looked in some strange way more suited to Dr. Grant than his wife. Everyone was holding up well considering their world had just been destroyed by a man with a razor blade.

Hemingway sat down in one of the wing chairs facing the sofa and explained that they had a few questions that they had to deal with now—things they needed in order to move forward with the investigation. She ran through the questions she had put to the Rochester boy's parents, focusing on new people in their son's life.

Mrs. Grant's mouth barely moved as she talked about her missing child. She began by saying that he was a good boy. Hemingway had interviewed many parents and they always began with that same heartbreaking expression. After that, Mrs. Grant went on in an orderly fashion, almost a summation of Bobby's life. He excelled at school, particularly science, taking MIT's Young Achiever's award this year for a robot he had designed and built that cleaned countertops using black light to target bacteria. She nodded at the piano in the corner of the living room, a shiny art deco Bösendorfer; she thought he played too much but when she approached the subject, he had reacted like most kids when told they had to cut back on video games. With pride she related how he had written two piano concertos over the winter and had a recital coming up at the Brooklyn Academy of Music in late July.

Bobby's driver, Desmond, had worked for them for six years now, driving the boy to and from school, to his extracurricular activities and piano lessons from the first time he had stepped out of the apartment on his own. Dr. Grant had purchased the pistol they found in the glove box. It was clear to Hemingway that both Dr. and Mrs. Grant were upset about Desmond's death. They seemed like compassionate, decent people.

The deeper they got into the questioning, the tighter Dr. Grant's face got, until he stood up, nodded at the door, and told them that they would better serve his son if they were out trying to find him.

After cards were exchanged, Dr. Grant walked them to the elevator, telling them to do anything necessary. If they faced any budgetary restraints, they were to come to him. The bell pinged and the doors slid open. Phelps stepped into the car and as Hemingway turned to shake Dr. Grant's hand, he held it and looked into her eyes.

"After everything we went through to have Bobby, it will kill his mother if something happens to him. Find my son."

Hemingway did her best to look confident as she nodded. Then she turned and stepped into the elevator. As the doors slid closed, Dr. Grant stared at her, his face still locked in disbelief. On the descent to street level, something told her that he was still standing there, staring at the elevator doors, trying to figure out who he had to speak to in order to trade his soul for a time machine.

They moved through the lobby and out to the no-standing zone where she had parked the Suburban. When they reached the SUV, her phone chirped.

"Hemingway."

"Yeah, Hemi, it's Lincoln. I got you that appointment you wanted at the Manhattan office of the Department of Waterways and Estuaries. Your contact is Dr. Inge Torssen . . . Torssen . . . Torssensomethingorother. It's up near the Bronx—One Hundred and Forty-fourth on the West Side. Can you be there in fifteen minutes? This Torssen woman has a flight out of Newark in two hours and she won't be there for much longer."

"Fifteen it is," she said, hung up, and pulled a U-turn in a smoking arc of rubber.

||| FIFTEEN

DR. INGE TORSSENNSON was tall, blond, intelligent, and hypereducated. A quick Internet search showed that she had started her career as an undergrad at the Norwegian University of Science and Technology, studying particle theory under the loose rubric of general physics. She eventually moved to fluid dynamics, garnering a PhD in a branch of wave refraction from MIT. Her specialty was Doppler current profiling. She was at the Manhattan office of the Department of Waterways and Estuaries on a one-year sabbatical before accepting a professorship at UC Berkeley.

She had the stride of a wide receiver and as they descended into the basement of the building, Phelps whispered to Hemingway that he now understood why the Vikings had kicked so much ass.

"I've looked over the maps and times you forwarded and have come up with a few things that might help with your investigation." Her English was excellent but flowered with the soft consonants Scandinavians are famous for. At the end of the hallway she pushed open the double doors. The blast of humidity was a much heavier presence than the New York summer five floors up at street level. The walls were literally sweating.

The scale model of the Hudson River rolled to the far end of the room, a complicated pool under a domed ceiling that could have housed a fleet of jumbo jets. The shorelines of Manhattan, New Jersey, and Brooklyn were recreated in scaled detail, the earth, concrete, stone, grass and glass represented by a uniform brown resin. Wires, cameras, and sensors monitored every square inch of the man-made island, sending the stream of digital information to several computer stations positioned around the installment. Hemingway's eye was immediately drawn to the scaled-down Statue of Liberty, roughly the size of a Barbie doll, at the far end of the pool.

Beyond the diminutive Lady Liberty, a couple of modelers stood in thigh-high water at the Jersey docks, wearing waders and double filter particle masks. They were modifying the shoreline to post-Sandy specs and they looked like giants in an Asian science fiction film.

"I've reverse-engineered the boy's most probable path based on the drop times you provided. You have to understand that there are numerous variables involved, not just current. I've factored in salt flux, wind, and tide—but this is all very speculative. The body may have hung up in debris somewhere for a while. The good news, if you can call it that, is that the particular area of the river where he washed up is subject to extremely heavy currents that have established patterns." She walked them to one of the platforms at the far end, a steel balcony above the northeast corner of the island of Manhattan.

"If the boy was abducted between six twenty-one and six thirty-one p.m. on Monday, as you indicated, and his body was found at nine twenty-one by a jogger," she said, pronouncing it *yogger*, "we have a window of a little under two hours. You suspect that the boy's body was dumped at—or just after—sunset, which was eight twenty-two p.m. If he was put in the water at, say, any time between eight twenty-five and eight forty-five, with wind and current factored in, I'd estimate that he was put in the water somewhere here . . ." The laser pointer came to life in Torssennson's hand, the red dot of its eye zeroing in on a stretch of water that boiled and bubbled with the diminutive currents fed through the simulated topography. It was a stretch where the Hudson River cut between Randall's Island and Astoria.

The red dot crawled along the shorelines of Astoria, then crossed the channel, and negotiated the terrain of Randall's Island, once again crossing water—this time the Harlem River—hitting the shore of Manhattan at 120th Street. "I can't be certain where the boy was dumped, but it was above here," she said, circling a bubbling epicenter of foam at the southern tip of a stretch of scaled-down real estate stenciled with the words RANDALL'S ISLAND.

Hemingway knew that stretch of water; she had kayaked around it hundreds of times, and knew that fickle patch of roiling anguish had a reputation of being evil as far back as anyone in New York could remember. It was one of the few places on the river that the pleasure boaters avoided, especially the weekend sailors with the expensive nav systems on boats tattooed with monikers like *Daddy's Li'l Girl* and *My First Million*. Only the big river barges—laden with garbage or stone—negotiated its wrath.

Hemingway focused on the scaled-down current and eddies. "That's Hell Gate," she said.

Then her phone rang, something that surprised her; she figured that this far into the earth there wouldn't be any reception. She mimed an apology to Dr. Torssennson and went to the far end of the platform.

"Hemingway," she answered. Across Manhattan the men in particle masks were busy mixing whatever it was they used for landscaping material and the visual was so surreal that she wouldn't have been surprised to see a guy in a Godzilla suit somewhere off to their right. The office parties down here had to be YouTube worthy.

"Hemi, it's Lincoln. I just got a call from a retired judge who saw the Rochester boy's story on CNN this morning. Name's Jack Willoughby. Lives in Boca. He said there was a remarkable similarity between the Rochester case and one he presided over back in eighty-four."

She didn't get the flush of elation or the push of adrenaline that most people would have; years of following leads that enticed her down the road to nowhere had hardened her hope reflex. "That's three decades ago, Linc." She wasn't being negative, just pragmatic—according to Dr. Marcus, the Rochester boy had been taken apart by a nascent killer, not someone with a history for this kind of thing. And these guys had a window that usually closed in their late forties as their testosterone waned. Something about this didn't seem right. "Did you run a check on Willoughby?"

"Thirty-eight years as a trial judge in the city—solid record."

"What did he have to say?"

"He had a case where a twenty-eight-year-old male was pulled over for running a light in Queens. After a shouting match that made the duty officer suspicious, he checked the car and found a pair of children's feet in a grocery bag in the trunk. The perp ran but the car was registered in his mother's name and they picked the guy up at his home a few hours later."

At that her adrenaline kicked in. "And?"

"The prosecutor couldn't prove that the feet had come

from a murder victim; Deacon's lawyer argued that his client had purchased them from a man who worked in a medical supply warehouse. And the body of an eleven-year-old Indian boy had indeed gone missing from one such facility a few weeks before. The perp served six months for disrespectful treatment of human remains. Probation afterwards—judge couldn't remember the details but I'm looking into it now."

"We have a name? An address?"

"Name's Trevor Deacon, that's d-e-a-c-o-n. I checked—he's on Crestwood in Astoria. Hasn't moved in all this time."

She hung up and turned to Phelps. "Jon, it's go time."

"Whacha got?"

"We have a line on a perp with a similar MO. Retired judge called it in. The guy lives right there," she said, pointing to where Dr. Torssennson's pointer had just walked across the water. "In Astoria."

III SIXTEEN

THE HOUSE was a little slope-roofed postwar with a garage, a small front yard taken up by an ancient elm, and a faded Post-it taped inside the screen door that told peddlers, Mormons, and Jehovah's Witnesses to take their business elsewhere.

Hemingway pulled up to the front of the house with two patrol cars as escort. She and Phelps hit the pavement and headed up the front steps while two of the patrolmen headed around back, guns out. The second pair of uniforms stood at the curb.

She and Phelps took up position on either side of the door. Thirty seconds after she pushed the bell, the front door opened and a small woman who had to be in her early eighties stuck her head out.

"Cantya read?" she rasped through a puff of tobacco smoke and jabbed a finger at the faded paper sign. "No Jesus. And no fuckin' Girl Guides." She stared at Hemingway for a second, then her eyes slid over to Phelps before coming back and settling on the undone top buttons of Hemingway's white cotton blouse. "Not if they know what's good for them."

Hemingway held up her badge, her other hand behind her, fingers wrapped around the rubber grip of her revolver. "We're looking for Trevor Deacon."

The old woman tightened her mouth around the cigarette and took a long haul, her lips wrinkled like an ancient, furry sphincter. "What'd he do this time?"

Hemingway took a step sideways so the woman would see the cruisers on the street. "Is Trevor Deacon here?"

From behind a cloud of smoke she seemed to teeter on the precipice of indecision for a few seconds before she nodded. "Yeah. He lives downstairs." She stepped out onto the porch in her ancient stained bathrobe and a pair of Pink Foil Nikes. "That's his door."

"Is he home?"

"How the fuckinell I know? I got X-ray vision I don't know about?"

Hemingway leaned down and looked the woman in the eyes. "Anyone else in the building?"

The old lady eyed her for a second. "Yeah, Elvis," she snapped, then tried to step back into the house and slam the door.

Hemingway grabbed her arm, swung her around, and Phelps had cuffs on her before her screaming started. Hemingway put her finger to her lips in a be-quiet gesture, and handed the old lady off to one of the uniformed officers. He dragged her down to the car, screaming that the cops were a bunch of assholes.

The two detectives ran through the upstairs part of the house, checking the rooms one by one. The door that led to the basement was boarded up. When they had finished, they headed down the steps outside. The old lady was still screaming inside the cruiser, every sentence accentuated with a subwoofer thud as she tried to kick her way out.

Hemingway looked for a buzzer at the basement door. The button had been taped over with another curled-paper ballpoint pen sign that read No Solissiters. She pulled the screen open and knocked on the heavy multilock metal door— the kind designed to keep people out. Or in.

They waited.

She knocked again.

Phelps eased sideways, took off his sunglasses, and leaned into the window, cupping his hands to see into the dark.

Hemingway raised her fist to bang on the door again when Phelps let out a low groan. "Jesus, no!" he said, and pushed her aside.

He hammered the door with two good bottom-foot kicks and the impact barely registered.

"Phelps, what the—?"

But he already had his automatic out. He leveled it at the door and blew out the two padlocks. Then he kicked it in. It flew into the wall and bounced back.

He screamed, "Call EMS now!" to the cops at the curb.

Instinctively, Hemingway went in first, crouching low and taking the left flank like they had done a thousand times in drills and a few dozen on the job.

As she swung the muzzle of her pistol around, she saw why Phelps had blown out the locks.

Whatever it was now, at one time it had been a human being.

"This must be Elvis," Phelps said, and holstered his pistol.

||| SEVENTEEN

BENJAMIN WINSLOW ticked off the final multiple-choice question, dropped his pencil, and raised his hand.

The scratch of graphite on paper around him ceased and a shuffle whispered through the lecture hall; he was the first one finished. *Again.* All three parts. Benjamin picked up his knapsack, walked to the front of the hall, and dropped his test paper and the Number 2 pencil onto the monitor's desk. He didn't bother nodding at the man; he often found the openmouthed look of awe annoying.

He pushed through the polished bronze doors and stepped out into the day. A photographer leaning against one of the massive limestone columns that flanked the door snapped a photo and gave him the thumbs-up. "Congratulations, kid. How's it feel to be a genius?"

"*Lorem ipsum,*" he said and headed down the steps before the guy figured out that he was being made fun of.

Benjamin took out his phone and dialed his father as he had promised.

He answered in one ring. "Dr. Winslow here."

"Hey, Dad, I'm done with the SATs."

"How'd you do?" his father said in his usual monotone.

Tests of all kinds had been a constant in Ben's routine ever since he could remember. Beyond his vast library of talent was an acute ability for predicting test results. But it wasn't much of a prediction; it was simply the ability to recall the number of questions he had known the answers to versus the number of questions he hadn't—simple math, really. "One of the multiple-choice questions in the reading section was interpretive so it depends on the test bias. Other than that, perfect." He got to the sidewalk and headed west, toward the park.

"Why don't you come to the museum? I've got to finish up some notes for tomorrow's lecture but I'll be done by the time you get here. We can walk down to the Garden Vegan and get a nice salad. Bean curd for the genius."

"How about a cheeseburger?"

"Kings don't dine on cheeseburgers, son." His father was quiet for a second and Benjamin wondered if he was angry. "Grab a cab."

Benjamin stopped at the curb and looked both ways before crossing Madison. "It's a nice day. I'd like to walk."

This time there was no pause. "We've talked about this. I don't want you walking through the park. It's filled with all manner of miscreants in the summer. Take a cab."

Benjamin wanted to tell his father that technically it was still spring but settled on, "Dad, I'm not a kid anymore."

"To a predator you're just a ten-year-old boy. Take a taxi."

I can take care of myself, he wanted to say but it came out as, "Yes, sir."

"See you soon, son." And his father hung up.

Benjamin reached around and put his phone into his

knapsack, then he headed across the street to the gauntlet of yellow taxis. This was ridiculous—who did his father think he was, a baby?

He got into the cab, smiled at the driver in the mirror, and said, "Central Park West between Eighty and Eighty-first, please. In front of the museum." Then he settled back for the ride across the park—a trip he would much rather have done on foot on such a nice day. What could happen to him out here?

HEMINGWAY STARED at Trevor Deacon. He had been a pedophile.

Had been.

Past tense.

Trevor would not be molesting children anymore. Trevor would not be doing much of anything anymore. What was left of him was neatly placed on the various pieces of furniture in the basement room, mostly the bookshelf and the old Telefunken record player/television combo under the window with the heavy bars.

His parts were all there, displayed like a collection of prized Franklin Mint plates. But the Franklin Mint wasn't going to be putting out decorative dinnerware to commemorate Trevor Deacon's accomplishments. Not now, not ever.

The forensics team was done with everything but the garage—the main body of the basement apartment was now open—so Hemingway busied herself learning what she could from Trevor Deacon's home. She stood with her hands in her pockets, her head tilted to one side as if she were scanning titles at the library, examining the demented performance art that looked like it had been lifted from a Rob Zombie story-board. Deacon's body had been reduced to its unarticulated components. Everything from his jaw to his feet was neatly placed in the cubbyholes of the teak shelving and on top of the stereo.

Hemingway was no stranger to violent death, and she was certainly no stranger to the closed-in world of the psychopath, but she needed to concentrate and with the old lady screeching through cigarette smoke from the door it was impossible to get a single thought going.

"Who's gonna clean this mess up?" she barked. "Me? Oh no. Not me. I've cleaned up after this piece of shit his whole life and I ain't gonna do it no more, I can tell you. He's a pig. And a sonofabitch. Just look at this place. It's a mess. A mess—"

Hemingway turned her head and nailed Papandreou with a hard stare. "Officer Papandreou, would you please escort Mrs. Deacon back out to the car. This is a crime scene." She turned back to the chunks of Trevor.

"Oh no you don't!" the lady screamed when Papandreou wrapped his fingers around her elbow. "I gotta keep my eyes on you sonsabitches. Last time you were here you ripped the place to shit. I ain't gonna clean up after you, neither. Take me upstairs, I ain't leaving my purse lying around with all you thieving cop assholes skulking around. I got experience with you guys."

Without taking his hand from her elbow, Papandreou said, "Mrs. Deacon, the last time we were here was 1984 and the police report said you opened the door and threw hot bacon grease at a police officer before he could open his mouth."

"I thought it was Trevor. I told the judge and he believed me. Check your fancy computers, ya dumb Greek cop bastard."

She turned her head back to the basement and barked, "You still ain't said—who's gonna clean this mess up?"

Hemingway resisted the temptation to walk over and slap the woman. "Nick?" she said, stretching it out to two irritated syllables.

Nick began pulling the old lady from the door. "We will have people come in and take care of that. But we have to record the evidence first. We can't do that with you standing here screaming. Let me take you upstairs and we'll get your purse. Then I'll have someone take you to the local precinct where a social worker will handle the logistics. You'll go to a hotel for a few days so we can catalog and clean up. While you're there, someone from social services will help you fill out the papers—as the victim of violent crime, you are entitled to compensation."

The old woman's eyes narrowed and her mouth pursed up again. "Compensation? How much compensation?"

"It depends on your current income but somewhere around six hundred dollars a month."

"Six hundred dollars a month! That sonofabitch over there is worth six hundred dollars a month! I wish he would have got this years ago." She picked up her pace. "Well, dipshit, you gonna take me to get my pension or not?"

Papandreou led Mrs. Deacon away and the rat-tat-tat of her voice was finally swallowed by the ambient noise in the apartment. Hemingway stepped back into character. Yesterday at this time, none of this had existed. Tyler Rochester had still been alive and the world was spinning happily on its axis. Less than a full turn of the planet later and little Tyler, a driver named Desmond, and a pedophile named Trevor Deacon had been turned into headlines. And then there was Bobby Grant—a child who looked so much like Tyler Rochester that they may as well have been brothers. Still missing.

Still gone. Still on his way to joining the others in the headlines unless they got lucky.

Deacon hadn't shown up on the predator list because he had never been registered on any of the databases. They were running down the case jacket but she already knew what they'd find. The guy had walked on a technicality and then got lost in the massive paperwork of the record-keeping engine. Three decades had gone by and he had slipped from communal memory because he had been careful. Until that judge had remembered him.

Of course, someone else had remembered Deacon as well: a guy with a saw and a lot of time to kill. What was the connection?

Hemingway turned back to the room—back to the task lighting and the strobe of the photographer's flash—and was grateful for the sudden silence. She walked around the space, a rec room turned apartment where Trevor had spent his life hiding from the world. His bed—an old iron frame—sat in the bedroom. The mattress, pillows, and sheets might have been another color yesterday—maybe white, maybe yellow— but were now a sopping mess of cracked red and black.

Deacon's torso lay on the bed. No arms. No legs. No head. No genitals. Just a big blood-spattered hairy roast waiting to go into the oven.

There wasn't much to look at in the rest of the apartment. There was an old Formica table with one chair, a toaster oven, a plaid sofa and the Cold War stereo/television combo. A coffee table with a book on birds and an ashtray on top. Not much of a place when you really looked at it.

The only thing that seemed new was the computer system set up near the fridge. Alan Carson, from the cybercrimes division, was in the process of dismantling Trevor's PC—a sleek red plastic tower with two forty-two-inch monitors.

Carson looked like a guy tinkering in his garage, not a man working a few feet from a chopped-up human being.

The forensics guys moved around in their space suits, hoods off now that they were done black-lighting the carpet and plucking samples with tweezers. The one thing that didn't make sense was that for a place so full of blood, there were no footprints or fingerprints, handprints, or glove smears. The only immediate evidence was on the Naugahyde covering of the single kitchen chair: a dried red crescent of blood that had come from the tip of a shoe.

But the crescent of blood frowned toward the back of the chair—an impossible position to tie your shoe, unless you had eight-foot legs.

He had stepped on the chair. Why?

The ceiling was barely seven feet tall and, with the exception of three ceramic sockets armed with bare forty-watt bulbs, was popcorn Sheetrock. Nothing had been taken down, nothing put up.

Carson looked up from the tower he was working on. "No hard drives." He pushed the Buddy Holly glasses up on his nose. "Panels were pulled, at least four hard drives gone. We can go after Internet records but if he pirated a neighbor's bandwidth it's gonna be tough."

If Deacon had been logged into the databases all those years ago—even on one of the "to watch" lists—there would have been a yard of ironclad conditions tacked on to his parole terms. Convicted pedophiles were not allowed within two hundred yards of anywhere children could be found, parks and schools in particular. They were not usually permitted to use the Internet; and if they were allowed to access the Internet, they had very strict access. Since Deacon had never been entered in the system, he had been completely unsupervised.

Mat Linderer from Dr. Marcus's office came over, sweating in his breathable antistatic suit. He had a wavy red line on his forehead where the sweatband had cut in and combined with the cornrows of a hair transplant, it looked like the top of his head had recently been sewn on. "Detective, there's not much here that looks out of place. Plenty of genetic material but most of it looks like it belongs to the vic. I found a pair of expensive telephoto lenses in the bottom drawer of the dresser." His tone was much friendlier than it had been that morning at the Huntington Academy.

"No camera?"

"No camera. But I did find this in the fridge." He held up a plastic Parkay container and peeled back the lid to show her the contents. It was lined with small clear polyethylene bags filled with a pink powder.

"What is it?"

Linderer shrugged. "I'll know when I get it back to the lab. Could be drain cleaner. Could be anthrax."

Hemingway took out her iPhone and snapped a picture for her files. "I want the results as soon as you've nailed them down."

He nodded, closed the lid, and eased it into a refrigerated cooler. "I'll call when I have something."

She walked over to a spot on the wall where four yellow pushpins were tacked to the fake paneling, the corner of a torn photograph hanging off one. The pins were spaced out for an eight-by-ten. What was missing?

Phelps, the Iron Giant, cycled slowly through the place, somehow managing to not be underfoot. Of all the people Hemingway had seen around crime scenes, no one had Phelps's uncanny ability to avoid being in the way. It was more than a skill, it was some kind of magical power.

Linderer waved him over and said, "I don't think this was a B and E but Detective Phelps's .45 did a lot of damage so I can't be sure. Both rounds went into the tumblers. But if the perp didn't break in, he was let in—those locks are very difficult to pick."

"The windows?" Hemingway asked, pointing at the two in the front and one in the bedroom. All three had heavy steel bars set into the sills. She had seen jail cells with leaner security.

Phelps, who had examined them carefully, said, "My grandson would have a hard time squeezing his skinny ass through there. No getting in."

"Or out," she added. "So whoever killed Trevor Deacon was let in and he locked the doors on the way out. Or had keys."

"We found one set of keys but not a second," Linderer said. "Everyone has a spare set."

Phelps pointed at the three steel doors to the basement: one that led upstairs to the boarded-over house passage; one for the garage; and one for the side entrance he had shot open. All the doors were secured with an array of security locks from the best manufacturers in the world. Thousands of dollars' worth of locks per door. "This guy liked his privacy."

Hemingway examined the door to the garage, painted over with the scribbly effigy of what could only be a spider, an image out of the dark recesses of Trevor Deacon's diseased mind. The forensics guys still weren't done in there but from the look she had seen on the face of the photographer, she knew it would be more of the same.

"What's with the spider?"

Phelps shrugged. "It's beyond me. Maybe he was a fan of *Charlotte's Web*."

Hemingway wasn't so sure.

With the thought still hanging over her, the task lighting from under the door blinked out and the door opened up. Two of Marcus's men came into the room, pulling off their hoods as they stepped over the threshold. They didn't look shaken—they were beyond being shocked on the job—but they did look upset.

Phelps headed into the garage. Linderer followed.

Hemingway stood at the threshold to the damp space under the house, examining the mad scribbled effigy of the spider, wondering how it had fit into Trevor Deacon's world.

Had it been his god?

His tormentor?

His confidant?

His lover?

From somewhere beyond Trevor Deacon's spider, Phelps said, "Hemi, there's something in here you should see."

She stepped through the steel door with the array of padlocks and security crossbars, past the arachnid sentinel, and into the gloom.

The garage was an ancient damp shadow that felt like the perfect place to keep a monstrous spider. The floor was patched and fissured and there was a filthy carpenter's bench in the middle of the room under the single bulb. Garden tools and lengths of welded chain hung from spiral nails planted in the concrete. The garage door was upholstered in pink insulation and part of the wall near the door was covered with moldy egg cartons—improvised soundproofing.

She passed another dark crescent of what could only be blood near the door—another shoe print like the one in the kitchen. It, too, had been covered with an evidence hood.

Phelps stood in the corner, beside an old coffin freezer. Linderer held the lid open with a rubber-gloved hand. Phelps was looking at her, not the freezer, and a feeble light that washed up onto his face gave his skin a yellow cast. Frozen vapor wafted over the lip of the appliance and slunk down to the floor.

She moved toward the light. Toward the open space that looked as if it were smoking. Her line of sight crawled over the lip of the metal box and she saw the neatly stowed plastic sandwich bags. It took a minute for her to figure out what she was looking at.

She closed her eyes, kept them shut for a second, then opened them, hoping that it had somehow taken on another form.

It hadn't.

Hemingway stepped toward the freezer, summoned by Trevor Deacon's madness.

She no longer felt Phelps or Linderer in the room. She could see them. But they were so far away that they could have been in another time zone.

The psychotic rendering of the spider on the door wasn't a representation of his god—it was something else, something a lot more basic; that drawing was Trevor Deacon's version of a Beware of Dog sign.

Inside the freezer, stacked like dumplings, were dozens of little blue-white feet in Ziploc bags.

NINETEEN

MARCUS SPENT a few seconds cleaning his glasses on the tail of his lab coat. Then he returned them to his nose, yawned, and pulled a file from a rolling trolley that sat in the aisle between the tables. He cracked the folder and read from the cover sheet. "Deacon, Trevor A., male, fifty-six years old. Case number 551.2101.677." The medical examiner peeled back the plastic sheet, bundled it into a sloppy knot, and put it in a bucket on the floor.

All the king's horses, all the king's men, and every forensic specialist in the land couldn't put Trevor Deacon together again. He was arranged in a more or less orderly anatomical position, except that his parts were not connected. His feet were at the end of the table, sitting on the soles, the sheared-through ankles pointing up at the ceiling like bloodless osso buco about to go into the oven. Deacon's head was in two parts, cut in half at the jaw. The top part of his skull sat at the head of the table, a meat helmet with slightly open eyes, one pupil dialed in toward his nose, cross-eyed in a way evolution had never intended.

Phelps stood on the other side of the stainless steel slab,

across from Hemingway. She knew that he would rather be somewhere else from the way his head was cocked to one side. Which was understandable—it was hard to gather any sympathy for the disassembled man laid out on the table like a set of wind chimes waiting to be strung together.

Examined from one angle, Deacon amounted to little more than another piece of human garbage subtracted from the cesspool of predators. Another broken person who did little other than transfer his own pain to the people he came in contact with. It wasn't hard to look at his remains and think that whoever had broken out the saw had done the human race a giant favor. But this was connected to Tyler Rochester and Bobby Grant; there was too much coincidence at play for it not to be. So they would be spending a lot of time thinking about the man on the slab before they put this one to bed.

"TOD was somewhere between midnight and two thirty a.m. last night." Dr. Marcus looked up. "And he did not die of natural causes."

Phelps snorted. Hemingway shook her head; this wasn't her first time in a lab, and certainly not her first time around a dead body, but she believed that a certain amount of respect was due the dead, even life's monsters. "What did he die of, Marcus?"

"Exsanguination."

"From one of these cuts?" Hemingway asked, sweeping her hand over the general area of the corpse.

The ME put the file down on the edge of the trolley, then picked one of Deacon's feet up. He pointed to the neat line of stump. "Sometime while his feet were being cut off is my guess."

At this Phelps said, "And he was alive when this happened?"

Marcus put the foot back in its place and as it touched the table, the flesh on the heel dented in, like a wax candle on a hot day. "Yes, he was."

Hemingway answered the sixty-four-thousand-dollar question. "This was done by the same guy who chopped up Tyler Rochester."

Marcus nodded. "This time the cut lines are straight, with very little travel. He's better than he was with Tyler Rochester. Smooth, long strokes and a lot of stamina. Taking a big guy like Deacon apart would have taken a good hour, maybe ninety minutes. But it's the same small-toothed saw—twenty-four teeth per inch."

"Same anesthetic?"

"The initial scan says yes. Again, thiopental with no analgesic is a fair guess. I'll know more in a couple of days when the tox screens come back but the MO is identical. If you look at his right eye you can see the damage where he was injected. A jab in the vitreous humor and then to work." Dr. Marcus paused, removed his spotless glasses, and cleaned them with a static-free wipe from a dispenser.

"Would it have taken thirty-five seconds to take effect, like the Rochester kid?" Hemingway asked.

"Longer if the same dosage was used; Trevor here was a big boy and he'd absorb it a lot slower. The effects might not even be as debilitating. But on top of the anesthetic I found heroin in his system. Heroin combined with something like thiopental would have made him a big, slow-moving target. Might have even killed him."

Phelps jammed his hands into his pants pockets and rolled up on the balls of his feet. "To get close enough to jab a guy like Deacon in the eye, it had to be someone he knew. Or at least felt comfortable enough to let in. The doors are fitted with back-locked Abloys and the bars on the windows are so close together a pygmy would have a hard time squeezing in."

Marcus readjusted the foot he had just put down, aligning it to some invisible grid that only he could see. "Even then, when someone jabs you in the eye with a hypodermic, a few seconds is enough time to take a swing. There were no defensive wounds. No tissue or fabric under his fingernails. Teeth were clean. No bruised knuckles. Nothing knocked over in the apartment. The only damage to the body was a broken toe on his right foot—probably when it hit the floor after it was removed. Technically it's postmortem even though he was probably alive when it broke."

Hemingway knew that this kind of work was nothing new but it took a special kind of someone to saw up a human being and place the parts around a room like accessories from Pottery Barn. And there had to be a purpose to the act. What had been the motivation?

"The similarities don't stop there," Marcus continued. "Like the Rochester boy, the inexperience in anatomy left some signature wounds. The right upper arm was cut an inch too far into the humerus then torqued to separate it from the body, like my grandkids do with chicken wings." He pointed to the corresponding joint but Hemingway didn't bother to lean in and examine it. "But he was already dead at that point."

The medical examiner went back to his notes and flipped through a few pages as if making sure he hadn't missed anything. "More than a little ironic that Mr. Deacon should meet his end by vivisection."

"Live by the sword." Phelps smiled and it was not a friendly expression. "Die by the sword."

AFTER FINISHING with Dr. Marcus, Hemingway and Phelps headed down to the sequencing and analysis labs, the backbone of the city's missing persons initiative. It was a maze of quarantined cubicles walled off from one another with frosted glass. Behind those walls was a twenty-four-hour horror show that never got canceled.

They moved past the sally port, through the main space, passing locked rooms where bodies in an advanced state of decomposition were being examined. In a discipline where DNA was now the defining factor in solving many cases, every effort was made to keep remains—or partial remains—from coming into contact with one another.

They found their way to Dr. Dorothy Calucci's lab. The two detectives had worked with her a year back on a case where a mother had locked her twin daughters in the oven as punishment for spilling milk on the floor. It had taken four screeching minutes for the girls to die. The mother was doing twenty-six years upstate but would be eligible for parole before she was thirty-five.

Calucci led the two detectives to one of the frosted rooms off the main lab where a few dozen stainless steel containers were distributed over as many tables. Each container was numbered and had a glass window in the hinged cover. Hemingway didn't have to look inside to know that they held children's feet, the handiwork of one Trevor Deacon.

Calucci lacked the bedside manner and dark humor of Dr. Marcus, a temperament a little more in tune with a case where the common element was live humans taken apart with a saw.

Calucci began the briefing without any greeting or salutation; she operated on the let's-not-waste-time frequency. "There were seventy-five feet in the Deacon house. Swabs determined that they belonged to boys. Sizing dictates that they were between eight and eleven years old. All of them were removed with a hacksaw or similar-type tool while the victims were alive. Out of seventy-five feet, there are thirty-one pairs and thirteen singles. So far we have identified six children—four pairs and two of the singles—by matching prints to online hospital registries that have been sistered to missing children networks. We expect to garner more matches through tissue samples submitted to the FBI's missing persons program within the CODIS database."

Hemingway didn't have to ask how long the process would take—as a lead detective in a squad specializing in child murders, she knew that nuclear DNA could be sequenced in about forty hours. Once sequenced and submitted to the FBI for identification, it took less than an hour for the software to find a match if there was one; there was no way to rush the process.

"We should start getting results Thursday morning." Calucci nodded at the protocols she had handed over. "You have six children identified there, detectives. The oldest case dates back to August 1992—a boy named Victor Roslyne. Disappeared on his way home from school."

Hemingway's pen stopped over the paper and she raised her eyes. "You mean to tell me that there are more than twenty years' worth of missing children's cases here?" she asked, indicating the stainless steel graveyard.

"So far, yes. There might be older cases but we won't know until we identify all of the victims. *If* we identify all of the victims."

Hemingway's focus wandered over the bins and she saw the diminutive feet beneath the clear windows. Staring down at the fruits of Trevor Deacon's labor, it was easy to understand Phelps's indifference up in Marcus's lab.

Hemingway wondered where, precisely, the system had failed—and it *had* failed. How else could you justify the disappearance and murder of at least forty-four children? Why hadn't Deacon been stopped years ago? How had his sickness managed to survive for so long? To flourish? Lincoln was hunting down the files now—they needed to know why this guy had walked.

Calucci continued with her briefing. "No heavy decomposition in any of the remains; they were frozen when fresh. There is a lot of cellular damage due to less than ideal freezing and improper storage conditions but we have usable DNA from all of the vics."

Hemingway scanned the forest of little feet then went to the files that Calucci had given her. "Are all six boys that you've identified from New York City?"

"Every one."

"Jesus," Phelps said in a low whistle. "This guy was a one-man plague."

Like Phelps, Hemingway knew the stats. Sixty-five

hundred children go missing in Manhattan and the surrounding boroughs each year: ninety-seven percent of those are runaways; a hundred and fifty cases turn out to be abductions by noncustodial parents or family members; and fifteen simply disappear from the known Newtonian universe. "Whoever killed this guy just reset the statistics." She tried to focus on the white field of her notebook instead of troughs filled with the screams of little boys. "Anything unusual with the remains?"

Calucci nodded and flipped through the sheaf of papers in her hand until she found what she was looking for. She folded back the page and handed the clipped bundle to Hemingway.

She read the page then looked up. "Are you sure?"

Calucci nodded. "On all of the single feet we found traces of competing DNA. I can black-light them if you want."

Phelps cleared his throat and held up his hand as if he were in grade school. "Can we have the dummy talk?"

Hemingway passed him the file. "Read."

He pulled out his glasses—cheap dollar-store grandpa deals—unfolded them, and plunked them onto the tip of his nose. For an instant he looked like he would begin with, "'Twas the night before Christmas," but the color quickly dropped out of his face. "You gotta be fucking kidding."

The grim line of Calucci's mouth barely moved. "It hasn't been matched to Trevor Deacon yet but there is no doubt that it's semen."

||| TWENTY-ONE

HEADMASTER FREYTAG stared at the boy, trying to figure out a way to bridge the communication gap. The headmaster had been at this a long time, and he had ushered the school through twenty-one years of minor catastrophes with a character that was strict, intelligent, and fair. But there were times when he needed to be creative. Maybe even a little vulgar. Times like now.

"Miles, do you know why you're sitting here?"

Miles Morgan shrugged as if it didn't make a difference. And in a way, it didn't. Like all the boys at the academy, Miles Morgan's future was written on watermarked paper. Whether he managed to finish his education at this institution or at another, he would walk into a life devoid of financial worries. He would spend his summers in Montauk, winters on Mustique. Except for the divorces coming his way, Miles Morgan would ride a worry-free wave to the cemetery.

But this was where Miles Morgan differed from the other boys at the school; he didn't care about any of that.

And Freytag found this refreshing.

Morgan followed his shrug with, "You're pissed about those four faggoty seventh graders."

Freytag sighed and leaned forward, his hands on the leather top of the desk. "Miles, you can't use language like that. Sexual orientation shouldn't be equated with weakness."

Morgan stared at him for a few seconds. "What?"

"You can't call someone 'faggoty'—it's not proper. Choose another term."

The boy shrugged again. "Can I call them assholes?"

Freytag wanted to sigh again but this time he held it in. "How about calling them bullies?"

Last Friday, four of the older boys had cornered Morgan in one of the bathrooms, thinking his heavy-lidded gaze revealed a victim in waiting. Their intentions were less than noble but fundamentally innocent—they tried to give him a wedgie. By the time a teacher had responded to the yells of terror and pain echoing from the bathroom, Miles Morgan had a broken finger and a crushed nose. But he had doled out nine lost teeth, one broken foot, one ruptured eardrum, one chewed-off nipple, two broken noses, and myriad cuts, contusions, and bruises—smiling a bloody smile the whole time. A younger boy, hiding in one of the stalls, had relayed the story—and the older boys had confessed; the only reason they hadn't been expelled was because Morgan thought the whole thing had been "a hoot."

"Bullies?" the boy asked. "Sure, bullies." He laughed, an inelegant, unselfconscious yodel.

"Miles, I know I don't have to tell you that fighting is not acceptable here at the school." Morgan didn't seem to grasp much; it didn't make the boy bad, of course, but it did make the job of explaining things to him somewhat difficult. "There are other ways to solve problems. It's not always necessary to—to . . ." he paused and scanned the report, ". . . bite someone's nipple off. There are ways of diffusing these situations."

Morgan yawned. "Yeah? Like how?"

"You can always try to talk your way out of trouble."

"I don't try to talk my way out of anything, sir."

Freytag thought of the newspapers, of the missing boys out there, and he wanted to impart some caution to Miles Morgan—it might help him at some point. "All I'm saying, Mr. Morgan, is that you can't always fight your way out of a bad situation."

Miles looked up and smiled. "Wanna bet?" he asked.

III TWENTY-TWO

THERE WAS a commonality between the Rochester and Grant boys. On the surface, it was appearance, and while sometimes that might be enough, it wasn't here. Not with Trevor Deacon thrown into the mix. Hemingway didn't know what the link was, only that it existed out there in the mind of the man who had lopped off the feet of one child and abducted the other. They could have passed for brothers. This one had a very specific fantasy to feed. There was an exactness to it.

There had been no real cooldown period: fifteen hours could hardly be called downtime. These guys needed a refractory period to recharge the batteries. At least usually. But not this one. He was on a mission. This was not happenstance. This was not wrong place wrong time. There was planning behind this. Good old-fashioned analytical thinking.

Which translated to purpose.

And woven into the geometry of the problem, was Trevor Deacon, predator extraordinaire. Someone had jabbed old Trevor in the eye with a hypodermic, then gone to work on him with a hacksaw. Trevor's death had taken patience, a taste for inflicting star-spangled agony, and time. A boy and two grown men killed, another child missing. They had an overachiever on their hands.

How did Deacon fit in with Tyler Rochester and Bobby Grant?

The first thing they had looked into was the financial standings of the two families. The shortest distance between a murder and a motive was usually a dollar sign. Every large city had come across someone who wanted the police to think that they had a serial predator on their hands when in point of fact all they really wanted was one single victim dead, usually someone with a life insurance policy. But neither Tyler Rochester nor Bobby Grant had been insured and a cursory glance into their parents' financial holdings showed that money wasn't a problem for either family.

So who was doing this? Why was he doing it? And how was he picking his victims?

Where was the link?

She wanted to find it while there was still time to get to Bobby Grant. Not in a day, after he was dead. Not in a week after another—God forbid—boy had disappeared. Or washed up with his feet missing. No, Hemingway needed to see it now.

"You okay?" Phelps asked from his desk.

Hemingway looked up, blinked. "*What?* Yeah. Why?"

"You were grumbling. When you grumble, it usually means that you're going to shoot someone or stab them or some such shit."

Even in the cold of the air-conditioned office, she was sweating. She put her hand up under her collar and slid it over her shoulder, feeling the muscle just below the skin. Her fingers found the familiar disc of scar where a red-hot chunk of metal had exited her body and thunked into a barstool. It was burning.

She looked up and smiled at the expression painted on Phelps's face; he looked troubled.

She pulled her hand from under her shirt and her palm was moist and smelled of Irish Spring. How the hell could she be hot when it was sixty degrees in here?

"I'm good. Just trying to figure out what makes this fucker go ticktock."

"You know, for a woman educated at Yale, you sure sound like a cop most of the time." And he smiled a little, more of that fatherly approval coming out.

Alan Carson walked in, wearing Chuck Taylors and pressed jeans. He had the unmistakable air of nerd about him. His department was allowed a certain leeway in the unwritten dress code of the NYPD, mainly because they never interacted with the public. And they would have cried if they weren't allowed to wear their hipster-geek T-shirts and skinny jeans. "Beware of strangers bearing gifts."

"And it doesn't get stranger than him," Phelps mumbled to Hemingway. Like a lot of the old-timers, Phelps mistrusted both technology and the people who worshiped it.

"What do you have for me?" she asked Carson, ignoring Phelps.

He held up a portable hard drive. "I've got three years' worth of Trevor Deacon's Internet records here: every click-through in a thirty-six month period—more than ninety-one thousand pages. Some will be dead links but his entire online life is here."

"Anything interesting?" Phelps asked.

"Plenty to work with. But therein lies your dilemma— weeding out the relevant from the irrelevant." Carson slaved the hard drive to her computer. "Knock yourself out."

Hemingway opened Deacon's Internet log and it didn't take long to see that the man had spent a lot of time visiting school websites. She did a quick search and found that he had visited the Damien Whitney Academy for Boys and the Huntington Academy a little over three months back—Tyler Rochester's and Bobby Grant's schools.

The big question, of course, was could it be a coincidence?

"Once we identify the remains of his victims, we'll be able to cross-reference it with these websites." She lifted her head, waved Lincoln over.

"Yeah?" he asked. After their time at the Deacon house, Lincoln and Papandreou had spent the morning running down files on anyone associated with the Damien Whitney Academy for Boys and the Huntington Academy. They had not yet found a single thing to link Tyler Rochester to Bobby Grant.

"Do a search on these schools," she said, tapping the screen. "See if any children have gone missing in the past three years."

"Sure. Can you put it into a PDF?"

She looked up at Carson. "Can we?" Carson had a crush on her—it was one of those obvious things that, had she been of a different makeup, could have been the poor man's undoing. But she kept him at arm's length, always being polite because she didn't want him to think he had a chance with her.

Carson leaned over her shoulder and she heard him take in a breath of her scent. "Sure. Just . . . let . . . me . . ." His fingers tap-danced across her keyboard, then he stood up and nodded. "Done."

Lincoln thanked him and went to the printer.

"What was with this guy and the feet?" Carson asked.

"Feet are the most common nonsexual body part to be

fixated on. Research suggests that foot fetishism increases during times when sexual epidemics are an issue; by sexualizing feet, participants avoid diseases transmitted through regular sexual channels. With a guy like Deacon it was probably a further step in desexualizing his actions. He was probably taught that sex was a depraved act; by focusing on feet, he was able to live out his fantasies yet not bend the fundamental principles of the shame he had been taught—technically, it could be justified that the act isn't sex. We'll know more once the psychologist talks to his mother."

Carson's face squinched up but Phelps just nodded as if this were common knowledge. He had been hunting child predators since the mid-seventies and understood the power play at work in many of their minds, usually the result of some deep trauma inflicted upon them as children.

"Thanks, Al. I'll call you if I need anything."

Carson nodded and his eyes dropped to her chest for a split second. Then he flushed, brought his eyes up to hers, and nodded. "Sure. Anything at all. I'll let you know if I find anything else. This guy wasn't big on encryption."

When Carson was gone, Lincoln made smooching sounds. "He's got it bad for you, Hemi. I hear Club Med in my ears. Maybe Aruba. A hut on the beach. A hammock. You and Carson . . ."

"What are you guys? Twelve? I pity the women in your lives."

Lincoln smiled. "So do they."

She turned back to Trevor Deacon's life reduced to bits and bytes, a bread crumb trail that led back into his fantasies. No sane person would want to peek in there.

Her phone rang. "Hemingway."

"Detective Hemingway, Mat Linderer here. I have the results on that pinkish powder we found at the Deacon residence and I've analyzed the torn photograph corner you wanted me to check out. First the powder. It's—"

"Heroin," she interrupted.

There was a stunned moment of silence. "Um, yes."

"The autopsy," she explained. "What's the cut?"

"It's about thirty-five percent pure, sixty-five percent baby laxative."

"Low-end street grade."

"Yeah."

"Why is it pink?"

"The color was added *after* the manufacturing process— there's no molecular binding. It's a vegetable dye of some sort. My guess is it's not supposed to be there. Maybe it was smuggled in something red."

Hemingway added the information to her notes. "And the corner of that photograph?"

"Printed on a home printer, not commercial grade. I can tell you it's an HP—manufactured within the last twenty-one months due to the toner it takes; I found traces of their new magenta. The paper is by Fuji, and it's available everywhere. I can't tell you what the image was. Could be sky. Could be water. Could be a cloud or smoke or a reflection in wavy glass. I handed it over to our digital guys and they ran an image search on the web and it doesn't match anything that's out there. Deacon's thumbprint is on it. That's all I can give you."

"Thanks, Mat. Appreciated."

Hemingway put the phone in her pocket and lifted her head to see Phelps staring at her. She filled him in on the vegetable dye and the printer.

When she was done, Phelps reached over and lifted his own notes from under a cup of long-cold coffee. The chair squeaked under his considerable bulk. "How the hell did Deacon walk all those years ago?"

It was one of those things that made you wonder if the whole system wasn't completely broken, or corrupt, or both.

Phelps found the page he had been looking for. "As per Nick's findings. I haven't seen the files yet.

"The initial jacket from 1984 states that the arresting officer—a street cop named Ronald Weaver—deceased May twenty-third, 2004—made a wrongful search. And since they couldn't find a body, and the feet didn't match anyone who had been missing, they couldn't prove that it was murder. Deacon's attorney, Marcel Zeigler—deceased July 2010—alleged that Deacon had purchased the feet from a man who worked in a medical research facility, and that they came from a donor. They ran down all possible cadavers in storage, from medical supply companies to hospitals, schools, and private research labs. They couldn't positively match the feet to a donor, but the body of an eleven-year-old boy had been stolen a month previously. Zeigler made a reasonable argument that Deacon had unknowingly purchased the feet of a stolen cadaver. They clocked him on disrespectful treatment of human remains.

"Zeigler argued that Deacon was guilty of bad judgment, not murder. The judge bought the story and Deacon went home after a six-month vacation at a minimum-security facility upstate. Enjoyed shop class. Model guy all the way around." Phelps looked up, took off his glasses. "In the three years set by the parole board, he was never late for a meeting. Followed up with therapy. No felonies. No misdemeanors. Gold stars across the board. When parole was over, he dropped off the face of the earth and no one thought to look at him ever again."

Hemingway thought back to Deacon's garage. The memory of those frozen little feet, blue and brittle, had been popping up in her head all afternoon. "Did they ever ID the feet found in his car?"

"Before DNA by almost a decade. Blood-typed but no tissue sample. Incinerated as medical waste. Nope. Unsolved."

The sky was hazing over in late afternoon and Hemingway knew they had to get out there and do something. Even if it was empty motion, it had to be better than sitting in here second-guessing everything that made sense. Which was very little. "I hate the waiting," she finally said.

"You and me both, kiddo."

She looked at the conference table with the neatly stacked files, then at her computer screen, then back up at the clock. "I've gotta go," she said and stood up, pulling on her jacket. "I can't sit here."

Phelps began to rise, then his body locked in a half crouch, as if a silent message had been radioed in from headquarters. He lifted his head, looked at her face, took in her body language, and sat back down. He nodded once. "Say hi for me," he said, then turned back to his work.

TWENTY-THREE

WHENEVER SHE was here, it was as if she had never left. When she was away, she couldn't remember what the place looked like at all. And she knew it would always be like this.

Her shadow stretched over the grave and wavered on the headstone, a small rectangular chunk of black granite with the words MOSES MANKIEWICZ chiseled in tight, noncursive hammer strokes. He had chalked forty-one years up on the fuselage before being shot down. A long time compared to some, short compared to others. A fucking miracle when applied to Mank.

Hemingway stood there for a moment, the whir of traffic on the Jackie Robinson Parkway close enough that she could hear the ricochet of gravel off the curb just beyond the trees. Mank lay with his parents—they had died in a car accident when he had been six.

The headstone was small and simple, a totally incongruous monument to a man who had lived as large as Moses Mankiewicz. A man who had epitomized the saying that too much can never be enough.

A few small stones rested on the marker, left by her on

previous visits. She reached into her pocket and pulled out the one she had picked up on the esplanade last night, fifty feet from Tyler Rochester. She knelt down on the grass and put it on the edge of the granite slab. It wobbled for a second.

It took her a few minutes to build up the courage to talk to him—it always did. It seemed weird, foolish, even, that she was here. It was surprising that Phelps didn't say more about it. But when she needed to open up to someone, coming here seemed like a justifiable pilgrimage.

The sound of the cars faded away and she sat down on the grass, facing the headstone. Each time she came here she was surprised that it didn't destroy her. Wasn't that what was supposed to have happened? This was Shakespearean territory. Gabriel García Márquez, at least.

"Hey, Mank—" She stopped, pushed her hair away from her jaw with her finger and tucked it behind her ear. She liked to think of Mank looking up and seeing the new her. She had walked through fire and made it. He'd be proud.

"It's been a busy couple of days." She felt the tears getting ready and she stopped them, consciously pushing them back to where they would be forgotten, shut down for safekeeping. "I'm pregnant. Really pregnant. And I don't know what to do."

A warm dry wind fluttered her hair off of her ear and then went still. She pushed it back, took a breath, and wondered what she was doing here. She didn't need advice. She needed conviction. One way or the other. Something definitive. After that, it would all be fine. "Girly, huh?

"And there's this guy. He took a little boy last night. Name was Tyler Rochester. Kid walked off the face of the planet on the way home from school. Three hours later he's found in the East River. His feet were cut off." She went on, laying the case out piece by piece.

Mank had always been a great detective. His knack for figuring cases out had only been matched by his knack for getting into trouble. Real trouble. David Shea kind of trouble. Sometimes she came here and all they talked was shop. A one-sided conversation that always helped her see the method in the mayhem. With everything unfolding in her new life the way it was—with work and Daniel and the possibility of a baby—she worried that she might lose these times, another ill-fated long-distance relationship.

When she was done laying out the case, she went back to the baby, eventually getting around to Daniel. She didn't talk to Mank about him all that much—something about it felt like a betrayal—but she had talked about him at first, so Mank would get a feel for the guy.

She doubted that Mank would have given a shit anyway. He would want her to be happy. And he wasn't one for handing out judgment. *The guy treat you well? Yes. The sex good? Yes. You get butterflies in your stomach when he touches you? Yes. He put the seat down some of the time? All of the time. Open car doors for you? All the time. Then we're done here, sweetheart. Thank you. Good night. Please leave your 3-D glasses in the bin by the door on your way out.*

She never expected to have any kind of a therapeutic breakthrough when she was here, but something about the ritual was comforting. Even now, when she didn't really have the spare time to piss around playing Ouija phone with Mank, it did her good. And maybe that was the problem. She was here talking to a dead guy when back at home she had what was supposed to be the next phase of her life. No matter which way she turned it, it was a little self-destructive.

What would Mank have done if she had told him they

had been having a baby? He'd have laughed. Then hugged her. Then started calling her *Mother*. Never stopping to ask if it was something she wanted. And if she told him that she wasn't sure, the walls would get hit, plaster cracked, knuckles maybe even broken.

Mank had problems with his temper. He had never hit her, never even hinted at it, and after that first time, when she saw that his rage was focused at the world, she had never worried for herself again. He was nuts, but he was a good man. When he let go, he took it out on a wall or a fridge or the hood of a car. Sometimes on some poor schmuck who ended up in the hospital breathing through a tube, grateful that he hadn't been kicked into a vegetative state. Mank had been dangerous. The kind whose unsmiling mug shot showed up on the news every now and then accompanying a story about a cop who had crossed the line. But he never would have hit her.

And he had made a lot of enemies along the way. Enemies like David Shea.

One afternoon he had embarrassed Shea in front of his boys. And that had been the final *fuck you* Mank had ever handed out. The next morning his heart was no longer beating.

When it was over, and she was in the hospital staring up at the acoustic ceiling tile, calculating the number of holes per square foot, she realized that she had peaked. There was no greater test ahead of her.

And now she was pregnant.

Her hand was on the tightly clipped grass above where his chest might be. She closed her eyes, whispered the words, "Sorry, honey," and stood up. "I gotta monster to find."

She walked back to the truck, grudgingly leaving Mank back there in the ground. The sounds of the world slowly came back—first the wind; then the traffic on the expressway; finally her own footsteps.

Hers was the only vehicle in the parking lot. She opened it with the remote, climbed in behind the wheel, put on her seat belt, and began to cry.

TWENTY-FOUR

HEMINGWAY, PHELPS, and an NYPD patrolman named Paul Kowalski headed upriver at a forty-knot clip. They had been combing an abandoned dock in Queens, not far from Trevor Deacon's residence, when the sun dropped behind the skyline of the city to the west. Hemingway watched it the last few minutes, wondering if the final gasp of daylight going out would be punctuated by the scream of a child.

Of course, she heard nothing but the indifference of the city.

Theoretically, it was too early in the investigation to discern patterns of behavior beyond broad generalities, but something told her that sundown was the witching hour. When the day had run out, so had Bobby Grant's time. She didn't know how she knew, only that she did.

The police boat was a twenty-foot Zodiac center console outfitted with a pair of 75 horsepower Mercs. Kowalski had the engines open and their wake spread behind in a mercurial jet stream, a deep white V that reached out for the shores of the river.

Phelps held on to a handle bolted to the side of the

console, the same even expression on his face that he wore throughout the almost seven years of their partnership. Even out here, on water that was piss hot, coupled with a wind that did nothing but magnify the humidity, he looked like he was fine, missing child notwithstanding. If she asked him how he was, he'd just shrug—the steam-driven Iron Giant in a suit, old school down to the soles of his shoes.

She licked a line of sweat from her upper lip and tried to focus on the shore zipping by starboard, an endless maze of jetties, parks, restaurants, condos, industrial buildings, and myriad places where you could dump a dead kid into the drink without being seen. Especially after dark. Patrolling the shoreline was a last resort but it was better than contacting psychics, if only marginally.

They were cutting due north, toward Hell Gate, fighting the outgoing tide. She was running on the belief that it was just a matter of minutes until another footless boy was surrendered to the East River. He was probably already out there, being drawn south by the careless hands of the current, heading for the Atlantic. She hoped she was wrong—she hoped that they'd get another day. But hope wasn't a strategy. Hope was passive.

The radio squawked to life, a single blurt that startled everyone in the Zodiac except for the Iron Giant.

"We found him," a nameless officer said, identifying his boat as an afterthought. "This is Search two-two-four-seven."

Hemingway checked the GPS and straight-lined their azimuth to 2247—a boat the roster said was piloted by a man named J. Smilovitch. The distance on the screen was an inch and a half—a little over half a mile west-southwest.

Kowalski keyed the mic. "This is three-one-one-five, we'll be there in two minutes." And he spun the wheel and opened up the throttle.

Hemingway took the mic. "This is Detective Hemingway. What *exactly* did you find?" she asked.

Through the distant static of radio contact Smilovitch said, "Someone's chopped off his hands. He looks awful. Just fucking awful—"

She thought back to Trevor Deacon, the child murderer extraordinaire who had taken the feet of at least forty-four children, forty-five including the pair found in his trunk. He hadn't been killed by an angry parent or a vigilante.

Trevor Deacon had been killed by a competitor.

THE DOCK at the police quay was lit up like a Hollywood premiere, the concrete span lined with officers. But they were not there to celebrate the launch of a studio production; they were there to welcome Bobby Grant. Hemingway was with the boy, his body cocooned in a polyethylene bag to keep new contaminants out and to lock in any evidence that had survived the waters of the East River.

Two of the ME's people climbed down into the boat, slid the folded tarp into a disaster bag, then strapped the lifeless child onto an aluminum stretcher. After he was on his way to the van, Hemingway and Phelps climbed out of the boat.

Dennet was waiting and he steered them through the throng of officers who parted in a sea of silent blue; even men who have seen death in all its permutations are humbled in the presence of a murdered child. The captain didn't ask any questions, didn't make any demands, he just pushed them toward the white NYPD Tahoe parked inside the fence, beside the medical examiner's van. Dennet got in the back with Hemingway; Phelps sat up front with the driver.

When the doors were closed and the engine started, the

captain opened the ceiling vent on his side of the backseat and waited until cold air was pumping out before he spoke. For a man under as much pressure as this case was bringing down, he seemed to be in a relatively calm mood. Of course all of that would change in a few minutes when he started yelling. The equation was pretty simple: bring back results, not more dead kids.

The driver followed the Econoline as it pulled through the gate out onto the Parkway.

When they were up to speed, Dennet turned to Hemingway and said, "Please tell me you are making headway. Please tell me you have leads. Please tell me that this thing isn't a scrub. We have two dead children, Alex. I don't need to tell you how bad this is going to look on the news. By the time we get to the station, it's going to be like the villagers outside of Frankenstein's castle." He paused and turned to the traffic outside the window.

The driver said, "We have two news vans following us."

Dennet waved it away. "Parasites. No marketable skills except frightening the uninformed. Christ, I remember when the news conveyed actual information via educated opinions. If we dug up Walter Cronkite and showed him what has happened to network news he'd ask to go right back to the dirt." He turned to Phelps in the front seat, then to Hemingway, the voice of the team. "Tomorrow morning we are going to hold a press conference. You are going to give these monkeys something that they can work with—and something they can work *on*. Let's use these people to our advantage. They like snooping, get them to work for us. I don't care how you do it, only that it gets done. I'll book it for eight a.m. so it'll make the morning cycle."

What could she give him? There were no concrete leads. When she thought about it, there was no concrete anything except those crescents of blood in Trevor Deacon's basement apartment. Man's size ten or ten and a half.

And two dead children. One with no feet. Another with no hands.

The Chevy hit 60th Street and cut east, leaving the white Econoline to go on to its destination.

"Where we going?" Hemingway asked.

Dennet didn't bother looking over. "To the Grant boy's apartment. You are going to tell two people that their son is dead. Then you are going to go to the morgue and walk through the autopsy with Marcus." He let out a sigh that might as well have been a curse. "And then you are going to go out there and find me the man who is chopping up these children."

SHE PULLED into the garage on autopilot—parking and getting out of the truck without exercising anything even remotely resembling concentration. She was halfway around the block when she realized she hadn't checked her mirrors before getting out and she hadn't checked the alley before leaving the garage; it was things like that that got people killed.

The trip to the Grants' apartment had been an exercise in agony. Mrs. Grant broke into hysterical weeping that her husband tried to quell but couldn't stop. The mother-in-law had collapsed into the sofa and stared ahead, comatose. Dr. Grant poured himself a drink but left it on the bar when Hemingway began to explain that they had fished his son from the river and someone had taken his hands off with a hacksaw.

The whole time Hemingway had talked to him, he stared at the Bösendorfer in the corner.

Dr. Grant made himself three drinks he never touched.

Of course, the time with the Grants was punishment from Dennet; a way to tell them to make inroads or they'd be doling out bad news to the parents of dead children until they stopped this guy.

Dennet had also been very clear that if they didn't make headway soon, they'd get pulled. The city would load more detectives onto the case. The FBI would be brought in. They'd be gone.

And all the bullshit she had put up with over the years would be relegated to the wasted effort bin. She'd end up in burglary or vice or some other career dead end where the intent was to push her into quitting. And then where would she be? What would she do?

After the Grants, she and Phelps had taken a ride to the grim land of the medical examiner to look at the boy. When they had walked in, the doctor was up to his elbows in the boy's chest, fishing out the mass of organs referred to as *the block* in-house. They wouldn't have tox screens back until the morning but it was the same perp; the boy's left eye was punctured and the bones in his wrists had the same twenty-four-teeth-per-inch saw marks.

And like Tyler Rochester, Bobby Grant had been alive when it had happened.

This time the killer had cut in the right place, putting the saw through the sweet spot between the ulna and the capitate. He was getting better at this.

Bad guy: *Four.*

Good guys: *Sweetfuckall.*

She rounded the corner and stopped. There was no traffic on Riverside and beyond that the Jersey shoreline glittered against the flat Hudson. She wondered where the monster was. What he was doing. What he was wearing. What he was thinking.

And who he was thinking about.

Hemingway stood on the sidewalk, staring out at the lights sparkling off the river. What had happened to all of Trevor Deacon's children? Had he released them into the arms of the river? If he had, why hadn't they been found?

Her hand went to her belly and she fell back into thinking that bringing a child into the world took a lot of guts, a bucketful of wishful thinking, and more than a bit of denial. Of course she had thought about all of this before—every time, in fact, she had seen one of life's discards in a parking lot or alley or any of the other places where people dumped the dead. But the exercise had crossed from academic to practical when she had peed on the little plastic stick yesterday morning and been rewarded with a big blue check mark.

Two dead children. A dead driver. A dead child murderer. There was a rhyme, a reason, to all of this. Some formula that she did not understand, could not see. Was the baby growing in her crippling her in some way or would the cellular revolution going on in her body add some vital insight?

Part of the solution?

Or part of the problem?

She unlocked the door and stepped into the entry. On her way up the stairs she passed the four equestrian portraits Mank had bought her the last time they had gone out. She paused for a second, thought back to the cemetery that afternoon, to the pebble she had laid on his gravestone. Then she turned away and walked into the loft.

The space was dark; Daniel wasn't home. Without turning on the light she went to the three big arched windows in front of the loft and stared at the distant shore of New Jersey. The only thing she was sure of was that this guy would keep going until she stopped him.

||| TWENTY-SEVEN

THE NEWSPEOPLE hummed like a horde of talentless vain insects. They laid cable, tested lights, ran through lead-ins, coiffed and primped and chattered into cameras. There was a sense of triumph in their actions, as if they had discovered something important even though all they would really do was fill time with empty speculation.

Hemingway and Phelps sat in Dennet's office, prepping for the press conference. Mike Babanel, the precinct's counsel, stood behind the captain's desk, looking like a leaner, balder Tom Hagen.

Dennet leaned forward and looked at Hemingway for a few seconds. "Are you ready for this?"

What could she say to that? "I can't wait."

Phelps stood against the wall that held the captain's citations and golf photos. The Iron Giant hadn't said much. Until now. "This could be putting you in his crosshairs, Hemi."

She just shook her head. "A six-foot chick with a gun isn't his type."

"The Grant kid's driver wasn't this guy's type, either." Phelps didn't sound convinced.

Babanel looked out the window, then at Hemingway. "Remember to think about your answers before you say anything. They are going to try to trap you. And remember that you will be on televisions all over the world. Those two things should help."

Had he said *help*? "Sure. Televisions all over the world. Think before I speak. Easy-peasy. What about swearing?"

Babanel, whose sense of humor was south of zero on the laugh-o-meter, shook his head. "Swearing's not recommended either, detective." He pointed to the document they had spent fifteen minutes going over. "Stick to the release and you are most of the way there. Answer seven questions. That's it. Keep the answers brief. Tell them that you will keep them informed of any breaks in the case, but that you need to be left alone so that you can pursue all relevant leads. When they ask 'What leads?' thank them for their time and leave the podium."

It made more sense to put Phelps out there; he had received every award, honor, medal, and citation there was— from the department and the city—some of them twice. The unsaid logic was that he was too valuable an asset to hang out for the vultures, while she was expendable. Focus would irrevocably shift to her; if someone had to be thrown to the dogs, she'd have the shortest fall and the largest impact. It was business, not personal.

And of course she had gone through this before. During the investigation into David Shea's death she had been hounded mercilessly; six weeks of intense scrutiny that ended as soon as she was found innocent.

She looked at Dennet, then Babanel, then turned around to see Phelps still leaning against the wall, looking like he'd rather be somewhere else. "Let the games begin," he said.

———

Standing in front of the podium brought her back to the weeks after Shea's death. She remembered the noise, the stench of hair spray, the forest of shiny-eyed idiots staring her down. But she had somehow forgotten how hot the lights could be. Or how loud the cameras were.

She stood on the front steps to the precinct with the morning sun bisecting the island from east to west. She tried not to wince into the bright halogen spots that came at her like a wall of headaches but she wasn't succeeding. But she wouldn't look down, or to the side—because that was negative body language.

". . . and last night we recovered the body of a second victim, ten-year-old Bobby Grant."

She paused as a murmur went through the crowd of reporters. She stared straight ahead.

"Like the first victim, Bobby Grant had been mutilated. I am unable to discuss or release the particular nature of his wounds at this juncture in time but I can say that his body was found in the East River by a police patrol."

And that was pretty much it—the department's peace offering.

"And if you can keep it civil, I'd be happy to answer questions." She stared into the lights, squinting to see hands.

She pointed and nodded.

Miles Rafferty: *Can you tell us if either of the boys were sexually assaulted?*

Hemingway wished she could shoot reporters based on nothing more than dislike. "Actually, that's something that we can neither confirm nor deny at this point because it still has bearing on the case." By wording it like that, the press could conjecture for days without figuring out if that had been a *yes* or a *no*.

She picked out another hand.

Donald Cox, CNN: *Can you be more specific in reference to the mutilations?*

Hemingway stared into the lights and shook her head. "Not at this time, no."

Edwin Choy, MSNBC: *Could you be more specific as to where Bobby Grant's body was found?*

At that she took a breath, and gave a general—and evasive—answer. "The body was found in the East River. I'm sorry I can't be specific because it still has bearing on the investigation." With that it sounded like they had something.

Another hand, this one belonging to Anderson Caldwell, fluttered in the dead air: *Did the two boys know one another?*

"That's a good question, Anderson, and one we're trying to figure out. It is possible that they crossed paths in some way but as of now it appears they did not know one another."

Jennifer Mann, Fox News: *Do you have any suspects?*

Babanel had said this was a given and prepped her. "We are investigating a lot of leads right now but I cannot at this time say whether or not we are considering any suspects."

Can I take that as a no?

"You can take that as neither a yes or a no. I am not being vague to hide information. I am being prudent in order not to jeopardize the investigation in any way. There is a difference."

Alistair Franklin, the *Washington Post*: *Do you think you have a serial killer on your hands?*

That was the one she was waiting for. She appreciated Franklin for wording it like he had—it allowed her to give a yes or no answer. "Yes, I do."

More camera flashes and hands and Horshack grunts.

Cameron Gillespie for *Nancy Grace*: *Do you think you will find the perpetrator?*

And at that Hemingway smiled. Now was the time to cash in on her past and maybe help the investigation go forward. She looked at Gillespie and paused, swiveling her head over the crowd. Then she took a breath, stared straight ahead, and slowly said, "I am going to find him and I am going to put him in prison."

While everyone was snapping photographs and yelling out questions, Hemingway leaned into the nest of microphones taped to the podium, and said, "If you would please calm down, Captain Dennet will fill you in on our plans—and recommendations—for keeping the school children of this city safe. He will run through the support networks that have been set up all over the city as well as our plans through the end of the school year on into the summer. Please check out the website at the bottom of your screen."

As she stepped away from the podium she saw Phelps look at his shoes and smile. "What?" she asked, and took her place beside him.

Still looking down, he said, "You know, for a chick, you got the biggest set of balls I ever saw."

"I get that a lot."

||| TWENTY-EIGHT

CAPTAIN DENNET got his wish; Manhattan looked like a police state. A pair of cruisers was assigned to every school on the island and surrounding boroughs. This blanket effort was extended to all institutions—public, private, male only, female only, coed—to keep the specter of favoritism from rearing its politically incorrect countenance. Those who criticized this overuse of manpower felt it would have been better utilized at schools where white ten-year-old boys were to be found—after all, that seemed to be the victim of choice. The champions of the citywide display of force said that even though the killer had chosen a certain demographic up until this point, there was nothing to say that he wouldn't change his taste, especially if another vast segment of school-age children were left unguarded. The logic, of course, went against all known research but the loudest voices got their way. Which meant that the NYPD had to be everywhere.

Hemingway and Phelps were assigned to the James Crichton Prep School in Morningside Heights. Papandreou and Lincoln were thirty-one blocks up, at the Esther Marring

School of New York—an all-black girls' school. The rest of the day's shift, culled from precincts as far south as Staten Island and as far north as the Bronx, were out en masse. They had a single message to convey: *we mean business.*

The news teams did their utmost to make the police look like the twenty-first-century equivalent of the Keystone Cops. They interviewed people on the street about security, as if the population had suddenly become surveillance specialists. They interviewed parents. Children. Registered sex offenders with computer-garbled voices and blotted-out faces. All in the name of constructive criticism.

They talked about Detective Alexandra Hemingway's oratory skills. Discussed her clothing. Brought up old news footage of the bloodbath she had left behind in David Shea's bar. Before and after photos of her where they discussed the scar tissue that made up the side of her jaw—as if she had chosen a bad pair of shoes, or worn stripes with plaid. They discussed the investigation into Shea's death and how Shea had killed her boyfriend, Moses Mankiewicz—a cop with a violent past.

They fixated on Hemingway's refusal to admit or deny that there were any suspects. Many hinted that this meant the police had a suspect, because that's what would bring in the ratings. But they were careful of being too certain of what they said, just in case they were wrong; no one wanted to risk damaging their imaginary integrity.

They focused on the easy money by generating fear.

They reported that attendance was down all over the city and that the poorer schools had higher absenteeism than the wealthier institutions. They went on that this was likely because the socioeconomically disadvantaged felt the police were there to protect and serve the rich, not everyone else.

And the higher attendance at the wealthier schools seemed to support these thin accusations.

The simple truth was that the rich believed their money bought them some kind of divine protection.

But belief often fails when tested against reality and at 8:13 a.m. another boy disappeared.

||| TWENTY-NINE

HIS NAME was Nigel Stuart Matheson. It was no surprise that he had brown hair and eyes. Or that he was thirteen days older than Tyler Rochester—three older than Bobby Grant. He was handsome. And wealthy. And gone.

Nigel disappeared while walking to school with a group of boys who lived in the same neighborhood—part of a strength in numbers program that many of the schools had adopted; a measure that made parents feel a little more secure. Everyone thought it was a good way to protect the children. After all, who would grab a child from a group?

One minute Nigel was there, waxing poetic about Curtis Granderson's strikeout record.

The next he was gone.

From the group.

From the street.

He came back in a big way: within fifteen minutes his picture was on every television and news website in the country. Smiling. Happy. Alive.

HEMINGWAY AND Phelps spent an hour individually interviewing the sixteen boys who had been with Nigel Matheson when he vanished.

After the first boy, Hemingway had to coach Phelps on his approach. These children were brought up to believe that they were special. They were taught that they were smarter and more gifted and when they looked at their lives they had to believe it. They would inherit the world and they knew it.

Phelps called them entitled little fuckers.

Hemingway just shrugged.

They were identical in dress and manner, and all had the easy comfort of certainty in who they were being groomed to replace. They were identical in their perfect hair, sly smiles, and blandness. Their versions of what had happened to Nigel Matheson were also the same.

They had passed a few other groups of schoolboys—one from Saint Dominic and another from the Jasper Collegiate Institute.

They crossed two intersections.

Went past a park.

Were captured by a surveillance camera inside the door of an apartment building.

He was there, among them.

Then he was not.

III THIRTY-ONE

THE APARTMENT opened up onto a lush vista of Central Park that stretched away to the north. There was a big balcony with a stone railing where bronze hawks sat watch, a leftover from before urban renewal had destroyed most of the building's original charm. The space was a combination of chrome, leather, and plastic that had all the earmarks of a collection rather than being merely well decorated. Hemingway saw that most of the paintings were by the top black American artists, something not usually collected by whites.

Wendy Matheson was tall and graceful, with a fat-free body and natural beauty that resembled Hemingway's in some lateral way. Besides wealth and photogenic DNA, she did not appear mean, jealous, or hypocritical but it was obvious that Mrs. Matheson had always been very happy that life was about her.

Until now.

Mr. Matheson had been boarding a flight at LaGuardia when the school called. The NYPD offered to pick him up but he insisted on making his own way back. Until then, it was Hemingway, an uncomfortable-looking Phelps, and Mrs. Matheson.

Mrs. Matheson did not say much; she answered in monosyllables and had the same distant expression of Mrs. Rochester, but none of the slurred speech.

As they talked, Hemingway's hand was on her stomach again—something she found herself doing too frequently now. Sitting there, staring down a woman whose son had just been taken, the gesture felt disrespectful, blasphemous.

They ran through the usual questions, from the basic to the invasive. With two boys down, Trevor Deacon dead, and the Grant boy's driver squirted all over the interior of the Lincoln, there wouldn't be a happy ending to the Nigel Matheson story unless they asked the tough questions.

They were at the point in the interview where they focused on lists and routine. The people Nigel Matheson spent time with and the places he went. They didn't bother asking about a life insurance policy.

They sacrificed poise and tact for truth and results. And it was obvious that Mrs. Matheson wasn't used to being hammered like this. Hers was a world of afternoons at Bergdorf's and weekends on the ocean. The only time she bothered to look at a cop was if she was pulled over and even then she probably didn't pay much attention; to people like this, the police were something to be dealt with, not listened to.

After a few moments of listing Nigel's friends, she stopped in mid-sentence. At first Hemingway thought she had remembered something, an important detail or a significant event. She looked up and said, "He was special." Her eyes went from Hemingway to Phelps then back to Hemingway again. Then she reached over and picked up a leatherbound book from the coffee table. "He wrote a play." And she began to sob.

Hemingway did something that was out of character but she couldn't stop herself. She went over to the sofa, sat down beside Mrs. Matheson, and put her arm around the woman.

"I'm sorry about this. I know that right now you can't believe me, but I know what you're going through. This isn't fair or right or anything else that makes sense. But now—I mean *right now*—we need you to be focused. Can you do that?"

Mrs. Matheson turned, buried her face in Hemingway's collar, and let out a scream so primal and rooted in anguish that it jolted Phelps in his seat.

Then she pushed herself up, wiped her nose in a handkerchief, and gave a single solid nod. "Okay."

Hemingway kept her arm around the woman. She felt the skin beneath the blouse, the muscle beneath the skin, the piston of her heart below that. Her whole body vibrated as if the molecules were on the verge of dispersing. "You want a coffee? Detective Phelps makes a great cup of coffee."

Mrs. Matheson seemed to actually consider the offer, then gave a soft, almost childlike nod. Her housekeeper materialized out of what appeared to be thin air, asked the detectives if they wanted some coffee as well, then disappeared.

"Look, Mrs. Matheson, we need—"

The front door kicked open, blowing Hemingway's question off the road.

Mr. Matheson barreled in, eyes red, tie in his fist. He ran to his wife, picked her up off the sofa and drew her into a hug. Over her shoulder he said, "I'm Andrew Matheson. What happened to my son?" He was tall, black, with close-cropped hair and the no-nonsense air of a man used to getting things done on a schedule.

"I'm Detective Alex Hemingway and this is my partner, Jon Phelps. Your stepson is missing, Mr. Matheson."

Andrew Matheson's face went brittle. "He's not my step-son, he's my son, detective."

Hemingway felt the saliva hit the back of her mouth in a surge of adrenaline. "Are you Nigel's biological father?" she asked.

"Of course not. Does it matter?"

Hemingway looked over his shoulder, at the family photograph on the console beside the Bang & Olufsen stereo. She focused on the boy between his parents.

Same as the others: brown hair, brown eyes.

White.

Dr. Grant said that after all the trouble they had gone through to conceive, this was going to destroy his wife.

Tyler Rochester's mother said that it had been hard to get pregnant. *Twice.*

Phelps said they could have been brothers.

All of a sudden she had it. "Mr. and Mrs. Matheson, I need you to tell me where you went for fertility treatment."

THIRTY-TWO

PHELPS TOOK the driver's seat and Hemingway strapped herself in, lit up the cherry, and pulled out her phone as they swung into traffic. They wound their way south and she cycled through her call log, looking for the Rochesters' number. She found it and dialed.

"Yes, hello. This is detective Alex Hemingway of the NYPD. I need to speak to Mrs. Rochester right now."

Pause.

"No, it's urgent."

Pause.

"Yes, very."

Pause.

"Sooner. Yes. Thank you."

She hung up and scrolled through her data for the Grants' number.

Dialed.

"Yes, this is Detective Alex Hemingway of the NYPD. I need to speak to Mrs. Grant immediately. It's urgent. Yes. Yes."

Phelps swung the big four-by-four around a double-parked

limousine and Hemingway suddenly wished she was driving. She hated the passenger seat. Always had.

"Yes, Mrs. Grant. I am very sorry to trouble you right now but I have an important question to ask you. It's personal and you have to keep it confidential—is that clear?"

Pause.

"Yes. I understand. Are you alone?"

Pause.

"Yes, I'll wait."

Pause. She covered the phone and said, "She's going to the bedroom." Pause. "Yes, I'm still here. Was Dr. Grant Bobby's biological father?"

She listened. Then punched the dashboard. "What was the name of the clinic you went to?"

Pause.

"Thank you."

She hung up. "Same fucking place—Park Avenue Clinic. Hit it."

And the big man in the gray suit flew the truck south on 7th Avenue.

||| THIRTY-THREE

THE SUBURBAN slid around the corner with the grace of a smoking cathedral. Hemingway kept one hand protectively over her stomach as she tried not lose the phone. "Nick, do we have anything on the Park Avenue Clinic? Or on a Dr. Sylvester Brayton who works there?"

"Park Avenue Clinic? What kind of a fuckin' name is—?"

"Jesus Christ, Nick, just do it without the commentary."

"Sure. Sorry. Okay . . . all right, the Park Avenue Clinic is a swanky place where a hundred grand buys you a bun for the oven—"

Hemingway closed her eyes and tried to push the blossoming headache away. "Forget the goddamned brochure stuff. Do we have anything in the system?"

"Let's see . . ."

Hemingway opened her eyes just as Phelps punched around a bus and missed clipping a taxi that had stopped on a stale yellow—possibly the only cab in history to not run a yellow.

Papandreou came back. "They're stock market country. They pay their taxes and look legit. One OSHA infraction during a renovation a few years back but that's it. Owned by big pharma."

Hemingway filed that away. "Now the doctor—Sylvester Brayton. B-R-A-Y-T-O-N."

There was the sound of fingers on a keyboard and he came back with, "Here we go. Brayton, Sylvester. Graduated George Washington School of Medicine. Then Johns Hopkins. On staff with the clinic as of a year before it opened its doors. Disappeared from staff rosters a little over a year ago."

Phelps slalomed through the tight crosstown traffic that seemed oblivious to the red flashing light clamped to the dash.

"Where is he now?"

The sound of typing was followed by, "I don't know."

"Nick, give me something."

More typing. "The guy just dropped off the face of the planet. No driver's license. No car registration. No cell phone contract." More typing. "Sweetfuckall. He just disappeared."

Hemingway ran through her conversations with the Grants and when she was done, Papandreou swore in Greek, a peculiar oddity; he was a fourth-generation New Yorker who didn't know a word of his ancestral tongue.

"We're on the way there right now. Find Brayton. And get a black-and-white to the clinic."

"Could be a coincidence," Papandreou said with no conviction at all.

This wasn't monkeys typing Shakespeare; Hemingway had already confirmed that two of the three victims were conceived at this clinic. There were no odds this good. "Get someone to the Rochester funeral—someone with a little tact— to find out about Tyler. I bet we're three for three." The dashboard clock gave them nine hours until sundown—nine hours that would sweep by like they had never been there at all. "And check out the other principals at the clinic. From the ground up. Find out if any of the MDs there have malpractice or ethics cases being reviewed—check with the medical board and the courts. If you find any cases, check out the plaintiffs. I'm guessing it's not a doctor—Marcus says whoever is taking these kids apart has no prior knowledge of anatomy."

"You think it's someone there?"

"I think it's someone everywhere. Do it. Put it all in motion."

||| THIRTY-FOUR

THE PARK Avenue Clinic was a renovated brownstone sandwiched in between a law firm and a glass building that housed an art gallery. It had passed the status of clinic and entered into the realm of corporation more than two decades back and it wore its muscle proudly. There was valet parking and three limousines sat at the curb.

Phelps rammed the truck across two lanes, plugging a hole a Rolls had staked out with its massive gauche ass. The driver looked up, acknowledged the flashing bubble with a shake of his head, and pulled out into the cars heading downtown. Hemingway was on the curb before the Suburban came to a halt, her shield out, feet pounding the concrete. By the time she was at the front door to the building, Phelps was patiently bringing Dennet up to speed with that no-nonsense diction he was famous for. The next call would be to the District Attorney.

Hemingway yanked the big metal handle and the ten-foot polycarbonate door bowed out, then flew open.

The welcome desk was sculpted from a single chunk of volcanic rock, cut to show the negative space of a mother and child swallowed by the ash of Pompeii. The handsome woman behind the counter backed up when Hemingway came at her with the badge. Outside, the screech of a police siren stopped at the curb and the sound of car doors slamming punctuated her footsteps.

"Detectives Alex Hemingway and Jon Phelps, NYPD. I need to speak to your CEO right now."

The receptionist was mixed race but her dialogue was heavy Brooklynese. There was a tiny black microphone peeking out of the hair beside her ear. "May I ask what this is about?"

"You have ten seconds to get the CEO or director or whatever you call the head cheese down here. At the end of ten seconds, I am going get annoyed. You don't want me to get annoyed," Hemingway said.

The receptionist's eyes shifted from Hemingway's badge to the restructured line of her jaw, then back to the badge. She took a step back. "That would be Marjorie Fenton."

"Then phone her, sweetheart. You get Fenton down here right now." She leveled her finger at the microphone. "Ten seconds," she repeated.

It was then that a woman appeared beside them. Her face was a perfect blend of poised calm and subtextual annoyance. Five hundred pounds of security squeezed into two suits stood behind her. Whatever her title, there was little room for doubt that she was a major player in the clinic's ecosystem. "*I'm* Director Fenton, how may we help you—detectives, is it?" She was small, maybe five foot one. Close to sixty but could pass for fifty if the light and makeup were right. She put her hand firmly on Hemingway's elbow. "I am happy to make an appointment. We are terribly busy and can't operate with the police barging in and—"

HARVEST | 145

Hemingway saw how this was going to go—or at least how Fenton imagined it would go—and she had no intention of letting the woman railroad her. "I am going to shut you up right now." At that, the wall of suit behind the woman flexed and Hemingway heard Phelps's shoes scrape the travertine behind her. She knew he had taken a step forward and that his hand was probably on the big automatic under his arm. For a man of his size, Phelps was able to move with surprising speed.

Hemingway continued in an even cadence. "You have heard about the two boys who were found in the East River? The other who was abducted this morning? Very shortly he is going to have parts of his body sawn off while he lies in the dirt somewhere, wondering why bad things are happening to him. If I don't get your help—and I mean *right fucking now*—I will go outside and call a press conference on the sidewalk. I will tell Wolf Blitzer and the rest of the cackling idiots that patients of this clinic are being murdered and yet you refuse to cooperate with us and I am going to emphatically state that the commonality between these victims is that they were all conceived here. You, Mrs. Fenton, can piss your retirement right down the toilet." Hemingway knew that this would all come out eventually anyway, but she was going for a knee-jerk reaction, not a rational response.

Fenton opened her mouth and Hemingway cut her off. Again.

"You may consider threatening me personally, but you'd be wasting your breath. I have a family attorney on retainer: Dwight Hemingway of Hemingway, McCrae and Pearson. They're a few blocks up, in nicer digs than this. I won't have to make meetings for three years, by which time the story of our little conversation here will be at the film stage and you will be on record as the director of Jeffrey Dahmer, Inc." Hemingway, almost a solid foot taller than the woman, pulled her elbow out of Fenton's grip and leaned over, her hands on her thighs as if reprimanding a child. "Now do you still want to play Queen Bitch with me?"

The door opened and the clink of cops in gear had everyone but Hemingway turn their heads. She kept her eyes locked on Fenton's, but this was a woman who gave nothing away. She just stared back, her expression frozen in the indifference that seemed to be her prime emotion.

Fenton turned to the receptionist. "Maya, we'll be in the big consultation room." Then she led the two detectives away.

Hemingway beckoned the two uniformed policemen to follow. Fenton moved fast in her heels and Hemingway recognized the rhythm of a runner in the way she timed her shoulders. The two security men and the two street cops closed up the rear. They rounded two ground-level corners and just before they came to an elevator, Phelps—still on the phone—said, "Yeah, we're there now," loud enough that Fenton shifted in her designer one-off.

They dropped into the building's guts in a backlit car, three of the walls decorated with Keith Haring acrylics—happy linear representations of parents and children with rays of goodness shooting out of their bodies. Hemingway's parents had a moderate collection of American modern, the brunt of their focus on Georgia O'Keeffe and Jacob Coleridge, but they owned a Haring or two; it didn't take a dealer's acumen to see that there had to be a million dollars' worth of canvas hanging on the walls. Money was evidently not an issue here.

That would change when the lawsuits started.

Hemingway was neither spiteful nor petty, and she wasn't holding Fenton at fault for her Sarah Palin imitation downstairs. She wondered if Fenton had an inkling of what was about to happen. Probably not—too much confidence in the way the world was supposed to treat her—which meant that Hemingway would have to bully her.

The elevator opened to a subterranean conference room that could have been under the White House if the president was into Ralph Lauren. The walls were paneled in bamboo and fitted with an array of multimedia presentation equipment, tools to help talk prospective parents out of their money. The table was a block of polished concrete and the chairs were high-backed leather deals that looked like they were lifted from a fleet of Bentleys. A heavy silver coffee service sat in the center of the table, along with sandwiches, muffins, and cookies.

They stepped out as a procession, Fenton doing her best to look authoritative. Hemingway was annoyed at the time they were losing and she could feel Phelps vibrating behind her like an angry infection. No doubt, this was one of those times when he would be silently lamenting the loss of the old days he always talked about, a time when the letter of the law hadn't been obscured by red tape and bureaucracy.

Fenton gestured to one side of the table and reached for the chair at the head but Hemingway grabbed it. Phelps dropped into the seat to her right. The two uniformed officers took up position at the door and Fenton was forced into one of the cheap seats with her security men behind her.

Fenton opened her mouth and Hemingway nailed her

again. "Mrs. Fenton, there is no discussion here. My patience and time is running out." She checked her watch. "You are almost at the end of my rope."

"Do I need counsel present?" Fenton didn't ask politely, courteously, or even as if it were any kind of a real possibility. She wanted to show she couldn't be pushed.

Hemingway turned on her predator face. "You know about Tyler Rochester and Bobby Grant?"

Fenton stared at her. "I read about it in the paper, yes."

"A third boy, Nigel Matheson, was abducted a few hours ago."

Fenton just stared, waiting.

"Bobby Grant and Nigel Matheson were conceived at this clinic and I expect to have the same news from the Rochester family in a few minutes. Dr. Brayton handled the pregnancies. Your clinic—or Dr. Brayton—are what links the victims. Very soon, the media will descend on this place and you can forget the right to a due process. You can forget the right to a fair trial. They will paint this institution black. And for just a second, I want you to imagine what the parents of the next child who turns up dead with his leg or his arm or his foot chopped off is going to do when they find out that we came to you." And she stopped cold to let that sink into Fenton's core reactor. "And you told us to go fuck ourselves." She looked into the points of anger that had replaced Fenton's eyes.

After a protracted pause, Fenton said, "First off, I do not know the name of every child we helped to conceive—the number now totals in the thousands."

"Would a doctor remember his patients ten years later?"

"I expect so, yes."

"So where is Dr. Sylvester Brayton?"

"Brayton left us a year ago and I am not in the habit of staying in touch with former employees. I heard he took a position somewhere in Europe."

"How long had Brayton been with the clinic?" Hemingway wanted to see if Fenton would be up front with information.

"I can't be certain, but an easy twenty years. Since before we opened this facility at least."

"Why did he leave?"

Fenton paused for a second. "We had mutually exclusive visions for the future of this clinic."

"So you won't tell me?"

Fenton shook her head. "I cannot discuss internal politics unless it has bearing on your case."

"Who picked up Brayton's patients?"

At that Fenton reached for the phone and punched in a four-digit extension number. "Yes, Maya, is Dr. Selmer back from Paris? Good. Could you please get him on the phone? Yes. Yes. Immediately. Then put him through."

Fenton hung up and looked at Hemingway. "Dr. Michael Selmer picked up Dr. Brayton's files. You have to understand that we are a fertility clinic, not a pediatrics ward. I doubt even Dr. Selmer will know that these boys were conceived here." She reached over and poured herself a cup of coffee. "What do you want from me, Detective?"

"That phone call to Selmer is a good start. Anything you can give me in the way of due diligence. I understand the doctor–patient privilege; I understand that we need a court order to access Dr. Brayton's files; I understand that we have to be very specific in our requests and that you can only release information that pertains to this case—we can't go fishing and we can't guess. But I am making the not-too-far-reaching assumption that these two—and soon to be three—children are not the only children at risk. There are more of Dr. Brayton's patients out there. Which means other children may be in danger. Until we have a court order in our hands, which will take—" She turned to Phelps and raised an eyebrow.

"Two hours," he said flatly.

"Since you cannot give me the names of Dr. Brayton's patients without breaking your fiduciary responsibility to this clinic and its patients, I expect you to get on the phone and contact each and every one of them. You will give them my coordinates and you will ask them to call me. You will be persuasive. They need to know that their children are in danger."

Fenton shook her head. "I don't have the legal authority to do that. They are Dr. Selmer's patients, not mine. Maya should have him on the phone any second." She pointed at the phone in the middle of the table beside the coffee and food.

The elevator opened and the receptionist came in. She was out of breath and held her pumps in her hand. "I can't find Dr. Selmer. I've called his apartment and he's not answering. I—"

Fenton pushed her chair back and stood up. "Did you call the doorman?"

Maya nodded, and with her mouth frozen in a perfect circle, she looked like an umlaut O come to life. "The doorman says there's no answer. He's not allowed to go in."

"Are you sure he's home?"

Maya nodded again. "He landed at nine thirty-five this morning. British Airways flight . . ." She pulled a crumpled sheet of paper from inside one of the shoes still dangling in her hand. ". . . flight two-two-nine-two. JFK. George, our driver, picked him up and dropped him off. Gate to apartment door. I called him. George left him at eleven oh five a.m. and the doorman says he hasn't left and no one answers his door. His car's in the garage."

Hemingway stood up. "We need an address."

IT WAS earlier than yesterday; they had forced him to advance his schedule and from here on out time would be in short supply.

He looked down at the body; the best of what the boy was about was now missing.

He held him for a second, looked down on his face, on his features, and felt as if he were looking at part of himself. Nigel Matheson had been handsome. And talented. And many more things that no one could understand.

But all of those things were gone now. The handsomeness most of all.

He held him in the current as he said goodbye. He smiled down at the boy—his friend, really—and let go of his ankle, giving him up to the cold hands of the river.

Nigel Matheson floated out a few feet, scraped between the rocks and bumped the decoy that floated there. Then the current fastened its fingers on him and took him away.

He picked up the insulated knapsack with the Canadian flag sewn to it, the one he used to transport their parts. He slung it over his shoulder and scrambled up through the scrub.

||| THIRTY-SIX

DR. MICHAEL SELMER had an apartment on West 86th Street and Amsterdam. The doorman wore a green suit wired with ten yards of gold braid and looked like he had forgotten his tuba somewhere. His name tag read PEPE and after a few seconds of pressing his finger to the buzzer, he shook his head. "I told the lady on the phone—he ain't answerin'."

Hemingway let Phelps take this one; it was his turn to do some heavy lifting.

Phelps knocked and put his ear to the door. Then he leaned down and went to work on the lock. There was a soft click and he swung the door in.

They went through the apartment, weapons out, communication reduced to hand signals. Pepe stayed in the hallway.

The living room, dining room, kitchen, and study were empty.

Then Hemingway held up her hand and they listened. There was an odd, raspy sound coming from somewhere at the opposite end of the apartment.

They found him in the master bedroom.

He was asleep: plugs in his ears; a mask over his eyes;

mouth open to the ceiling; snoring a jet-lagged slumber. He wore silk pajama bottoms and nothing else.

Phelps reached out and touched his toe.

Selmer lifted straight off the bed in a screaming cat launch. He had the mask off and was up against the headboard in a single startled move. Then Pepe walked into the room and the fear in his face converted to confusion.

Hemingway had her badge out. "I'm Detective Hemingway and this is Detective Phelps. We need to speak with you."

He put his hand to his forehead and for a second it looked like he would faint. "Jesus Christ, why didn't you knock?"

———

A few minutes later they were in the living room, overlooking a church. Dr. Selmer still had his silk pajama pants on but had thrown a Paul Frank T-shirt over his chest. He had a coffee in his hands and looked like he was about to fall over, his squinty-eyed stare not dissimilar to the monkey logo. "Sorry, I took two Seconal about—" He checked the gold Cartier on his wrist, tried to focus, and gave up. "Hell, I don't know. Before I went to bed." He took a sip of his coffee and tried to follow Hemingway as she paced.

"Dr. Selmer, have you read the news?" she asked, indicating the iPad sitting on the coffee table.

He shook his head. Slurped more coffee. He clearly just wanted to get back to bed.

Hemingway stepped forward, yanked the iPad up off the exotic wood surface, and found the *New York Times* website. Then she handed him the tablet. "Maybe you should."

His eyes ratcheted down and he tried to focus on the print. When he couldn't, he reached for his glasses.

He scanned the screen and the tired look dropped away. Without taking his eyes from the screen he leaned forward and placed his mug down on one of the coffee table books neatly stacked on the table. He swiped through the content and what little color remained in his face drained away. He went to put the iPad back onto the coffee table but it slipped from his fingers and bounced on the floor. "Oh Jesus."

"So you recognize those names?"

He no longer looked like the drugged-out monkey on his T-shirt. "Before I say anything, what are you doing from a legal standpoint?"

Hemingway was glad he wasn't another Fenton. She ran through the chain of events, starting with her epiphany at the Mathesons' apartment and ending with her showdown with Fenton. "Our captain has this before the DA right now. From there it goes in front of a judge. We should have a court order giving us access to your files by the close of business today. Which is five hours closer to sunset and if this guy sticks to his routine, we'll find Nigel Matheson in the river just after sundown."

Selmer shook his head as he put it all through his processor. "This is bad."

"Your career?"

At that he laughed a single, derisive snort. "My career? When my name becomes associated with these horrors, what do you think will happen to me? I might as well move to Finland. My career, Detective Hemingway, is over.

"I am thinking about my patients—and they are my patients now, regardless of how they began their association with the clinic. Or with Brayton."

Something about the way he said the doctor's name set off some low-level alarm in her mind. "What can you tell us about Brayton?"

He shrugged. "Great doctor. Smartest guy in the room. A narcissist, but that's not uncommon in exceptional people."

"You know where he is?"

He shrugged again. "Scandinavia somewhere. Norway, I think."

She smelled bullshit behind it all.

"If the link between those three boys is Brayton, there are bound to be others. I can't tell you who they are. Not yet. Not legally. But I can put them in touch with you. I can warn them," he said, mimicking Hemingway's thoughts. He stood up. "I have to get to the clinic. To my files." He ran to the bedroom, pulling off his shirt. There was nothing sluggish about his movements now that the adrenaline had kicked in.

Hemingway stood up and her cell phone went off. She nodded at Phelps who went after the doctor and she answered her phone.

"Hemingway here."

"Hemi, it's Marcus. I found something you need to hear. The Rochester and Grant boys were half brothers."

"How is that possible? They were—" And then it hit her. "Sonofabitch, they had the same father."

"He's not hunting them because they're his type. He's hunting them because of who they are. It's not a phenotype; it's a genetic link."

||| THIRTY-SEVEN

THE ELEVATOR was large—an anomaly for Manhattan no matter what the price point. There were no Keith Harings hanging on the paneled walls but Dr. Selmer's parents had to be proud.

Selmer stood in a corner, staring at the floor. They would escort him to the clinic where he would begin calling the parents of other children who had been sired by the same donor. At least that was what he said the scope of his activities would be. Papandreou and Lincoln would stick with him until the footwork was done and they had a list of parents. Always the list.

Hemingway's phone made him jump.

She pressed it to her ear. "Hemingway."

"Hemi, it's Papandreou. It looks like they found Nigel Matheson in the East River."

She felt the air leave her lungs and she checked her watch. It wasn't yet 1 p.m. "What do you mean, 'looks like'?"

"It's hard to tell; the bottom of his face has been sawn off."

|¦| THIRTY-EIGHT

HEMINGWAY DROVE, Phelps rode shotgun. The lights and sirens were dialed to their apex as they pushed through traffic. The early-afternoon sun was behind the rolling sheet of clouds that stretched to the horizon but it still felt like the streets were heated to within a few degrees of combustion. A storm was coming and everyone hoped it would bring a brief respite from the heat and humidity.

She and Phelps had switched out with Lincoln and Papandreou who were now with Selmer at the clinic. They would act as chaperone until the court order came through. No one thought he would run but they were all concerned that Fenton would offer him a check to keep a united front for their house of secrets.

Hemingway pulled around a florist's truck, then rocked through a hole between two taxis, her tires screaming across the hot city pavement. Phelps held tight, his face the same impassive mask he had sewn to his skull whenever they were at work.

"He's early," she said, hating that she expected anything of this guy. There was an old cop rule that said the most you could count on from the other side was nothing. And even that was often hoping for too much.

Phelps shrugged, as if it all amounted to the same thing—which it did—another dead child.

A lane opened up in front of them and Hemingway pounded down on the gas. The truck lurched forward at nearly sixty miles an hour.

Rochester and Grant were half brothers.

They shared a parent.

A father.

A donor.

Which was as narrow a commonality as they could hope for. They had more than a lead—they had their case. She didn't know where it was yet, but the boys were the key. If they busted their asses, they'd find him. Hemingway didn't know how long it would take, only that it would get done.

THE BOY looked like a mechanic had taken his head apart to get at the transmission inside. Only there was no transmission. And there was no putting it back together again. He was waxy, lifeless, and horrifying.

Phelps looked down at the child, coughed once, then walked out of the room, leaving Hemingway and Marcus in silence.

Hemingway had seen a lot of damage done to the human body but she couldn't get used to what this guy seemed to feed on. There was no way to hammer this into any kind of comprehensible geometry. No. Way. At. All.

She looked down at the boy and gulped in a lungful of air. She could smell the river in him. "What am I looking at?"

Since Phelps's departure, the only noise had been the scratch of Marcus's pencil and the distant tidal force of her own heart. His pencil stopped and Hemingway looked up to see him staring at her. "His jaw was cut out," he said.

She forced herself to lower her eyes, to focus on the boy. "With our hacksaw?" It seemed a pointless thing to ask.

Marcus didn't add any body language to his response.

"Same saw. Same anesthetic. Same type of victim. Same injection point. Same everything. Except for the parts he took."

Hemingway tried to make sense of the ugly thing she was looking at.

"And he learned something from taking Deacon's skull apart. As opposed to going straight through like last time, he used two cuts, one straight back into the condyle, the second up from under his chin. Saved himself having to go through the ramus and spinal column."

"Was Matheson alive when this happened?"

Marcus waved the question away as if it were academic. "Of course."

Bobby Grant's half brother; Tyler Rochester's half brother.

Hemingway stared down at the boy. His lower jaw was gone and the meat on the skull above was swollen and distorted. The corners of his mouth were opened up to his temporomandibular joint. His top teeth and uvula hung in the wreckage of his face—a purple mass of bloodless anatomy that looked like it lived on the bottom of the ocean. Part of his larynx poked up through the top of his neck, like an exposed pupa. He looked worse than dead; he looked defiled.

For a second, Marcus put aside his professional demeanor and asked the question that was running through everyone's head. "Hemi, do you know the kind of person it takes to do something like this? What kind of experiences a human being needs to have under his belt to do this to a live child?"

Hemingway had no answer, she doubted anyone did. She stared at the boy. This hadn't been done by a human being at all.

The door to the lab opened and Phelps came back in. "Sorry about that," he said.

Marcus continued, business as usual. "Again, there are no defensive wounds. His hands are clean. Washed by the Hudson—true—but in good shape. No ripped nails, abrasions, cuts, bruises, lacerations, ligature marks, or fractures. I can see that on one victim. But all three? They don't fight and they don't see it coming." He looked up. "Our boys are comfortable around the killer."

"So was Deacon," she said.

DR. MICHAEL SELMER wasn't prone to greed and this had always made him suspect in the eyes of Director Fenton; there is nothing a medical corporation values less in an employee than moral rectitude, even in the abstract. The clinic and its principles were fundamentally positive but the ends-versus-means formula that was dictated by corporate survival often cast it in an unsympathetic light. Like now.

Selmer wasn't afraid of Fenton as much as he was worried about her. She wasn't evil, but she *was* devious. And tenacious—a trait worth ten times its weight in brains. In medicine it was all about staying power, and in his thirty-one years in the industry, he had never worked under anyone more driven than Frau Fenton.

She ran the clinic with relentless precision. She didn't outlaw the thieving of office supplies or begrudge her employees parking passes—no, if anything she was overly generous with benefits: Hermès briefcases each Christmas; a new Benz each spring. But there was a price for her love: you had to perform. Continually on. Continually perfect. Continually nervous.

This hypercompetitive atmosphere ensured that only the strongest survived and competitive mechanics had refined the clinic's personnel to the top stratum of American medicine. Which in turn attracted the top stratum of clientele. And the self-feeding machine acquired the finest research facility in reproductive endocrinology anywhere in the hemisphere.

Fenton had been waiting for him in the lobby and had insisted on walking him to his office. She had been alone, her two security baboons conspicuously absent. She had talked about loyalty. About the greater good. About finances and bright futures.

Before she left him at his desk, she pushed a copy of his contract into his hand, reminded him that he had a legal responsibility to the clinic and an ethical one to his patients. She didn't mention Brayton; she didn't need to. Then she had left him alone with his conscience.

Right from the start Brayton had been her golden boy, a handsome dark-haired wunderkind. He attracted all the right clients. All the right money. Until he had been found out.

As soon as Fenton left his office, Selmer had called his lawyer, his *personal* lawyer, not the clinic's people. Counselor Harwick had listened carefully, then told him that the press would catch on to this within twenty-four hours. He said Selmer could forget distancing himself from the great big mushroom cloud painted on the wall—it would make no difference that none of this was his fault.

He didn't ask Harwick about Brayton.

Harwick said the best path to a future was to have everything ready for the police when they arrived with the warrant. Legally, he couldn't tell Selmer to coach them ahead of time as to what portion of the files they'd be looking for, but he suggested that reaching out to the NYPD might not be the worst idea right now; being a live dog was better than being a dead lion. He closed by saying that in ten years Selmer would look back and tell him he had been right. Then he hung up.

He couldn't tell them about Brayton—he had signed a confidentiality agreement—but he could help protect the children.

The matter of confidentiality was largely one of interpretation and Selmer had a broad range of choices here, from helpful to near criminal. They could subpoena information they believed was there, but they could not come in like the gestapo and confiscate said information if he refused to hand it over. And they might not request the correct information.

Selmer worried about Frau Fenton, upstairs concocting a plan of defense with the clinic's battery of legal help. She wanted him to hold out until the last moment—the best thing for the clinic and maybe even for him, she had said. Which was bullshit.

She was worried that Brayton's indiscretions would be made public.

Brayton had crossed so many lines—ethical, moral and legal—that no one knew how far-reaching the consequences would be. He had been sent into exile. But he would be found—it was only a question of time. And when it all came out, the fires of hubris would burn the clinic to the ground.

He could call the parents, but he knew these people, knew the filters he'd have to go through. He was looking at three days if he was diligent. And they didn't have three days. So he went over his options. He could do this without breaking the law but he couldn't do this without violating the nonnegotiable tenets of medical practice. But he would never practice medicine again—so what did he care about doctor–patient confidentiality?

And of course he'd be sued after this. The Rochesters or

the Grants or the Mathesons would go after him in civil court and the litigious judicial system would take away everything he owned. But he wouldn't do jail time because he had done nothing illegal. Strictly speaking. So why not give it away with his head held high instead of letting them take it while he fought a losing battle?

Detectives Lincoln and Papandreou were in the lobby, as both protection and reminder that he was now under the eye of the law. If he walked out the front door, they would be with him. Which might be a good thing.

But Fenton would know. And she'd slap the lawyers on the NYPD faster than anyone could imagine. He'd go under glass and the bickering would start.

He looked at the spreadsheet, a list that had taken him a year to piece together. By law, the clinic was required to report this information to the Society of Assisted Reproductive Technology, under directives from the Centers for Disease Control. But government forms do not always ask the right questions.

It didn't take very long to see the pattern the police were onto: Tyler Rochester, Bobby Grant and Nigel Matheson had all been fathered by the same donor.

He wondered how long it would take them to figure out that the father was Dr. Brayton.

| | | F O R T Y - O N E

HEMINGWAY AND Phelps threaded their way through traffic from the medical examiner's office downtown to the Deacon house in Astoria. Deacon and the boys were somehow linked; the question was how. Maybe they had missed something at the house.

When they pulled up outside, Phelps let out a protracted "Fuck me," stretching the first word into three syllables.

Without the cavalcade of police cars out front, it should have looked like any other house on the block. But the villagers had tried to exorcise the demons from its walls and it looked like the setting for a lynching. The big elm in the front yard was toilet papered and dozens of bicycle tires hung from the branches like black sightless eyes. The sidewalk was dotted with pentagrams laid out in bloody bright epoxy paint. The bricks and garage had been spray-painted with the words *monster, motherfucker,* and *beast.* The planters that had been by the door were smashed on the driveway. Evidently things were just hunky-dory in Walley World.

Hemingway maneuvered the two-ton SUV into the empty

space in front of Deacon's and they stepped out into the humidity.

A man in a wifebeater sitting on a stoop across the street yelled, "I wouldn't park there if I was you."

Hemingway crossed the street and pulled out her badge. "Yeah? Well you're not me, fuckface. And if anything happens to that truck while I'm inside, I'm going to come back here and kick the shit out of you. We clear, cupcake?"

The man spit into the brown bush beside the steps. "Yeah."

As they walked up to the door, Phelps said, "He's either a fuckface or a cupcake—he can't be both."

"What are you, the grammar police?" They approached the cracked concrete steps and Hemingway caught the movement of a shadow by one of the windows. "And what was with the Virginia Woolf reference the other day? You start reading them book things?" she asked, in a fake hillbilly accent.

"Discovery Channel."

The door opened before they had knocked. "You got my check?" Mrs. Deacon barked into Hemingway's face.

Phelps took a step back and Hemingway did her best to smile. "That's a different office than ours, Mrs. Deacon, and I'd—"

"The name's Bergen, lady. Deacon was that bastard's father. A bum. Like his kid. Knew it from the moment he was born. Didn't do nothin'. And now them people spray-painting bad words on *my* house, toilet papering *my* tree, like *I* had anything to do with the stuff what went on downstairs. How's I supposed to know, huh? Damn stupid people. They think I'm gonna move, they got another think-a-dink coming. Tryin' to scare an old lady in her golden years. That's just mean."

"Why aren't you in a hotel?"

"They let me keep my per diem—don't mind if I do—if

I stayed here. Don't need niggers going through my suitcase when I'm in the shower."

Hemingway closed her eyes, wondering where they made people like this. "We're here to look at your son's apartment," she said, trying not to sound angry.

The old woman's mouth pursed up, reprising its role as a furry sphincter. "I already told you people. I ain't been down there in years. Can't get there through the house—he had it locked up like the floor was paved in gold or somethin'." And with that she slammed the door.

They turned and headed around to the basement entrance. On the bottom step Phelps leaned over and said, "I know hit men got bigger hearts than her."

What could she say to that? She had hunted these men long enough to know that for the most part monsters weren't born, they were made; it didn't take a lot of imagination to see how Deacon's mother could be worked into the flowchart.

Hemingway punched her code into the lock box, took out the big ring of keys, and opened the door—Phelps's entry shots were now repaired with a neat plywood patch fitted with new locks. They stepped under the bright yellow X of police tape into the gloom of Trevor Deacon's lair.

Just below the scent of disinfectant and ammonia was the stench of death and misery. It felt like a living presence. It wasn't the way Deacon met his demise—being sawn apart in his own bed—that rippled across the pond of her conscience; no, it was the thought of the children he had taken apart down here that made the place feel like a dark corner of the underworld.

They didn't know what they were looking for, only that it might be here, hidden in the gloom. The boys were tied to the clinic—which would probably be enough. But they still had a long way to go, and until it came together, they had to run down everything they had. And right now that meant Trevor Deacon's world.

She flicked on all the lights and even without Deacon's parts neatly displayed on the teak wall unit a feeling of sadness seemed to emanate from the very pores of the dwelling. It was difficult to imagine any happiness in this room. She couldn't picture anyone laughing or watching old movies or throwing birthday parties. But misery and mutilation and screams and loneliness were no stretch at all.

Hemingway laid the initial crime-scene photographs out on the table and they each took half, Phelps the kitchen/ living room, Hemingway the bedroom and garage. The metal bed frame was still there, stripped down to the springs. It had once been a glossy white but was now a chipped dirty gray that cried rust at the rivets. She stood in the doorway and opened up her mind, willing herself into Trevor Deacon's headspace. It wasn't profiling or channeling or any of the populist ideas of how a detective worked, it was merely an effort to understand the man's thoughts and how he had acted on them. If she could see who he had been, she might get a line on his killer.

She stood at the foot of the bed and reached out, touching her fingertips to the cold metal. This was where Deacon had ended his time. The four main posts were scarred and scratched and she remembered the padlocks and lengths of chain in the garage, hanging on big spiral spikes. She wondered how many children had been in this room. And as much as she wished the bed could talk to her, she was grateful for its silence; she wasn't sure she could handle the things it had witnessed.

There were the children they knew of back in the medical examiner's office. But how many had been erased from the planet? How many would never be put to rest? They would remain ten-year-olds forever, grinning out from photographs on mantels and nightstands and websites for parents who hoped that they were out there somewhere. Lost, maybe, but alive. Growing up calling someone else Mommy. Not disassembled in a garage in Astoria.

What had Deacon done with their bodies? The forensics team had gone through the property with every available technology and found nothing. There was no backyard, the foundation had been scanned and there were no bodies set in the concrete. They had interviewed Deacon's coworkers and no one knew a thing about him. He hadn't owned a car in years and the neighbors said they never really saw him around much. He went to work, came home late, never spoke to anyone. It would take months, at least, to figure out how he had snatched the kids, where he had snatched them, why he had snatched them. But that shit could wait. What they needed right now was to find out who had killed him.

Other than the bed, the only furniture was a dresser that contained clothing and the two camera lenses Linderer had catalogued. They were hidden behind the shirts in the bottom drawer.

She pulled them out—both were Nikon telephoto lenses. One was a massive 500 mm affair that looked like the barrel assembly of a howitzer and the other was smaller but only marginally so. She was familiar with photography equipment and the lenses looked like the ones Daniel was always packing and unpacking for work. She dialed his number.

"Hey, baby," he answered. "All good?"

"Yeah. Look, can you tell me the price of a couple of lenses?"

"Maybe."

Hemingway picked up the box of the largest one, a beige cardboard carton with black writing. Deacon's name was on the box in felt tip marker. "Nikon f2.0, five hundred milli-meter."

"The sports guys use them for fieldwork. Ten grand new. Maybe five secondhand. What's this about?"

She didn't have time to explain. "Work. I can't talk about it."

"I see," he said, but it was clear he didn't.

She read the next box to him, "Nikon F2 in two hundred millimeter."

"Another sports lens. It's got a fixed focal length but it's perfect for low-light shots—say if you were shooting volley-ball in a gym. Five grand retail, three used."

"Thanks, baby, you're the best. I'll talk to you later." She hung up and pocketed the phone.

She took the lenses out of the boxes and Deacon's name was professionally etched into the focus ring that ran around the optics of each. The warranty registration cards were in both boxes, stamped by B&H Photo in Manhattan. She took a snapshot of each card with her phone and returned the lenses to their hiding spot.

Where was his camera?

Phelps was still going through the kitchen cupboards, working with slow precision.

The kitchen chair still had the protective box over the seat, the single crescent of dried blood from a shoe sole vis-ible on the vinyl under the protective capsule. Man's ten or ten and a half.

The focal point of the room was still the spider scrawled onto the door to the garage, as haunting as when she had first seen it.

She opened the locks and stepped into the garage.

The space was as neat and sparse as it had been when Phelps had called her in to see the freezer full of feet. The single red crescent of the leather-soled man's shoe was there, under a protective polycarbonate box fastened to the floor with yellow tape.

The freezer stood in the corner. Unplugged. Door propped open. The lengths of welded chain still hung on rusty spiral spikes.

The workbench was back in the lab, secrets being pried from its wood. There were the feet of the children that they knew about of course. But what about children who hadn't shown up in the freezer? Maybe they'd be able to isolate their DNA from samples taken from Deacon's improvised operating table.

She held up the photo and the wood looked like it was swollen with old motor oil. So far they had identified thirteen different sources of DNA—and all had been matched to feet in Deacon's collection. Maybe that's all there were.

Had she really just thought that? *"All there were"?* Had she examined the remnants of the broken and ill and plain old evil for so long that she no longer thought in terms of right or wrong—only in terms of numbers?

Don't get all girly, she told herself. Do your job.

Her hip buzzed and she pulled her phone out. "Hemingway," she said automatically.

"Detective, this is Dr. Marcus. I've got news from the FBI's CODIS database on the Deacon victims."

"That was fast."

"We got lucky."

"How lucky?"

"They identified all but two of the boys. We don't have the case files yet but I can give you the dates they disappeared. The first case dates back to July of eighty-eight. It looks like Mr. Deacon was responsible for the disappearance of two children a year from that point on. There are holes in the schedule—I only have one child from 1994, 1997, and 2004 and there are no children for 2006. Other than that, it's pretty close to a schedule. I've e-mailed you the spreadsheet."

Hemingway pinched the bridge of her nose. "So the guy was active for a quarter century?"

"Whoever killed Trevor Deacon just cut down child abductions in New York City by eighteen percent."

Hemingway looked down at the empty space where the dirty, bloodstained workbench had sat. Whoever had killed Deacon seemed intent on carrying the torch, only at an accelerated rate. "Dr. Marcus, I appreciate it."

Back in the living room she paused in front of the four holes where the yellow pushpins had held a photograph. Less than twenty-one-month-old HP personal printer, Fuji paper, no discernible image, Deacon's thumbprint on the front surface.

She took out her phone and dialed the precinct, clicking through to the evidence department.

"Evidence, Rhea here," a man said in the bored tones of someone marking off time.

"Rhea, this is Hemingway. We found a Parkay container filled with baggies of heroin at the Deacon murder scene yesterday."

She heard the tap-tap-tap of fingers on a keyboard. "Yeah, got it here. Sixteen baggies, three grams a crack. Pink heroin. Never seen pink heroin before. What about it?"

"I need to check one out. Prep the paperwork and have it waiting for me."

"Hemi, this is a class A narcotic. You'll need to process the reqs and they gotta go through the prosecutor's office. After that you'll have to—"

"Call Dennet. If it's not ready when I get there in half an hour, I'm going to pull you through that little hole in the window on your cage. We clear?"

There was a moment of awkward silence followed by, "Sure thing, detective."

When she got off the phone, Phelps was staring at her. "You okay, Hemi?"

"Yeah, why?"

He stared at her for a moment.

"No reason." Then he opened the door and stepped into the light.

III FORTY-TWO

THE DISTRICT attorney was a man named Edward
Schlesinger, a perfectionist extraordinaire. Hemingway, Phelps
and Dennet stood off in the shadows, conserving energy and
trying not to distract the man from his task. He was going
over the warrant, ticking off points, underlining sections, and
making corrections in the margins.

No one wanted an oversight rendering the investigation
null and void. Not only did all the *t*'s have to be crossed
and all the *i*'s dotted, but there had to be a scope of seizure
that was defensible as legitimate and broad enough to net
them the information they needed. There would be no going
back to the judge for a second warrant because the first one
had overlooked something. And since the DA was the man
to defend the writ, he had to be certain that they hadn't
missed anything.

The DA stopped, brought his pen up a paragraph, and
reread a passage. He circled something in a broad flourish of
his fountain pen, capped it, placed it on the leather surface
of his desk, and leaned back in his chair. "We do not get a
second chance at this, gentlemen—and lady," he added with

a nod. "You are asking for a very limited scope of information in what could turn out to be a much larger picture. I'm not complaining—this makes my job of selling it to Judge Lester much simpler—but there are still a few areas where you're overreaching."

Hemingway stepped away from the bookcase and came over to Schlesinger's desk. He was a small man and sitting there, with Hemingway's six-foot frame towering over him, he looked positively tiny. But not the least bit uncomfortable; true to his ilk, he relished confrontation.

"Mr. Schlesinger, we know from the parents of the three murdered boys that they were conceived at the same clinic and their parents were treated by the same physician—Dr. Sylvester Brayton."

"And you are unable to find Brayton?" It was a good question.

It was Phelps who answered. "It's obvious he doesn't want to be found."

"Or that Fenton doesn't want him to be found," Hemingway said.

At that Schlesinger held up his hand. "This is exactly what I am afraid of, Detective Hemingway. We all want this to go well. Don't paint bogeymen on the wall unnecessarily."

Hemingway stared at him for a moment. "Something's wrong at the clinic. There's something that Fenton's not telling us."

"What do you know for sure?"

"That the parents of all three boys were patients of Dr. Brayton; we need to know the names of his other patients because they could be on a hunting list."

Schlesinger nodded. "Granted. But what does that give you? That gives you a doctor and three children. What you are requesting here is the identity of the donor. This man, whoever he is, has not been implicated in any crimes. By asking—"

"Not been implicated in any crimes? His children are being murdered—as far as I'm concerned, he's the only suspect we have."

"Yes, but how do I sell that to the judge? It's reaching."

Hemingway felt the room get a little smaller. "The one common link we have here is the donor."

"I agree. And I'm sure the judge will agree. But is it grounds for a warrant? The names of the boys I can sell; by all indications they are in imminent danger. But the donor has not been implicated in any of these crimes. There is no evidence to suggest that he knows anything about these children."

Hemingway stared at Schlesinger for a few moments and she felt the muscles of her jaw tighten. "Where else are we reaching?"

"You cannot ask for a list of all the couples who had a child fathered by this donor. Again, there's no evidence to suggest that they are all in danger. Not at this point."

"No offense, Mr. Schlesinger, but you're shitting me, right?"

Schlesinger steepled his fingers in what looked like a practiced pose. "I'm not the bad guy here, Detective Hemingway, I'm just telling you what the judge is going to tell me. If I can't defend every part of this request, the judge will dismiss it and what do we have then? Wasted time.

"So far you have three boys who were fathered by the same sperm donor. That's solid. But you can't ask for the names of all children fathered by this donor, because that's reaching. What about girls he fathered, if any? What about older children? Younger children? That clinic has been in business since . . ." He leaned forward, checked his notes. ". . . nineteen eighty-seven and Dr. Brayton practiced there since it opened its doors for business. Selmer came on board ten years back. This donor may have a history of providing sperm as long as that clinic has been around. Does that mean that children he may have fathered who are twenty-five years old are also at risk?" He opened his hands in a well-I'm-waiting gesture.

Hemingway's jaw clicked again. "No, it doesn't."

"No, it doesn't," he repeated, a lilt of condescension in his tone. "So we have to be narrow in our scope of request. Since all evidence points to boys with a very narrow range of age, I would like to propose an age limit." He leaned forward again, flipped through his notes. "All three boys were born in April and May ten years ago—they were all ten years and one to two months old. Would you be happy with a range of nine years and six months to ten years and six months?"

Hemingway stood up and backed away from the desk because in a second she was going to start swinging. "And what happens if a boy is found in the river who is aged ten years, six months and one day? Are you going to be the one who goes to his parents' home to explain they weren't warned that their son was on a psychotic hit list due to a decision you made?"

Schlesinger stared at her, his expression unreadable. "No, detective, that will be *your* job. *My* job is to go before Judge Lester and ask him to open the medical files that will help *you* solve these murders. Asking for every piece of paper in Dr. Selmer's files is a mistake."

Hemingway's jaw clicked again. "I'll settle for nine to eleven." It sounded like betting odds.

Schlesinger looked over at Dennet who shrugged. "Try," he said.

Schlesinger looked back up at Hemingway. "Okay, I'll try. And I'll be convincing."

Phelps came forward and threw a photograph onto the district attorney's desk. "Convincing's good," he said over the picture of Nigel Matheson laid out on the table at the morgue, his face opened like a mortar round had taken it apart. "Because this guy ain't fucking around."

||| FORTY-THREE

SELMER TURNED away from the electronic medical record and pressed his fingers to his eyes. He felt like his heart was pumping a viscid epoxy that was being rejected by his body. He concentrated on his breathing, taking deep gulps in through his nose and forcing them out through his mouth in a steady chug.

In.

Out.

In.

Out.

Over and over and over until he felt like his body was ready to breathe on its own again. He focused on his chest, ignoring the vomit he felt pushing at the back of his throat with its sour, coffee-tinted fingers. In a few minutes he felt better. Not perfect. But good enough, which was a minor miracle considering what he had just learned from the EMR of Tanya Everett.

He stood up, went to the fridge, and downed half a bottle of grapefruit Perrier. Selmer wanted to walk back to his desk, to look at the list with his notes scrawled in the margins, but he wasn't sure he'd be able to read it without feeling sick again.

He finished the water and dropped the bottle into the trash. Then he went back to his desk and looked down at the numbers.

He read the names over again, still making a conscious effort to oxygenate his blood.

The machinery of justice would roll over this place as soon as the ink from the judge's signature dried on whatever warrants the cops were smart enough to write up. Somewhere in his files was the information the police needed to find a man who took little boys apart with a saw.

But they didn't know about the girls.

The two detectives seemed bright and aggressive. But were they creative? Lateral thinkers? A court order could give them the information they requested but it wasn't the key to the kingdom. They could only ask for specifics, for information that they knew existed and that they believed would help them solve these murders. They couldn't fish.

They did not know about the girls. Ergo, they would not look into them.

Selmer looked at his wall of diplomas and citations and thank you cards and realized how deep inside the bubble he had become. Fuck it. His career was over anyway.

He swiped the pages of notes and the printed-out EMR into his messenger bag, slung it over his shoulder, and walked out into the hall.

The lawyers would do what they did, the media would do what they did, and he'd be able to hold his head high through the whole bloodletting even if he could no longer practice. It was just one of those things. Bad timing. Bad luck.

He knew that Fenton was upstairs, trying to slow the inevitable.

Fuck her and her little empire.

If he walked out the front with those two cops, she'd send one of the clinic's lawyers with him. If he protested, she'd have one waiting for him at the precinct. He had to do this the old-fashioned way.

Before he left his office he took a piece of the clinic's stationery to write Fenton a letter of resignation. The pen stayed poised over the paper for a second as he decided what to write. He finally settled on two words and an exclamation point.

Selmer took the small staircase at the back, the one they used to use back when they still hired people who smoked. He dropped down to the loading dock and out the back door, nodding a hello to a maintenance man in coveralls who was unloading paint from the trunk of an ancient, rust-riddled van—no doubt more beige and off-white for yet another useless "refreshing."

The dark pewter sky vibrated with the coming rain. He cut across the alley, walked past a hundred feet of Dumpsters and back doors, then stepped out onto the sidewalk. A man on the corner was screeching like Chicken Little, hocking umbrellas for five dollars apiece to a sweating populace who did their best to ignore him.

Selmer crossed between the cars waiting at the lights and the heat off the radiator grills warmed his pant leg. He looked up at the sky again; it was bending under the weight of the rain in its belly.

There was a throng of schoolboys in front of the electronics store, ogling the latest gadgets. The boys parted to let him through and he squeezed by, ducking into the parking garage. The attendant, Eddie, handed him his key without being asked and Selmer gave him a ten and a thank-you, realizing that he might never see Eddie again.

His leased Benz was on the second floor near the back. He threw his bag in the backseat, climbed in, drove down the ramp, and paused at the mouth of the garage.

By the time he got the car down to the entrance, the city looked as dark as the garage. The schoolboys ran by his grill and he thought of the boys who had died.

Maybe he could help stop it from happening again. He thought about how hard he had worked to get here. Then he thought about the note he had left for Frau Fenton. He was leaving with as much pride as he had started. Not a bad way to go, he thought, then pulled out into traffic.

Selmer hit a red light a block west of the garage and the schoolboys crossed in front of him, young and full of life.

Dr. Sylvester Brayton had sold the clinic's wealthiest clients on the idea of purchasing their sperm from a catalogue of rarefied samples. High IQs, handsome, healthy. Five hundred thousand dollars a crack.

The profiles were fake—Brayton had simply provided his own semen.

Fenton had figured it out that night at the opera. The next morning Brayton was gone. From the city. From the country. No doubt shuffled off to some dark corner of the globe in exchange for keeping quiet. A classic example of the win-win Fenton was always talking about.

Only it wasn't looking so win-win for Fenton now, was it? She looked like Charlie Sheen on a binge, spouting delusional rhetoric. Sure, Brayton was gone but his legacy would be around for a long time, like a curse lifted out of a fairy tale.

The heat came off the asphalt and licked up the side of the car.

He caught movement in the mirror, at the edge of his

peripheral vision. He glanced at the reflection and saw someone come around the back bumper.

It was stupid to dodge the lights at rush hour, almost
suicidal.

The engines around him changed pitch and he looked
up. The light was green.

Traffic began to move.

He took his foot off the brake and once again saw something at the edge of his sight—this time it was a face. He
turned. Recognized the face. Began the last expression that
would ever cross his features—a smile. There was a flash and
something whistled through his throat. He instinctively hit
the gas.

Blood spurted across the windshield and for a bright
panicked second he understood that he was already dead.

He lost consciousness and the Benz rolled west for half
a block before detonating a fruit stand and slamming into a
lamppost.

Then the sky opened up and the rain began.

FORTY-FOUR

THE OUTER office had been redecorated since the last time she had been here, the architectural symmetry of French Empire traded in for Midcentury Modern. The receptionist—a woman named Karen who had been here as long as Hemingway could remember—ushered her straight through the maze of cubicles to the big corner office. The plaque on the door read DWIGHT R. HEMINGWAY III.

When she walked in, the man behind the desk got up, came to her, and embraced her extended hand in both of his. Then he gave her a kiss on each cheek and held her at arm's length—something that seemed to be happening a lot lately.

"You look wonderful, Allie." He smiled as he spoke. "Radiant, even."

"Thanks, Uncle Dwight, but I'm a little old for compliments."

Her uncle laughed. "Ah, yes, Alexandra, the eternal pragmatist. The Hemingway women are never too old to be told they're beautiful—just look at your mother."

"How's Miles?" she asked. Even though she was here on

business, a certain amount of respect was due. Besides, a lot of her family information came from these moments.

"He's glad to be out of LA, I think. That series was killing him. Broadway's been good—"

"I've read the reviews."

"Well, we're spending time out in the country. If you ever want to get away from the Big Apple . . ." he let the sentence trail off.

"Uncle Dwight, I don't have a lot—"

"—of time." He nodded and mixed a smile in with the movement. "I know. What can I do for you?"

She hadn't seen him since last Christmas. He had taken her to lunch. They ate at Atelier, sitting at the family's usual table. The meal had started out full of awkward silences but eventually they found common ground and the afternoon disappeared over Scotch and catching up. He dropped her off at her place and she promised to keep in touch. To do this more often. But even as the Bentley pulled away, and he waved from the backseat, she knew they wouldn't. And here they were, more than six months later, and she hadn't so much as sent him an e-mail.

"This is all confidential," she said.

Uncle Dwight waved it away. "Everything we talk about is confidential, Allie." He was talking about her parents.

She was talking about a man who took children apart with a hacksaw.

"Have you heard about the boys we've found in the East River?"

He nodded and his handsome face tightened up. "Of course." He walked around his desk and sat down in the big leather chair. The skyline spread out behind him was wiped out by the thunderstorm hammering down. Every now and then the gray throbbed with lightning, as if a giant fuse had blown.

"We're lean on leads and I need a favor. A *big* favor."

He stared at her, his lawyer side trumping the uncle. Listen first; ask later.

She reached into her pocket and pulled out a padded envelope. She handed it across the desk. He peered inside then dropped it to the desk.

"That's heroin," she said.

"Okay."

"It's been colored with some sort of vegetable dye. I assume the color should make it easier to track down a point of origin."

"Okay."

"That heroin was found in the house of a man who murdered a lot of children." She handed a photograph of Trevor Deacon across the desk.

Her uncle didn't bother picking it up, as if contamination might be an issue.

"His name and address—including his former telephone number—are on the back. I don't care about the drugs, Uncle Dwight. As far as I'm concerned, they're a nonissue. Whoever sold them; whoever supplied them; whoever cut them—it doesn't matter to me. But I need to know about this man. I need to know where he went, what his habits are, and I've hit a wall. There's not a lot of pink heroin out there, so that's something."

Her uncle leaned back in his chair and crossed his arms over his chest. "I'm not that kind of a lawyer, Allie, you know that."

"Look, Uncle Dwight, I know the corporations you represent. I'm not asking for secrets. I'm not asking for names. You have my word—my *personal* word—that I want nothing from these people except information that will help me figure out Trevor Deacon's habits. You still represent Redfoot Industries?"

He nodded. It was a tentative, almost guarded, gesture.

"I don't care about Mr. Yashima's business dealings. But his beginnings are not as auspicious as his Wikipedia entry portrays. If anyone can find out where that comes from, it's him. I am asking *you* for the favor.

"I need to speak to the man—the actual street dealer—who sold this stuff to Deacon. I can't get down the food chain that quickly. All of Deacon's phone records and e-mail accounts are clean. I don't have any leads."

He stood up and turned to the rain beyond the window. For a few moments he stared out at the dark gray that had swallowed the skyline. When he turned back, his face was a mix of doubt and indecision. "These are not people that like questions, Allie. I can do this. But if you are lying to me, if anyone is prosecuted because of this, there will be repercussions. Do you understand what I am saying?"

"I promise this is not about drugs."

Her uncle dropped his eyes to the desk, to the photo and envelope she had given him. "Give me three hours," he said. Then he steepled his fingers and looked at her. "But I need something in return."

Here it is, she thought. "What?"

"Don't be so suspicious. I want you to call your father."

"I called him last month. He was out."

"That was the month before."

She thought about it for a second, then nodded. "You're right. It was."

"I'm not trying to get between you two because personally I don't see a need for it. You and he have a relatively good relationship. He worries about you. He'd just like you to be—"

"More like Amy."

Dwight shook his head. "That's not fair. To him *or* to you.

He doesn't want you to be anything like Amy. He has bound-less respect for you and for what you've done with your life. Sure, he would have wanted more grandchildren, but only if you wanted to have them."

She felt her hand head for her stomach and she con-sciously stopped it.

"He just worries about you being bombarded by the worst that humanity has to offer. Any father would be." He nodded at the envelope on the desk. "Maybe a career where you didn't carry around heroin."

"Is this you talking or him?"

"Both, I guess. But he misses you. So do I. I'm not asking you to take family vacations. I would just like a little—" he paused, which he rarely did "—*damage control.*"

She thought about calling him on that. Because they both knew it was bullshit. Her mother—her father's second wife—cared very little about anything except for her Bergdorf charge card and the bells and whistles that went along with being the wife of Steven Hemingway. It had always been that way and Hemi had long ago come to accept it. "Okay," she said after a moment of silence. "I'll call but I want him to stop sending me those checks. I'm fine. I don't need anything. When I needed help, he was there. I took the money for the down payment on my place."

"Which you *paid back.*"

"I don't want the money."

"What should he do with it? Burn it?"

She had thought about this one on the way up—as the family lawyer, Dwight knew what was going on. "It's not that I don't want any of the money, Uncle Dwight. I just don't want it now. I don't expect him to leave it to the church—it will probably end up being left to Amy and Graham and me.

When that happens, I'll worry about it. Until then, I haven't earned it."

At that, Dwight smiled. "It's not about you earning it. It's about your father wanting to give you something while he's still here. He doesn't send you any more money than he sends Amy. The difference between the two of you is that Amy cashes the checks."

"I'll call him."

"I'm flying out to the North Shore on Sunday. You want to come along?"

She pointed at the envelope on the desk. "I can't leave this case right now but I'll call him. Pinky swear. And as soon as I get a break, you and I will play a few rounds of tennis. How's that?"

He smiled and shook his head. "Why is it I always believe you when you lie to me? I always have."

She got up and came around the desk, gave him a hug and kissed him on the cheek. "Because I have good intentions."

"Evidently you've never heard about the road to hell."

She thought about the mutilated children they had found. "It's not a road, Uncle Dwight, it's a superhighway."

A VAST capillary system of interconnected hallways, corridors, and passages wormed through the earth beneath the American Museum of Natural History. If you didn't know where you were going, it could be an unsettling place to spend time. Benjamin Winslow had grown up in the subterranean world. His father had never really believed in babysitters and ever since he could walk, Benjamin had spent most of his nights and weekends here, three stories below the streets of the city, wandering the storage rooms while his father worked.

Mother Nature had let go outside and even here, burrowed deep in the earth, the boy could hear thunder pounding the city. The sound waves shook the bedrock and the foundation shuddered with each crack of electricity.

His father was an anomaly within the closed world of the museum. Most of the staff, including the department heads, lived under the continual threat of financial cutbacks. Where the other staff members were forced to deal with the endless internal politics of a massive institution, his father was beyond the petty pressures—and whims—of the museum chairs and departmental financial officers. He accomplished this by providing his own endowments for the department.

When the other departments in vertebrate zoology wanted to pursue research or acquire rare or exotic specimens, they had to deal with endless bureaucracy to make it happen. They had to beg, borrow, and steal. Not so the Department of Ornithology: when Dr. Winslow wanted something, he simply wrote a personal check for it. And received a tax write-off in the process. For this reason, the museum would never get rid of him.

Dr. Neal Winslow was monumentally wealthy; during the early part of the twentieth century, his grandfather's firm had been the largest manufacturer of surgical instruments outside of Germany. The postwar boom had grown the family fortune to a size where it could not easily be measured.

Benjamin walked by one of the storage lockers, a massive room the size of a gymnasium. He was friends with a lot of the museum's staff—most of them got a kick out of asking him questions they thought were difficult—and he had visited all of the storage rooms. They were lined with miles of steel shelving that reached up into the darkness, piled with the world's forgotten secrets.

Benjamin's favorite locker was the one that housed the specimens from the Department of Entomology—there were hundreds of thousands of drawers filled with glass-cased insects that he found absolutely fascinating. He knew more about certain species than many of the people in the department but a passion for invertebrate zoology had no practical application in his life so he had focused his attention on hyperbolic geometry and writing, two disciplines that got him the right kind of attention. Along with the paper the Harvard mathematics department had published, the school had been surprised by the six-volume, 1,200,000-word collection of biographies he had completed. It seemed that not many ten-year-olds were interested in the lives of Julius Caesar, Niccolò Machiavelli, Charles Darwin, Homer, Molière, and Nicolaus Copernicus. The newspaper coverage had started soon after that. And the scholarship offers.

Benjamin Winslow even had a Wikipedia entry; he loved being touted as a polymath.

Benjamin walked down the dark hallway that looked like it reached out into forever. Then he heard it, a soft scraping behind him. It wasn't much of a sound—hardly loud enough to qualify as noise, really—but it had been enough.

Benjamin spun around and saw the dark figure looming over him. Its arms came out and clamped on his shoulders. Then it squatted down and looked into his eyes.

"I've been looking for you, son. It's time to go. I have a schedule to keep to." His father didn't sound angry but his father never sounded angry.

"Sorry, Father. Of course."

Dr. Winslow patted him on the head. "Let's go home."

Benjamin hated going home early—more than anything else in the whole wide world.

III FORTY-SIX

FOR THE first time in as long as Hemingway could remember, she was alone, something that rarely happened at the station and never happened during daylight hours. The rain filled the air with static that blocked out ambient noise. She stared out the window, watching the buildings across the street flicker through the heavy downpour.

Her corner of the floor was abandoned and quiet; Papandreou and Lincoln were at the clinic waiting for Dr. Selmer; and Phelps had gone for food when they came back from Uncle Dwight's. The DA was still with Judge Lester. The Matheson boy was with the coroner. Fenton was with her lawyers. All was at rest for the moment.

Except that he was out there, gearing up for another child.

She was tired but that was nothing new. Ever since the incident with Shea she had slept badly. She didn't suffer nightmares or have residual flashbacks, but for no reason she could understand, she never woke fully rested.

Hemingway didn't think about Shea anymore, not really. Along with the hospital and the surgeries and the physiotherapy, the memory of him had slowly faded away. Mank was a different story. He came back sometimes, mostly late at night when Daniel was asleep beside her and she was alone inside her head, staring at the shadows on the ceiling. She'd think of him, remember some little thing they had talked about, and she'd start to wonder what they might have had. She'd lie there in the dark and cry. But lately those moments were becoming rarer, and part of her worried that she'd forget about Mank altogether.

It wasn't fair to Daniel. She loved him; he loved her. What they had seemed to be right for both of them. And she felt safe with him, something she had never felt with Mankiewicz. And now they might be having a baby.

But it wasn't just a baby; it was a human life. From cradle to grave and all the pain in between. How could she bring a child into a world where the people who told you they had a handle on goodness tended to be the first to judge and to hate? Where genocide was taking place all over the world and torture was deemed okay by the government? Where a monster was out there sawing children up while their hearts were still beating?

She closed her eyes, focusing on the thrum of the rain against the world outside and the roof above her head, and everything else ceased to exist. She was back in the river, on the Hudson, feeling nothing more than the wind in her hair and the resistance of the water. She felt her body swaying a little, riding the swells in her kayak. She gripped the arms of the chair and the steel warmed to her touch like the carbon shaft of her paddle. For an instant she was under the George Washington Bridge, being pulled downriver by the tide, traffic rumbling across the spans high overhead.

And it all fell apart to the chirp of her cell phone.

"Hemingway."

"Allie, it's me."

Hemingway pinched the bridge of her nose to stave off the pounding she knew would soon start up in her head. She didn't want Amy and her neediness. Not now. "Amy, I'm at work and it's not a good day." Which was code for *fuck off*.

"I know. I saw you on the news this morning." Brief pause. "I've left Patrick. Left DC. I was hoping maybe we could talk. Help me get a little perspective. Have a drink."

That last part sounded like the goal. "Where are you?"

"I'm on the train right now but I'm staying at the Plaza."

Hemingway knew it was a mistake before she opened her mouth but it came out anyway. "Forget the hotel. Stay with Daniel and me. We can talk." Why had she done that? Daniel didn't like Amy.

Diagnosed as acutely narcissistic when she was sixteen, she had been a problem her entire life. She had always been theatric, very much to the detriment of herself and those around her. Every family has its tortured soul and Amy was the Hemingways'.

"Why don't you come to the hotel? We'll have a massage, order in some booze. I can tell you what happened."

She wouldn't make the mistake of inviting Amy to the loft again. "I'm on a tight schedule right now. Things are . . ."

The door blew open and Phelps came in. She knew something bad had happened when she saw his face. She said, "I gotta go," and hung up.

Phelps stared at her for a moment before speaking. "Someone cut Selmer's throat at a traffic light."

"Where the fuck were Papandreou and Lincoln?"

Phelps shrugged. "I don't know. Dennet caught me in the staircase. Nick and Linc are on the way in. Apparently Selmer gave them the slip."

"Why the fuck would he do that?" Hemingway couldn't

believe what she was hearing. She thought about what had happened and where it now put them. It took a few seconds for her to think of an upside. "At least now we get our warrant."

Phelps's eyebrows raised in a *how-you-figure-that?* expression that hung there for a bit. Then his face broke into a grin. "For a lady, you sure are smart."

"I get that a lot," she said.

THIS TIME they rolled into the Park Avenue Clinic with an army of cops and a docket full of warrants from the DA's office. Fenton was waiting for them, her two security boys flanking her like a pair of backup singers. Behind the backup singers stood the lawyers. No one looked happy, least of all Fenton.

"Nice to see you both again, detectives." If an electric fence had a voice, it would have sounded like her.

Phelps had the honor of handing over the sheaf of warrants the DA had secured, the only positive consequence of the death of Dr. Michael Selmer. Fenton didn't bother to look at them, she just handed them back to the lawyers.

Hemingway stepped into character. "Mrs. Fenton, Dr. Michael Selmer was murdered an hour ago. Someone cut his throat."

Fenton's expression twitched for a second, then snapped back to its former impassivity. "I didn't know."

Hemingway nodded at the warrants the lawyers were flipping through. "Those warrants entitle us to any and all computers, cell phones, fax machines, tablets, and other

electronic devices that *may have* been used by Dr. Michael
Selmer in the past twenty-four hours. We are also entitled to
a list of any and all phone numbers that he may have used
in this building within the same period, including fax numbers. The failure of anyone employed by this clinic to follow
directives issued from any of our people will result in the
charge of obstructing an investigation. Mrs. Fenton, would
you please have someone show us to Dr. Selmer's office?"

Fenton stared up at Hemingway for a moment and her
face had that same flat expression. Then she turned back to
the wall of legal advice. They shook their heads in unison,
and for a second it looked like the security men would break
into a gruff harmony. Fenton rotated her gaze back up to
Hemingway. "Please follow me," she said.

||| FORTY-EIGHT

IT WAS well past supper and the precinct was set to its usual voltage in the ever-present battle of good versus evil. Once the rainstorm had finished throwing its tantrum, the heat had come back, baking the streets and sucking the rain back into the atmosphere. Before the puddles had gone, it was hotter and more humid than before the cloudburst. The air-conditioning did its best but the computer lab was stifling, the heat magnified by the red-hot processors humming within the server towers. There seemed to be a thousand little plastic fans spitting out air and even the Iron Giant looked irritated.

Alan Carson—the senior analyst from the cybercrimes division and the brains of their IT lab—had gone to work on Selmer's off-the-shelf encryption software. The clinic had provided all of the doctor's passwords but he had added a few of his own and it was chewing up time. Carson kept knocking back Yoo-hoos and throwing more horsepower at the problem.

Hemingway hated reducing anyone to a stereotype but there was no other way to look at the man. He was probably the same age as her—somewhere in the tail end of his thirties—but everything about him said teenager, from his black Chuck Taylors to his silly T-shirts. Probably had a doll collection at home—only he'd call them *action figures*. But he was good at his job—gifted, even—and never threw around any of the macho bullshit like some of the other cops. Besides, she got an admitted kick out of the crush he had on her. It was nice to cash in on free ice coffees every now and then. And the guy always remembered the sugar.

One of Carson's minions had hooked Dr. Selmer's hard drives up to a server. This computational life-support system was one of more than sixty such setups in the lab—now the second most well-funded sector in the department.

The goal was to retrace the doctor's last few virtual hours on the planet, an exercise that in the new digital world was usually more productive than retracing real-world hours. They had his phone records—both office and cellular—and Phelps and Hemingway were going over the list, running each number through the system and marrying it to a name.

Would someone he had called turn out to be the killer?

Until they knew, they'd keep digging into the patient files. That was the pressure point—everything met there. Somehow.

Between the time he had been dropped off and his final run-in with a razor-sharp piece of steel, Selmer had been a busy man. He made a total of one hundred and three phone calls. Of those, sixty-six were to residences in Manhattan, eleven were to directory assistance, and twenty-six were to out-of-state numbers, including three to Italy, two to Sweden, four to Australia and one to Mexico.

Hemingway went over the column of calls, short-listing anyone who was within driving distance of the clinic. The closer they got to Selmer's time of death, the shorter the distance had to be. There was still a chance that the killer wasn't any of these people but when you had nothing else to go on, you went with anything you could.

Carson punched the desk and howled, "Motherfucker!"

Phelps asked, "Motherfucker *good* or motherfucker *bad*?"

Carson flicked the screen. "I've cracked his off-the-shelf encryption. What do you want?"

Hemingway took up position over Carson's shoulder. "Start with the donor: bring up Tyler Rochester, Bobby Grant and Nigel Matheson's files." Her shirt was stuck to her body and the air held the hot oil smell of a tool shed. It was stiffling; how did Carson take this, day in, day out?

Carson clicked through the system, rapidly opening and closing fields. It took a few clicks for him to figure out how the patient files were organized but once he had it he went straight to Tyler Rochester's file. "Here you are. Donor 2309432. Guy was a Scandinavian atheist," Carson said.

At any other time, Hemingway would have smiled—for now, the reflex was turned off. "Check Bobby Grant's file."

Carson clicked around until he had the information up on the screen. "Here you go. Just like the Rochester kid. Another Nordic atheist and—" Carson pointed at the donor number: 4022393. "If they had the same father, how is that possible?"

Hemingway commandeered the mouse and clicked through to Nigel Matheson's file, reading the attributes of his donor: 3249023. "This guy came with the same options."

"He's a man, not a BMW," Phelps said.

Hemingway looked over at him. "This is marketed by men for women—trust me, there are options."

"You're a cynic," Phelps said.

She clicked around the page. "Height: six one; weight: a hundred and eighty-two pounds; hair color: brown; eye color: brown; complexion . . . blah . . . blah . . . blah. Here we go— religion: atheist; ethnicity: Scottish/Swedish; education level:

PhD; area of study: medicine/biology; blood type: O positive; CMV status: negative; pregnancies: n/a; accumulated number of pregnancies: n/a; IQ: Stanford-Binet (version five) score of one hundred and seventy-one." Hemingway turned to Phelps. "Still think these aren't options? And they're identical to the Rochester kid's." She nodded at the screen. "The donor number might be different but the rest of the information is identical. What do you make of that?"

"If it's the same donor, why give him different numbers?" Phelps sounded frustrated.

"Look at the donor numbers—they're all seven digits and they all contain zero, two, two, three, three, four and nine. Which is different," she said, and negotiated to a random file, "than the other donor numbers the clinic used—they are ten digits long. Didn't you see that when you were flipping through?"

Carson looked embarrassed. "I must have missed that."

"Why would he do that?" Phelps asked.

"He wanted people to think they were different donors."

"So what do we do?" Phelps asked. "If he lied about the donor identity, how can we find other children with the same donor?"

Carson raised his hand. "That's easy. I just enter the search parameters using the profile values that are specific—how many six foot one, hundred-and-eighty-two pound brown-eyed Scottish/Swedish atheists with a PhD in medicine and biology who have O positive blood and an IQ of one seventy-one can they have in the database? And I make sure the donor numbers contain those seven digits. Here, let me try something." He took back the mouse, set up a search with the donor's stats as parameters, and hit enter.

The results were instantaneous. "Here are the kids you're looking for," he said, raising his hand for a high five.

They ignored him, both leaning in to better see the data. After a few awkward seconds Carson lowered his hand. "Right back at ya."

Hemingway read the screen and shook her head. "Is this wrong?"

Carson ran the search again and the same total came up. "Nope. It's right. This guy fathered sixty-seven children."

SIXTY-SEVEN SUCCESSFUL pregnancies?" Hemingway asked. "You're kidding."

Carson flicked the screen again. "It's right there."

The more answers they found, the further they seemed to be from any kind of a solution. From a technical point of view it was progress; from a practical standpoint it was more work.

It was Phelps who spoke up. "It's actually very common. Fertility clinics are not subject to any kind of demographic responsibility. There have been multiple cases where kids who are dating find out they are related. Some donors father hundreds of children and usually in the same neighborhood—almost always in the same city. The Scandinavian countries have limited the number of times a doctor can use a specific donor in any given year. The UK is thinking about legislation."

Carson stared at him, his mouth open.

"Discovery Channel," he offered. "I started watching for Shark Week and it kind of became a habit. Ask me about Stonehenge."

"Or the Bloomsbury Group," Hemingway added.

Phelps shook his head. "You're mean."

She kept her eyes locked on the list of successful pregnancies. "And this should be criminal."

It was Carson who spoke. "Why? Look at this guy. Six one, PhD in medicine, Scandinavian, athletic, high IQ. Flip through their catalogue and I'll bet he comes with fucking cup holders and clear coat."

"Where's his name?"

Carson shrugged. "This is his donor profile, my guess is this is the preliminary stuff when you're trying to make a decision on which model to download. If you like what you read, it's probably on to . . ." He clicked around until he was back in the main directory then ran a search. "There's nothing on this guy in the system." He ran all the different donor numbers through the database. "Nada."

Phelps started up with his Discovery Channel education. "There should also be a profile detailing his hobbies, favorite food, allergies, medical background, and other assorted shit."

Carson smiled. "I'm sure that's exactly how it is worded on their website: check out your donor's food allergies *and other assorted shit.*"

And then Hemingway had another of her lightbulb moments. "It's him."

"Him? Him who, him?"

"Brayton. Jesus, just think about it. You guys are men. If you needed sperm, where's the first place you'd go to get it?"

Phelps closed his eyes and shook his head. Carson blushed.

"That's right. You've got your own dispenser." She went to the worktable and pulled Brayton's file out of a banker's box she had lugged over from the squad room. She read off her notes. "Height's right. Weight's right. Brown hair, brown eyes—check. Scottish-Swedish—mother's name was

Lindenberg—and Brayton could be Scottish. PhD in biology?
Check. Very smart? Check. Like I said, options." She leaned
forward, her face a few inches from the monitor, as if trying
to smell out meaning in the lines of information. "Get me
the names of all sixty-seven of this guy's children. If we
don't figure this out soon, this is nothing more than a hunting list."

Carson wiped his palms on his thighs and reached for
the keyboard. "You know, for a woman you can be pretty
grim."

"I get that a lot."

FIFTY

HEMINGWAY AND Phelps were on their way to visit the first family on their list—the Atchisons, parents of a ten-year-old boy named William. They lived on the Upper East Side.

Hemingway was calling Daniel to tell him not to expect her home. There were things they had to talk about and she didn't want him to think she was avoiding him.

He answered immediately. "Hey, babe."

"Hey yourself, Mr. Man. What's what?"

"Your sister's here." There was a pause. "She said *you* told her to come by."

Hemingway mouthed the word *fuck* without saying it out loud. "I might have."

"Yeah, well . . ." He let his voice trail off and she knew Amy was within earshot.

"She's with you now, right?"

"What are you, a detective?"

"Has she started drinking yet?"

"*Yet?*"

"I'm sorry, baby. She called me from the train, said she was checking into the Plaza. I told her to come by and she said she'd rather be at the hotel. I thought we had worked it all out."

"Yeah, sure." He didn't sound angry, just unhappy. The last time they had seen one another she called him a fag and a peasant, in that order. She had been pretty drunk and didn't remember it when Hemingway called her the next day but the damage had been done—Daniel had been raised with the belief that there was no greater sin than being a bad drunk. "I made the guest bed up for her. She told me that was *quaint*."

Hemingway flinched. Daniel had stayed as far away as he could from her family's money, and her sister took a spiteful joy in pointing out the financial shortcomings of their lives compared to hers. Not that Daniel gave a shit about money, but he hated being insulted—for all his Bohemian artsy fartsy weed-smoking patience he was still a proud man. That Daniel hadn't thrown her out was yet another testament to his goodness. "Sorry, baby. Can you take it for tonight? I don't know when I'll get back. If at all."

"That case? The one with the camera lenses you called me about?"

"Yeah. Can you cover for me? Be charming and shit."

"I won't be her punching bag." There was a pause on the other end of the line that ended with a deep breath and, "Okay. Sure."

"Thanks. I only have one sister."

"That's more than enough."

"You're a good man."

"You mean I'm a pushover."

"No. I mean you're a good man. Did you have plans for tonight?"

"Iggy has a gig downtown and I was going to head out with Matty to take some photos but that's kind of changed now."

"Go. Work. Have fun. She'll be fine by herself. Give her the spare key. We have lives to live, bills to pay. Get drunk, stay out all night, and keep your hands off the wimmens."

He laughed. "There ain't no wimmens but you, Allie."

Why did she hate it when her family called her that but loved it when it came from him? "Later, baby."

"Later," he said, and hung up.

She slipped the phone into her jacket pocket, and Phelps said, "Tell me, Hemi, how the hell does a guy like Brayton just disappear? He's making—what?—seven figures a year? Guy like that only disappears if he wants to disappear."

"You think he's hiding?"

Phelps shrugged. "Could be. If he's the donor, and if Fenton found out, I can see the logic in the decision. Would you want her on your ass? He's probably vacationing at Lake Vostok." When she looked over at him he said, "Discovery Channel."

If Brayton had indeed crossed all the lines they suspected—and Fenton found out—she would be a force to fear. "Think she has the balls to put him away?"

"Nothing would surprise me about that woman."

Her phone rang and she answered in typical Pavlovian form. "Hemingway."

"Detective, it's Dr. Marcus. I'm finished with Michael Selmer's body."

"And?"

"He was killed with a right-to-left sweep across his throat. Long, sharp blade. It was thin, so it's not a hunting or fighting knife. I'd say we're looking at either a fishing knife or one of those Japanese chef's knives. Single incision. He would have been unconscious almost immediately."

"No needle in the eye?"

"The MO matches the Grant boy's driver to a degree.

Something was removed from the car before your people got to the scene. The surveillance camera from the back door at the clinic showed that he left with a black leather bag—it looked like a Ghurka Express. It wasn't found in the car and there was a smudge of blood on the backseat, as if something were pulled from the car."

Selmer had printed up all of his files earlier in the day. There was a good chance that the killer might now have the same information as they did. "Thanks, Marcus. If anything else interesting comes across your table, I'm here."

"Not me. I'm going home. All work and no sleep makes me a cranky boy."

"You have any idea what I should be looking for in this guy?"

"Classic psychopath. Disarming. Friendly. Smart as hell. Manipulative and narcissistic. I can't see anyone with this kind of pathology living a totally normal life. The more murders he gets away with, the more his confidence grows. He is good at this. But he's running. The more you push, the sloppier he'll get."

Hemingway didn't agree. "I get the feeling he knows *exactly* what he's doing; I don't think *we're* pushing *him*, I think *he's* leading *us*."

"We're allowed to have our differences."

"Keep me informed." She hung up and the heavy summer smell of the city, that mix of exhaust and baked asphalt and electricity, hit her and took her back to that last summer with Mank.

They had moved in together. Stopped fighting. Things were going well. Or at least less shitty than they had been. She remembered their last night together. They had gone for a walk and ended up at a little Italian place in Morningside. It was good, maybe one of their best nights. They had walked slow, holding hands, ending up in an antique shop that for some reason was still open. Mank bought her those four equestrian portraits, the ones hanging at the top of the stairs. There were fireflies on the way up Amsterdam and Mank carried the paintings under his arm, wrapped in brown paper and twine. They bought a bag of plums from the fruit stand on the corner. They had gone to bed, made love and fallen asleep in a happy sweaty knot.

The next day Shea and that tumor of a sidekick, Nicky, had walked up behind Mank and put two rounds into his spine and two more into his brain as he lay screaming in pain on the pavement. There were three witnesses who identified Shea and Nicky. After the first witness didn't come home from work one afternoon, the remaining two decided that they had not seen a thing. Shea and Nicky walked.

After three weeks of sleepless nights and more tears than she thought she was capable of producing, she got into her car, drove across the Brooklyn Bridge, and paid Shea a visit.

The investigating officers put a lot of horsepower into tracing the anonymous call that had warned Shea. They chased it down to a prepaid AT&T cell phone, purchased five months before the shooting and prepaid for a year in advance. It had never been used except for that one time. Then it dropped off the face of the earth. The wiretap had recorded an electronic— not modified human—voice generated by an AT&T text-to-speech program available for free on the Internet.

Since there was no way to tie the call to Hemingway, and since her placing the call would have endangered her own life, all charges were dropped.

And it all came back because the city smelled like the last night she spent with Mank.

Her cell vibrated, signaling a text, and she snapped out of her memories, consciously removing her hand from her belly.

As Phelps pulled the heavy truck through traffic, she scanned the message, thinking it was from the medical examiner.

It read:

I'M NOT FINISHED.

BUT YOU ARE.

The message had come from Tyler Rochester's phone.

||| FIFTY-ONE

HEMINGWAY CALLED Carson on the car's wireless and had him slave Tyler Rochester's signal to the GPS function on her phone, remotely downloading the appropriate software patch. The process chewed up nearly four minutes including a phone reboot.

She checked the screen and held it up for Phelps to see. Then she asked the disembodied voice of Carson, "You certain?"

There was the distant tinny sound of keys being struck. "Absofuckinglutely. He's on a boat. The coordinates are right in line with the Staten Island Ferry. It just left the Whitehall Terminal. ETA St. George Terminal is twenty-two minutes."

"We'll be there in five," she said, and the big man in the gray suit punched his foot to the carpet and the Suburban rocketed south.

————

The collective hive of the NYPD had pulled together and when they arrived at Battery Park, a departmental boat was waiting for them. As they climbed aboard, the pilot told them they'd do it with a little over four minutes to spare. They had already called the captain of the ferry and told him to slow the boat down as much as he could—a maneuver that would get them two more minutes.

The inside of the St. George Ferry Terminal looked like a small-town airport in Cold War Eastern Europe, a dreary cavern of gray paint over concrete block. After the police boat docked, Hemingway and Phelps swept through the building with Frank Delaney, the head of security for the MTA South Ferry terminal. Delaney was a small wiry man who looked like a kid playing grown-up beside the two cops, but his thirty-one years of experience were evident in the way he had set things up. All the exits were manned and everyone in security had been told no one was to leave the building except through a single manned set of doors until one minute before the ferry docked. After that it was on a person-by-person basis and all passengers had to go through the cops.

As they ran through the building, Hemingway's stomach tightened up, rebelling after twelve minutes pounding the waves in the Zodiac. She wasn't normally prone to any kind of motion sickness but the mix of exhaust, heat, and an MSG-laden lunch seemed to be doing some previously unknown voodoo on her. She hoped she wouldn't have to chuck in a garbage can.

"You okay?" Phelps asked, trying not to sound concerned but unable to hide it.

"I'm not convinced that this is a good expenditure of resources."

The killer wouldn't be on the boat. She knew it and Phelps knew it. And Delaney probably knew it, too. Their killer wasn't the kind of guy to send a text from a ferry; ghosts didn't do things like that. He was long gone.

What was he up to? He didn't make a move that hadn't been rehearsed in his head a thousand times.

"You gonna have a lotta upset people coming off the ferry," Delaney said.

Hemingway made an effort to respect anyone who functioned under the umbrella of security—public or private—and she had a lot of respect for the MTA guys, who were continually bombarded with the sleaziest kinds of crimes. She had fought her way up to the rank of detective, busting her ass to overcome sexism and good old-fashioned ignorance, and she refused to dole it out to anyone else. Although many of the other detectives never actually expressed disdain for anyone of lower rank or station on the job, Hemingway had seen enough guys lose valuable allegiances due to mine-is-bigger-than-yours situations. Even Phelps, who she considered the last of the old-school gentlemen, sometimes pulled rank for no reason she could see. She thought of it as testosterone poisoning and ego massaging for the most part. But a man like Delaney could be their best asset—or their worst enemy—and she refused to lose a case because of ego.

They followed him to the ramp where the ferry would dock. Hemingway was glad that the running portion of the program was over but her stomach still felt like it was being squeezed by an oily fist.

Silty gray clouds deadened the Hudson as the sky geared up for more histrionics. The ferry was a few minutes out, a moving part in the much larger clockworks of the city behind it.

Hemingway leaned on the railing and took in a deep breath, hoping that the upset stomach wouldn't come back. She asked Delaney, "What did you tell the captain of the ferry?"

He shrugged. "Just what you told me to—to slow it down

as much as he could and to dock according to protocol. From there your people would run the show. Your uniformed officers will handle screening the passengers as they disembark."

It was time for a little diplomacy. "I know that technically this is an MTA affair, but we are looking for someone who is—"

"Above my pay grade?" he asked, smiling like this was one grand adventure.

Hemingway hadn't given Delaney any specifics but she needed him to understand that this guy was dangerous. "It's not a question of pay grade, it's about safety. I don't want you to lose any people because we downplayed the situation."

"This guy some terrorist asshole? I ain't never had a terrorist asshole on one of my boats."

"I'd take a terrorist over this guy anytime."

From where they stood, the city didn't look that far away unless you tried to see movement, then you realized how distant it was. There were no gulls riding the breeze and when she swiveled her head toward the dock cranes of Jersey the sky was empty of any movement except a few errant jet streams over Newark. She looked down at the water, at the garbage floating in the dark waters, and wondered if they'd get this guy before they found another boy floating out there.

Once again she found herself drawn back to wonder what had happened to Trevor Deacon's victims. Forty-four boys that they knew about—and probably more that they didn't—had been subtracted from society by that creep. Had they floated by here on their way out to sea? Would they ever know?

Standing there, watching the gentle slosh of the waves against the pilings, she felt her stomach tighten again, threatening to send their earlier lunch of dumplings and root beer scurrying for daylight.

"You sure you're okay?" Phelps asked from her right.

"Yeah. Fine. Fuck." She sounded irritated and immediately regretted it.

Delaney, sensing a weak spot in the conversation, jumped in. "You're the same Hemingway who shot those guys in Brooklyn a few years back, ain't ya?"

She nodded, hoping that he'd leave it at that; they rarely did and Delaney was no exception.

"That took some guts, detective. Walking in there and all. Musta seen that video a hunert times on the news. No bulletproof vest or nothin'?"

She shook her head but closed her eyes, hoping her stomach would settle down. If she waited him out he'd eventually change topics. They always did when faced with silence.

"They shoulda made you chief after that. How many guys—or ladies, excuse my French—can walk into a room full of armed assholes, draw second, and clean the place out? I been in security all my life and I ain't never seen anything like it. That was Dirty Harry kind of shooting." He leaned forward. "Don't take this the wrong way, but you got big balls for a lady."

With her eyes still closed she said, "I get that a lot."

Delaney pulled out a pack of cigarettes, held it up. "You mind?"

She opened her eyes, stared at him. Besides Phelps and the cops standing back in the shadows, the dock was empty. She couldn't very well protest on their behalf, even if it was a law—this was his turf and he was doing them a lot of favors. "Not at all." And that little voice that had not yet said anything—had only made its presence known by occasionally nudging her subconscious—reminded her that she was pregnant.

And it sunk in a little more. The irrevocability of the coming decision. Maybe she and Daniel would have the baby. Maybe a few. Raise a family and grow old and maybe nothing bad would ever happen to their children.

Why not?

Because that would take a commitment. A commitment to Daniel. A commitment to the baby. And, more importantly, a commitment to herself. Jesus, how did people say yes to this? A child wasn't like a house you didn't like or a marriage you no longer wanted to be in; there were no outs. It was a commitment until you stopped existing. Which in practical terms meant forever.

What kind of a choice was that?

She stepped sideways to avoid the smoke. It was a forgivable compromise. After all, how much carbon was she sucking down each and every day in the way of car exhaust?

Phelps pulled her aside and held up the schematics Delaney gave them. "We'll sweep the ferry from front to back. Delaney's guy says it's easy if we put men on the stairwells here, here, here, and here. And two more over here. It should be a ten-minute job."

Hemingway turned to the boat coming in. "He's not on the boat. He gave Tyler Rochester's phone to someone else. Maybe even a kid—wouldn't that be a sick fucking joke?"

"You want to call it off?"

"We can't do that on the off chance that he really is there and I don't want to send a bunch of cops onto the ferry unless they're in combat mode. It's all in or all out. This guy has killed enough people already."

The ferry was closing the gap and the faces of the people on board would soon be discernible.

"You can't be standing on the dock when the boat pulls in, Hemi. This guy knows you. Stay out of sight."

That Phelps was right didn't make it any easier—she was point man on this case and the idea of anyone else walking into her mess felt wrong. "I'll go wait inside."

Delaney, whose attention seemed to be nailed to his smoke, waved her over. "Come on, you can watch the whole thing on our security system." He dropped his cigarette over the railing and headed up the ramp.

||| FIFTY-TWO

HE FACED the door, waiting for it to open. The noise—the hum of people, the sound of engines—did not exist. His focus was reduced to the bright polished bronze knob. He wanted to reach out, to touch it, but that was not part of the plan. He was to wait until she came through. He had played this moment out in his head and now was not a time to make adjustments—this was a time to act, not react. No changes could be made. No substitutions.

She would open the door and see him. Smile. Maybe even recognize him. He would smile back, because that was what should be done—what was expected. She would come to him. And he'd lift his arm.

She might see the blade.

There would be that tiny instant when she would flinch. Maybe step back.

Then her fingers would go to her throat.

She'd hit the floor.

And he would lean over her and watch her die.

Because that's what he did.

III FIFTY-THREE

THE BOAT, though technically female following nautical tradition, floated under the moniker the MV *Andrew J. Barberi*. She was a big bitch, measuring more than three hundred feet in length with a width of almost seventy and tipped the scales at a solid 3,334 gross tons. Able to carry up to six thousand passengers through the worst that the Hudson had to offer at a respectable sixteen knots. Orange and yellow. Without grace. Or elegance.

Hemingway's focus shifted from one monitor to the next as she tried to see into the two-dimensional representations of the *Barberi*. Delaney stood at her side, chomping on an unlit cigarette, instinctively following Phelps and the uniformed officers as they wove through the 2,361 passengers.

The city had gone crazy with surveillance systems after 9/11 and the MTA was no exception; she was looking at millions of dollars' worth of paranoia.

Hemingway stayed in contact with Phelps through a headset Delaney had given her—more toys from the new antiterrorist budget. "Where is he?" she asked, and the image of Phelps on the monitor shrugged in response.

She slid her line of sight across the monitors, searching the crowd for someone—anyone—who might be their killer, looking for . . . What exactly *was* she looking for? Some looked tired; some looked pissed off; some looked high; some even looked happy.

But none of them looked like they got their jollies by taking little boys apart.

She watched Phelps set his shoulders and plow through the crowd, a pair of patrolmen in tow. She had come to love him in their almost seven years of protecting and serving. Not because he had adopted the role of surrogate father in her life. And not because he bought her shrimp shumai every Wednesday. But because he was a good man.

And he had never asked her about that phone call to Shea.

Phelps moved forward. His head swiveled back and forth on his stubble-dusted neck as his eyes took in the people and reactions around him. Down there, in the arena, Phelps would smell him out because that's what he had been designed to do.

Hemingway watched the monitors, wishing she were there with him. They had stared down everything from a Bell Atlantic employee with nine sticks of TNT strapped to his chest to a hostage taking at the Met, and sitting here looking at Phelps do this alone felt like some form of acute betrayal.

Phelps pushed through a throng of passengers, following the beacon on the screen of Hemingway's phone.

Hemingway's eyes slid from one passenger to another; none of them seemed to notice Phelps. They stared ahead, shuffling forward in uneven baby steps like cattle.

Phelps's voice came out of the speaker. "It's right here." He stopped and his head swiveled back and forth.

The two uniformed cops spun in place.

"We're right on top of the signal," he repeated.

"He's below you, Jon." She glanced sideways and Delaney nodded. "Or above you."

Delaney picked up a headset that was patched in but not being used. "Go to the far end of the deck. Take the stairs down. There's a pair of doors on the landing—on either side of the staircase. The codes are . . . ," Delaney reached into his pocket and brought up the notes he had jotted down before Phelps had gone on board. "Eight eight oh one three."

"Eight eight oh one three," Phelps repeated.

"Both doors go down to the maintenance corridor that leads to the engine room. If he's below you, he'll be in one of the tool rooms. They're marked in red. We don't have surveillance cameras down there." He kept the headset in his hand.

"Why not?" she asked.

"Passengers are not supposed to be down there. And we don't hire no terrorist assholes."

Phelps nodded and headed for the stairwell to the door that would take him to the engine level. She keyed the mic again. "Jon, be careful. If he's there, he's waiting for you."

Phelps nodded and she saw his head tilt to the side like it did when he smiled. The action said, *Don't worry about me, little lady.*

Phelps moved down the steps and stopped on the landing in front of the door. He reached out and grabbed the handle.

From her perch in the control room, Hemingway saw his fingers connect with the metal and twist. The door swung in. He stepped forward. And off the screen.

THE SOUND of the engines was no longer a subtle vibration that hit his inner ear but a full-blown presence that shook the floor. Phelps couldn't hear the men behind him or the sound of his own feet on the deck so he slowed down like he had learned back in the jungle all those lifetimes ago. The maintenance hallway was clean but hadn't been painted in years and grease and dirt had worked into the cracks. The engines superheated the air down here and the humidity was off the charts. The bright space of the stairwell behind them threw weird spidery shadows across the wall—a dark mass of arms and legs and heads that looked like a misshapen creature moving down a tunnel in search of prey.

Phelps took in the smell of diesel fuel and heat and solvents. And something else buried beneath it.

He reached into his coat and wrapped his fingers around the grip of his .45. He slid it out and swept his thumb down over the frame, knocking the safety out of its notch.

And then the engines stopped.

They came to the first door and Phelps reached out and touched the bronze knob. It was hot in his palm. He twisted his wrist, took a breath, held it and flung the door in, lining up on the opening with the big automatic.

It was a supply room, loaded to the ceiling with Styrofoam cups, cases of empty beer bottles, napkins and toilet paper.

They moved on.

The second door was stenciled with the words TOOLS/ ROPES in a red Boston Traffic font. Phelps stepped in front of the metal portal and stopped dead center. He raised the pistol and gently turned the knob with his free hand.

Then he pushed the door in.

And found a room from hell.

THE DOOR swung in.

He was waiting for her.

He saw a shadow. Larger than himself. Coming through.

He reached out with the blade.

The shadow stumbled backward. Reached up. Gripped its throat.

Blood pissed out in a fan-shaped arc. Splattered the wall. The sill. Shoes.

PHELPS STUMBLED back.

And stared down at the destroyed architecture of the child.

Between his time in the jungles of Southeast Asia and four-plus decades as one of New York's Finest, he had seen the human body exposed to unimaginable indignities. But this tipped the scales in a whole new sport. Tyler Rochester's phone sat neatly on an overturned bucket beside the body. It was covered in bright happy stickers.

Phelps backed away from the door and keyed his mic. "He ain't here, Hemi. But he was. He left another one behind. He's been—" He paused as he tried to make sense of what he was looking at. "—Destroyed."

FIFTY-SEVEN

HE STEPPED over the body of Mrs. Atchison. Blood still thrummed out of her neck in a steady pulse but instead of the bright pyrotechnics of a moment ago it was now a thick diminishing throb. She was already brain dead. He moved cautiously by, lifting his feet over the blanket of red that had already filled the low points in the floor and was now reaching for the corners with thick rounded fingers.

He thought that she was alone with the boy but thinking something was not the same as knowing it. He checked the main floor. William was upstairs—he had seen him from the street, through the window of his bedroom. Now the boy was in the bath, singing and splashing while his mother bled out on the floor in the foyer.

On the other nights he had watched them from the park across the street, the housekeeper left at five; they were supposed to be alone now. But better safe than sorry.

He went through the house quickly, starting with the living room, the study, then on to the dining room and kitchen. A quick peek down the basement steps told him that the wine cellar was empty because there were no lights on. Besides, anyone in the basement would have heard Mrs. Atchison's body hit the floor and would have been drawn upstairs by the sound.

He went back to the foyer. She was dead now, sprawled out in an awkward pose that was almost comical because one of her hands was on her peepee. He smiled at that.

Then he walked up the stairs with the long filleting knife hanging from his hand.

The master bedroom, en suite, three guest bedrooms, main bathroom, and powder room were all empty. He went through the closets and even stooped to look under the beds.

William was in the tub, singing an old-fashioned song that he didn't recognize. The boy couldn't sing at all. But there was another thing that William did well and that's why he was here; to extract the boy's other gift.

After placing the filleting knife down on the antique console beside the bathroom door, he unslung the knapsack with the Canadian flag sewn to it and slid it to the floor. He removed the syringe from the plastic case in the side pocket and held it up to the light.

He didn't bother to tap out the bubbles but he did give it a quick check to make sure that it was still primed with anesthetic.

He reached out, placed one gloved hand on the bathroom door, and pushed it open.

William's singing echoed off the tiles. He was in the tub, head back, eyes closed, singing about being a lonely boy without a home. He had a wig of suds on his head.

Listening to whatever instinct was running through him, William opened his eyes. He saw the figure in the door. He smiled, maybe thinking for a split second that it was his mother.

And saw that it wasn't.

His smile grew puzzled. "What are you doing here? I thought that we were getting together tomorrow."

"I couldn't wait," he said, and stepped toward the boy in the tub.

||| FIFTY-EIGHT

BY THE time Delaney got Hemingway through the terminal, over the evacuating decks of the ferry, and down to Phelps, he was sitting on the bottom of the tight metal staircase to the maintenance corridor with his head in his hands.

"Don't go in there, Hemi." His voice sounded a little off in the confines of the space and she took it as echo. But what he said bothered her; in all their time together, he had never babied her, never tried to protect her from the sometimes horrifying realities of the work. If he had, they never would have made it as a team. That he was doing so now was unsettling.

Hemingway walked by, putting her hand on his shoulder as she passed. He was shivering, something that seemed impossible in the hundred-and-ten-degree heat that made the place feel like a terrarium. And then she realized the Iron Giant was crying.

The two uniformed cops leaned against the far bulkhead across from the stairwell. One looked like his brain was unplugged and the other had his eyes closed, fingers pressed to his sockets.

The hallway was tight and smelled like a hot engine after a day on the road. The space was lit with caged overhead bulbs that lent an extra air of malignancy to the stifling atmosphere and dark passage. She moved slowly toward the light spilling over the sill, across the floor, and up onto the wall in a flickering weak oval. It looked like a television was on in the room.

The engines were turned off and Manhattan-bound passengers would be taking another of the MTA's ferries, boarding at the secondary dock. The corridor was quiet and all she heard, other than the sound of her shoes on the boilerplate deck, was her heart chugging away in her ears.

She paused in front of the open door but didn't look in. Something else was mixed in with the smells of the engine deck and she recognized it as the stench of death. She turned slowly, swinging her eyes around, and focused on the dimly lit body spilled across the floor of the tool room.

The lubrication had left her sockets and she could not swivel her eyes. All she could do was stand there. Dumbly. Mutely. Staring at the dead child.

When the image had finally been absorbed, her CPU came back online and she ran down the hall, skidded to a stop at a garbage can, and threw up.

THEY STOOD on deck, staring at the city across the water. Phelps cradled a Styrofoam cup of coffee Delaney had been kind enough to provide and Hemingway sipped water she hoped would wash the taste of puke and Tic Tacs out of her mouth. They hadn't said anything for a few minutes and both were busy repairing their hard drives after what they had seen.

They were waiting for Marcus to finish in the tool room.

After what could have been an hour or a minute, Phelps asked, "How pregnant are you?" He took another sip of coffee, eyes still locked on the distant spires of Sodom and Gomorrah across the waves.

She thought about lying to him. She thought about asking him if he was nuts. She thought about punching him in the arm and saying, *Good one*. She even thought about crying. All she said was, "About six weeks."

Phelps pulled the cup away from his mouth and nodded a single, authoritative time.

"How'd you know?"

At that, he smiled. It was a shy, gentle smile and it always caught her off guard when he pulled it out during working hours. "I'm a detective, Hemi. I know you think I'm old and blind but I'm not that old *or* that blind."

That hadn't been an answer. At least not the kind she was looking for. "That doesn't explain the *how* part, Jon."

He took another sip of coffee. "You've been eating a lot lately—even for you." At that his smile broadened—her eating habits were a continual source of amusement to him; they had been since the first time they sat down to a meal together. "You keep your hand on your belly a lot. You're not touching alcohol. And you're glowing."

"Glowing? Did you say *glowing*? Now I know you're lying."

Phelps shrugged like it didn't matter one way or the other. "I remember how Maggie looked when she was pregnant with Francis. She had that same look you got now. I saw it again when Shane came along—hell, I knew she was pregnant before she did. And I seen Francis's wife when she was pregnant. I know what it looks like and it looks like you."

"That doesn't sound very scientific to me."

"What do you want me to do, lie?"

She took another swig of water and heard the clank of the gurney being wheeled over the steel deck on the way to the stairway to the basement. She thought about the boy in the tool room and she burped and tasted Tic Tacs again.

"And in all the time I've known you, nothing has made you throw up on the job."

"That was pretty bad, Jon."

"We've seen worse."

"When?"

"Remember the Dionne lady? That was worse. A *lot* worse."

She thought back to that one and the Tic Tacs spit a little

mint up the back of her throat again. "Isn't it supposed to be called morning sickness?"

"We got odd hours," he said. "Daniel know?"

He wasn't trying to walk her—he was pitching fastballs. "Yeah."

"You don't have to do anything you don't want to. Keeping it, not keeping it—it's up to you."

And now it was her turn to ask a question. "Why would you say something like that, Jon?" She hoped that hadn't sounded as accusatory to him as it had to her.

He paused this time, as if deciding if what he was going to say was a smart thing to do. "I was just wondering about Mank. I know you miss him."

"Of course I miss him—I was in love with the guy—but what the fuck does *that* have to do with anything?"

Phelps turned and looked at her—*really* looked at her. "Hemi, I don't stick my nose in where it doesn't belong. But we're friends. Hell, we're more than friends in many ways, and I want you to be happy. But I know you. I've watched you chew through a few guys in the past couple years. Mank's death killed a little piece of you. And that shit with Shea afterwards didn't help. You've always said you never wanted kids. I just assumed that you meant you didn't want kids right then. But maybe you never do. It's none of my business, except to be your friend. You love this Daniel of yours?"

She felt like he had just punched her in the stomach. "Yes. Yes, I do."

"You love him enough to have him in your life forever?"

Phelps was saying all the right things—all the things a friend would say—all the things that she had asked Mank at the cemetery yesterday. "I hadn't thought about it like that."

"Now who's lying? You know me—I'm not big on

handing out judgment—so this ain't about any kind of right or wrong. But you and I see the worst that people have to offer. We see the world as a broken damaged place full of broken damaged people who inflict the most frightening kind of pain on one another. That ain't an easy thing to forget.

"When Maggie got pregnant with Francis I had only been a cop for two years but that's long enough in this city. Hell, I think it's long enough in *any* city. I didn't want kids, not after what I seen in 'Nam and at work. But Maggie did. And you know what? My family helped me stay sane while I waded through all this shit over the years."

She jabbed a thumb over her shoulder, at the medical examiner's team fighting the stretcher down the stairs to pick up a child who had been defiled with a sharpened blade. "And what if something like that happens?"

"You know, after Shane was born I went to get a vasectomy. I was in the doctor's office and I was worried that I was making some kind of mistake. What if my children died? I talked to the doctor about it and he said one of the smartest things anyone has ever said to me in a time of crisis. He said, 'You can't plan your life on tragedy.'"

"Sure you can, Jon. Just ask the parents of that little boy downstairs. Ask them if bad things happen. They'll tell you that bad things happen all the time."

"Good things happen all the time, too. You got a guy who loves you and you love back. He ain't Mank and you know what? Good he ain't because you know and I know and everyfuckingbody knows that a life with Mank would have been a goddamned disaster. The only thing that guy could be counted on for was being angry. Everything else—as sunny as you want to paint it—was just wishful thinking."

He had never spoken to her like this, and she knew the

process had to be difficult for him. And he wasn't wrong—maybe that's all Uncle Dwight had tried to tell her. It was time to move on a little. Mank was dead. He wasn't coming back.

"I've been thinking about all those things, Jon. And I'm thinking myself into a hole. I don't know if I can do it." And that was as truthful as she was ever going to get with anyone.

Phelps took a deep breath of hot, heavy air. "I'm going to tell you one thing, and if you ever repeat it, to me or to anyone else, I'll never forgive you. When I was your age, I had a fourteen-year-old and a twelve-year-old. And I was never there, so Maggie raised our kids. I love Maggie with all my heart—she's the best thing that ever happened to me. And those boys. But she thinks that the South Pole is hot because people head south in the winter, she's convinced that Ikea is the capital of Sweden, and she hasn't read a single book that doesn't have pictures in it in the forty-one years we've been married. But I fucking love that woman. And she did a phenomenal job with those boys, all while taking care of her dying mother."

She focused on the new Manhattan skyline. The Freedom Tower still looked odd, foreign to her eye. She wondered how long it would take to become familiar.

"You got everything it takes to be a great mother, kiddo. And I don't just mean your family's money. Maybe I'm reaching, but your brother and sister have to get a very nice allowance to live those lives—so I assume that there's some there for you if you want it. And a child might be a good reason to want it. At least to pay for good schools and tennis lessons. Trips to Europe, maybe see a few museums. Braces and a fucking pony. Maybe you can give your kid a better life than most cops can. If you want to. If Maggie could do it, you sure can. I'm with you no matter what. You need someone to drive you to the clinic, and you don't want to tell Daniel about it, I'm there. This is your life. And that's all I am going to say about that. I am sorry if I hurt your feelings."

She had to pull her focus away from the city at that one. She turned, looked at him. He was a big, goofy-looking man who had been shot three times, stabbed once, had his nose broken more times than anyone could remember and had hands that looked like they were salvaged from a broken prizefighter. And she realized that in Daniel she had found a man who would measure up to Phelps, if not in battle scars, at least in caring. And the way they both cocked their head to one side when they were thinking or smiling. "Why is it that no matter how lousy I feel, you always manage to make everything seem just a little bit better?"

"Call it a gift." He nodded over her shoulder. "Speaking of gifts, here comes Dr. Death."

Dr. Marcus was in pants and shirtsleeves, the jacket and tie of earlier lost somewhere along the way. "Detectives," he said. "I am not in the habit of telling other people how to do their job, but you two need to make some headway and you need to do it fast."

"Same guy?" Hemingway asked, knowing it was a stupid question as soon as it was out of her mouth.

The medical examiner ignored her. "You have any suspects?"

"The only thing we're going on now is a connection to Dr. Brayton."

"Still haven't found him?"

Hemingway shook her head. "We've got it out to the FBI—if he's alive, we should know something soon."

"He your only suspect?"

There was no satisfactory way to answer that so neither cop said a word.

"I am going on the record as saying that I am sick and tired of looking at dead kids."

Hemingway ran a hand through her hair and straightened up, pushing the kinks out of her back. "Come up to the control room, you have to see the surveillance tapes. The Rochester boy's phone was programmed to send that text at a predetermined time. Did he set it before the murder or after? He had the processor in hibernation and the phone went on just before it sent me the text. And we damn well know he was here, on the boat, at the TOD."

"At around two p.m."

They walked across the yellow boilerplate ramp. The walk felt good. She felt her chest and head clearing out again. Her stomach, too.

The control room had seventy feet of river frontage with a clear view of Manhattan across the bay. How long had they been at this now? It felt like a lifetime.

Hemingway steered Dr. Marcus over to the back corner where Delaney was waiting.

"Show him," Hemingway said.

Delaney fiddled with a few buttons then paused to point out four monitors, "Here, here, here, and here." The displays flickered to life, showing the doorways on the passenger deck. "These are the doors to stairwells that drop to the engine deck." The time stamp started at 6:50. "This is ten minutes before the ferry's first cycle of the day." He hit a button.

The timer began spinning in hyperdrive. People danced by, paused in front of it—all in the jittery mercury-poisoned body language of fast-forward. The seconds on the counter turned into minutes turned into hours. No one said a thing as the past closed on a little boy's future—a little boy who was being strapped into a stretcher as they took a trip in the four-monitor time machine. The hours zipped by and not a single passenger—or employee—approached any of the doors.

1:30:21 . . . 1:34:30 . . . 1:38:15 . . . 1:41:10—Delaney cued back the knob and time slowed down.

"Right here," Hemingway said.

Delaney spun the dial down to real time and the seconds began ticking off in a familiar beat. A child approached one of the doors.

"That's the staircase between the main deck and the saloon deck—the same one Detective Phelps went down—the same one we've been using."

It was a boy. Dark brown hair, dark school jacket, light—probably white—shirt, school tie. He had a knapsack over his shoulder.

"That's the victim," Hemingway said.

Marcus moved closer to the screen, trying to see into the past.

The boy hunched in front of the door for a few seconds, his back to the camera, the knapsack jostling back and forth as he worked his hands. After a few seconds he put his shoulder to the door, turned the handle, and pushed into the staircase.

Delaney spun the knob and the clock began fast-forwarding again.

Eleven minutes later the boy was back at the same place and he entered the same door again. This time he wasn't carrying his knapsack.

Marcus held up his hand. "He went back up, then down again?"

Delaney pointed to a schematic. "There are some small grates at the end of the downstairs corridor here and here that lead to a pipe that runs up to an emergency hatch where the cars used to park before those terrorist assholes brought a war down on our asses. The hatches open up here and here. He had to have used one of them as a passage."

"And his killer?" Marcus asked.

Hemingway shook her head and went back to the monitors. "You can't open the escape hatch from the outside. Linderer said one of the hatches was opened—they aren't picked up by any of the surveillance cameras and they're not wired into any alarms because they can only be opened from belowdecks—MTA personnel only. We have the boy coming onto the ferry once, going through that door twice."

Marcus shifted his gaze to the schematics. "And you don't see his killer go down there at any point?"

"Like I said," Hemingway offered in what sounded like a defense to her. "A ghost."

The medical examiner stared at the screen for a few moments. "And we know it wasn't anyone on the crew." His people had black-lighted the staff and hadn't found a single trace of genetic material—whoever had taken that child apart would have lit up like phosphorescent plankton. And no one had been out of sight of the cameras long enough to have made the mess they were cleaning up downstairs.

It was Delaney who spoke. "None of my guys have records—as MTA employees they've had their assholes—excuse my French," he said sideways to Hemingway, "X-rayed. They're on camera all morning. They're good."

Hemingway waved it away. They were back to *ghost*.

Phelps pointed at the screen again. "Nowhere do we see anyone going in any of the access points to get to the basement. No one went through any of those doors. No one went down that corridor today."

Marcus shifted and a bead of sweat on his forehead shook loose and rolled down behind his glasses. He scooped it out of his socket with a finger that had just been probing a mutilated child, blinked, then squinted like a cartoon character.

"Carson will take apart all the footage that the MTA has for the past three days, to see if anything's been doctored."

Delaney shook his head. "That means they'd have to get by my people. And our surveillance system isn't online, it's autonomous. It ain't us. That video hasn't been touched. But knock yourself out."

"We have one crescent of blood downstairs. Looks like a size ten or ten and a half man's leather-soled shoe."

The same as the two back at the Deacon house, on both sides of a door guarded by a giant spider. "Anything different?"

Marcus looked down at Delaney who nodded his head. "I know, below my pay grade." He disappeared.

"I can't tell if the anesthetic was administered through either of the eyes for obvious reasons, but he's added a new tool to his repertoire."

"Which is?"

Marcus shrugged. "I won't know till I scope some metal I found in the spinal column, but it looks like a chisel. Probably driven by a hammer."

They still hadn't identified the victim. They had his school tie and Papandreou and Lincoln were running that down. The boy went to—or at least had a tie from—St. Mark's School for Boys on the Upper East Side. They'd start with the list of patient names they had culled from the Brayton/Selmer files.

From there they'd narrow it down to a student at St. Mark's. But they'd have to rely on DNA for the final say-so. They couldn't get an ID based on a photo of the remains—there was no legal way they could show pictures of this boy to anyone. And if they did, it wouldn't do any good; it was impossible to identify a child without a face.

"We gotta go." It was too hot in here and this wasn't even movement, let alone action.

On the way out they said goodbye to Delaney and thanked him for his help. Cards were exchanged, promises to phone if anything new was discovered were made, and the two cops headed for the staircase that led out to the terminal.

As they passed the ramp, Hemingway saw the guys from the medical examiner's office rolling the too-big stretcher over the painted boilerplate. It didn't look like there was anything under the plastic.

Hemingway and Phelps headed to the police boat. The air felt as oppressive as it had down in the basement with the dead child and she wondered if a trip on the water would help cool her off or make her feel worse. One thing was certain, the empty stomach was no longer agreeing with her. She looked up at the sky, wondering when it was going to let go again.

When they hit the steps down to the police Zodiac, Phelps stopped and turned back to her. "You do whatever you feel is the right decision. And I promise no one will think any different of you." Meaning: *me*. "Just make the right long-term decision, not the easy short-term one. And if that means you need a place to stay if it comes to that—me and Maggie got the guest suite out back. You can stay—for a reasonable rent—as long as you want. Babies. No babies. It's all the same to me."

She stared at him for a second, and realized that was the nicest thing anyone had ever said to her. "Thanks for worrying, Jon." Code for *I love you back.* "Now let's go get some food."

"You know, for a lady, you sure can eat."

"I get that a lot."

THEY WERE drilling through the Brayton/Selmer patient list. One call after another. Alphabetically. Some people were home. Some weren't. Black-and-whites had been sent out. The parents they reached had initial reactions ranging from horror to disbelief yet were all tinted with the same underlying timbre of fear.

Two parents had directed them to their legal representation and hung up. Hemingway was on her eighth family—the parents of Casey Dorf.

"The Dorf residence."

"This is Detective Alexandra Hemingway of the NYPD, may I please speak with Mrs. Angela Dorf?" They always started with the mother—it was only a matter of statistics until they came across a couple where the father had no idea he wasn't the child's biological parent.

A pause.

"This is Mrs. Dorf." The tone was suspicious.

"Mrs. Dorf, I need to talk to you about a very private matter and I need to make an appointment for a pair of local officers to come around and talk to you in person. Until that can happen, there are some things I need to warn you about. Are you in a position to speak freely?"

"Yes." Still suspicious. Maybe even more so.

"I need to talk to you about your daughter."

In a farmhouse somewhere in Connecticut, Mrs. Dorf gasped.

"Where is she right now?"

There was a long pause. "She's dead, Detective Hemingway. She died last summer."

"I'm, I'm sorry."

"Yes. Well. Of course you are."

"May I ask what happened?"

"Casey fell on the playground. Middle of the afternoon. Lots of children around. She was there and then she wasn't." And the tone of her voice said that the conversation was over. She hung up.

Hemingway wrote the word *deceased* beside the Dorfs' name. She lifted her head to find Phelps staring at her. He had a phone in his hand and his finger was on the cradle. "The Everetts' child, Tanya, died last year. Drowned at the beach in Greece—middle of the day."

Hemingway stared at him. It hit them simultaneously.

They rifled through Brayton's folders, looking for the same page in each. It took the better part of five minutes and when they were done, they went down the list pregnancy by pregnancy.

Of the sixty-seven children, there were fifty-nine boys and eight girls.

Two of the girls—a full twenty-five percent—were dead. Which was either a remarkable coincidence or a red flag.

It took Hemingway five more minutes to locate the next patient on the list, the mother of Stephanie Gordon. She had moved a few blocks down Fifth Avenue.

Hemingway asked to speak to Mrs. Gordon.

After a full minute of waiting, there was the sound of high heels on marble and Mrs. Gordon answered.

Hemingway introduced herself, then asked Mrs. Gordon about Stephanie.

There was the sound of a single deep breath, then Mrs. Gordon said, "My daughter is dead, Detective."

"I'm very sorry." She paused—the next part felt cruel. "May I ask what happened?"

There was another pause. "She was at a playdate with some other children. At the park—"

Hemingway didn't have to hear the last part to know what it was going to be.

"—in the middle of the day."

She thanked Mrs. Gordon and hung up.

Three out of the eight girls were dead. This was something much, much grimmer than bad luck.

She wrote the word *deceased* beside Stephanie Gordon's name before picking up the phone to call the mother of the next girl on the list.

THE BOY they had found on the ferry was named Zachary Simmons. He had been a brilliant painter. He was scheduled to start studies at the Sorbonne in mid-July, which would have been his tenth birthday.

Phelps and Hemingway suited up in silence, far too familiar with the routine of talking to the parents of dead children.

SIXTY-TWO

THE SUN had crawled below the skyline to the west. The air still felt like fluid and everything glistened but the rain had not come down. The offices were still sinister and if the garbage cans suddenly burst into flames, no one would have been surprised. It felt like hell. With bad coffee.

After talking to Zachary Simmons's mother, they had come back to the precinct, loaded up on coffee, and gone after the patients who had had baby girls.

Hemingway made the calls—a woman was less threatening than a man. At least that was the theory. She was met with anger, bewilderment, and hysteria.

They had the eight names up on the board.

They stood in front of it for a few moments, taking it in.

They now had another commonality: all of the female children from Brayton's files were dead.

Eight little girls had stopped being alive at some point last year.

All had died in freak accidents.

In most of the deaths there were dozens of witnesses.

Not one of the mothers so much as hinted at a suspicion

of foul play; the general consensus was the old wrong place, wrong time catchall.

Casey Dorf: *fell on a playground and died in the hospital two days later—June 24.*

Tanya Everett: *drowned while swimming at a beach in Greece—August 20.*

Stephanie Gordon: *fell off her bike in Central Park and broke her neck—July 22.*

Cynthia LaColle: *fell off her bike on the East Side Esplanade, driving her jaw up into her brain—May 27.*

Belinda Marsh: *fell off a swing, landed on a bolt that secured the iron base to the ground and it speared her in the throat; she bled to death in front of her mother—Sept 2.*

Heidi Morrison: *fell off the subway platform in front of a train—August 5.*

Tiffany Rostovich: *drowned in the bathtub at home—June 10.*

Pamela Zager: *died of an apparent heart attack in her sleep—July 8.*

Hemingway took out her pen and began a new page on her legal pad, arranging the deaths chronologically. "With the exception of Tanya Everett—who died fifteen days after Heidi Morrison, but thirteen before Belinda Marsh—these girls died exactly two weeks apart from one another."

"And then there were none," Phelps said.

III SIXTY-THREE

HIS FATHER stood at the window, his eye fastened to the antique brass telescope, watching the birds in Central Park across the street. The only time his father seemed at peace was when he watched his beloved birds. He barely moved. Barely breathed. Barely seemed there at all. He could be found here every night, scanning the foliage for rare taxa.

What was it about them that fascinated him?

Like the birds he hunted, Benjamin's father was anomalous to the general population. Even in the world of academia, where eccentrics were the norm rather than the exception, his father was misplaced. He couldn't help his physical appearance—a car accident before Benjamin had been born had crushed parts of his spine and done irreparable damage. He walked with a pronounced, stooped-over gait that made him look like one of his avian subjects. Some of the boys at school laughed at his father, but that was to be expected from people who couldn't grasp the concept of fractions. Things would be better at Harvard. Hopefully.

Their apartment was unlike the home of any of the other children he went to school with. Whereas their parents decorated with porcelain vases, bronze busts, and modern art, his father had filled the house with glass-cased birds. Most of the boys he knew had stopped coming over because his house was simply "too weird," as they put it. It wasn't as if he had a lot in common with these boys in the first place, but it was interesting to interact with people his own age. Even if they couldn't read Homer in the original.

His father slowly swung the scope around, looking for wildlife where it shouldn't be. Sure, the park was filled with trees and grass and water, but it was artificial; everything was primped and manicured to within an inch of its life. Why would birds gravitate to the park when a ten-minute flight could carry them clear of the concrete landscape and put them in real nature? Maybe that was the origin of the expression "birdbrained," because they sure didn't seem to use their heads.

A few weeks back *Scientific American* had published an article comparing Benjamin to William James Sidis, the youngest child prodigy ever to be accepted to Harvard; Benjamin was younger than Sidis by a whole year.

He was also a lot smarter.

Benjamin was special. His father had always told him so. Which was why he loved him so much.

And Benjamin wanted nothing more than for him to stop.

SIXTY-FOUR

HEMI FINALLY found Brayton. He had thrown a rope over a pipe in the basement of a rented apartment in Helsinki some eight months back. No note. No life insurance.

The body had been cremated.

Brayton's last employer had been a traveling clinic that served Lapland. The head doctor, Mika Jula, said that Brayton had been exemplary and wondered why he had chosen to work for so little when his skills would obviously be much more valuable elsewhere.

Jula had agreed to send a copy of the death certificate to Hemingway, and stressed that he wished there was more to share about Brayton.

Hemingway got off the phone and stared at Phelps. "Brayton's dead. Has been for months."

"Shit."

"Yeah. Shit. I'm hungry."

Phelps got up and started to put on his jacket. "Why am I the one always getting the food?"

Hemingway tapped her index finger to her temple. "Because I do all the thinking."

———

While Phelps was out hunting down more coffee and food, Hemingway called Marcus at home. She filled him in on Brayton then moved on to the eight dead girls. Lincoln and Papandreou were at the far end of the office, making calls to parents of the boys on the list.

She spent ten minutes laying out what she probably could have done in five—but she wanted no misunderstandings. When she asked him to start an inquest he didn't pause, didn't start any of the usual pissing contest conniptions he tended to do simply because he could; he just listened patiently. When she was done he asked if she'd send her notes over. He would need the night and some of the next morning to get his ducks in a row.

Hemingway understood: he'd have to mobilize massive amounts of manpower to open the deaths of these girls. Eight court orders. Eight sets of grieving, and not necessarily rational, parents. The newspapers. The injunctions. The scrutiny. Overnight seemed more than reasonable, it seemed like a gift.

Hemingway was not naive; Marcus also needed this mess behind him as soon as possible. The CSI effect had already gripped the talking heads and everyone was yakking about carpet fibers and DNA and all kinds of fancy shit they knew nothing about. People wanted answers; in lieu of answers, media-driven public opinion would accept scapegoats. His detractors were already spewing stupidity on the television, newspapers, and Internet. Marcus wanted this gone as much as she did.

There was no challenge in convincing him the girls hadn't died in random accidents. By the third girl he was a silent presence on the end of the line. And this didn't fit the MO of the ghost with the hypodermic and saw who had added a hammer and chisel to his toolbox.

He figured out the timeline as fast as she had.

"There were sixty-seven successful pregnancies in Brayton's files from the donor. We've lost four boys plus the Grant boy's driver, Dr. Selmer, and the eight girls."

"And the inimitable Trevor Deacon."

"Yeah. Deacon. I better get back to work. Call if you need anything, I'll be here all night."

"Maybe you should go home, get some sleep."

"That's not happening." Until they had a breakthrough, she'd be running on caffeine and adrenaline. "A cup of coffee and a sandwich and I'll feel a lot better." *Or at least less shitty.* She paused again, and realized that she felt like she had died and nobody had bothered to tell her about it. She hung up.

Before she had put the phone down, it rang again. She answered without checking the display.

The voice was reptilian. "Detective Hemingway, someone asked me to call you about a man who bought pink powder."

Trevor Deacon's drug dealer.

Hemingway snapped up. "Where can I meet you?"

There was a pause. "I'm not sure that's such a—"

"All I care about is information about the man you met. That's all. I can meet you anywhere."

Another pause. Then, "Twenty-seventh between Tenth and Eleventh there's a bar called Mitch's. Come alone. How long for you to get there?"

She checked her watch, looked outside and factored in traffic for this time of the night. "Give me half an hour." Then she hung up.

Phelps showed up with two paper bags stained with grease.

"Trevor Deacon's dealer just called. Twenty-seventh between Tenth and Eleventh."

Phelps put the bags down. "Haven't been there since it was gentrified. The Minnesota strip. Remember those days?"

"Before my time, Jon."

"Sorry, I keep forgetting that not everyone was around before the Internet."

Dennet marched in. He had a folder in his hand. "Where are you two going?"

Hemingway was in the midst of threading her arm through her jacket. "Got an appointment with Trevor Deacon's dealer."

"It can wait three minutes," Dennet said, putting the file in Hemingway's hand. Then he turned to Lincoln and Papandreou. "Linc, Nick, get over here."

They came over.

Dennet leaned forward, putting his knuckles on the table. "The Rochesters' attorney sent that over." He stood up, and began circling the table. "Ten years ago Brayton offered membership to an exclusive unique-donor fertility program at the clinic."

"Meaning?" Lincoln asked.

Hemingway opened the docket and took out a slick, leather-bound brochure with PAC embossed across the front in foil lettering. She scanned it.

"Instead of a patient picking a donor from a catalogue, which lacked exclusivity, Brayton offered an option where patients could purchase the proprietary rights to a donor."

Lincoln interrupted. "Some rich broad doesn't want to pick sperm out of a catalogue because some other woman might have used the same guy?"

Dennet nodded.

Lincoln shook his head in disgust. "Purchasing proprietary rights to a guy's sauce just ain't right."

Hemingway held up the folder. "This outlines Brayton's vision as one donor, one patient, one pregnancy."

"Which is bullshit," Phelps said. "We know the boys are half brothers."

Lincoln tapped his breast pocket. "But none of the parents did. This explains why."

Phelps was still sitting with his arms crossed. "What did he charge for this exclusivity?"

It was Dennet who answered. "Two hundred and fifty K for the donor, another two fifty for the paperwork and procedure."

Papandreou said, "Half a mil is a good motive for murder."

Hemingway headed for the door. "Linc, start looking at the parents. We'll be back in a few hours." Some people were paying a half a million dollars for something she wasn't sure she wanted for free. "What do you think, Phelps?"

The Iron Giant followed her to the door. "I think I shoulda stayed in school."

BENJAMIN WINSLOW lay on the bed, his face buried in the down pillow. He tasted blood from his cheek, feathers and tears. The apartment was silent except for the sound of his father showering.

Benjamin lay in the dark, hurting, crying, hoping for someone to come and take him away from this place.

Someplace beyond Harvard.

He'd even settle on the world swallowing him up.

As long as his father stopped touching him.

III SIXTY-SIX

IN ITS heyday it had been known as the Minnesota Strip, a place where kids from the sticks with no marketable skills could make it in the city. Twenty-seventh between Tenth and Eleventh used to be lined with boys, from young twinks up through the stereotypical Joe Bucks. Around the block, on Twenty-sixth, was where you could find *Coal Miner's Daughter* types competing with Pam Greer wannabes. This chunk of real estate had kept the porn industry saturated all through the VHS revolution.

Now it was just a section of town that gentrification had stripped of most of its character. Hemingway pulled the Suburban up to the curb, across the street from a bar sandwiched between an office supply store and a courier company. Mitch's Bar had been there so long it looked like a geological formation that had grown up from the bedrock. It reminded Hemingway of Bernie's; all that was missing were the ancient, greasy piñatas. There were places like it peppered through the city, holdovers that had survived a hundred years' worth of economic fluctuation. The street looked deserted and what little movement there was came from the dark humps of sewer rats milling around the base of a Dumpster down the street, big black shadows moving slowly in the heat.

Hemingway checked her cylinder, tucked the revolver into the holster at her waist, and said, "Wait here."

Phelps finished his coffee in one loud slurp. "I could use another coffee—this one's empty."

"I gave my word, Jon."

He was silent for a second. "Okay."

They stepped out onto the baked asphalt and the air tasted like a ticking engine. There was still no wind. No reprieve from the heat.

Phelps walked down the street, eying the dark corners and alleys. Hemingway walked into Mitch's alone.

The place was a bigger shithole inside than she had pictured, and she had a developed imagination. They served hobo juice for two bucks a bottle and Motörhead played out of one speaker, a machine-gun bass track that rattled the glasses. The Rockford Files was playing on a television suspended over the ancient feltless snooker table. There were no neon beer signs—this wasn't the kind of place beer company reps loaded up with free advertising—and she wasn't sure which was stronger, the smell of sweat or the stink of piss.

Two drunks were staring at empty glasses in a booth and an old woman at the bar looked like she had died in place a few days back but no one had noticed. The general population looked like they were hiding from something, life probably. Business as usual for the down and out.

"She okay?" Hemingway asked the bartender, a skinny kid with an open mouth in a stained Hertz Rent-a-Car T-shirt. He shrugged without taking his eyes off James Garner.

Hemingway found the dealer at the back, his hands on the plywood tabletop—a street fighter's signal that he meant no harm. As she walked up, he said, "You're here to talk to me."

She reached for the chair and he lifted his head. She froze for a second, something that rarely happened.

His face was tattooed with Gene Simmons makeup, bat wings that spread out from his nose, covering his cheeks and flaring up onto his forehead. Male pattern baldness had taken hold and he wore a greasy once-white T-shirt embellished with a rhinestone skull that had lost half its shine. The shirt rode up past his distended belly.

She sat down. "Thank you for meeting me. I'm Detective Hemingway."

"I'm Roy." He kept his eyes down, locked on the rings that sweating glasses had branded into the plywood. "You wanna buy me a drink? You don't hafta or nuthin' but it would be nice."

Hemingway waved at the bartender, signaling a round for Roy. He looked over, then turned back to the TV without acknowledging her.

"Ain't that kinda place," Roy said. "You gotta go to the bar."

Hemingway got up and walked over to the television. "Can we get a beer?" she asked.

The bartender shrugged. "You suck my cock if I bring it over?"

At that she stepped forward and grabbed him by the wrist, wrenching it around and forcing him off the stool. She cranked it again and he went to the floor. "How about I make you suck it yourself?" she said, twisting. "Or do you want to skip the dating so you can bring me a beer?"

"Yeah. Yeah. I was just being friendly. Fuck."

She let go and he fell over.

He stood up, massaging his shoulder. "No means no. I

get it." He walked over to the bar, capped a Pabst and brought it over, the swagger back in his step.

When the bartender had gone back to James Garner and friends, Roy took a draft and wiped the back of his hand across his mouth. "What you want?"

"I'm not wearing a wire. I'm not interested in any narcotics you may or may not have been involved with. And now that I've said that, it would be entrapment if I went back on my word. All I want to know about is—"

"Arnold Palmer," he said.

"Um, no, actually—"

"That's what he called himself. That guy on the news. Deacon." He pulled out the photo she had given to Dwight and slid it across the table. "He told me his name was Arnold Palmer."

"Where'd you meet him?"

He gave her a sad smile. "Staten Island Ferry."

And an image of the Simmons boy exploded in her head.

"I took it from Battery Park one night and he sat down beside me. Nobody sits down beside me except maybe fags and those hard-core hipster kids. At first I thought he was gay. He told me that he had been watching me. Following me, even. Knew what I did. Said he was a customer. I told him I didn't know what he was talking about. He knew what I had, where I picked it up, who I had picked it up from."

"When was this first meeting?"

"A year and a bit. May, I think. Met him about twice a month after that."

"On the ferry?"

"No. Never on the ferry. Mostly he just showed up sitting beside me on the subway or a park bench or buying beer. Weird guy." At that he stopped, looked up at her. "Weirder than me, I mean."

"You ever catch him following you?"

Roy shook his head. "Not once. Never saw him coming. He was a ghost or something."

"What can you tell me about him?"

"He liked watching kids. And I ain't just saying that because it was on the news. I met him at parks a lot. At first, I thought it was because he was trying to look like he fit in. I do lots of deals in pa—" He stopped, looked up at her. "Look, Detective, I ain't got a lot of skills. I can cook and that's about all I know. If this is about busting me, and I go to the joint, life ain't gonna be easy for a guy that looks like me, you know? How I know you ain't here to bust me?"

"All I can do is promise. If I was wearing a wire, I've been recorded telling you that I am not interested in your narcotics activity and if I later arrested you—or allowed this tape to be used to help arrest you—I would be breaking the law. It wouldn't hold up in court. You'd win."

"Not me. I don't win at nothing." He paused and took a sip of his beer. "I met him at Randall's Island a lot."

Hemingway remembered Dr. Torssennson's pointer crawling over the patch of earth where she figured Tyler Rochester had been dumped—Little Hell Gate was off the southern tip of Randall's Island.

Then she remembered the school schedules she had gone over with Phelps—the year-end track-and-field meet that was scheduled for next week—nine thousand private school boys on the same patch of earth. Randall's Island again.

"What's *a lot*?"

His eyes scrolled up as he retrieved the information from wherever he kept it. "Wednesdays for about two months. He liked baseball diamond forty-eight. It took a little while until I figured out that he liked looking at the kids. I ain't making excuses or nothing—I should have seen it right away—but my brain ain't wired to see that kind of stuff. Pickpockets, three-card monte—that kind of shit I can figure out. But people that like kids? Not part of my thinking. I may not be the most law-abiding guy out there, but some shit is broken. What I do, selling drugs, is pretty much all a guy that looks like me can do. Every now and then I get a job in some restaurant but something goes missing and they accuse me. Spago's ain't hiring a guy like me. So I deal a little tar cut with brown sugar or instant coffee. That's it. I never wrote a bad check. I don't steal. And I don't look at kids. It made me sick.

"I tried to shake the guy. I laid low for a while, changed my schedule, my routes. I thought he was gone. I hoped. Guy like him has a bad smell following him. Worse than failure, know what I mean? Didn't see him for a bit. Then one afternoon I'm sitting on a bench feeding pigeons an' he sits down beside me with a box of Chicken McNuggets. Said he was disappointed I didn't keep up my end of the friendship. Friendship? Jeezus, some people got a way with words. You could tell he thought of himself as some kind of supergenius—you know, the kind of guy thought he was so much smarter than everyone else. I told him the travel time uptown and across the bridge was killing me. I told him to find his own dealer up there. He was pissed. I think he liked that I sat there while he watched the kids. Made him feel like he had"—Roy looked at her—"a friend, I guess."

"He ever have anyone with him? A real friend, maybe?"

Roy laughed, a loud giggle that overrode James Garner getting his ass whipped by some truckers. "He didn't even like himself. No friends. Just a knapsack. Black, with a Canadian flag sewn on like he was pretending to be a tourist. And he had a camera. It was digital but it looked like one of those old big cameras, not like the small ones we got now. Had one of those—what do you call 'em? Telephoto lenses."

She thought about the lenses in Deacon's bottom drawer and the question of the camera came up again.

And Deacon's hard drives.

"I saw him talk to kids a lot. He'd mosey up to the sidelines of a game and snap a few photos, pretend like he belonged. And then he'd start talking to some lone kid. At first I thought he was just being friendly. And then I started to see how he looked at the kids and decided that I didn't need no more trouble than I got."

"You ever report him?"

"For what? Talking to kids? I never seen him do anything bad to the kids. He never even put a hand on their shoulder or nuthin'. All he did was talk to them."

"You ever hear what he discussed with them?"

He shook his head. "No. No. No. Whenever he did that, I split."

"Did he ever tell you anything about his life?"

Roy shook his head. "Said he had a nice house. Big car. Said he liked watching the kids because he was a sports fan. It was bullshit. You know how you can tell when people are bullshitting? They tell you they used to be this and they used to be that when all they are is a bum. I get a lot of that. I attract it like some kind of a magnet."

"Anything else you remember about him?"

At that Roy smiled. "He said that he was going to be famous someday."

Hemingway slid one of her cards across the table. "You think of anything else, you call me. I appreciate this."

"I was told to call you. I do what I'm told." Roy eyed the card for a moment, as if it held some great meaning.

"You have a number I can reach you at?"

Roy thought about it for a minute. Then he scribbled his number on a piece of cardboard he tore from a pack of cigarettes. "Yeah. Sure. We can have cocktails at the Ritz."

She stared at him for a moment, and her eyes unconsciously dropped to his belly It was pale. Hairy. She nodded a goodbye. "Thanks for everything." Then she walked past the old woman who still looked dead, past *The Rockford Files*, and into the night.

||| S I X T Y - S E V E N

LINCOLN AND Papandreou looked like they had been sleeping in their clothes and Hemingway couldn't decide if it was the heat or the hours that had done the damage. They limped across the street like a pair of broke-dick dogs and came into Bernie's.

Papandreou dropped into the booth and Lincoln grabbed a chair, swung it over to the table, sat down and threw his notebook onto the Formica. Then he reached for Hemingway's plate. "Leaving food behind? That ain't like you," he said, grimacing at the taste of the cold fries soaked in catsup.

"My stomach's acting up."

"I seen you eat a sandwich with bones in it once. You ain't got no stomach, you got a valve." Papandreou waved Bernie over, signaling for two coffees.

"How many of Brayton's patients did you get to?"

"Quite a few. You gotta meet the Borenstein woman."

Lincoln swung a fry around like an accusatory weapon. "The real prize is the Morgans. Totally fucking nuts."

"We're all nuts. It's part of the human condition."

Papandreou pulled the sugar dispenser over in preparation for the caffeine he had just ordered while Lincoln continued to pick at Hemingway's fries. "Then they're weird."

Phelps finished off his soda. "They're not weird, they're *eccentric*."

Bernie came over with their coffees. After he walked away, Papandreou upended the sugar dispenser into his. "No, Jon, they're fucking weird. One looks like some kind of freaking lesbian vampire, the other a redneck cop got lucky and inherited a bazillion dollars. Winslow is like that guy from *Psycho* with all the stuffed birds. Me? I collect shot glasses and back issues of *Popular Mechanics*. These folks? They collect weirdness."

Hemingway pushed her plate over so that it was in front of Lincoln; something about the congealing grease was beginning to turn her stomach. "As in?"

Lincoln shrugged. "It's not the shit we saw, it's the shit we didn't see. I don't know what it was."

"You're supposed to be a cop. Short-list it, Linc."

"Doris Borenstein. Fifty-three, married five times, looks like a taxidermied piranha–"

Hemingway held up her hand. "Don't do that."

Lincoln nodded an apology. "Sorry. Like I said, these people freaked us both out a little. Ms. Borenstein has no employment history and her name is listed as administrator or senior fundraiser for eleven charities—emphysema, MS, general big-time stuff like that. Nice apartment but she's cold as a mother-in-law's love."

Lincoln wiped the catsup and mayo off his fingers with a napkin and opened his notebook. "Next up we have Cindy and 'Ace' Morgan. Guy builds battleships and shit. Rich Texan. Their place is decorated like Keith Richards' bedroom. Gold leaf and leopard print and naked gold cherubs bolted to everything. He's seventy-five. Wears a cowboy hat and sounds like Ross Perot. His wife, Cindy, is thirty-five. Former veterinary technician and before that she was an 'Internet model.' They think this is all one big hoot, some kind of role-play or something. They thought we were fucking joking. And you should meet their kid, Miles. Christ, what a goof."

Lincoln flipped forward a few pages. "Then we get the McDaddy of them all, Dr. Neal Winslow—chief ornithologist for the American Museum of Natural History. Specializes in endangered and extinct taxa, most notably the—" he went back to his notes and haltingly read"—*Pinguinus impennis*, whatever the fuck that is. Some kinda bird, I guess.

"His kid Benjamin is some kind of genius. I mean totally off the charts. Smarter'n any of the other ones, and they're all weird little rain men. The kid's ten and has a full scholarship to Harvard. Wrote a collection of biographies of famous people just for the fun of it.

"Dr. Winslow is something else. Fifteen years ago he busted his back in a car wreck. Spine's held together with screws. Wife died seven years back—fell overboard on a cruise—inquest reported death by misadventure. Insurance never paid out because they couldn't rule out murder. Winslow didn't contest the judgment. Now he does Scouts with his kid. Owns a bunch of corporations. Lives in the Dakota. Plenty of zeros in the bank. Odd guy."

Papandreou nodded over his coffee. "Freak," he said. "Hunched over like some kind of bird."

Hemingway flicked Lincoln's notes. "What's wrong with you guys? His back was fucking broken. Don't be disrespectful." She leaned back in the chair and knitted her hands together on top of her head and she saw Lincoln's eyes automatically dial into her bust. "So what *don't* we know about these people?" she asked, taking her arms and crossing them in front of her chest.

Benjamin Winslow
Donor 9332042
Age: Ten years, three months, fourteen days

Dr. Neal Winslow was a single father.

His wife had promised him that it would be her job, her sole responsibility. He could pretend to be interested on birthdays and Christmas, maybe even Thanksgiving. Parent–teacher nights would, of course, be required at least once a year. He would never have to go to recitals or endure finding a piano teacher, or put thought into the child's schooling. She would handle all of it. He would be notified of events via a weekly memo. He wouldn't have to sleep with her. The details would be handled by medical professionals. And it would keep her happy. So he had agreed.

His wife went to a clinic specializing in such things. The child was born. And soon after, his wife disappeared from a cruise ship somewhere off the coast of Portugal. Her body was found three days later by fishermen, so badly bloated by the expanding gases in her system that they thought she was a blue crab–covered life raft.

Benjamin became his sole responsibility and he spent countless hours teaching his son, molding him. And by the time he was five, the boy could outpace his father at anything he took an interest in.

Benjamin had an aptitude not easily measured by standard testing methods but it was generally agreed that he had an IQ that topped 220. The boy excelled at multiple disciplines, not the least of which were mathematics and language. He was touted as a polymath, and Dr. Winslow nurtured his son's gifts.

Solomon Borenstein
Donor 2323094
Age: Ten years, one month, nine days

Five husbands littered Doris Bornstein's past, no small feat for a woman of forty-one years of age. Three had been rich, one had been nice and rich, and one was gay and rich. But they had all been smart. And good in bed. Except maybe for the gay one—unless he was high. But she had come to the table with her own money and had walked away from each without a battle. There had never been any forethought put into any of her divorces: one minute she was contented, maybe even a little happy, the next she was asking for a divorce. The first divorce was over poached eggs; the second, just after coming while he was giving it to her in the ass (the poor sonofabitch never even got to finish); the third, ten minutes after he bought her a nine-million-dollar beach house in Montauk; the fourth, during a Knicks game—she hated basketball—and the last one over a glass of wine on a British Airways flight.

Of course she was up front with numbers Two through Five about the way she had left the previous marriage(s). Like all men, each thought he was different than his predecessors. And they were, but only from one another. Three years was the average.

Solomon was conceived when she had been married to Herrik, her gay Norwegian god as she had called him. She had wanted a baby, he had wanted her to have a baby, but they had one rule—he didn't go near her vajayjay. So they had compromised and opted for a surrogate and a sperm donor. It was amazing what a socioeconomically disadvantaged woman would put her body through for a mere three hundred thousand dollars. Morning sickness and stretch marks? No alcohol or—God-fucking-forbid—drugs for nine months? It was absolutely unthinkable.

So Doris and Herrik had rented a womb, bought some sperm from the tall smart sexy donor that Dr. Brayton recommended, and settled in for the wonderful role of parenthood. Five months in—while they were on their way to London to see Van Morrison at the Royal Albert Hall—she looked over at Herrik and decided that the relationship had run its course. When they touched down at Heathrow, they each took a different car and had not spoken since.

Of course she loved her son, Solomon.

Miles Morgan
Donor 4032239
Age: Ten years, two months, three days

Forney Morgan, who everyone called Ace, had done it all himself. No rich daddy. No bank loans. No credit. And no fucking woman telling him what to do, how to do it, or how long he was allowed to do it for. Amen. Thank you. And fuck the cheese loaf on the way out the door.

Morgan Industrial was OPEC's leading manufacturer of petroleum barrels. He had started the business in his garage in Odessa, Texas—marking up outsourced barrels by a buck apiece. By the time Texas was producing nearly three million barrels a day he had gone from brokering to manufacturing. Now, at the Christmas end of his life, his interests had expanded to include shipbuilding—an endeavor that led him to Uncle Sam, for whom he was now producing nuclear submarines. Life was grand.

And then he found Cindy. Working in the veterinarian's office where he took Rumsfeld and Adolf—his Great Danes—

for their monthly checkup. She was twenty-three and had a big smile and an even bigger pair of tits. He had always been a boob monkey, ever since he could remember. It was good old-fashioned love at first sight.

She had agreed to a dinner. Over wine they found out that he was almost exactly forty years her senior. And besides her tits, she was fun to listen to.

She could also fuck the orange off a traffic cone.

They got married after a quick visit to the lawyer for a prenup that stated, should the best of intentions somehow not be enough, she would be taken care of and he would not lose enough to make him hate her, which seemed like a healthy compromise.

He didn't need any of the little blue pills to put the steel to her. When she clamped her cans together, stuck out her tongue, and licked one of her nipples, he almost ripped through his pants.

Two years in she asked for a baby. He thought about it and figured *what the fuck?* They tried. No pregnancy. She went to a doctor who specialized in correcting those kinds of women's problems. She checked out. And after two months of prodding, he had grudgingly gone to have the joystick examined. He knew what was up before the visit—an old motorcycle injury. He had been sixteen and the surgeon who had put him back together said that he might not have children. Turned out he was right; the boys just weren't swimming.

She had somehow gotten him to agree to the handsome spermcicle people. The joke had ended up being on her; instead of the Brad Pitt model she had ordered, the delivered product bore an undeniable resemblance to the Hamburglar, as if Ace himself had magically entered the very core of the child's being. Ace loved his son.

But the kid was a dolt. Yet somehow smart enough to realize that getting angry about it was a wasted effort.

He also had an unbelievably high pain threshold. Good old farm stock, Ace guessed.

Fuck Brad Pitt.

||| SIXTY-EIGHT

THEY WERE dealing with a breakfast of BLTs and NYPD travel mugs filled with the precinct's finest blend from the machine in the corner. Mother Nature had cranked the thermostat back up into the red zone and Hemingway's skin was having a hard time breathing.

Papandreou and Lincoln had come by to drop off their interview notes from a night spent running around the city, visiting Brayton's patients. After a quick rundown, they had left to get some much-earned sleep. True to habit, Papandreou had flicked the television on but left the sound off. Now, an hour later it was still flashing over Hemingway's shoulder as she put the breakfast away, wondering in some distant corner of her mind if she was having too much coffee for the baby.

Baby? There was no baby.

Not yet.

Not until she decided there was.

Keep telling yourself that, sister.

She took another bite of the sandwich.

Phelps chewed mechanically, his eyes focused on the television. She looked at her watch and figured that the local morning cycle had started, the newscaster delivering the night's mayhem with insincere gravity.

Without taking his eyes from the screen, he said, "Hemi, go home. Get some sleep." He looked ready for the trenches—fresh shaven and smelling of some not-too-bad cologne. "The world can get by without your help for a few hours."

||| SIXTY-NINE

SHE WAS sound asleep, somewhere beyond the point where a phone call or human voice could penetrate, deep in a slumber only the incessant ringing of the doorbell could shatter.

She forced an eye open. Sat up. Looked around for a robe. Yanked it on over the nightie she had slept in.

She moved slowly down the stairs, coming to the main nave of the loft. The place was a mess and it looked like Daniel still hadn't come home. Her head felt like it was too small for her brain.

The bell jingled again and she rounded the banister to the staircase. She moved past the four equestrian portraits and almost slipped on the polished wood. She hitched the robe a little tighter. Opened the door.

She saw a smile. She smiled back. Something came at her. She never registered the blade whistling through her throat but she did feel the giddy high.

She saw her own blood spurt across the doorway.

Then she saw nothing at all.

III SEVENTY

PHELPS WAS still engrossed in the news. He had weathered so many media shit storms that he no longer took it personally. He thought most of the people on television were idiots anyway and he watched with the sound off, reading the chyron and the headlines. More than enough to get the gist of what they were saying.

He was no longer a young lion but he hadn't been hit by age as hard as a lot of his contemporaries. Many of them had opted out of active street duty years ago, deciding to spend the tail end of their careers perfecting their Microsoft Office skills. He had never felt the need to slow down. He liked what he did, was good at it, and rarely took his work home with him at night. Why fix what ain't broken?

Something flashed across the top of the screen and the announcer stared into the camera, looking graver than she had a second ago. They cut to a remote camera—a live report from the West Side.

The camera captured a body lying in a doorway, legs inside, torso, arms and head flopped out onto the limestone landing. There was a massive jet of what could only be blood sprayed across the white Sheetrock inside the entrance. The head was twisted on sideways, buried in a mess of black hair. A paramedic stooped and covered the body with a sheet.

Phelps recognized the door. He stood up, knocking his chair over.

Across the bottom of the screen the chyron read: *Detective Alexandra Hemingway of the NYPD murdered at her home.*

III SEVENTY-ONE

PHELPS STARED at the television for a moment, mouth open, disbelief swirling around in his head like an angry weather system. "Hemi," he said slowly.

Hemingway looked up from her sandwich. The tremor of wrongness in his voice made her stop chewing.

"I think something very bad has happened."

She came around to his side of the conference table and looked up, eyes on the screen for a second—maybe two—before she said, "Oh, Jesus," and was gone.

Phelps grabbed his holster and ran after her.

||| SEVENTY-TWO

THE STREETS had not yet clogged up with the morning rush hour and Hemingway punched the big truck around the corner in a smoking drift that sounded like an angry *Tyrannosaurus rex*. The lights thumped and the sirens screeched and she had her foot to the floor as they drifted west, the city's architecture sliding sideways across the windshield.

Phelps was belted in, one hand on the holy shit handle, the other on the center console to keep him from slamming back and forth as she screeched through the corners and punched to the red line on the straightaways. A cruiser closed up their path; it had started out in the lead to clear the way but she had quickly grown tired of sitting behind it and had barreled past after two blocks.

Phelps hadn't so much as flinched. But he swore.

The ride usually took about twenty minutes at night, forty in traffic. Hemingway made it in seven.

They rounded the final corner in a swinging arc of smoke that scattered the reporters lined up at the edge of the road. She didn't slow, but hammered up the middle of the street, skidding to a stop a foot from the side door of the cruiser that blocked the road.

She ran through the tape, past the uniformed officer, through two more cops who tried to stop her, and pushed aside the EMT men crouching in her doorway. One tumbled back and fell down the stairs.

There was a white plastic sheet over the body that lay across her threshold. One of the EMT guys started back up the steps but Phelps stopped him.

Hemingway stood there, looking down at the sheet. The world went prismatic as tears filled her eyes. She closed them and the tears shook loose. She crouched down, reached out, and wrapped her fingers around the sheet.

There was nothing else in her focus except her fear.

She needed to see. Needed to know. And then she could fall apart.

She needed him. Loved him. He had been taken by a killer who enjoyed disassembling little boys.

Another bad man who wouldn't leave her alone.

She tightened her grip. The plastic was warm and humid, and her hand shook so badly that the sheet vibrated with her touch.

A big shadow that could only be Phelps blocked out the sun. She felt a hand on her shoulder.

Hemingway pulled the sheet back, and looked down at the twisted black blood-spattered grimace on her sister's face.

ⅠⅠⅠ SEVENTY-THREE

PHELPS LED her to a cruiser where she took up position leaning against the grill. He pushed a cup of coffee into her hand and she stared at it for a moment as she tried to figure out what had happened. The initial fear and disbelief were replaced by an eerie sense of calm that she knew was a form of shock that would eventually come out in one big scream.

She had her back to the news cameras parked at the end of the block. She heard Phelps go back to the line, talk to the cops on the scene. He dipped his head into the ambulance. There was a commotion at the edge of her vision.

Phelps headed back and stood in front of her, shielding her from the cameras. "Okay. Look at me. I am going to tell you something and you have to act like I haven't said anything because it will be all over the news and you don't want this guy knowing any more about your personal life." He stepped in. "Okay?"

She was back in the present, back to the hot hood of the car and the too-warm coffee in her hand, and the sun already cooking the city. "What?"

He squared his shoulders. "Daniel's fine. He's the one who found her."

She stood up, searched over his shoulder. "Where?"

Phelps reached out, steadied her with a hand on each shoulder. "We walk over nice and slow. What would that film asshole you love so much say?"

"Bitch, be cool."

"Yeah, well, some people got no class."

"Where is he?" A tinge of hysteria had crept into her voice and she took a breath, willing the panic inside her to shrink.

"He's in the ambulance. He's fine but he's in shock."

She headed around Phelps, toward the ambulance. She was aware that the cameras were there but she was back in cop mode now. Long stride, hand on sidearm, her eyes hidden by her aviators.

Daniel was sitting on the edge of a stretcher, his head in his hands—just a skinny guy with long hair and too many holes in his jeans for a forty-five-year-old. There were bloody patches on his chest where he had wiped his hands. His camera bag sat on the floor beside him, the strap smeared with blood.

Until that second she forgot that he had gone out last night. Iggy, wasn't it?

Hemingway snapped her fingers at the tech and when his boots hit the street she climbed in and pulled the door closed behind her. She crouched in front of him, and the grip of her pistol clinked on the frame of the stretcher behind her.

Daniel looked up at her. He didn't smile, nod or acknowledge that he had even seen her. But he began talking, very matter-of-fact, a little too fast. "I was a few seconds late getting to her. Fifteen. Maybe twenty. I stopped at the diner to get a coffee. Came down the street. Passed some schoolkids. Guy walking his dog. When I got there she was still bleeding. Blood pissing out all over the place." Their eyes connected and they knew one another again. "I'm so fucking sorry, Allie. I tried, I really did."

The tears filled her eyes. She took a breath, pushed them back. Then unfolded from her crouch and sat down beside him. She put her arm around his shoulder. All she could think was had he been there, she might have lost him, too.

"I called nine-one-one. I wanted to call you but I couldn't remember your number. I tried to find it in my contacts but my hands were shaking so hard I dropped my fucking phone. And all of a sudden the police were here. And now you're here and I don't know what I saw but I want to unsee it."

"Daniel, it'll be fine. It's the adrenaline in your system. You're in shock. We'll get you some shots; B12 will help. You'll start shaking in a few minutes."

"In a few minutes?" He held up his hand—it was vibrating as if it were plugged into a hummingbird's central nervous system.

"You're going to be okay."

"Okay? Your sister is out there spilled all over our doorway—oh, sorry, *your* doorway—and you tell me it's going to be okay? No, Alexandra, it's not going to be okay. This is so fucking far from okay that it's in another language. Your sister is dead. I should have been here. You should have been here. How can we keep doing this? We never see each other. We never . . . Ah, fuck it." And he stopped, stiffened and slid into himself.

Phelps opened the door, stuck his head inside. "The medical examiner's people just showed up. And your sister has to leave." He jerked his head in the general direction of the cameras. "The less we give those assholes, the better."

Hemingway stood up, putting her hand on Daniel's shoulder. She gave it a squeeze. "Tell them what you saw, then we'll get you into a shower and bed."

Daniel waved her away. "Leave me alone."

She stopped to say something and then realized that she had nothing to offer. "I'll be outside if you need me."

But Daniel's head was back in his hands.

Hemingway and Phelps took up perch on the front bumper of the ambulance as the people who tended to these things came and went. They recorded, filmed, measured, black-lighted, dusted, collected, catalogued, and conversed.

It was slow in coming, but when it hit her it didn't feel all that different than the time she had been shot. There was that same weird burning in her chest, as if the machinery had stopped working, but none of the noise.

She had to call her folks. To tell them what had happened to their daughter. And for the second time in their lives, they would have to bury a child.

Hemingway pulled out her phone and stared at it for a while, trying to figure out how to handle this. It came alive in her hands, lit up with her parents' number in East Hampton; the summer cocktail circuit must have started.

She stared at it for one ring.

Two.

Then three.

Phelps pointed at her phone. "It's sooner or later, kiddo."

She accepted the call, took a deep breath, and pressed it to her ear. "Hemingway here." It was a lousy save, one that would only buy her a few seconds.

"Allie! We saw the news and we were so worried. Mom said it was some kind of mistake but I wasn't so sure. You know how I get. It's—"

Her father was yammering on, something that went against his Anglican poise. "Dad?"

"—a father thing. If you ever have children, then you'll know what I'm talk—"

"*Dad*?" A little louder.

And he stopped. "What?"

"Dad, it's Amy." She felt her voice waver just a little, but to a parent's ears it was enough.

There was a long pause. "Is she all right?"

"I'm sorry." And with that she held the phone out to Phelps.

They sometimes did this for one another, took up the slack. When Ernie, Phelps's brother, had lapsed into a coma after a fall, she had been the one to deliver the decision to not continue with mechanical assistance; Jon just couldn't say the words. At the time she hadn't understood what it meant to him. She did now. Some things have to be said to—and for—the people you love when they can't express themselves.

As he took the phone from her hands, her chest tightened. She leaned over and took a deep breath, grateful for the big sunglasses.

III SEVENTY-FOUR

PHELPS KEPT the front end of the Suburban at a single car length from the back bumper of the van carrying Amy's body to the morgue. On their left, the East River flashed between the traffic and the concrete as they headed south on the FDR.

Hemingway rode shotgun, her thoughts slowly and steadily creeping toward anger. Amy had died, and even though she could keep herself from crying, she couldn't keep the tears from forming. This was not allowed to derail her. Because that's what that prick out there wanted: for her to go away.

She would not let that happen.

No.

Fucking.

Way.

They already had him, they just couldn't see it. He was close, buried somewhere in the lives of these children. Now they knew it wasn't Brayton. But it was someone connected to him. They might already have spoken to him. Interviewed him. Shook his hand.

In that spooky way Phelps had of reading her thoughts,

he asked, "You gotta be all in or you gotta be all out. There ain't no middle position on this one, kiddo."

"We have him, Jon. Our perp is buried somewhere in the files and medical reports, in the hundreds of names we're looking into, in the way he's killed these people, and in the way I've pissed him off. I'm in. Until it's done."

Phelps pulled back as the van ahead took a tight right off FDR Drive, heading for home, the office of the underworld. "There's Amy's funeral, which means your parents. Daniel will need a little maintenance. And you got other shit on your plate, too."

Couldn't forget the baby.

She thought back to the ambulance, to the shell-shocked fear in Daniel's eyes. This had been his first real peek into her other life. It might have been too much. This luck had followed since forever, some kind of negative space in the universe that sucked in and destroyed the people she loved the most. Two sisters now. Mank. And everyone they had lost since Tyler Rochester had been found hugging a bridge piling in the East River.

"Your dance card's kinda full."

"Either my dance card's full, or I have a lot on my plate. It can't be both," she said, mimicking his tone in Deacon's driveway yesterday. "Do you really believe that?"

He shrugged. "Not really. No."

"Then stop being a prick. We go to the morgue. Then we go back to the office and finish up with the Brayton/Selmer list. Someone out there knows our ghost. We have a lot of people to visit."

"You need to sleep."

"Not as much as I need to find this guy."

III SEVENTY-FIVE

THEY STARTED with Doris Borenstein. She was the first of the morning and she had sandwiched them in between her beautician and her spiritual advisor, code words for plastic surgeon and psychiatrist.

A disembodied electronic voice asked them to hold their identification up to the camera. The man who let them in was ten percent larger than Phelps in every conceivable measurement and had a head that fit his shoulders like a five-gallon bucket slapped onto a snowman. He had pink eyes and white hair, a perfect albino. He introduced himself as Elio.

Doris Borenstein was a nervous woman. She was coiffed and perfect and looked like she had stepped out of the early seventies in a pair of bell-bottom linen trousers, a tailored button-down and a pair of sunglasses that would have done nicely as welding goggles. Her skin also looked three sizes too small for her skeleton.

Everything was carefully chosen and beautifully lit, including Doris Borenstein, who sat under a softened light that did a good job of masking her wrinkles. Elio hung back, mute, arms loose by his side. There was a large-caliber automatic in his belt that he didn't bother to hide.

"I apologize that I couldn't meet you later but my advisor only has one-hour slots available. Why, exactly, are you here?" she asked, hand held to her chest.

"First off, does your companion over there have a carry permit? I do not enjoy being uncomfortable."

Mrs. Borenstein smiled. It was an expression that belonged on a spider. "Elio is licensed to carry a concealed sidearm in nineteen states, branching out from his New York resident carry card. He has been in my employ for fourteen years."

Hemingway nodded but that didn't make her feel any more comfortable about the big sonofabitch standing there with a chrome Desert Eagle sticking out of his waistband.

"You spoke with Detectives Lincoln and Papandreou. Did they tell you that Dr. Selmer was murdered yesterday afternoon?"

"I heard. We are not required to like everyone we meet. I have a very biased opinion of anyone connected with that clinic. Especially considering what your two colleagues told me about Dr. Brayton's hit list. Incidentally, have you found him yet?" She looked from Hemingway to Phelps, then back to Hemingway.

"Dr. Brayton is dead. He committed suicide a few months back."

"Who says the police never bring good news?" Mrs. Borenstein smiled. "Now what, specifically, can I do for you?"

Hemingway looked up at Elio but spoke to Doris Borenstein. She didn't bother to ask if she wanted some privacy; Lincoln had underlined that she had insisted Elio stay in the room during questioning.

Hemingway chose her first question carefully, avoiding the subject of the girls. "Do you know anything that might help us? About the clinic; your son's siblings; Dr. Brayton—"

"—That reptile, Fenton?" Borenstein interrupted.

Hemingway waited.

"I am not a stupid woman. I love my son, he is a remarkable child. But that clinic misrepresented the package I purchased. Marjorie Fenton is not concerned with patient care, she is concerned with making money. She is a greedy little rug merchant and yes—I can't say that I'd be all that broken up if someone killed her as well. And that is not a threat of any kind—just wishful thinking."

"Please tell us about your son, Solomon."

At that she changed poses. "Solomon is a singer. Opera. The voice of an angel. If anyone ever took him," she turned her head and looked up at Elio, "I'd kill them and everyone they ever loved."

———

When they were back in the street, Phelps said, "That woman is trying to be Alexis Carrington."

Hemingway smiled and got in behind the wheel. "She's just bored."

Before pulling out into traffic she checked the patient list.

One down.

A million to go.

SEVENTY-SIX

MARY ZRBINSKI attended to the general needs of the Atchison household. Her tasks ranged from picking up dry cleaning to arranging lifts to the airport. She made sure the cook had a well-stocked kitchen for the days he came in, and she made sure that William made his appointments. The Atchisons were decent people.

It was morning, the one day she came in at 10 a.m. as opposed to 7 a.m. She noticed that the black carriage lamps were still on as she came up the street. She put her key in the lock, pushed the door in, and stepped inside.

She closed the door and the stink hit her. What was that? She took a step and her feet went out from under her, wishboning her legs in a clumsy almost split that tore her skirt. Her head hit the hardwood and she lay there for a second.

The house was unusually quiet.

She pushed herself up and her hand slipped. The sensation of oil seeping through her clothes cooled her skin.

She fought to a sitting position.

Mrs. Atchison lay against the wall a few feet away. Blood was everywhere.

WHEN HEMINGWAY and Phelps pulled up to the Atchison house, a uniformed officer met them at the curb. A woman sat in the back of his cruiser, wrapped in a kit blanket, sobbing. The other officer squatted by the open door, talking to her.

"Dispatch said two? One a kid?" Phelps asked.

The Atchison house was on their list—they had been on the way here yesterday when Hemingway had received the text from Tyler Rochester's phone. She wondered if it was a coincidence. Either way, it was disturbing.

The cop nodded. "Maid came in for the day. Walked in and found the lady of the house at the front door. Called nine-one-one and we responded. Did a walk-through." He swallowed. "The kid's upstairs in the tub."

"You guys touch anything?"

The cop shook his head and swallowed again. "No light switches. Nothing."

Hemingway and Phelps headed into the house.

Mrs. Atchison was sprawled out on the floor. There were slip marks through the pudding-like scab, the sloppy hand-prints and thrash marks where the housekeeper had fallen.

The smell was so bad they had to breathe through their mouths.

They had their service pieces out; they had been at this too long to trust anyone else's work.

They moved around the stagnant puddle of Mrs. Atchison's blood, almost resorting to rock-climbing moves on the paneling to step over the mess on the floor. It seemed impossible that all this blood had fit into one person's body.

The ground floor was clear. As was the basement—a well-stocked wine cellar.

They moved up the stairs in file, Hemingway point.

Another wave of death hit them, this one mixed with the scent of lavender. They cleared the floor from front to back, quickly working their way to the bathroom. The door was ajar and a bright slash of light spilled out across the hallway.

They paused at the door, nodded a final *Are you ready?* to one another, then Hemingway reached out and pushed it in with the nose of her revolver.

Phelps staggered back and coughed, putting his hand to his mouth.

Hemingway stood in the doorway. There was no way to equate the mess she saw with a living, breathing child.

The boy lay in the bathtub, head back, tear streaks through the blood that spattered his face. His ribs were spread wide and he looked like a bloody cryptid insect in the process of becoming something else—his lungs had been lifted out and flopped back over his shoulders where they hung like scabbed bloated wings that had not yet formed. The rest of his internal organs were gone.

III SEVENTY-EIGHT

THEY SENT the Atchison boy off to the stainless steel table in Dr. Marcus's lab where he'd be reduced to evidence. The last two bodies should have given up more than the first two; they hadn't been scrubbed clean by the river.

Yet they were still shy on trace evidence. And completely lacking in suspects.

Something was bound to turn up; it was physically impossible for a person to enter a room and not leave a little of themselves behind. Hemingway and Phelps were becoming almost superstitious about this one, though: the only thing that denoted his passing were the dead children.

They had more interviews to do. New information to sift through. An ever-widening gene pool of potential killers; it felt like half the population of Manhattan was under suspicion.

Marcus had already signed out the autopsy reports on Brayton's eight dead girls. And then he had been interrupted with Hemingway's sister and William Atchison. One step forward, two steps back.

But Papandreou and Lincoln were out hunting down

whatever they could on the girls—half sisters in an equation no one understood.

Hemingway and Phelps still had patients to speak to. Parents to warn.

But how did you warn someone about this? You couldn't. Not really. There was no way to look the parents in the eye and tell them about bloody butterfly boy. That would be cruel. Hell, it would be more than cruel; it would be sadistic. But they needed to know their kids were in danger.

Hemingway was frustrated. "So he kills all of the female children first. Then he goes after the boys. Whoever is doing this had the information in Brayton's files before the first girl died. Before they took Selmer's bag out of the backseat of his car. It's someone who had access to Brayton's files at some point."

"Who has legal access to a doctor's files?" Phelps wondered aloud.

"Any of the nurses at the clinic. Receptionist. Cleaning staff. IT people. Maintenance. Movers. Shredding service. Delivery people. There are a thousand ways to get to a doctor's files if you're not interested in the legality of the situation. But everyone in the clinic—from the cleaning people to the guy who used to deliver the sandwiches at lunch to the coffee machine repair people—had been cleared. One guy with a twenty-year-old DUI and one with a domestic violence arrest—no conviction. Three people with parking violation problems. No one fits this."

At that Phelps looked over at her. "Hemi, when we find this guy, he's just gonna be some bum we've never heard of and no one ever paid attention to."

She wasn't so sure.

THE SKY had knitted over again in a gray foil, as if the storms of yesterday had come back to tease the city with the promise of rain. But the heat and humidity held on with sticky fingers and if Hemingway didn't get a shower soon, her blouse could be used as a biological weapon.

She hoped that the weather would stay ugly and they could forget about the final track-and-field day at Randall's Island. The place seemed tied to everything that had happened so far, from Deacon using it as a spectator and drug-buying hangout, to all the schools of the dead children using it as their physical education grounds.

Phelps's voice brought her back to the present. "There. Up ahead on the left. Green awning."

She glanced in her mirror, then over her shoulder, and cut across three lanes, pulling the truck into the fifteen-minute loading zone in front of the Fifth Avenue apartment.

After what felt like their hundredth ride of the day in a lushly appointed elevator, the apartment door was opened by a small woman in a perfectly tailored Chanel suit. She introduced herself as Carmen, said she was the Morgans' personal assistant, and that she would be happy to take their drinks request.

They thanked Carmen, told her that coffee would be fine and that they had very little time.

Lincoln hadn't been far off with his Keith Richards bedroom crack—the place looked like Donald Trump's with less restraint. Everything was animal print, gold leaf, and sparkled.

Carmen led them through a wall of floor-to-ceiling bronze-framed doors, out onto a stone terrace that wrapped around the corner of the building. The haze of Manhattan spread out like the world's largest canvas—the Morgans owned at least half of the top floor. They rounded the corner and Mr. and Mrs. Morgan were at a wrought iron table, wearing matching robes and having breakfast even though it was coming up on eleven o'clock.

"Mr. and Mrs. Morgan, I'm Detective Alexandra Hemingway. This is my partner, Detective Jon Phelps. Thank you for making the time to see us."

Everything about Mr. Morgan said self-made. He was a heavyset man who sported a pair of floral swim trunks and a diamond-encrusted Rolex that pinched his pink wrist. He stood up and shook hands. When he was standing he wasn't much taller than when he was sitting. "Glad to do it, detectives. Glad to do it. Call me Ace. The little lady's Cindy."

Mrs. Morgan was in her thirties and had the tight toned body of a gym bunny. Her skin was tanned the color of maple syrup and her blond locks were the best weaves that Hemingway had seen outside of *Charlie's Angels*. She giggled when she shook hands, and a good sixty carats of stones jingled on her wrist in a coil of tennis bracelets. Every movement she made seemed to be done with the intention of jiggling her breasts and it was obvious that even the Iron Giant had a hard time keeping his eyes off of them.

"You guys want some food? Bacon's flown in from Texas—double smoked. And we got some great cheese—smells like turds—but it's the best there is."

Phelps shook his head and gestured to Hemingway. "Detective Hemingway, are you hungry?"

She ignored him. "Thanks. No."

"Well, it's there if you change your mind. What's this shit with the kid?" Ace asked, and went back to eating.

The table was set with gold-plated flatware and water lilies floated in a low crystal bowl shaped like a woman's face. There were bagels and rolls and an assortment of fruit and cheeses that seemed to be there purely for presentation; Ace's attention was nailed to a plate piled high with bacon. A big cigar smoldered in an ashtray at the edge of the table.

Phelps smiled. It seemed like the Morgans were his kind of people. "As we went over on the phone, the boys who have been killed share the same biological father as your son. We think that Miles might be in danger."

At that Ace threw his head back and guffawed. "Shit, you haven't met little Miles." Mr. Morgan reached over and picked up his wife's cell phone in the rhinestone case on the table. He tapped the screen and said, "Oh Jesus fucking Christ, Cindy, what's with this password bullshit? I can't ever find my phone and you know I don't give a sweet flying fuck if you have a boyfriend just as long as he ain't got some disease that I can catch from your coochy-poochy. What's the fucking password?"

Cindy's nose crinkled up. "Don't swear so much, Daddy. It's two-two-two-two."

Ace smiled. "Sure you can remember that?" He punched it in.

"I think so."

A man in a black suit and tie showed up carrying a silver

service of coffee. He laid it down on an iron server and filled two cups for the detectives. Then he disappeared as silently as he had come.

Ace tapped around on the screen and returned the phone to the table. "Just don't sleep with any Democrats—I hate those fucking pussies. Fuck a real man, for Chrissake."

"Yes, Daddy," she said, and went back to picking at her low-fat cottage cheese.

Ace turned back to Phelps who had lost the look of comfort from a few minutes earlier. "All right, so we disagree that my son's in danger. I texted him—he should be here in a minute. What next?"

"Mr. Morgan—"

"Ace! I told you to call me Ace!"

"Ace. Yeah. Sure. We'll need a list of anyone your son knows—everyone from his hairdresser to—"

"Barber," Ace interrupted. "My kid does not go to a hairdresser, detective. He ain't no fag."

"We'd be grateful for a list of everyone in his life: his teachers; tutors; anyone who drives him around; friends he sees on a regular basis; parents of friends where he does sleepovers or playdates; stores you take him to; tradespeople you may have had in the house."

"Goin' back how far?"

"Three years would be good. Can you think of anyone who seems odd or suspicious?"

"All of her friends," Ace said, nodding at his wife. "They're a bunch of freaks."

Cindy slapped him on the arm. "Don't be mean, Daddy. You like Jezebel."

At that Ace nodded with the corners of his mouth turned down. "You got a point. I do like her." And he winked at Phelps.

Hemingway was about to stand up, to tell Phelps that they had to leave, when a little boy appeared at the edge of the table. He had come silently up on them and was standing there, arms crossed, staring at Ace. "You texted me, Father?"

She had yet to see one of Selmer's boys alive. Lincoln's comment about him being a goof was pushing it, but it was obvious that the kid wasn't like the other children on the list. He was heavy, stood with his mouth open, and had a dull expression on his face. Other than the brown hair and eyes, he didn't look like he had anything to do with Dr. Brayton's *Boys of Brazil* program.

Ace put a hand on the boy's shoulder. "This is Detective Phelps and his partner, Detective Hemingway."

The boy turned and extended his hand, first to Phelps, then to Hemingway. "Miles Morgan, a pleasure to meet you both." He had a good handshake but looked like he would rather be somewhere else.

Ace went on. "They tell me that there's a bad man out there running around killing little kids and that you might be in danger. Does that frighten you, son?"

The boy shook his head.

"And why not?"

With the speed of an adder, Miles Morgan's hand flashed up and he had a knife to Phelps's throat. It was an airframe knife with a black carbon blade that dented Phelps's skin. The boy backed up, flicked his wrist, and the knife was gone. "Though I walk through the valley of the Shadow of Death, I fear no evil because I am the meanest motherfucker in the valley, sir."

Phelps stared at the child.

Hemingway's hand was on her pistol. "Don't you ever draw a weapon on a police officer, Miles."

Miles looked her in the eyes. "I was answering his question."

"I don't care. You do that to a police officer and you can end up dead."

The boy looked over at his father, searching for some kind of qualifier to Hemingway's lesson.

"She might have a point, son."

And with that the boy smiled. "Is that all?"

"You ever get into any kind of trouble at school, Miles? Fighting?" she asked, looking at the bandage over his nose, his two black eyes.

"Fighting isn't trouble. Fighting's fun."

After Miles had walked away, Ace threw a few more strips of bacon down his throat, then opened up his hands. "When you want that list?"

Hemingway pulled out her three-by-five and a pen. "We can go over it right now. If you think of anything later, we can add it."

Ace eyed her for a second. "You know, you're pretty hot for a cop."

At that, Mrs. Morgan dropped her head and stared over the top of her sunglasses. She nodded. "You are."

Hemingway didn't bother smiling. "I get that a lot."

THEY SPENT the rest of the morning and all of the afternoon running down the balance of Brayton's patients. The ones who had moved away were interviewed on the phone and local PDs were sent out to do a formal report—if Tanya Everett hadn't been safe in Greece, this guy could go anywhere, even if the brunt of his focus seemed to be aimed on New York right now. Lots of new information came their way. More teachers. More tutors and drivers and butlers. More dead ends.

The last patient they saw was Dr. Neal Winslow, father of ten-year-old Benjamin. Benjamin was the oldest of Brayton's children by five days, and by all reports an exceptional child.

Dr. Winslow and his son lived in the Dakota facing Central Park. Signing in—even for the two detectives—was like going through airport security on Kentucky Derby weekend.

In the ride up in the elevator, a little old lady cradling a Pomeranian in one arm and a crocodile bag in the other eyed the two detectives warily, as if they might try to squeegee her dog. She got out on the third floor. They rode on to the seventh.

When they stepped out of the elevator Phelps looked around and whistled, taking in the unique architecture. "Who designed this place, Gomez Addams?"

Hemingway had been in the building before; she had dated a boy whose parents lived here back when she was in college—still did, as far as she knew—and the place hadn't changed at all. She rang the bell.

A thin man in a good English suit answered the door. He could have passed for a butler in an old Lon Chaney film. He stood in the doorway, leaning slightly forward as if he were caught in the midst of a bow. This had to be Dr. Winslow.

"I am Detective Alexandra Hemingway and this is my partner, Detective Jon Phelps. We called you earlier."

"Yes, you did," the man said. After a moment of what appeared to be indecision, he said, "Please come in."

As Phelps stepped over the threshold his mouth fell open. The apartment looked like a professionally curated museum. A pair of taxidermied birds the size of German shepherds flanked the door, glass eyeballs focused on infinity. And instead of the usual center table prescribed by most decorators, the entry was taken up with an Edwardian display case where six massive birds sat regally—and permanently—watching the door with imposed disinterest. They looked like a race of ancient penguins bred for fighting. Phelps paused in front of the case and it was obvious that he was wondering just what the hell he was looking at.

"*Pinguinus impennis*—the Great Auk," Dr. Winslow said lovingly. "The largest collection on the planet. Under one roof, at any extent. Declared extinct in 1844 but with unverified sightings up until 1852. Overpredated by man, of course."

He closed the door and walked past them, as if he had somewhere else to be. He moved deeper into the apartment.

The two detectives followed but Hemingway had a hard time not stopping to admire the birds that were everywhere.

Unusual taxidermied specimens filled most of the available space but somehow it didn't feel cluttered; the display cases were tastefully arranged as if at a good gallery, and the effect was mesmerizing. The hallway was lined with custom-made bronze and iron shelving filled with books on ornithology, mostly large leather-bound volumes.

On one of the shelves sat a common dove in a display case, a stained baseball beside it under the glass. The brass plaque read: MARCH 24TH, 2001—THROWN BY RANDY JOHNSON OF THE ARIZONA DIAMONDBACKS. THE ONLY FASTBALL TO KILL A BIRD. The piece hinted at a sense of humor lacking in the rest of the space.

They passed a King Island Emu, an ivory label stating that it was the last known member of its species—it had died in Paris in 1822. Most of the cases had similar labels, either LAST KNOWN OF ITS SPECIES or the more chilling, ONLY KNOWN OF ITS SPECIES, POSSIBLY A SUBSPECIES OR HYBRID. There was education and dedication behind the collection; this was a major passion that had taken generations to build.

There were none of the hand-tinted Audubon prints Hemingway expected. Instead, the walls were decorated with antique oil paintings of birds in atypical poses—cockfights and still lifes of hunting trophies. They passed a large canvas in a rocaille frame that depicted a sideboard piled high with dead pheasants. As they moved by, Phelps's body language became less fluid and Hemingway recognized the unease—this was not his kind of place.

A few of the smaller walls were decorated with framed photographs and Hemingway paused in front of a color print depicting a great blue heron with a frog in its beak, a duck decoy behind it, sun-bleached and weed-covered, riding the swirl between two rocks.

Dr. Winslow brought them to the living room, tastefully decorated with period Arts and Crafts furniture. The room was surprisingly dark for a building where properties started at twenty million a crack and she remembered that back in college she had been surprised that a place with such high ceilings could have such little ambient light.

A pair of telescopes stood at the window pointed out at the park—no doubt for bird-watching—one seemed to be tailored for a child. Several digital SLRs sat on a small table beside the telescopes, a collection of telephoto lenses neatly arranged like the spires of a small city. Like Daniel, Dr. Winslow was a Nikon man.

He gestured to two big Morris chairs and said, "How may I help you?"

Hemingway liked reducing people to stereotypes—it had helped her growing up and it was an invaluable skill as a detective; often, generalities were all there was to go on. Winslow had the air of a trust funder who had chosen the cloistered world of academia because it filled out the job requirement imposed by a certain kind of upbringing—old money that said a man had to fill his time with work. And with a passion as evident as his, it was easy to see that he wasn't bored.

"Dr. Winslow, first off we appreciate your taking the time to see us. We want to go over what you discussed with Detectives Lincoln and Papandreou yesterday."

The man nodded and closed his eyes. Hemingway had a hard time telling if the expression that came over his face was one of sadness or of being inconvenienced.

Hemingway glanced at her notes. "Did you suspect that Benjamin might not be as . . . unique as you had been promised?"

Dr. Winslow shook his head. "My wife handled the details. I had no expectations one way or another. Biology," he said, waving his hand through the air, gesturing to the dozens of cased birds, "has its limitations."

"Were you upset when you found out?"

Dr. Winslow thought about the question for a moment. "Detectives, when I was a child my mother purchased a dog. She bought it from the finest breeder in the country—a wonderful little whippet named Grosvenor. Around Grosvenor's first birthday he developed some health issues—health issues my mother had been told he would not have. The dog, it appeared, was guaranteed. The breeder said he would be happy to take Grosvenor back. He'd put the dog down and replace him with a pup from the newest litter. But my mother already loved that dog. Some things cannot be undone."

Hemingway found the comparison distasteful. "So you weren't upset?"

"I don't care how Benjamin came into my life, only that he has."

Winslow was one of two single fathers on the list. "Where is Benjamin now?" she asked.

"At school, of course."

"Did you think about keeping him home?"

He stared at her. "Keep Benjamin from school? No."

Hemingway thought about William Atchison cracked open in his tub. If Dr. Winslow had seen that, little Benjamin wouldn't be going anywhere until he was fifty. "You know about the boys who have been murdered in the past few days?" Winslow didn't look like the kind of guy who spent a lot of time in front of the television.

He nodded in that weird blinky fashion again and it made Hemingway uncomfortable.

"The link between the five victims is the donor—the same one as Benjamin's."

Winslow didn't say anything, he just stared at her as if awaiting the good news part of the conversation.

She continued. "We believe the killer may have had access to your file sometime in the past. We don't know how or when but it's one of the possibilities we are examining. Someone knows these boys share a father. We just don't know how."

At this he lifted his head, straightened his back as much as he could, and peered at her from under bushy eyebrows. "What about the opera invitation?"

"What opera invitation?"

He stood up and lifted a handsomely framed photograph from an oak sideboard, handing it to Hemingway. "Benjamin and I went in matching tuxedos. We had a lovely evening. We had punch and the music was wonderful." He sounded happy, childlike.

"When was this?"

Dr. Winslow picked up his iPad and clicked through his e-mail. Then he handed the tablet to Hemingway. "That's the invitation," he said. "May twelfth."

Hemingway looked at it. It was an invitation to an evening at the opera for friends of the clinic. It congratulated them on a happy nine years.

"I don't understand," she said.

"Instead of blind carbon copying everyone's e-mail address, they cc'd them. Everyone who was to get a nine-year invitation was probably on that e-mail list. Here, let me show you." He reached over and clicked on the address.

A list of e-mail addresses appeared. She read through

them, ignoring the cutesy e-mail handles and focusing on those with real names—she recognized at least thirty from Brayton's patients. The e-mail addresses for the Rochesters, Grants, and Simmonses were on the list.

She looked up at Phelps. Someone at the clinic had made a mistake and sent this out to all of Dr. Brayton's children. She counted the addresses—there were sixty-seven of them.

They had their hunting list.

Why hadn't anyone told her about this?

"Can you print this up?" she asked Dr. Winslow. "And please forward it to me—there might be something hidden in the metadata. You're not obliged to do so—I would need a court order to make you hand it over—but you would save us some time. It's your call."

Dr. Winslow waved it away. "Not a problem." He tapped in a command and walked out of his room, coming back in thirty seconds with a crisp full-color invitation printed on glossy paper. Then he handed the iPad to Hemingway. "Please forward it to yourself."

"Who sent the invitation?" Phelps asked.

Hemingway held up the tablet, touched her fingers to the screen, and magnified the text.

The e-mail had come from Marjorie Fenton.

HEMINGWAY CALLED CNN and the news teams descended on the clinic with a well-coiffed vengeance; all that was missing was the Reverend Samuel Parris, a bullhorn, and a gallows. Papandreou and Lincoln were across the street, Papandreou working on a hot dog while Lincoln cautiously sucked a Rocket Pop in a stooped over pose so he wouldn't drip red, white, and blue all over his shirt. When Hemingway pulled up in the Suburban, Papandreou chucked the last of the dog down and Lincoln tossed his Popsicle in the trash.

Hemingway plowed her way through the gauntlet of camera flashes, halogen lighting, and rhetorical questions. She yanked the door open and stepped into the skating-rink cold of the clinic. There wasn't a patient in sight.

Director Fenton was behind the receptionist's desk with her two security men, a troop of blue-suited lawyers behind her—they looked like Custer's boys just before the shit went down.

"Detectives," Fenton said as she checked her watch, "as of four minutes ago, the Park Avenue Clinic initiated bankruptcy proceedings. We have willfully placed a significant portion of our capital in escrow to go toward possible resti-tutions." The statement was practiced and vague.

"Mrs. Fenton, may we speak with you in private?"

Fenton's eyes twitched in their sockets and her mouth went flat, and for a second it looked like her operating system had crashed. Then her mouth opened very slowly and she said, "Yes, of course."

They followed her to the subterranean boardroom and Hemingway noticed that the artwork was gone; empty nails stuck out of the walls at every turn. Papandreou and Lincoln waited in the hallway with Fenton's legal counsel while Hem-ingway and Phelps talked to the woman. Fenton dropped into a chair and Hemingway perched herself on the edge of the table. Phelps leaned against the door, arms crossed, the Iron Giant at rest. Or waiting for an attack command.

"Mrs. Fenton, since I left here last time we have learned that Dr. Brayton has killed himself and you held an anniver-sary celebration last year for the patients."

Fenton just stared at her.

Hemingway's knuckles tightened on the edge of the desk and Fenton looked down at them, as if realizing for the first time that they were alone.

"If we had known about Brayton, we wouldn't have wasted valuable resources looking for him. And if you had told us about the opera, and that almost all of your patients had been there together, we might have been able to warn them. Two more children might be alive." And with that, Hemingway handed Fenton a photograph of the cryptid child from the bathtub.

The director looked at it for a second, then quickly turned away. Her jaw moved in its mounts and for a second it looked like she might gag.

"That's William Atchison. He was at the opera that night."

She stabbed another photograph into Fenton's hand, this one of the Simmons boy on the ferry. "And that's another patient of Dr. Brayton's—Zachary Simmons. He was at the opera as well." She followed these with the color copy of the invitation that Dr. Winslow had printed up for her. "You should have told me about this the first time I sat down with you." She wanted to knock this woman around.

At that Fenton held up a folder. Hemingway opened it. It was a clipping from the Style section of the *Times*, dated May 13 of last year. It was a photo taken in front of the Met, Dr. Brayton exiting a limousine. In front of him was a family, a little brown-haired boy in their midst. There was another to his left, and two more in the background. At first Hemingway thought you'd have to be blind to miss the similarity between the children but quickly realized that was what these women had ordered—what they had expected: handsome little men to be.

Fenton began to speak, and all the bite , all the swagger, had left her voice. She sounded tired. "I knew right there. At the opera. It was obvious that they were his. All of them. They were in different sections of the hall, so none of the parents caught on. But I didn't get to where I am by believing in coincidences. I called my lawyers that night. I had his samples destroyed and I fired him the next morning. He signed his life away to me; I could have put him in jail for the rest of his life. I honestly didn't know where he had gone—I wanted nothing more to do with the man. This clinic wasn't built on deceit and I find it very sad that this is its undoing. We have helped a lot of people build beautiful families over the years." Hemingway thought for the first time that Fenton sounded sincere. "I didn't know Brayton had killed himself but I can't say that I'm upset by it."

"Can you prove that Brayton is father of these children?"

Fenton nodded. It was a defeated gesture. "I have cheek swabs locked away."

"Whoever is killing these children has known about their connection to one another for a while. Who had access to your files—legally, ethically, physically? How are the files protected? We need to find this guy and we need to do it now. He's going through these children like some kind of a bad dream."

"From a legal standpoint, only those directly involved with a particular patient are supposed to access their files: it's not like a library where browsing and choosing is permitted.

"Actual access to a patient's record is restricted almost exclusively to physicians, health care providers, nurses, and medical assistants. A receptionist would potentially have access to, and occasionally handle, records, but would be technically prohibited from opening them. It's not in the job description. From there it gets worse."

Had she said *worse*?

"The number of people we employ in the billing department, the medical coders, and the records department is very robust. It's part of what makes—*made*—us efficient. These employees have access to a massive amount of information. When they come across any personal information while billing or filing they are supposed to read what was done, code it, bill it, and forget it. Half of the time they don't even read the patient's name, only their patient ID number.

"Our paper charts are kept in both the vault as well as a personal fireproof safe in each doctor's office. They are not left lying around. Our record and chart rooms are locked at all non-practice times but when the office is open, they are unlocked and available to our employees. Our medical records department physically stores all of our records. The runners who work there have total access to all of the patient records but they're not supposed to look inside them.

"Then things get a little more complicated. At the beginning of last year we transferred all of our patient files to electronic medical records—it's a new federal law. Access to electronic medical records is limited to authorized employees who need a password. Doctors and nurses are notorious for logging in and leaving their panels open because logging in and out all day long is annoying.

"There are complex security systems within the EMR networks but the measures are not infallible. There are apps that work from laptops, iPhones, iPads and other mobile devices. If a doctor were logged in and not physically with that device, it would be like leaving the file room open for anyone."

Hemingway thought of the text she had received from Tyler Rochester's phone; whoever was killing these children was comfortable around technology.

Fenton continued: "Anyone working in coding, billing, medical records, or medical transcription would have all the legal rights in the world to be looking into files. It's the cornerstone of their job. But there's a difference between legal and ethical. People check files all the time without any ethical reason whatsoever. Just not my people.

"Federal law mandates that patients' records be made available to them. If Jane Doe demands a copy of her medical record, she gets it. We return files to patients all the time. Once they are printed and released, who knows who has access to them?" She shrugged.

Fenton had just spread suspicion to most of the people in the country.

Her voice box started back up. "But none of this shifts

blame away from Dr. Brayton. We wouldn't be here if he hadn't been such a narcissist. I think what he did was unforgivable."

Hemingway looked down at the photo of William Atchison. "So does the guy who's killing these boys."

||| EIGHTY-TWO

HEMINGWAY'S UNCLE had called; her parents would be at the Helmsley in a few hours and her brother was coming in from Los Angeles sometime during the night. Dwight—in his customary role as family mediator—wanted to know if she had a minute to drop by, if only to make an appearance.

She told him that she'd make it as soon as she could.

Papandreou and Lincoln still looked like tired, disheveled extras from a road movie. Phelps, on the other hand, was his same immutable self—hair combed, not so much as a yawn in the past twenty-four hours. Hemingway and Phelps had both managed to steal a shower; a change of clothes and freshly brushed teeth helped, at least until the heat needled back into everything.

"Okay." Hemingway held up her hand, indicating that it was time to focus on the pile of dead children and the collateral murders of five adults. "We need to figure out what's next on the flowchart."

Papandreou finished off a slurp on his drink and shook his head, the cream mustache making him look like that guy from Hall and Oates. "He ain't giving us time to breathe.

The more people he kills, the more people we have to interview. My brain's gonna explode and I haven't had ten
minutes to put any of this together."

Hemingway stared at him for a moment. "You don't get
to stomp your feet and say *not fair*. I'm really sorry that you're
tired and that you still can't see shit, but then I wonder how
the hell you became a detective in the first place. Did you get
anywhere with your interviews?"

Once the photograph of the opera became part of their
armament, Brayton's patients seemed more approachable, less
defensive, as if the police were now in on some grand little
secret that entitled them to civility. There was something
fundamentally wrong with a few of these people; this was
The Stepford Wives in wealthy Technicolor. They were so isolated, so used to things being done as—and when—they saw
fit, the thought of an interloper penetrating their cloistered
little terrarium was frightening.

Tyler Rochester's and Bobby Grant's deaths had made
little impact on many of the parents they had tried to warn;
that had been someone else's child, not *theirs*. Theirs was
special. She had never seen this level of worship to the cult
of children. It was beyond jaw-dropping, it was downright
disturbing.

"These people breathe a different oxygen than I do."
Lincoln pushed a stack of yellow interview jackets across the
table.

"Find anything we can use? Any video, photographs or
news footage? Tweets? Blogs? Cell phone pictures? Smoke
signals? Suicide notes? *Anything at all?*"

"We have the surveillance video of Heidi Morrison's death
from the MTA."

"And?"

"And nothing. She's standing on the platform with her

mother at the Hunter College station. Lots of kids milling about and just as the train pulls in she jumps out onto the track and gets grated by fifty tons of steel." He reached for his laptop, pried the top open, cued up a video, and let it play out.

A section of platform at the Hunter College station came to life. There was no sound.

The platform was molecularly packed, it was clearly rush hour; men in suits, corporate-looking women and schoolchildren made up the bulk of passengers.

"That's her," Lincoln said, indicating a smudge amid a sea of smudges that translated to the top of the girl's head. She was bouncing up and down—dancing. "And that's her mom." He indicated a woman to the smudge's left. Lincoln fast-forwarded through time.

Hemingway's focus stayed locked on the girl, now dancing in a manic pogo as the film played at thirty times normal speed.

The pulsing crowd slowed as Lincoln cued it up. The girl, still dancing, slowed down as well.

Interchangeable schoolboys ran through the frame, like fighter pilots dodging flak. An old lady eased her way from screen left to screen right, trying to get close to the tracks. A cop walked by. An old man with an umbrella came into the frame and leaned against a beam. Someone dropped a cup of coffee. Hemingway kept her focus on the girl.

For some reason the crowd moved to the left, like a flock of birds in flight, then back right as the lights of the approaching train became visible at screen left. People moved by her. Kids ran behind and around her. The old lady tried to strong-arm her way to the front of the queue.

All of a sudden the girl lurched forward, off the platform. And the train rolled through.

"Rewind that."

Lincoln shrugged. "It won't do any good. Me and Nick watched it fifty freakin' times. She just flies off the platform like she's magnetic. No one pushed her. No one touched her."

"Just rewind it."

She watched it a few times and Lincoln was right: there was nothing to see. One minute the child was there, bopping up and down, the next she was under the train.

Lincoln reached over and tapped the files. "In every single instance we couldn't find a reason to be suspicious."

"Except?"

"Except those numbers don't make any kind of sense in the real world. A one hundred percent accidental mortality rate for eight ten-year-old wealthy American girls in one summer doesn't add up."

Hemingway stared at her notes. All they really had were names and times of death and—

Hemingway reached over for the photograph of the party that Dr. Winslow had given her. She stared at it for a second, then reached for her notebook. "Here we go. May twelfth last year. *Six o'clock at the Metropolitan Opera House at Lincoln Center. Evening dress. Cocktails followed by dinner and music. RSVP by April 29th.*"

She wrote *May 12* down at the top of the page, above the dates column. The party was held on May the twelfth."

"And?" Lincoln said, irritated.

"And those girls started dying exactly two weeks to the day later." She underlined the dates, one at a time. "It started with the party. It had to. It's someone who was there."

||| EIGHTY-THREE

IT WAS here somewhere.

But where—*exactly*—was here?

A room full of boxes—everything from protocols to autopsy reports, to the medical examiner's notes and crime-scene photographs, the FBI's CODIS returns and stacks of interview folders and known associates of everyone concerned.

Hemingway knew that it would come at them out of the blue. A criminal record. A text or an e-mail or a changed name. A parking ticket. A size ten or ten and a half leather-soled shoe that lit up in the lab. Someone with a faulty fuse box, an axe to grind, a debt to collect. Someone who listened to their Rice Krispies. Or God.

The news battalion camped across the street had fewer answers than the police did. They had thrown around so many bizarre scenarios that even the late-night shortwave conspiracy nuts thought they had lost their minds. The talking heads were calling it everything from payback for Area 51 experiments to biblical justice against mad science, and no one seemed to think his chatter was the least bit unethical.

The newspeople had become a pack of braying animals, and Hemingway wondered who would start the grassroots riot that was surely coming—it would start when someone finally stood up and made the ghost of the great Joseph N. Welch proud. An equivalent of, "I'm mad as hell and I'm not going to take this anymore!" might just do it.

Christ, she was tired. And amazed at the crap swirling around in her head. She needed to go home to get some sleep. Maybe talk to Daniel. And her folks. It was time for a little of the damage control Uncle Dwight had mentioned.

But first there was the case.

Out there, somewhere, was a very smart man with a saw who enjoyed doing terrible things to little boys.

In absolute terms, that was the effect, not the cause.

The cause was something much older—some deep childhood trauma that had melted the insulation off the wire. Bad home. Bad parents. No home. No parents. Evil done and evil now revisited. Somehow, doing those terrible things made him feel—*better* wasn't exactly the word; *less anxious* was probably closer to the truth. And there was a fantasy at play that she didn't know, couldn't understand. Some specific pathology that internally justified these monstrous acts. Some basic belief that she couldn't see but desperately needed to.

These boys were being destroyed by him.

Wrong—that was passive voice.

He destroyed them.

Active. And accurate.

There was planning behind it all. He had murdered eight girls on a clock that the Swiss could nail their train schedule to. And no one had noticed any of it happening. From a certain perspective, the whole thing tasted of black magic.

Had he been at the opera that night? Or was it some

random nut who had glommed on to some insane fantasy that involved cutting up these boys? It wasn't aliens or Jesus and it wouldn't turn out to be anyone who believed in those things; there was too much critical thinking in this for it to be someone who believed that the Force existed or Jonah had actually lived in the belly of a whale. There was too much creativity at work for it to be someone of such limited vision.

Lincoln and Papandreou were at the computer lab picking up the lists of family, friends, business associates, practitioners, employees, tradespeople, neighbors, and anyone else remotely acquainted with the victims and their parents. They would also have the same lists from fifty-one of the fifty-nine former patients of Drs. Brayton and Selmer who had been interviewed in the past day and a half. The computers would cross-reference the lists, narrowing their search. Then they would weed out the natural happenstance of six degrees of Kevin Bacon and find the real common link—some little piece of connecting tissue that would set the whole thing on fire.

Hemingway had dealt with dozens of families who had lost fathers and mothers and children to violent crimes over the years. When she took the academic exercise one step further, the murder of her own baby sister all those years ago had set her on this path; her own defining genesis had come out of a death. She remembered reading an old Russian proverb that said a tree can't grow healthy if the roots are sick.

And it was hard to get sicker than a nobody killing your baby sister for no other reason than it seemed like a good idea.

And now Amy was gone. She'd have to look her parents in the eyes knowing that it was her fault. Amy had been murdered because the killer had confused her with her sister. Which was understandable; when they were together, people often thought they were twins. Or had. Past tense again.

She needed to give the old power plant a rest; it was time for sleep.

Phelps came in with a pair of paper bags and held them up. "Coffee, shumai—the pink ones, right?—and sweet and sour soup. Breakfast, lunch, and supper all rolled into one."

She pulled her hand off of her stomach, pushed her chair back, and stood up. "I should marry you, Jon."

"I snore and watch fishing shows. It would get old real fast."

She smiled and it felt like it took all of her energy. "That's okay, I shoot people and never come home." And she realized that had sounded a little bitter.

As she took a Styrofoam cup from his hand she knew that she still had a big decision to make, one that would either allow or prohibit her intake of coffee—her favorite food group. And she'd have to make it soon, because there were tipping points for these things. There was a difference between unsure and irresponsible.

She stirred in a sugar. "What do you think makes this guy tick, Jon?"

"It's not ritualistic but it has purpose."

Hemingway thought about William Atchison. What had been done to him. "What kind of a purpose could drive a human being to do this? He's not angry, he's too controlled for that. He knows the difference between right and wrong, so he's not crazy. He sends me a text message, so he's confident. He knows we're coming for him, and he's hasn't run. So what could be driving this guy?"

Phelps pulled a coffee out of the bag and peeled the lid off. He raised it to his mouth and paused, staring at her above the rim of the Styrofoam cup for a few seconds. "What's the best motivator there is?"

And it hit her.

"*Fear*," she said.

||| EIGHTY-FOUR

HIS FATHER was waiting for him in the kitchen when he got home. He didn't look angry but he did look like something was wrong. Which was never a good thing.

Benjamin hoped it wasn't something he had done.

He came in, put his knapsack down on the bench by the back door, and took off his jacket. His father was sitting at the island with a Scotch in his hand, the kind he only took out when he was having one of his "moods." And lately, his moods were getting closer and closer together, as if he were plugged into a diminishing timer.

Benjamin thought of an innocuous greeting, something that wouldn't tip the scales one way or another. "Hello, Father."

His father looked down at him and his eyes had that faraway look that Benjamin didn't like. "Son. I need to talk to you."

He didn't sound angry, which was a good sign. But that distant stare wasn't going anywhere.

His father stood up from the island and he wobbled a bit.

Benjamin went to the sink and washed his hands, then

he dried them. He tried to act casual, as if nothing were wrong. But there was plenty wrong—he could tell. His stomach started to rock back and forth, something it always did before the bad things started to happen.

Benjamin stared up at his father, his hands clasped in front of him, and nodded. "Did I do something wrong, Father? Did my SAT scores come back?"

"What? No, son. No. Not at all." His father looked puzzled for a moment, then angry. "The police came by today. They wanted to talk to me."

Benjamin felt his legs go cold. He hadn't told anyone. Not a soul. He always kept the promises he made to his father. That was the Golden Rule: *Keep the secret.*

His father came forward and touched his cheek. Then he helped him climb up onto the island, on the cold stone by the sink.

He leaned in and whispered in Benjamin's ear. "They say you might be in danger. They said that you should be careful."

Benjamin didn't like hearing this. Not one little bit. "Ca-careful of what, Father?"

"Someone bad, son."

This sounded like a trick, so he chose the best answer he could; he was adept at making fast decisions. "I don't know anyone bad."

At that his father smiled and he knew he had said the right thing. "I know that, son. But there's a bad man out there, and he's hurting boys and they came by to warn me. I don't want to worry you—because there is nothing to worry about—but I wanted to tell you, just in case they ask. You tell them I told you, okay?"

Benjamin nodded because he knew that had been another trick question. "Yes, sir."

"The police don't know what they're talking about. You'll

be fine. After school's over next week we'll take a vacation. Maybe go back to Greece like last year—you'd like that, wouldn't you?"

Benjamin had liked Greece. And there were plenty of things that had occupied his father's time, lots of birds. "Of course."

For a second his father's focus seemed to go away, then snapped back like an elastic band. "Boys have been taken, Benjamin. When he's finished hurting them, he dumps them in the river."

"Why does he take them?"

"Because he's unhappy, son." At that his father looked down, at the floor. "You haven't spoken to anyone, have you? About . . ." he looked up at his son ". . . me?"

At that the needles in Benjamin's legs exploded and he thought he might pee himself. "Of course not, Father."

But his father did not look convinced. "This man has taken some of the boys we met at the opera last year."

"They seemed like a nice bunch of kids. Most of them, anyway. I didn't like Miles Morgan but I suppose he can't help himself. Not everyone can be like me."

His father smiled at that. "Son, you are singularly unique. I've always told you that. There's no one remotely like you out there." His father smiled, then kissed him on the cheek. "My little genius. Now go wash up."

At that his stomach started swinging again. "Yes, sir."

"And don't forget to wash your peepee."

||| EIGHTY-FIVE

THE PRESS were going absofuckinglutely apeshit. Every news outlet on the East Coast, from the little local cable stations that had avoided being plowed over by the Internet to the big boys who owned the airwaves from Chicago to Manhattan, were stationed in front of the precinct. The talking heads wanted justice; they wanted answers; they wanted a suspect; they wanted details. But mostly, they just wanted ratings.

Hemingway was in that place of uncomfortable limbo located behind the podium and in front of the bright lights. The heat had redlined and most of the newspeople looked like they were about to blow their radiators. Dennet thoroughly believed that with her sister's name indelibly recorded on the victim list, the reporters would grant her a degree of slack. Hemingway wondered if he really believed that or if it was just a clumsy attempt to blindside her; she knew the reporters would go after her like dingoes playing with a honey-covered baby.

Phelps stood behind to her right and she could feel his presence, a perfect mixture of sentinel, moral support, and guardian angel. She couldn't keep her eyes from dancing around the crowd—she was too tired to fight instinct—and she wouldn't be surprised if *he* was here in the room with her. It seemed like the kind of thing he might do.

She ran through the developments in the case and now that all of the relatives were notified she had been instructed to use names. Which meant that more newspeople were camped out on the sidewalk in front of the Rochesters, Grants, and the rest of the families—more bad luck they didn't need.

Hemingway recapped the timeline, starting with Tyler Rochester's disappearance. Trevor Deacon was added to the mix. She discussed where the bodies had been discovered. Confirmed their grievous injuries but left out lurid details. She didn't connect any of the dots for them. She didn't lead them through Deacon's involvement or tell them that the boys were half brothers. She neither confirmed nor denied the Park Avenue Clinic's position within the ongoing investigation. And she paused before reading her sister's name off of the list.

"Any questions?"

A forest of hands flicked toward the heavens.

At this point she reminded herself to keep the answers simple, monosyllabic if possible; the press conference would be followed with a brief and bloody biography of Detective First Grade Alexandra Hemingway and the armchair therapy would begin. Maybe they'd get someone like that Harvard psychiatrist Dr. Justin Frank to discuss her unaddressed rage and daddy issues. What pissed her off was that he'd probably be right.

"Yes?" she said, pointing at a reporter from ABC. She didn't really want questions—what she wanted was to fire a couple of rounds over the crowd and head for her Suburban.

"Are you certain that your sister's death is, in fact, part of the current spree of killings that you are investigating? Is there a chance that it is somehow payback for your having killed Irish mobster David Shea?"

The bitch had hit that one out of the park. No warm-up. No easing into it. Bang, straight into the cheap seats. "My killing of Shea was in self-defense. We fought. He lost. That's all. My sister's death is linked to the serial murderer we are now hunting."

A hand to her left—the *New York Daily News*.

She took it.

"Detective Hemingway, don't you feel that your close relation to the killer's last victim hinders your ability to stay objective?"

Hemingway sensed Phelps's presence behind her, ready to rip the microphones out by the roots and use them on the reporters like suppositories. She leaned forward, the mic an inch from her mouth, and clearly said, "No." *Good night and go fuck yourself.*

She nodded at a seasoned reporter from the *New York Times*.

"How many suspects do you have right now? And what do you feel the timeline will be on an arrest?"

The reporter was smart, a better caste of journalist when compared to most of the people lining the sidewalk in front of her. But that first question wasn't really a question, he knew that they didn't have a suspect; if they did, they would have released his name—or at least details about his arrest—by now. It forced her to admit that they were still paddling in a river of shit and the exercise had been geared to put her on the defensive. "As you know, we have not yet released the name of a suspect." *Because we don't have one.* "And as to the second question, the mountain of information we are carefully and methodically analyzing and cataloging is staggering. I can't give you a timeline because anything I say could be outdated in a few minutes or even a few seconds. I can promise that I'll be standing up here in the not-too-distant future giving you whoever is responsible for these deaths."

"That sounds like you have someone in mind."

No, it sounds like I wish I had someone in mind. "Like I said, I promise that not too long from now, we'll be having a much less one-sided conversation." She was pleased at how she had handled that.

Jennifer Krantz-Domingo-Gomez was in the front, her hand politely raised, no malice in her face. Hemingway knew the woman casually and she took a chance. "Yes, Jen."

Gomez, a little woman with a face like a candy you wanted to unwrap, smiled. "Have you collected any DNA or other forensic evidence during the investigation?"

Gomez just got on her Christmas list with that softball. "The medical examiner's office has handled itself with the usual proficiency and professionalism we have come to depend on. I can comfortably say that besides being in constant rotation with the FBI's CODIS program at Quantico, our own labs have done an exceptional job in processing evidence."

Her peripheral vision picked up movement to her left. "Yes, Pete," she said.

"Besides the FBI and their CODIS program, have you enlisted the help of outside agencies—on either a state or federal level? And if not, at what point in the investigation would you consider seeking their assistance?"

Shit. "The NYPD has the necessary resources and skill to deal with this. We will be making an arrest on this investigation and we will be making it as soon as humanly possible—without the help of the BCI or the FBI. If their presence would advance the investigation, they'd be here by now."

Sashi Numrta from *People* snapped her fingers. Without thinking about the action, Hemingway nodded at her.

The reporter blinked her eyes and turned on the charm. "Detective Hemingway, do you understand the concerns some have expressed over your handling of such a high-profile case when the shooting of David Shea is still fresh in everyone's mind? Are you uncomfortable with this or—?"

"No, I don't understand the concerns. I am a valuable asset to this force. Every single inquiry into the Shea incident found me faultless. Or maybe you haven't seen the footage."

Even the reporters laughed at that one—Numrta had hosted a miniseries on the shooting and those unbelievably long thirty-eight seconds of video had been played three dozen times over three nights. She was more than familiar with the video—she was probably the world's expert.

The only thing Hemingway remembered about that brief snippet of time was the noise—the sound of her heart thundering in her skull and the punch of gunfire. She remembered walking out into the sunshine and sitting down and not being able to breathe or scream and then passing out. "So I think that personal attacks and libelous accusations should be avoided."

"I wasn't accusing—"

"Next question," Hemingway said, cutting her off and nodding at another reporter.

"Detective Hemingway, as a police officer who makes roughly seventy-one thousand dollars a year, how is it possible that you own a building valued at over five and a half million dollars?"

"My finances are not up for discussion. I file my taxes every year on time and have a private firm handle the paperwork for me."

"I wasn't suggesting that your money is in any way ill-gotten—"

Had he said *ill-gotten*? What was this, Elizabethan England?

"—I thought that listeners would find it interesting that a woman who comes from such a wealthy background as yourself would make the decision to become a police officer."

Sonofabitch. He knew the story. Everyone knew the story. It had come out after Shea, when the media had taken her life apart with a scalpel, layer by layer. Maybe they were trying to convince the viewers that a real fucked-up human being was at the center of this story; nothing sells good television like the promise of weakness. "Do you have any questions about the investigation?"

The reporter shifted his feet and a few snickers echoed in the crowd.

"Next," she said.

A woman stepped forward, her pen pointed at Hemingway. "Detective Hemingway, with this many people dead in such a short period of time and no suspect in custody, are you worried about the possible damage to your career?"

At that Hemingway realized that they just wanted to film her losing her shit in time for the evening cycle. "To be honest, unlike yourself, I don't care about the ratings, I care about results. And if you'll excuse me, I have somewhere more productive to be."

PHELPS RODE up in the elevator with her, his presence making her feel a little less vulnerable in what she knew was going to be an unpleasant reunion. She had gone over this meeting from every conceivable tactical angle and no matter how she approached it, she knew she'd walk away from this feeling worse than she already did.

"You'll do okay," Phelps said, his voice a full octave below the pitch of a diesel engine.

"That's one way to look at it." The reporters had acted like the mean kids from Willy Wonka, she hadn't talked to Daniel all day, and she was about to be ostracized from her family. She shrugged.

"Family's family," the big man said.

"You come from different people than I do, Jon." He rarely spoke of his family, but when he did, it was with fondness.

Phelps seemed to mull the statement over for a few nods of his head. "Yeah, I do. My old man chased work all over the place so he could feed us, dragging the family across the country. My mom looked forward to spending her golden years doing all the things he promised her she'd do before they reached the end of the rainbow. But on the day they handed him his gold watch he crawled into bed and stayed there, sleeping, being afraid and depressed. That whole time my mother sat downstairs with her suitcase packed, waiting to go on a safari she'd wanted her whole life. Six years later he had a heart attack and two weeks after that my mother bought herself a seniors group ticket to see Kenya, a place she had always dreamt of visiting with her husband. She had a stroke while packing her suitcase and died with her head on the carpet. She never got to see Africa. Everybody's broken, Hemi."

"I'm just not looking forward to it."

At that he just shrugged. "Ninety percent of the shit we worry about never comes true. The other ten percent? Fuggedaboudit."

She had never been tight with Amy, not in all the years they had spent as children at home, not through primary or high school, and by the time they had both shipped off to prep schools on opposite sides of the country the wedge had been so firmly entrenched in the real estate between them that it could never be mended. They saw one another at family gatherings and every couple of years Amy would call, usually when she was in the bag, under the pretense of patching things up. But in all those years they never got to the patching things up portion of the program. Amy usually slipped into some alcohol-fueled diatribe about how their parents had always paid more attention to Allie, and the conversation would usually go into a flat spin punctuated by the sound of a dial tone.

Amy had gone to therapy for a while but eventually, like every other time in her life when forced to take responsibility for her actions, she had simply walked away from the process. The unhappy girl burgeoned into someone whose insides were ugly and broken. And of course it was never her fault.

Their mother had always sided with Amy, maybe because she had recognized some of her own behavior and felt a need to justify it. And Hemingway believed that her father had as well. It all came down to Amy's being more fragile; she needed them to hold her hand through life. Eventually she had done well on paper—husband, children, nice house in the country and a respectable handicap at the golf club. But even with all the propping up, her life had never really gelled, and everyone shared the unspoken expectation that one day it would all just implode.

No one had thought she'd have her throat cut after being mistaken for her sister.

Hemingway remembered how she had collapsed in the living room and howled like a gored beast when Mank had been murdered. And although there were a lot of emotions at play here—anger, disbelief, pride, vengeance, rage—she would not—could not—let loss factor into it. Not yet. Of course, her parents would translate that into noncaring.

The elevator stopped and the bell pinged. Phelps stepped out and put his hand on the door to keep it from closing. "You coming?"

A man sat on a chair in the corner, facing the elevator doors, the staircase beyond. When Phelps and Hemingway stepped out, he stood up. There was a folded newspaper in his hand that looked like it had weight to it.

He was thin, Japanese, and wore a well-tailored suit and an open-collared shirt. As they walked over to him, he placed the paper down on the seat. There was the grip of an automatic in the folds of the newsprint.

He bowed, then extended his hand. "Alexandra, you have

my deepest sympathies. I am terribly sorry about your sister."
His English was perfect.

"Thank you, Mr. Ken. You know my partner, Detective
Jon Phelps?"

Mr. Ken bowed a second time, and the ink under his
collar flashed against the white fabric—irezumi ink; old time
yakuza war paint. He had been a fixture in the family since
before she had been born, working first for her grandfather,
now for Uncle Dwight.

He gestured toward the door to the suite. "Your parents
are expecting you." He dismissed them with a bow and went
back to cradling his newspaper and watching the elevator
and stairwell.

Hemingway paused at the door. "You sure you want to
do this with me?"

"It's time you figured out I'll follow you anywhere."

She knocked.

Uncle Dwight answered the door. His tie was loose and
he had a Scotch in his hand. He smiled when he saw her.
"Allie, how are you?" He pulled her into his arms, holding
the glass away from her shoulder.

She hugged him back and realized that the last time she
had seen him felt like a thousand years ago. She could hear
conversation off in the suite, some music, the clink of utensils
on porcelain. The smell of flowers was almost overwhelming.

"You remember my partner, Jon Phelps."

The two men shook hands and Dwight kicked in with his
considerable social skills. "Detective Phelps, thank you for coming. This is all informal, just a little get-together for family and
close friends and as my niece's partner, you qualify as both."

"Mr. Ken is doing a nice job of intimidating people out
there."

Dwight smiled at that. "He has that effect, yes." Then

Dwight grabbed her by the hand and led her off into the suite. "Your parents are in here," he said softly, "and they're looking forward to seeing you."

She knew Dwight, the family mediator, and figured that he was lying to her; he had probably said the same thing to them.

"Where's Miles?"

"He's on his way in from the country—I sent the jet. He should be here in an hour."

"Give him my best," she said, then spotted her father by the window, a whiskey tumbler in his hand, looking as if he had stepped out of a Ralph Lauren ad. Her mother was sitting in a silk wingback, two of her shopping friends by her side. A barman stood in the corner, a selection of crystal, ice, and booze out on a cart. A few other people stood around, talking, drinking, and looking like they were discussing tax loopholes. Conversation skidded to a stop.

Her father saw her and his face changed from a waxy disinterest to a smile. He came over and gave her a hug. He smelled as good as he looked. "Thank you," he whispered in her ear. "I was worried that you wouldn't come."

"She was my sister, Dad, and regard—"

"Because of your job," he said, cutting her off. "I know you're busy, Allie."

And with that she realized that she had been wrong—that she actually liked it when he called her that.

They unclenched and her father extended a hand to her partner. "Detective Phelps, thank you for escorting my daughter." They had met a few times over the years.

Phelps shook his hand and said something about it not being a problem.

The three of them went over to her mother. She was elegant and trim and her hand glittered with a fistful of diamonds.

Her pupils looked like pinpricks and her eyes could barely focus. "Hello, Allie. How nice of you to make the time."

There had always been tension between them and Hemingway assumed it had to do with her complete rejection of the country club friends, the shopping, and the men who looked like Brooks Brothers mannequins—all the keystones in her mother's soulless universe.

Hemingway ignored the jab and gave her mother a hug. "Hello, Mother. You remember my partner, Detective Jon Phelps."

Her mother looked Phelps over with the exaggerated body language of a drunk trying to look sober. "That's quite the suit, Detective," she said.

Phelps smiled, took her hand, shook it, and said, "Your daughter picked it out for me." Then he excused himself, probably to hunt down a club soda.

Hemingway made the rounds, shaking hands, air-kissing, and telling everyone that she wished she was seeing them under better circumstances. When she was finished, her father led her back to the front room and sat her down on one of the sofas.

"Graham's flying in from L.A. in a few hours, I know he'd love to see you."

She nodded but didn't say much.

"And Patrick's in a suite downstairs. He's pretty beat up about this." Patrick was Amy's husband. He wasn't a bad guy but there never seemed to be much to him and Hemingway felt that if he turned sideways, he'd disappear altogether. Had Amy said anything to their parents about the breakup? Had it been a real split or just another plea for attention? She was always breaking up with him.

Hemingway felt petty thinking about these things; it was time to move on.

Her father leaned in and put a hand on her shoulder. "How are you?"

"Don't worry about me. How's Mom?"

Her father shook his head. "No, Allie, I want to talk about *you*. How is Daniel? How is being a police officer?" He paused, and looked into her eyes. "Are you happy?"

"Dad, you have your hands full here. And I can't even begin to think about Amy. I'm tired and I need some sleep and—"

He cut her off. "And you are going to talk to me. Because life is short and I won't let you be a stranger anymore. I thought, and I suppose *still think*, that there's a different life waiting for you out there. One where you don't have to worry about—" He stopped cold and his eyes dropped to his drink for a second. "Having your throat cut when you answer the door."

She held up her hand. "I do this because it's what I was built to do. Can you imagine me sitting in Uncle Dwight's practice? Or in one of your companies? They'd laugh me out of the boardroom."

He cupped both her hands in his. "No, they wouldn't. They'd respect you because you are not a woman people can ignore. You are a good detective because that's what you've decided to be. If you decided to be a horse breeder or a rally driver or an astronaut, you'd be the best there is, because that's who you are."

She pulled her hands out of his. "I like what I do." But that wasn't entirely correct. There were plenty of negatives that went with the job. More than she could count if she bothered to think about it.

"But it's not good for you."

"This is why we don't talk."

And at that his face changed. "When Claire disappeared, I promised myself that I'd be there for you, take care of all of you. But I can't do that, I can't be everywhere all the time.

And what happened to Amy . . ." He stopped, and his lip trembled for a second, but he was able to push it back into himself. "What happened to Amy today was supposed to happen to you. Someone was out to hurt *you*, and I can't take that. I just want you to consider doing something else." He leaned over and kissed her on the cheek. "And if you can't consider doing something else, I want you to sit down with me and explain why you do this. Is that fair?"

She didn't know how to react to this. "Sure."

"Look, I know I don't say much, but if you solve every single murder of your career, it's not going to bring Claire back. Bad things happen and they're not your fault."

What about Amy's death? she wanted to ask. "Let me put this case to bed and we'll talk. If you want, we can take a vacation."

At that her father smiled. "Deal. But I pay. And we go somewhere nice. Maybe France. We can tour Burgundy in the fall, drink some wine, get to know one another."

Pregnant women don't drink wine. "France? That sounds great, Dad."

Someone back in the living room brayed with laughter and her father's eyes glanced over her shoulder. "I have to go back to those people and you have to get back to work. Or at least get some rest—you look tired. Beautiful, but tired." He leaned forward and kissed her again. "Please be careful."

She felt tears start with that one but held them off. "I'm good at what I do."

"So is this guy you're hunting." Her father stood up and pulled her to her feet. "Don't forget that."

As the elevator doors slid closed, Mr. Ken waved a good-bye, the newspaper still folded in his hand. As the car dropped into the shaft, Phelps said, "I don't like that guy."

At that, Hemingway smiled. "You're not supposed to."

||| EIGHTY-SEVEN

THE POLICE tape was gone and the trauma-scene unit had cleaned up. Two uniformed cops sat in a cruiser out front—they'd be there until the case was over. Hemingway walked up to the car and leaned in the open window. She recognized the two officers from the precinct.

"Koombs, Dorsett. You can go home now."

Koombs, a little guy with big ears, shook his head. "Sorry, Detective. We got orders from Phelps. We are on you until you collar this guy."

Hemingway didn't like this—they would not have done this if she had been a man. "I'm lead detective on the case—I outweigh Phelps. Fuck off."

Koombs shrugged helplessly. "I can't."

"I'll call Dennet and have him pull you."

At that Koombs smiled, reached into his pocket. "Detective Phelps said you'd say that." He pulled out a folded sheet of precinct stationery and handed it over.

Hemingway opened it and read the short note. It was an order from Dennet for Koombs and Dorsett to watch over her residence until reassigned.

"Shit," she said.

"Sorry, Detective. Nothing personal."

She stood up and took in a deep breath, filling her chest and expanding her ribs. She looked up the street, then down, toward the water. It was empty. The guy wouldn't come after her again.

When she looked back at Koombs he was staring at her chest, grinning, those too-big ears lifted with his smile.

"Jesus," she said, and turned to leave. "Just don't get killed. I have that effect on the people around me."

"Phelps told us that, too," Koombs said.

The staircase was dark and she stood there on the threshold for a moment, trying to get her bearings. For the first time, the realization that her sister had been murdered came at her in a blast of air-conditioning that carried the smell of disinfectant.

As a precaution she went through all of the rooms in the apartment. Daniel was asleep in their bed, or at least pretending to be, his back to her.

She stood in front of the fridge for a few minutes, trying to decide if she was hungry. She settled on a glass of milk and a banana.

A new camera bag lay on the table, the tags clipped off, lenses and camera bodies halfheartedly jammed inside. She found Daniel's old bag in the garbage, the strap stained with a dark swatch of her sister's blood.

How had an evening at the opera mushroomed into a plague of visits by the Angel of Death? First the girls. Then the brown-eyed handsome boys started washing through Little Hell Gate. The Grant boy's driver. Deacon. Dr. Selmer. Mrs. Atchison. Amy.

But that's how things went: one minute all was well in the kingdom, the next fire rained down from the sky. That last night she took that walk with Mank through the East Side had been good, maybe the best night they ever had. A few short hours later it was blown away when Shea and Nicky had stepped from the shadows. The world didn't care about your plans because it was too busy turning. And the machinery seemed to be greased with blood.

She walked over to the window and took a sip of the ice-cold milk. She stared out at the street, at the cop car parked in front of her door, at the weird light on the asphalt. She could handle that it was not safe out there. It was, in fact, one of the few basic beliefs she held—it had taken hold the moment Claire had disappeared. But she couldn't handle that with a child. No how. No way.

So why did she even fantasize that she could have a baby? Maybe she'd get lucky, do something right, and her child would think of life as a gift, not a burden. But would that lessen her load? Would that help to quell the anxiety every time her child was out of her sight? What would happen if the kid was late coming home? Or at a sleepover? At school? She wasn't sure she could handle that. Day in, day out, year after year after year. You never stopped worrying about your kids, her father's talk was proof positive of that. Here she was, thirty-seven, and he still worried about her. And her particular background and pathology pretty much guaranteed that she'd never be at ease as a parent. Was the whole exercise worth it? She took a bite of the banana and turned away from the window.

Tomorrow promised to be worse than today; the final athletic day for sixty-two of the city's private boys' schools, a year-end showdown to weed out the trophy takers from the participation ribbon receivers. The buses would carry the boys from their various institutions to Randall's Island, the isolated chunk of real estate that did duty as recreational space for

many of the city's schools. Dennet's bid to shut the event down
had been quashed by the powers that be and Hemingway had
resolved herself to a day of fruitless paranoia.

Sixty-two schools translated to a staggering eighty-nine
hundred students; nine hundred and four who fell into the
right age group; forty-one who shared a father. Forget ulcers,
this kind of stress could cause cancer.

There was a lot that could go wrong, a lot that would be
out of her hands, and again she wondered if she was being
set up to take the fall. And with the paranoia came the realization that she needed some sleep. After a little food, she
told herself.

She put the milk and banana down on the coffee table,
sat down on the sofa, and fell asleep.

||| EIGHTY-EIGHT

PHELPS PICKED her up at 5 a.m., honking loudly and frightening the two patrolmen still out front. He brought coffee and bagels and drove slowly while she went through the process of waking up, bolstering her progress with slurps of caffeine.

Daylight was slowly seeping into the sky and the city was still magically silent except for early-morning delivery trucks. Phelps cut through the quiet streets toward Central Park. After crossing on 79th, he continued west until they found an on-ramp for the FDR.

"Sleep okay?" Phelps asked after she had absorbed a little of the coffee.

She thought about it. "Sat down on the sofa, and that's all I remember. You?"

"Me and Maggie are sleeping in the basement—much cooler than the rest of that place."

"Why don't you get an air conditioner, Jon?"

"Wife says it's cold enough all winter." He shrugged. "She's right."

She raised the coffee to her lips to take another sip and it hit her. "Jon, pull over!"

"There's no shoulder."

"Pull over. Now!"

Phelps flashed the lights and swung over to the rightmost lane. He glanced in the mirror and stopped the car. "What the fu—?"

Before the car came to a stop, Hemingway shoved the door open, stuck her head out, and threw up. Her stomach clenched a few times, forcing the coffee and bagel out between gasps for breath.

Then, as quickly as it came, it was over.

She pulled her head back inside, closed the door, and wiped her mouth with a napkin from the bagel bag. "This girly stuff sucks, Jon."

He looked at her, then down at the hand held protectively across her stomach. "I'm sure it does," he said, and checked his mirrors before he pulled back into traffic.

||| EIGHTY-NINE

SITUATED IN the East River, Randall's Island proper is separated from Queens by Hell Gate, and from the Bronx by Bronx Kill. Though technically deeded as part of Manhattan, it is separated from the city by the Harlem River and runs from roughly 100th to 127th Street.

Home to the New York City Fire Department's training facility, the New York City Department of Environmental Protection's wastewater treatment plant, the seventeen-floor Manhattan Psychiatric Center, a vast patchwork of sports fields and parkland, and roughly fifteen hundred full-time residents, Randall's Island was also one of the most coveted chunks of real estate in the Northeast. Nature lovers could visit the salt marshes and freshwater wetlands on either side of Little Hell Gate Inlet, and the sports minded could hit the batting cages or driving range.

Under the watchful eye of the Randall's Island Park Alliance, a vast chunk of the island's space had been allocated for sports and recreational purposes: there were sixty-three soccer, softball, baseball, field hockey, football and lacrosse fields; twenty tennis courts; and five miles of waterfront pathways. Major track-and-field events could be hosted at Icahn Stadium, a state-of-the-art facility that seated five thousand spectators.

Besides catering to the area's public schools, the island's recreational facilities also played host to the physical education programs of many of the approximately nine hundred private schools in the area. Schoolchildren can be found all over the island every day of the week.

———

As Phelps took the car off the Robert F. Kennedy Bridge and swung down onto Randall's Island, Hemingway marveled at the size of the place. She had paddled its shores when navigating her kayak past Little Hell Gate, and even visited it on a few occasions, but she had never looked at it as a reserve to hunt children. This morning it looked as large as a continent.

Phelps followed the Darth Vader instructions dictated by the GPS, driving past the psychiatric center and then swinging around to the tip of the island where a battery of police cars were ready for the day's task of keeping the children safe.

Lincoln and Papandreou were already there with the two dozen cruisers and an army of uniformed policemen, most drinking coffee. A few stood off from the crowd, smoking in little groups. Phelps parked off to the side and as Hemingway got out, more cars pulled up behind them.

The plan had come from her office and they had thrown it by both the State Association of Independent Schools, which oversaw the private schools, and the New York City Department of Education, which controlled the public schools—both bodies had rubber-stamped the idea of a police presence for the last games day of the year.

The plan was simple: there was one uniformed police officer assigned as security liaison to each school and it was their job to check the roster of each bus that left for Randall's Island; that same officer would ride with the last bus to the island and check return attendance at the end of the day when everyone packed up to head home. The math worked out to roughly one officer per seventy-five students plus the hundred extra policemen that would be manning crosswalks, parking lots, paths, the edge of wooded areas, bathrooms, on-ramps, off-ramps, and the island side of the footbridge that connected with Manhattan at 103rd Street.

But the real emphasis—the one Hemingway had tried to keep under the radar—was on the forty-one of Dr. Brayton's children who would be on the island today. Each had an officer assigned as a shadow—some uniformed, some plain-clothes. Hemingway had made the call, stressing that not focusing on these specific children was tantamount to negligence. This translated to forty-one shadows mixed in with the general population of police officers.

Along with the new day had come more heat. Papandreou wore a police T-shirt and jeans with white leather sneakers, Lincoln wore chinos and a Hawaiian shirt, and it was hard to decide who looked like more of a stereotype.

Phelps was in one of his many gray suits, this one a light summer wool. As usual he looked rested and ready. Hemingway had opted for jeans, engineer boots, and a cotton blouse. She couldn't remember when she had last worn girl shoes. Her badge hung from her neck on a beaded chain and her revolver was on her belt. She started to do the rounds.

She didn't like that she didn't recognize many of the cops who had pulled duty; the business of policing ran on respect and confidence, two things that were hard to come by when you hadn't worked with a person before. But she went through the group, introducing herself and trying to become familiar with as many as possible.

After half an hour of introductions, small talk, and more coffee, she got up on the gate of her Suburban. She went over handheld channels, protocol, and warnings. Then she went over the e-mail that outlined the parameters of their duties here.

By the time the coffee was gone, the sea of uniformed policemen and policewomen knew what was expected of them, but not what to look for; it was the old "anything out of the ordinary directive," which in New York City had a completely different set of boundaries than any other place on the planet. From the southwest corner of the island they dispersed to points northeast, heading out on foot, bicycle, golf cart, and car.

The buses started arriving around eight-thirty, filled with cheering bouncy children excited that summer vacation was almost here. Hemingway and Phelps made the rounds to the parking lots allocated to busses, intermittently checking attendance with the ride-along officers and making sure that the chaperones were up to speed.

Coaches and gym teachers lugged mesh bags of soccer balls, duffels of lacrosse sticks and baseball bats, and endless pieces of protective equipment. Everyone carried a water bottle. And the kids—from the grade school children to the high school seniors—bopped around with the boundless enthusiasm of youth.

After an hour of making the rounds, verifying that all was well, she headed back to the Suburban. They had a busy roster again today, and she probably wouldn't sleep for another thirty hours. Who said it was lonely at the top?

Hemingway saw Phelps moseying between two of the soccer fields on the way back to the SUV. He had a pair of old Wayfarers on and she wondered if he realized that fashion had come full circle and he was a style icon among the younger cops in the precinct; some of them sported thin ties and a flat top à la Chuck Yeager and it could be traced straight back to Phelps, an unwitting fashion plate in oxfords.

She nodded a hello and he waved back with a slow-handed boredom that said he had had enough, but she had learned a long time ago that you couldn't judge Phelps based on his enthusiasm.

He was probably right. After all, what kind of a self-destructive maniac would try to get through this kind of manpower?

The downside to such a massive display of force would be the news teams, contributing the usual more harm than good to the equation.

A breeze blew in off the river, smelling of salt and diesel and a general malaise that experience told her was a mixture of seaweed, garbage, and a long list of chemicals. She lifted her arms to get a little wind under her wings to cool her thermostat. As she stood there, enjoying the flutter of air against her clothes, Phelps came up.

"Hotter'n piss out here," he said, Oscar the Grouch with a badge.

"Eloquent."

"Fuck that noise. They don't pay me to be eloquent."

He turned to the south and stared out across the water at Manhattan's irregular skyline. Hemingway kept her arms spread and willed the wind to cool her; all it did was make her sweat a little more. Phelps was right—it was hotter than piss.

"What if he shows up here?" she asked.

Phelps unbuttoned his suit jacket and jammed his hands into his pockets. "He'd have to be insane to try and breach the security here. Anyone so much as goes close to one of these kids and he'll have a dozen cops bouncing up and down on his skull."

She closed her eyes and focused on the breeze and for some reason it smelled worse. "Okay, let's go get some food and head back to the precinct. I want to see what Carson and his übernerds have come up with."

As they swung around the asphalt of Wards Meadow Loop and back up to the Triborough hub, Hemingway surveyed the little uniformed specks mixed in among the frenetic flea circus of children. Even from a distance she could see the tension in the body language of the policemen, and she liked that. Nothing keeps a cop sharp like worry. And with nearly nine thousand kids on the island, forty-one who represented flesh-and-blood targets for a man with a saw, there was plenty to be worried about.

More than enough.

THE DAY was spectacular and he danced among the police officers and children. He did a little boogie at the edge of the field where Johnson's Academy and Maynard's Collegiate Institute were in the last quarter of the grade four tournament. He smiled and waved a good morning to the policeman to his left and the policeman waved back, like he had better places to be and bigger things to do than watch a bunch of kids kicking a ball around. And he couldn't argue with that; he had better things to do as well—Miles Morgan, for example.

He smiled at a couple of the chaperones and they smiled back. It was as if everyone were one big happy family. When he walked over to the water cooler, the lady in the MCI T-shirt asked him if he'd like a drink.

"Yes, please," he had said, because he assumed that was what she expected him to say. He took the plastic cup, nodded a thank you, and continued on his way.

He had been talking to a police officer a few minutes earlier, asking him what the big fuss was. Pedophile, he had answered. A real sicko, apparently. When the cop had excused himself to go to the bathroom, he had picked up his knapsack and headed out into the fields.

No one saw him. No one acknowledged him. He was invisible here, among his people.

It took fifteen minutes to make it to the lacrosse field where Miles Morgan was finishing his last game of the year—the last game of his life, really. Miles was like all of these boys—pretenders, ignoble blood and poor breeding. Worse than bastards. Sons of bitches.

He found the Morgan kid at the edge of one of the soccer fields. Three cops stood over by the goal, talking. The action over, everyone looked like they just wanted to cool down.

Miles was with some other boys, in the midst of a joke that involved several punches to the smallest one in the group. Miles picked him up in his peripheral vision and stopped, turned. He came over.

"You see all the cops?" he asked, once again demonstrating his finely tuned sense of observation. "Didn't think you were coming this week."

He shrugged and the knapsack with the Canadian flag sewn to it shifted on his shoulder. "When have I not come?" he asked.

Miles ignored the response. "Did you bring it?"

"Didn't I say I would?"

"You want to show me right here?"

They walked back between two buses.

He lowered his knapsack, pulled the two zippers, and pulled out a corner of the shadow box. Three hairy lifeless legs reached for the corner of the box, thick as pencils. "Biggest one in the world," he said, knowing the boy couldn't say no. They never did. "It feeds on birds."

"I can't pay you here. My money is in my shorts."

He pretended to think about this for a second. "I know a cool spot that's pretty private."

Miles Morgan's eyes narrowed. "I shouldn't."

"Why not?"

"Aw, man, they gave us this long-assed speech at school this morning. Said we need to stay in sight and to watch out for strangers. To keep on the fields where our classes are."

He shrugged. "What do you expect them to say? But all right, if you're scared to leave, I understand. If I was like you, I'd be scared, too." He zipped up the pack, stood up—subject closed.

The Morgan boy stopped him. "I really want it. And I'm not scared."

"Then I have the most private place in the world."

HEMINGWAY AND Phelps were in the cybercrimes lab with Carson, going through the endless data when her cell chirped. "Hemingway," she said automatically.

"Hemi, it's Nick. We lost Lincoln."

She felt something flutter in her stomach. "What the fuck do you mean *lost*?" At the edge of her peripheral vision Phelps stood up and reached for his coat.

Rising above Papandreou's voice was the static of cheering children. "Last time I saw him he was talking to the Morgan kid. Maybe five minutes ago. Morgan kid's gone, too."

She remembered Ace and Cindy's son—Little King Switchblade. "What happened?"

"I went for a squirt. I couldn't've been gone for more than five minutes. He was there when I left, standing by the buses watching a bunch of kids. Ten minutes later, he's AWOL. Poof."

She turned and headed out of the lab, Phelps holding the door for her. "Where are you?"

"Northeast tip of the island, the parking lot between softball fields fourteen and thirty-three."

Without asking, Phelps shoved a creased photocopy of a Randall's Island map in front of her face. She checked the top right-hand corner and located the two fields. "Below the wetlands?"

"Yeah."

"Where'd he go? Any holes?"

There was a pause and she could picture Papandreou standing on his tiptoes, squinting into the distance. "Everyone says they were doing their job but you know how it is. You close your eyes or turn your head, and they're gone. Hey— hold on. Yeah, you know what, he coulda gone that way, sorry—the only way I see out of here is under the railway bridge."

"You try his cell?"

"Yeah."

"And?"

"And he ain't answerin'."

"Find Lincoln and find that kid. We lose someone today, we lose this investigation to the Feds. And we'd deserve to." She checked her watch. "We'll be there in fifteen."

LINCOLN SCANNED the landscape for reporters; there weren't any—which was good. But he had lost the kid—Miles—which was bad; Hemingway would throw an Elizabeth Taylor if she found out. And where the fuck was Papandreou? He had gone for a piss—how long could that take, for Chrissake? He reached for his phone, then figured if Nick wasn't here, there was no point in making him run. He'd go after the little fuck himself.

Lincoln stepped up into one of the school buses, flashing his badge at the driver who was doing his best not to fall asleep. Lincoln grabbed the handle and swung out, using the added height of the steps to scour the landscape.

Where had that kid gone?

And then he spotted him, over near the trees, heading into the scrub on the way to the railway bridge. He caught a glimpse of the boy for a second just as he stepped into the bushes. Then he was gone.

"Thanks," he said to the driver, and went after the boy. He knew he could get the Morgan kid back before anyone noticed he was gone. He had to.

He moved quickly but didn't run—if any of the reporters caught sight of him, he didn't want to look like he was on a mission.

When he hit the trees he turned and looked back at the buses parked like a group of stagecoaches in Indian country. Papandreou still wasn't anywhere in sight. He looked ahead, toward the architecture of the bridge rising out of the earth, and figured that he could go get the kid and be back before Papandreou knew he was gone.

Like every other kid on the island, the Morgan boy was in blue shorts and a white shirt and he had never before noticed how many white plastic bags were strewn about. They all looked like the kid.

He cleared the trees and came into a field of uneven terrain strewn with rocks and construction castoffs. Sheets of plywood and concrete slag and roofing shingles littered the temporary construction yard and the railroad bridge stretched into the sky above. Lincoln could hear the children's shouting from behind the treeline and it sounded like a recording from a long-ago time. The Robert F. Kennedy Bridge was ahead, past the railroad bridge, and Lincoln headed toward it.

Miles Morgan was nowhere to be seen.

He threaded his way across the field, wondering what the fuck the kid was doing over here. If he wanted a smoke there were closer places. He cleared the railroad bridge and then came up on the cracked concrete foundation of the RFK. He looked back toward the sounds of cheering one last time, briefly considered calling Papandreou, then decided that he had come all this way on his own so a few more feet wouldn't matter. He stepped forward, under the RFK Bridge.

The shadow of the bridge rolled over him like a cloud bank. The heat didn't abate but the atmosphere changed and the humidity and stench beneath the concrete piling felt like a fever.

The walls of the abutment were spray-painted with graffiti that ran the gambit from sloppily scrawled FTWs and initials to multicolored masterpieces as long as motor homes. The garbage in there was the usual stuff of New York legend and it stunk of piss and damp earth and pigeon shit and the wind pulsed thorough but did little to improve the smell. The birds hidden in the overhead girders cooed like an eerie soundtrack and the sounds of the Triborough traffic rattling over expansion joints echoed down into the dark.

A handful of pigeons scattered and headed out into the sunlight.

The dark played with his head and the other side of the bridge looked like one of those mouse doors from the Tom and Jerry cartoons he had watched as a kid—a small arch not big enough to get a hand into. But it was a hundred feet high and probably fifty wide. And close. All he had to do was get there.

Lincoln moved slowly through the weird shadows, making a concerted effort to breathe through his mouth so he wouldn't have to smell the sour shit and mud and who knew what the fuck else that was rotting away down here.

He peered into the mottled gray geometry of shadow and the occasional glint of light off of broken glass. Where had the kid gone? Maybe it was time to call Papandreou. And say what? *Um, sorry, Nick, I lost a kid—yeah, the dull one.* No, that wouldn't work, they'd be laughing at him for days.

But something in here was wrong—he could feel it. He couldn't put his finger on the precise voltage of the problem, but he knew he had to be careful. He reached down and unclipped his service piece and the feel of the pistol in his hand triggered the combat mode setting in his brain. He moved forward, taking controlled breaths.

Water dripped. Pigeons whispered in the dark overhead. Cars rattled the concrete and steel. And the wind off the East River funneled through, stirring up dirt and dust that stung his eyes.

And then a soft voice to his right whispered, "Mister?"

He spun, leveling the pistol at the word. A child huddled at the wall. Miles Morgan.

Miles whispered again. "He's in here."

At that Lincoln spun his head, scanning the darkness. All he saw was shadow and garbage. And that arch that wasn't so far away but looked smaller and further away than it had a minute ago.

He reached for the boy. "Come here, kid."

The child's fingertips touched his.

Then he saw a second shadow come out of the dark off to his left. He swung the muzzle of his .38 around.

The figure stepped forward and when he saw who it was, he dropped his gun arm. "Jesus, you're gonna get shot sneaking around like that."

The figure twitched and Lincoln never really felt it. Not even the blood pissing down the front of his shirt.

He fell over in the filth and garbage under the Robert F. Kennedy Bridge.

And died.

||| NINETY-THREE

LINCOLN WAS dead by the time Papandreou stumbled over him in the shadow of the bridge. His throat was open in a sharp V that went through muscle and flesh and nicked the bone behind. His pistol was in his hand. He hadn't fired a round.

A boy's shoe was found a few feet away and the impressions in the dirt suggested the boy had been squatting there when Lincoln had come across him. Lincoln had knelt down near the child, the boy had taken a step toward him, and it was at that point that his throat had been cut from the other side.

There were no other tracks; it was as if the killer and child had simply flown away.

The word *ghost* was not far from anyone's lips.

Papandreou was angry. "No way, Hemi. I've known Linc for twenty years and there's no fucking way some guy with a knife coulda taken him down if he had his pistol out. Lincoln was a shoot-first-and-ask-questions-later guy, you know that."

"Then what happened in there, Nick?"

Papandreou stared her in the eye for a second. "I don't know."

The commissioner pulled in an extra hundred uniformed officers and they were canvassing the island from one end to the other. Roadblocks were set up at all exits and every car checked and recorded, the driver's identification logged. Trunks were opened, duffel bags unzipped, coolers inspected. School buses were loaded back up with the kids and their chaperones and were leaving the island on a ramp denoted for their use; every bus was checked by a five-man police team before being allowed off the island and the name of every driver, teacher and chaperone was recorded. They would find Miles Morgan. After all, a ten-year-old boy didn't simply melt away.

Hemingway and Phelps were at the edge of the path, near the tall grass that separated the baseball diamond from the fire department's training facilities. The heat was stifling. The usual reinforcements had gathered their wagons and were doing their battlefield magic—three Econolines from the medical examiner's office, a fleet of police cars, and a division command post that was there to coordinate the search for the missing boy. The space-suited technicians from Marcus's office milled about in slow motion in the eerie light of the halogens and the scene under the bridge looked like a set from a science fiction film, all that was missing were massive egg pods.

Hemingway left Phelps and moved away from the whirr of the emergency teams, drawn toward the flow of the river at the northeastern corner of the island. She needed to clear her head.

As she walked across the baseball field the wind came in and picked up dust devils that swirled out over the water. The sound of cheering children had been replaced by the squawk of seagulls flailing in the sky above a garbage barge in the channel and the crack of flames from the fire department's training facility. A squad of firemen were going through exercises on the other side of the chain-link fence, and smoke and flames billowed out of the brick building like a medieval tower under siege. Dummies leaned up against the fence, fire scarred and dead looking. She headed for the water.

This one was the death of a thousand cuts. Kids and cops and family and strangers. When this case was over—when this guy was locked away in some concrete hole a thousand miles beneath the crust of the earth—she'd have time to think. Maybe take that trip with her father. Maybe head to Key Largo to spend a little time in the mangroves, kayaking and soaking up vitamin D and recalibrating her life. Maybe even go away with Daniel.

Maybe paint the guest room for a baby. Maybe not. The future was still wide open. At least for a few more days.

She stepped off the baseball diamond and cut through the line of police vehicles parked on the service road, walking into the high grass that crawled up a hill, then dipped down toward the water. The natural shoreline was a mix of brambles, shrubs, trees, and bushes woven into a tight green curtain below the broken dirt of the hill. She followed it until she found a cutoff down to the water and stepped off the road.

The path was a dirt rut that cut through the tall grass, worn smooth, the humps of big stones poking up. She recognized the double trail of a kayak trolley etched into the surface of the earth and the semicircles of toe prints from a shoe that had climbed up from the bank. There was a dock ahead—part of the training facility. The water's edge was littered with garbage and she stood there doing her best to clear her head and calm her breathing.

She watched the barge make its way south toward the swirling eddies of Hell Gate. The air above the boat was haloed with a cloud of seagulls that picked at its cargo and filled the air with white noise. The generating plant across the river in Astoria looked close enough to touch.

Like the birds over the barge, it was as if this bastard had wings. Like some great mythical bird with a razor-sharp beak—but instead of taking a titan's life, this fucker took whatever he wanted. If she hadn't lived it, she'd have thought it completely unimaginable.

Yet here she was.

At the shore of the river of the dead.

She spotted some humps in the water to her right, just under the fire department's dock, almost hidden in shadow. She focused on them for a few seconds, something about them incongruous. A swell from the barge came in and they rolled in the pitch, bobbing up and down. There was an instant as they peaked, then rolled slightly, and she realized that she was looking at the toes of feet pointing at the sky—one shoed, one not—and beyond that a human face riding in the waves.

A body.

A boy.

"Phelps!"

The sound was ripped away by the wind that carried the dust off the baseball diamond behind her.

The body bobbed in the water.

Another wave came in and it rocked once, almost flipped over, and shook loose from the reeds. It spun a quarter turn and edged out between the dock pilings, into the channel.

Another swell rolled in and kicked it free. It floated out, away.

Hemingway stumbled down the bank and jumped into the water. In a step she was up to her waist. She waded toward the boy but the hands of the current grabbed him and he moved out toward the channel.

"Phelps!"

She dove forward and swam for him with strong even strokes.

The current fastened its grip on the body and started pulling it down toward Hell Gate, toward the city beyond.

Her arms dug into the river with solid strokes but her boots dragged her back. She splashed through the chop, heading for the boy. She didn't look forward, didn't think about what she was doing, she just concentrated on her stroke. On moving. On making it.

The boy swung out with the current and she knew that if he made it into the fast water, she'd never catch him.

She put a final burst into her kick and lurched forward.

In a few more strokes her hand hit his stockinged foot. She grabbed it and tried to move sideways but he had just hit the fast water and it yanked her out.

In another second they'd both get sucked into the current. She swung out, into the heavy pull of the water and pushed the boy toward shore. It had no effect—it was like trying to push a concrete wall.

She pushed again.

Then again.

And finally they began to move.

The shore started to swing by at speed.

She gave one final burst of muscle, a mindless thrash that carried her out of the fast water to the slow draft of the shallows.

And then she was standing.

She had the boy by the ankle and had time to look at him now. It was Miles Morgan.

His chest was opened up and filled with water and swirling tendrils of flesh and artery and bone.

"Hemi!"

She looked up to see Phelps at the water's edge a hundred yards back. He stumbled along the rock-strewn terrain under the dock, heading for her.

She walked the boy in, eased his body up onto the bank where he would stay until the medical examiner's people got to him. As she dragged him out, the water in his chest sloshed out in a red burp and tentacles of vein spilled down his sides.

She dropped down on the bank.

The barge was past now and the final smash of its swells lapped at the shore. Fifty feet south a great blue heron eyed her suspiciously, then raised its beak disdainfully, turned, and flew out over the river.

She watched the bird for a few strokes of its wings, then turned to see Phelps come crashing through the scrub beside her. Behind him came a platoon of cops.

He saw the boy laid out on the rock, the yawning mouth of his opened ribs. "You okay?"

Hemingway coughed, wiped the back of a hand across her mouth, and nodded. "Perfect." Her eyes went back to the heron heading away. She thought about how an experienced cop like Lincoln had been taken down with a knife. About the corner of the photograph taken from Trevor Deacon's basement cell. She thought about Dr. Selmer's throat being cut at a stoplight and about the musical chairs game the boy on the ferry had played.

Hemingway pointed at the rocks she had just swum through. "Look."

Phelps followed her line of sight. He stared blankly for a few seconds then the deadpan expression dropped out of his features and he slowly shook his head.

About fifteen feet from shore were a pair of rocks. A duck decoy rode the water between them, defiantly facing the current. Its paint was battered and the plastic was sun bleached and dented. How it had gotten here was a mystery.

"Sonofabitch." He came over to her, helped her ashore. "You know, for a chick you're pretty smart."

At that, Hemingway smiled grimly. "I get that a lot."

||| NINETY-FOUR

HEMINGWAY SWITCHED into the spare clothes she kept in the back of the Suburban, one of those old cop habits that she had picked up from Phelps. The clothes she had worn into the river went to the medical examiner's to be scanned for any trace evidence that might have come off Miles Morgan's body. They were on their way to the lab and the cherry blinked like a punk rock metronome. She slalomed through traffic in tight throws that pushed the big vehicle's center of gravity to its limit and when the big truck went up on two wheels Phelps tightened his grip on the holy shit handle.

Miles Morgan had been taken apart at the water's edge in a spot upriver from where he had been found floating in the reeds. Nothing but a burnt patch of red-black dirt by the water. The medical examiner called in another team, standard protocol to avoid contamination from Lincoln's murder; they came down the ramp as Hemingway and Phelps had raced up the other side toward the tollbooths.

Hemingway punched through holes in the traffic while Phelps called ahead to book the lab time they'd need. Then he gave Dennet a heads-up so he could put preemptive feelers out to the DA; if the science lined up like they believed it would, they'd have the ammunition for a warrant in a few hours.

The trip to the precinct took seventeen minutes, some sort of a minor miracle in the midday summer traffic. Hemingway stormed through the line of reporters, ignoring their questions, Phelps stuck to her side.

They ran up the five flights and she made it a full floor ahead of Phelps. The investigation room was stacked with countless bankers' boxes and Dennet was waiting for them. He was on the edge of the conference table, his hands in his pockets.

"What the fuck happened at Randall's Island, Alexandra?" Dennet never used her full first name. No one did. People called her Hemingway, Hemi, or Allie. Never Alexandra. Unless they were pissed.

"We have it, captain."

Dennet let out a breath like he had been kicked in the stomach. "Really? Because a few hours ago you had three hundred police officers at your disposal and what did that get us? Huh? Lincoln is lying in his own shit under a fucking bridge and another boy is on his way to the morgue. So it doesn't look like you have this. Not a little and not a lot."

She pulled the lid off of one of the boxes. "Give me an hour with the lab."

Dennet shrugged. "You can have all the time you need, but it won't do any good. Ace Morgan called in some heavy hitters from the Department of Justice and the FBI. The ink's not dry on the forms yet but I got a call from the New York Bureau office and they're in a meeting now. This goes to them before sundown. They'll keep you on as liaison but the horsepower will be coming from their people."

Phelps walked in and sat down, not huffing and puffing but looking like he needed rest.

Dennet didn't bother with a hello. He just stood there, his eyes on Hemingway.

She found the box she was looking for and pulled it out, opened it on the table, then snapped on her latex gloves and removed Dr. Winslow's invitation for the opera—the one he had printed up at home. She gently slid it into a large manila envelope. "Line up the DA—make sure he's available to file a warrant with a judge."

Dennet shrugged like it didn't matter one way or another. "You've got until the Feds take over. After that, you'll have to convince them."

She held up the envelope containing the invitation. "This is it, Ken."

He eyed her skeptically for a second before saying, "You have anything we can share with the press?"

She put the envelope under her arm and shook her head. "After I make the arrest."

"You want to tell me what you think?"

She came around the corner of the table and stopped. "Just make sure you line up the district attorney. We have this prick, all I need is the legal firepower to bring him in."

NINETY-FIVE

HEMINGWAY PULLED the Suburban over in a no-parking zone, the cherry flashing, a wheel up on the sidewalk.

Mat Linderer came out the front doors of the Office of the Chief Medical Examiner. He looked odd out of the space suit Hemingway was used to seeing him in. "We'll be at the cybercrimes lab with Carson," Hemingway said, and gave him the envelope. "Call my cell when you know."

III NINETY-SIX

THE MASSIVE spreadsheet ran across the wall of monitors in a widening pool of information that had been correlated in every conceivable manner. Alan Carson plucked out the name Hemingway asked him about and loaded it into a deep web search field.

The first pass brought up nearly sixty-one thousand pages from around the world. Hemingway pushed her notes in front of him and said, "Can you narrow it to anything around—or after—these dates?"

"August twentieth last year? Sure." He negotiated through the search fields and punched in the new parameters. The results narrowed from sixty-one thousand pages to just under five thousand. He checked her notes again and began to dig.

At that point Hemingway's phone went off. "Excuse me," she said, and left Phelps standing over Carson's shoulder.

"Hemingway."

"Detective Hemingway, it's Mat Linderer from the OCME. I have your results. You were right—"

Hemingway felt her stomach jump the rails. She closed her eyes and concentrated on Linderer's voice.

"—both the invitation and the photograph tacked to the wall in the Deacon residence were printed by the same printer. The feed lines match and there's a pixel lag that is perfect. The paper is from the same manufacturer but a different batch."

Her stomach was back on track and she opened her eyes. "How long to get a report together? Something I can take to the DA."

"Give me five minutes."

She checked her watch. "You've got three. E-mail it to me."

Hemingway hung up and went back to Phelps and Carson. Carson nodded at the screen. "I can't find any record of his presence on any flights for the two weeks before the death, but I have this . . ." He used the cursor to highlight a foreign Google page.

She leaned forward and examined the screen. "It's in Greek."

"Let's run it through the translation software. It won't be perfect, but it will give you a pretty good idea of what it says." He hit a button and a new window opened up.

Both Hemingway and Phelps leaned forward. Both held their breath. Both read silently for a few seconds until Phelps finally said, "Sonofabitch. You were right."

On the morning of August 19th the year before, Dr. Neal Winslow had given a lecture at the Hellenic Ornithological Society regarding the reintroduction of shorebirds to reclaimed habitat. The lecture took place at a library in Athens.

The next morning nine-year-old Tanya Everett—one of Dr. Brayton's girls—drowned while swimming with friends, less than an hour from Athens.

Phelps shifted on his feet. "What do you think?"

"All this proves is that the photograph from Deacon's apartment was printed by the same printer as the invitation and that Winslow was in Greece when the Everett girl died. It doesn't prove that he killed anyone. It's all circumstantial."

"So what do we do?"

"Get his Internet records; his phone records; credit card statements; air miles card; health club membership—anything that we are allowed to get. We dig. It's there, somewhere."

"He said he didn't care where his son had come from. He said he hadn't known. The guy looked cool about all this," Phelps said.

"The man is fascinated by rare specimens, Jon—many the only known example of their kind. He values rarity. He wasn't satisfied with an off-the-shelf model. He lied to us."

SCHLESINGER DIDN'T look skeptical anymore than he looked convinced. He sat at his desk, arms folded, stare locked on Hemingway. "Are you sure?"

"We found two Nikon lenses in Deacon's bedroom. Winslow has a collection of similar lenses by his window, part of his bird-watching arsenal. We ran the warranty card found in Deacon's sock drawer and Winslow shops at the same store—B&H in Manhattan."

"Half the world shops there," Schlesinger said, sounding unconvinced.

She knew he was right; Daniel was there all the time.

Alan Carson stood in the corner, his arms folded across his chest. Babanel, the precinct's lawyer, sat on the sofa, his tie open, looking as hot as the rest of them. Dennet and Phelps stood by the door, like a pair of carvings. But the prize was the district attorney—if they had him, they had the warrant.

Hemingway slid a photograph across the table. "Brayton's eight girls began dying exactly two weeks after the opera, May last year. Dr. Winslow was deeply upset by this party."

"Motive?" Schlesinger asked.

"Wouldn't you be upset if you had ordered a prized purebred and you got a mutt?"

Schlesinger held up the file on Benjamin Winslow. "Kid's got an IQ over 200. Youngest person ever admitted to Harvard. Hardly a mutt."

"It's not about what he has, it's about what he was told he'd have. All of the Park Avenue Clinic's patients expected a certain amount of exclusivity. When Winslow found out his son wasn't as unique as he had been led to believe, it infuriated him.

"He decided to go after these children, beginning with the girls. Eight executions on a very precise schedule."

Schlesinger shook his head. "A man like Dr. Winslow is going to hire excellent counsel. The first thing they will ask will be his motive. And so will the judge when I present this to him. Why would he do this?"

Hemingway slammed her fist into the desk. "Because he's a sick fuck. Who knows why? His mommy didn't breastfeed him. Or his daddy did. We have him." She ground her finger into the report from the lab. "We have him cold."

The district attorney stared at her for a second, then asked, "Give me a chain of events that I can work with."

"I think Winslow and Deacon met on Randall's Island while Deacon was out there staring at kids. Winslow was chaperoning his son's class, something he did often. Both Deacon and Winslow carried expensive cameras with telephoto lenses. Winslow hunted birds, Deacon children. They struck up a conversation, maybe bought a coffee at the canteen at the same time. Became friends or at least buddies. Turns out they have a shared interest. Maybe Deacon pushed Winslow over to the dark side. But a learning process went on. Some sort of a team effort.

"Things soured at some point. Maybe they had their

382 | ROB POBI

eyes on the same boy and Winslow was a sore loser. He killed Deacon. We wondered how the killer got into Deacon's apartment with all those locks; Deacon let him in or he had his own keys. They had probably shared the garage for sessions."

Schlesinger nodded as if she had good points. "A buddy system?"

"Some serial killers work in pairs; usually weak people who find confidence in superior firepower. The core system always comes from a dominant partner with a particular fantasy that he or she imprints on the weaker. Winslow could have been the dominant one, the one who wanted to take it to the next level, to this weird parts-taking ritual of his, and Deacon balked. So he finished Deacon off.

"If Deacon had been doing this as far back as eighty-six, he had the automatic role of master. Winslow was a lot smarter than Deacon and maybe he got fed up and decided to mutiny."

Phelps stepped in, offering a little outside perspective. "Pairs of male killers feed off one another. That's what they do. With someone else to record it mentally, it goes from being a participatory activity to a spectator sport. One is always the boss—always maintains psychological control."

Schlesinger leaned over and picked up the photograph Phelps had taken with his cell phone out on Randall's Island. There was nothing interesting about it except the battered duck decoy, head dented, blind with sun-bleached glaucoma that had whited out its eyes.

Hemingway tapped the table. "I saw that same decoy and rocks in a photograph in Winslow's apartment. It was taken where I found Miles Morgan. Printed by the same machine that printed the torn photograph in Deacon's apartment."

Schlesinger's expression was still anchored somewhere in the land of necessary objectivity. "And his wife's death?"

Hemingway shrugged. "We don't know. It's been ruled an accident but who knows? If it was, maybe that's what kicked this whole thing off. He wouldn't be the first person to go off the deep end after the death of a spouse. If it wasn't . . ." She let it drop off.

Schlesinger leaned back in his chair and ran his eyes over the people in the room. "Which brings us back to motive. Without it . . ." He let the question float out into the air above his desk.

Hemingway figured it was time to drop the bomb. "We think we have video of Winslow on the ferry."

"When?"

"The day before the Simmons boy was murdered."

"Not very convincing."

"It is if it's a dry run. He was carrying a knapsack Deacon's drug dealer identified—it has a Canadian flag patch sewn on." She pushed another photograph across the table, this one lifted from a security tape on the ferry. It showed a stooped figure carrying a knapsack.

"That could be anyone." Schlesinger shook his head. "My grandfather."

"Dr. Winslow has a pronounced stoop from a spinal injury." Hemingway tapped the photograph. "It rained that day and he stayed on deck in his raincoat, looking down. Five feet from the escape hatch just off camera. There isn't a single shot of his face but the body language is easily identifiable. He headed across to Staten Island. The cameras picked up his knapsack, and we can clearly isolate the flag." She handed another photograph over. "And he's wearing open-laced oxfords with leather soles. We were able to run down an account he has at Brooks Brothers and his foot is listed as a size ten wide, which is why the lab wasn't certain if the footprints left behind at the crime scenes were ten or ten and a half. We get warrants for his home and office I bet we find the shoes and the knapsack. The murder weapon as well."

"What about the day the Simmons boy was murdered? Can you place him on the ferry?"

At that Hemingway shook her head. She knew it was a pull in the skein of the investigation but they'd figure it out. It was only a matter of time. "Not yet."

"Does he have alibis for the murders?"

"At this point, all we can say for sure is that he was at Randall's Island this morning. Chaperone for his son's class. We looked at some video footage at the time of Lincoln's death and he's nowhere to be seen."

Schlesinger's eyes shut down for a second as he went into thinking mode. "Okay, let me put warrants in front of the judge. Let's see what he says." He leaned back in his seat and knitted his fingers together on top of his head. "While I'm doing that, you bring him in for questioning."

HEMINGWAY AND Phelps flanked Dr. Neal Winslow's door with two uniformed policemen. Alfred, the building manager, was along to make sure they didn't cause any damage.

Phelps gave one grave robotic nod and pushed the buzzer. A long peal of songbirds broke out on the other side of the oak door.

Phelps rolled his eyes.

They waited thirty seconds.

No footsteps.

Phelps pressed his finger to the button again. Another peal of songbirds.

Followed by more silence.

"So you're not sure if he's home or not?" Phelps asked Alfred.

"We don't keep tabs on our residents; this is America."

Phelps rolled his eyes just as Hemingway's phone vibrated. She answered.

"Detective Hemingway, Ed Schlesinger. I just finished with Judge Lester and you have your warrants. I've e-mailed it to you."

"Thank you, sir." She hung up, fired up her e-mail, and held the warrant out for Alfred to read.

"Which means?" he asked.

"That we are going to open this door."

———

Hemingway, Phelps and the two uniformed officers swept through the place. Alfred stood by the door. When they finished, they met back in the living room, amid the glass-eyeballed birds.

Hemingway pulled out her phone and dialed Alan Carson. "Yeah, it's Hemingway, can you get a lock on Dr. Winslow's cell phone? I've got an arrest warrant for him."

"Hold on."

Hemingway nodded off the seconds while Phelps looked around.

He opened desk drawers, looked behind paintings, doing a fast inventory of the place. He quickly branched out from the living room, one of the uniforms following him.

Carson came back on. "He's moving too fast to be on foot right now. Fifth Avenue and East Sixtieth."

"Keep somebody on him. We're on the wa—"

From somewhere deep in the apartment, Phelps hollered, "Hemi!"

He was in the kitchen, standing in front of one of the floor-to-ceiling Sub-Zeros. The uniform was puking in the sink.

Phelps held a shoe by a lace and it dangled in his hand, spinning in the weird light cast up by the open freezer drawer. In his other hand he held a knapsack with a Canadian flag patch sewn to it.

Even from the other side of the room, Hemingway could see the dark crescent on the leather sole of the shoe.

But the big news was the freezer.

The cop was still letting go, his supper coming up in spasms.

Hemingway stepped forward and looked down into the lighted box.

Inside, neatly wrapped in cellophane, were parts of children.

HEMINGWAY WAS still staring at the well-organized collection of hunting trophies when her phone rang. "Hemingway."

The cop was still vomiting in the background and she stepped away from the noise. "Hemi, it's Dennet. A boy disappeared on the way home tonight. Driver dropped him off in front of the building but the kid never made it upstairs. Sol Borenstein."

Two blocks from Winslow's last reported location.

Hemingway and Phelps left the two uniformed officers to wait for the medical examiner's people.

As she followed Phelps to the door, she grabbed the photograph of the decoy bobbing in the current from the paneled wall.

III ONE HUNDRED

HEMINGWAY SPOKE to Mrs. Borenstein on the phone. Elio had dropped Sol off at the front door—he needed to use the bathroom and couldn't wait for the ride up from the garage. Elio watched him run inside and assumed the doorman sent him off to the private resident's restroom behind the elevators. He figured the boy would meet him at the desk in the lobby.

Sol never made it inside.

He vanished between stepping through the front door and arriving on the other side.

Video from the surveillance camera showed the boy pulling the front door open, then looking off to his right. He smiled, waved, and stepped out of the frame.

Winslow's location was fed directly to the onboard laptop mounted to the dash of Hemingway's truck. Winslow was moving up Madison at twenty-seven miles an hour, between 71st and 72nd.

Hemingway and Phelps were three blocks down, at 68th. She didn't have the cherries on and didn't want to slow things down by being pulled over or—worse—alert Winslow up

ahead. But she had skipped a few lights that drivers punctuated with the standard *Fuck You!*

She caught up to him by 77th. Winslow's turn signal
blinked on at the 79th Street entrance to the park. It was an
easy car to spot, a black Bentley with heavily tinted windows,
detailed to the teeth. Hardly inconspicuous.

The black luxury sedan cut across Park Avenue southbound traffic in a gentle sweep and headed into Central Park.
The taxi up ahead balked at the amorphous opening and
Hemingway floored it, pulling the big four-by-four around
the cab in a fog of smoking rubber. She rocketed across the
southbound lane in a blare of horns, caught one final glimpse
of the museum off to her left, and was swallowed by the
shadows.

She gained on Winslow's Bentley, coming almost to its
bumper as they swung down, beneath the grass, then up past
the basketball courts.

Phelps fired up the dashboard cherry and the siren.

Winslow's Bentley continued on for a few seconds, then
the brake lights lit up. The car began to slow, to pull over.

The brake lights died, it lurched forward, then back to
the center of the lane.

"What the fu—?" Phelps had his hand out on the dash.

The car hung in front of them for a second, perfectly bal-
anced like a graceful bird in flight. Then the driver hit the
brakes again and it veered sharply right, scraped the front
quarter panel on the stone wall, jogged left, then swung around
and impacted with the side of the tunnel.

The ass of the car swung out across the road.

Hemingway stomped down on the brakes with both feet.
The dinosaur roar of rubber on pavement echoed in the
tunnel and the Suburban slammed into the Bentley. The air
was filled with a thousand different sounds and the framed

photograph on the center console detonated against the windshield.

Hemingway heard nothing but a high-pitched squeal that she somehow knew was inside her head.

Phelps reached over, put his hand on her chest.

"I'm good," she said, but all she heard was the sound nailing into her brain.

She didn't hear the squeak of his hinge or any words he might have said.

She looked out the fragmented windshield. The nose of her truck was buried in the flank of the Bentley and the big sedan's windows had blown out. There was a boy in the backseat: Sol Borenstein. Splattered with glass. Seat belt holding his head up at an odd, lifeless angle. Blood everywhere.

She caught the stooped form of Dr. Winslow as he lurched out the far side of the vehicle. Phelps was off to her left, a prismatic smudge in her peripheral vision.

Winslow had the boy with him.

His son.

Benjamin.

Winslow was screaming but she couldn't hear him through the squeal that was still rocketing around her skull.

The photograph from Winslow's was folded in half on the dash, the glass disintegrated. A corner of the picture stuck out of the splintered edge of the frame.

There was a spine-jarring suction as her hearing rumbled back in one big pressurized thump that shook her head with subsonic boom.

And she heard the distant screech of sirens and Phelps yelling at Winslow.

"Winslow, put the knife down."

"I can't. I have to do this!"

"*Helllllllllp meeeee!*" the boy screeched. "Shoot him! Shoot him!"

Hemingway slapped at her buckle and the seat belt let go and slowly crawled back across her body. She reached out to steady herself on the dashboard and her fingers clamped down on the edge of the picture frame. The frame came apart and the photo fluttered loose, into her lap.

Across the back, in the precise well-trained script of a gifted ten-year-old, were the words:

For Daddy.
I love you.
Your secret keeper.
Benjamin

And all of a sudden she knew.

She fought her way out of the car and stood on the pavement on borrowed legs.

Dr. Winslow was on the other side of the Bentley, his hand in the air, a bloody blade in his fist. He had Benjamin clamped around the throat.

"This has to stop!" Whatever constraint he had left ruptured, and the knife flashed toward Benjamin's throat.

Hemingway screamed, "No!"

And her hearing went away again in a final, pneumatic snap timed to the flash of Phelps's pistol.

Winslow shuddered once as a cloud of red mist vapor-trailed out behind him. He stepped back clumsily, pulling the boy with him. His arm came down and the knife sang into his son.

Phelps fired again.

III ONE HUNDRED AND ONE

IT WAS hot and windless and with the gentle roll of the swell, the effect was hypnotizing. Hemingway pushed her Ray-Bans up on her nose and squinted into the light bouncing off the water to the south where the roiling patch of Hell Gate bubbled with the outgoing tide.

She was here to get a little perspective on what had happened.

And what was about to happen.

Big things. Forever things. No-turning-away-from things.

She had launched from Randall's Island, not far from where she found Miles Morgan's body floating in the shallows under the dock that day. At first her strokes were steady and purposeful—her shoulder clicking with each swing of her arm—but the further she got from land, the less she felt like paddling. Now she just rode the current, following the gentle pull of water on the hull.

It had all been there in front of them from the beginning but they hadn't seen it. Not really. Not for what it was.

Because it was unthinkable.

They had been right about one part, of course: Trevor

Deacon *had* run into a fellow enthusiast out on Randall's Island. The friendship had come up out of nowhere, one of
those random pairings of fractured minds that come around
more often than anyone really wants to believe.

Deacon had been near the trees, taking pictures, when
someone came over to talk to him.

Benjamin Winslow was probably charming and friendly.
But that wasn't what had won over Trevor Deacon—no, that
had been accomplished with the photographs. In exchange
for keeping them secret, all little Benjamin had wanted was
to learn.

Deacon hadn't had a choice, not in any real sense of the
word, because Benjamin's intelligence had only been surpassed
by his sadism. Deacon quickly grew frightened of the child.

Then one night not too long ago he had squeezed between
the bars of Trevor Deacon's windows and injected anesthetic
into his eye while he slept. It was a battlefield anesthetic that
he had stolen from an old field kit in the museum. Then he
cut Deacon's feet off while he had still been alive. Just for
kicks.

Phelps had said that his grandson would have a hard
time squeezing his skinny ass through the bars. A hard time,
sure, but not impossible.

By the time he was finished, Trevor had been reduced to
the unarticulated parts. His body left on the bed.

Because a ten-year-old boy could not lift it.

And the shoe print on the chair? Benjamin had worn his
father's size ten triple-E brogues from Church's. He used the
chair as a ladder to reach the photograph he had given Deacon as a warning, taken at his dumping ground. He had given
his father a picture taken at the same place. His dad had had
it framed and put it up on the wall with the pictures of his
other birds.

Benjamin had been set off by the picture that had captured Dr. Brayton and all the little handsome men to be that he had created. His own little biological empire. The photo had shown up in the *Times* the morning after the opera and that had been it, the fire had started.

Like his biological father, Benjamin Winslow had been a narcissist. And his practical father—Dr. Neal Winslow—had nurtured that in the boy. He had raised him as special. The boy had grown up alone, in a terrarium built for his uniqueness—like an exotic poisonous reptile kept for display. And he wanted no competitors in his little ecosystem. The only-child syndrome taken to an extreme conclusion.

He began with the e-mail list. It hadn't been hard to hunt them down. Not for a boy with his aptitude.

Benjamin had started with the girls because there were fewer of them. As he moved down the list he had discovered that he had an aptitude far beyond geometry and language.

Phelps had spoken with Dr. Winslow's travel agent and the trip to Greece last year had been his son's idea. The agent remembered Winslow insisting on the dates and saying that his son really wanted to go. Because he had known that Tanya Everett would be there. He had swum out with her and the rest of the children and pushed her under and held her down between his legs. The police in Greece weren't noted for their forensic prowess and the two hundred witnesses had negated any suspicion of foul play.

The others had been just as easy.

Heidi Morrison hadn't jumped in front of that train, she had been pushed. Benjamin hadn't been visible on the surveillance tapes because he was too short to be seen on the packed platform.

The boys?

They hadn't been abducted. They had been lured.

Benjamin had had no trouble moving among the boys because he was one of them. And in all the eyewitness accounts, children had been around. Even Daniel had passed the schoolboys that morning. The Grant boy's driver would never have suspected a child. Miles Morgan would have felt superior around Benjamin—but Benjamin Winslow had been way too smart for a boy like Morgan to deal with.

The kid had even outsmarted a good street cop like Lincoln.

Solomon Borenstein had walked away from the front door to his building because Benjamin had called him over to the car. And just like in Tanya Everett's death, Dr. Winslow had been used as a dupe. It had all gone wrong when little Solomon had started to cry and asked to go home. Dr. Winslow didn't understand what the problem was—he thought Solomon and Benjamin had a playdate.

Dr. Winslow saw his son slit the boy's throat in the rearview mirror. He had grabbed the knife. Fought with him. Crashed the car.

And lost.

They had been blind on so many fronts. The garage attendant where Dr. Selmer parked his car had said that kids had been around when Selmer left the garage—his throat had been cut less than two blocks away. At a downward angle. Because the killer was only four feet tall.

A ten-year-old killer had never factored into the equation.

Bobby Grant, the docile piano prodigy, watched Benjamin cut his driver's throat. After that, he would have listened to Benjamin—either he forced the Grant boy to come along or he told him that he had killed the driver to save him. Ten-year-old children believed things like that. Even gifted ones.

Benjamin had been walking with Nigel Matheson's group when he disappeared. He had pulled the boy down an alley and off the face of the earth with the promise of basketball tickets.

The toughest one to figure out had been Simmons on the ferry.

The surveillance film of the boy entering the staircase to the engine level, not coming out, then reentering it a second time had stumped them. They thought he had gone out through the escape hatch, then gone back in by the staircase.

Wrong again. Just another old magic trick, like Pepper's Ghost. Smoke and mirrors and getting the observer to use their own preconceptions to work against them. Everyone believes their own eyes. Even when they are lying.

There were two boys in the video.

Two boys who looked so much alike—dressed in their school jackets—that they were virtually indistinguishable.

First on the screen was Benjamin Winslow. He opened the door with the access code—the one he had seen a crewman punch in the day he had taken the ferry with his father—and descended the stairwell to the engine level to wait. He told Simmons to meet him there where he'd show him something special.

And when it was over he had gotten out exactly like Delaney had proposed—by crawling through the escape hatch that came out on the car deck. Then he had disembarked with the rest of the passengers. And a knapsack containing more hunting trophies.

Benjamin Winslow, for all his mathematical acumen and encyclopedic knowledge, had still only been a jealous ten-year-old boy.

And his diary had outlined the sexual abuse he had suffered for years. Monsters aren't born, they're made.

Dr. Winslow followed a strict vegan diet and had fresh meals delivered daily; he never used the freezer. Which was why Benjamin had been able to store his little museum of trophies in there for the few short days his killing spree had lasted.

It was amazing what a child had accomplished with nothing but determination and a hacksaw. They would be talking about that kid for years.

Hemingway checked her watch. If she wanted to make the clinic she'd have to start back now. And she had people to speak to. Forgiveness to ask. Amends to be made. There was her father. And Daniel. More of Uncle Dwight's damage control in action.

Maybe she'd take that vacation with her father and tour the vineyards of Burgundy. She took her hand off her stomach, picked up her paddle, and dug the blade into the water. Her shoulder clicked with the movement and the bow of the kayak started to swing around, away from the roil of Hell Gate.

And across the river of the dead.

ACKNOWLEDGMENTS

I have to thank Charles Shutt, MD, FACOG—dedicated doctor, passionate writer and bruddah—for helping me get the business end of the fertility clinic right. His input on medical records and EMR access was concise and thoughtful, and his explanation of the way the client-patient privilege actually plays out from a legal standpoint helped me dig my characters out of one of the holes I always seem to write them into. The true parts are his. The rest is mine.

I would also like to thank Detective Alfred King (retired) of the NYPD, who unknowingly had a part in writing this novel—I hope he doesn't mind seeing his name in print.